MYSTERY WRITERS OF AMERICA
Presents

THE BLUE RELIGION

ALSO BY MICHAEL CONNELLY

Fiction

The Black Echo
The Black Ice
The Concrete Blonde
The Last Coyote
The Poet
Trunk Music
Blood Work
Angels Flight
Void Moon
A Darkness More than Night
City of Bones
Chasing the Dime
Lost Light
The Narrows
The Closers
The Lincoln Lawyer
Echo Park
The Overlook

Nonfiction
Crime Beat

ALSO FROM THE MYSTERY WRITERS OF AMERICA

Death Do Us Part
(Edited by Harlan Coben)

MYSTERY WRITERS OF AMERICA
Presents

THE BLUE RELIGION

NEW STORIES ABOUT COPS, CRIMINALS, AND THE CHASE

Edited by
MICHAEL CONNELLY

BACK BAY BOOKS
LITTLE, BROWN AND COMPANY
NEW YORK • BOSTON • LONDON

Little, Brown and Company
Hachette Book Group USA
237 Park Avenue, New York, NY 10017
Visit our Web site at www.HachetteBookGroupUSA.com

First Edition: April 2008

Library of Congress Cataloging-in-Publication Data
Mystery Writers of America presents the blue religion : new stories about
cops, criminals, and the chase / edited by Michael Connelly. — 1st ed.
p. cm.
ISBN 978-0-316-01251-5 (hc) / 978-0-316-01265-2 (pb)
1. Detective and mystery stories, American. 2. Crime — Fiction. I. Connelly,
Michael. II. Mystery Writers of America. III. Title: Blue religion.
PS648.D4M97 2008
813'.087208 — dc22   2007042278

HC: 10 9 8 7 6 5 4 3 2 1
PB: 10 9 8 7 6 5 4 3 2 1

RRD-IN

Printed in the United States of America

CONTENTS

The Blue Religion: An Introduction   *vii*

SKINHEAD CENTRAL, *by T. Jefferson Parker*   *3*

SACK O' WOE, *by John Harvey*   *15*

THE DROUGHT, *by James O. Born*   *35*

DIVINE DROPLETS, *by Paula L. Woods*   *56*

SERIAL KILLER, *by Jon L. Breen*   *74*

A CERTAIN RECOLLECTION, *by John Buentello*   *86*

A CHANGE IN HIS HEART, *by Jack Fredrickson*   *97*

THE HERALD, *by Leslie Glass*   *121*

SUCH A LUCKY, PRETTY GIRL, *by Persia Walker*   *140*

FRIDAY NIGHT LUCK, *by Edward D. Hoch*   *169*

THE FOOL, *by Laurie R. King*   *186*

BURYING MR. HENRY, *by Polly Nelson*   *219*

OATHS, OHANA, AND EVERYTHING, *by Diana Hansen-Young*   233

THE PRICE OF LOVE, *by Peter Robinson*   258

CONTACT AND COVER, *by Greg Rucka*   279

RULE NUMBER ONE, *by Bev Vincent*   299

WHAT A WONDERFUL WORLD, *by Paul Guyot*   317

WINNING, *by Alafair Burke*   337

FATHER'S DAY, *by Michael Connelly*   348

About the Authors   369

THE BLUE RELIGION:
AN INTRODUCTION

A long time ago, when my first book was published, the first review it received classified the novel as a "police procedural." This classification was news to me. I thought I had simply written a book, a crime novel, if it absolutely needed to be classified. Okay, a mystery, even. Sure, it was about cops and robbers and how the good guys work to catch the bad guys, but I never realized that I had ventured into what was called a "subgenre." I soon learned that crime fiction is a world of genres and subgenres and even sub-subgenres.

Nearly twenty years later, I sit here writing the introduction to a book that celebrates one of those subgenres. Welcome to the world of the cop story. Welcome to stories that explore the burden of the badge.

One note on these stories, however. While this tome and its individual stories will fall under the classification of police procedural, they are anything but explorations of procedure. They are explorations of life. They are explorations of character.

In my observations of the blue religion as both a journalist and a writer of fiction, I have found that most people who carry badges believe they are part of a misunderstood breed. And I believe they have a point. How are we to weigh the burden of the badge if we do not carry the badge? In these stories, we do it by exploring the many facets of character of those who carry the badge. As you will find, procedure is only window dressing for our true focus. We learn what it is like to corner a murderer, to unmask a hidden killer. We walk the line between justice and revenge. We see what it costs to do the job both right and wrong. We find resolution and redemption.

There is an adage attributed to Joseph Wambaugh, the great writer of police stories, that informs our effort here. It is as simple as it is true. It holds that the best story about the badge is not about how a cop works on a case. It is about how the case works on the cop. In the subtlety of that distinction is the axiom that gave the writers who are gathered here all they needed.

I know a detective who works cold cases in Los Angeles. He works out of a windowless office, with his desk pushed up against his partner's. He has a glass top on his desk. With such a basic setup in almost any other office in the world, one would almost invariably find photos of loved ones—children, wives, families—under the glass top. Smiling faces, reminders of what is good in life. Inspiration to do the job well.

But not this detective. He slips the photos of dead people under his glass. Photos of murder victims whose killers he still hunts. They are reminders of what is bad in life. Reminders of the job unfinished and inspiration to keep going and to do the job well.

To me, that gets to the heart of character, not procedure. And that is what this book is all about.

—Michael Connelly

MYSTERY WRITERS OF AMERICA

Presents

THE BLUE RELIGION

SKINHEAD CENTRAL

BY T. JEFFERSON PARKER

So we moved up here to Spirit Lake in Idaho, where a lot of Jim's friends had come to live. After forty years in Laguna Beach, it was a shock to walk outside and see only a few houses here and there, some fog hovering over the pond out front, and the endless trees. The quiet too, that was another surprise. There's always the hiss of wind in the pines, but it's nothing like all the cars and sirens on PCH. I miss the Ruby's and the Nordstrom Rack up the freeway. Miss my friends and my children. We talk all the time by phone and e-mail, but it's not the same as living close by. We have a guest room.

We've had mostly a good life. Our firstborn son died thirteen years ago, and that was the worst thing that's ever happened to us. His name was James Junior, but he went by JJ. He was a cop, like his father, and was killed in the line of duty. After that, Jim drank himself almost to death, then one day just stopped. He never raised a finger or even his voice at me or the kids. Kept on with the Laguna Beach PD. I had Karen and Ricky to take care of, and I took meds for a year and had counseling. The one thing I learned from grief is that you feel better if you do things for other people instead of dwelling on yourself.

We're living Jim's dream of hardly any people but plenty of trees and fish.

There's some skinheads living one lake over, and one of them, Dale, came over the day we moved in last summer and asked if we had work. Big kid, nineteen, tattoos all over his arms and calves, red hair buzzed short, and eyes the color of old ice. Jim said there was no work, but they got to talking woodstoves and if the old Vermont Castings in the living room would need a new vent come fall. Dale took a look and said that unless you want to smoke yourself out, it would. Two days later, Dale helped Jim put one in, and Jim paid him well.

A couple of days later, I went to dig out my little jewelry bag from the moving box where I'd kind of hidden it, but it was gone. I'd labeled each box with the room it went to, but the movers just put the boxes down wherever—anyway, it was marked "bedroom," but they put it right there in the living room, where Dale could get at it when I went into town for sandwiches and Jim went outside for a smoke or to pee in the trees, which is something he did a lot of that first month or two. Jim told me I should have carried the jewelry on my person, and he was right. *On my person*. You know how cops talk. Said he'd go find Dale over in Hayden Lake the next day—skinhead central—what a way to meet the locals.

But the next morning, this skinny young boy shows up on our front porch, dark bangs almost over his eyes, no shirt, jeans hanging low on his waist and his boxers puffing out. Gigantic sneakers with the laces loose. Twelve or thirteen years old.

"This yours?" he asked.

Jim took the jewelry bag—pretty little blue thing with Chinese embroidery on it and black drawstrings—and angled it to the bright morning sun.

"Hers," he said. "Hon? What's missing?"

I loosened the strings and cupped the bag in my hand and

pressed the rings and earrings and bracelets up against one another and the satin. It was mostly costume and semiprecious stones, but I saw the ruby earrings and choker Jim had gotten me one Christmas in Laguna and the string of pearls.

"The expensive things are here," I said.

"You Dale's brother?" asked Jim.

"Yep."

"What's your name?"

"Jason."

"Come on in."

"No reason for that."

"How are you going to explain this to Dale?"

"Explain what?"

And he loped down off the porch steps, landed with a crunch, and picked up his bike.

"Take care of yourself."

"That's what I do."

"We've got two cords' worth of wood and a decent splitter," said Jim.

Jason sized up Jim the way young teenagers do, by looking not quite at him for not very long. Like everything about Jim could be covered in a glance.

"Okay. Saturday."

Later I asked Jim why he offered work to Jason when he'd held it back from Dale.

"I don't know. Maybe because Jason didn't ask."

———

THE WAY JJ died was that he and Jim were both working for Laguna PD—unusual for a father and son to work the same department—but everyone was cool with it, and they made the papers a few times because of the human interest. "Father and Son Crime Busters Work Laguna Beat."

If you don't know Laguna, it's in Orange County, California. It's known as an artist colony and a tourist town, a place prone to disasters such as floods, earth slides, and wildfires. There had been only one LBPD officer killed in the line of duty before JJ. That was back in the early fifties. His name was Gordon French.

Anyway, Jim was watch commander the night it happened to JJ, and when the "officer down" call came to dispatch, Jim stayed at his post until he knew who it was.

When Jim got there, JJ's cruiser was still parked up on the shoulder of PCH, with the lights flashing. It was a routine traffic stop, and the shooter was out of the car and firing before JJ could draw his gun. JJ's partner had stayed with him but also called in the plates. They got JJ to South Coast Medical Center but not in time. One of the reasons they built South Coast Medical Center forty-seven years ago was because Gordon French was shot and died for lack of medical care in Laguna. Then they build one, and it's still too late. Life is full of things like that, things that are true but badly shaped. JJ was twenty-five—would be thirty-eight today if he hadn't seen that Corolla weaving down the southbound lanes. They caught the shooter and gave him death. He's in San Quentin. His appeals will take at least six more years. Jim wants to go if they execute him. Me too, and I won't blink.

————

THE NEXT TIME we saw Jason was at the hardware store two days later. I saw his bike leaned against the wall by the door, and I spotted him at the counter as I walked through the screen door that Jim held open for me. He had on a knit beanie and a long-sleeve black T-shirt with some kind of skull pattern, and his pants were still just about sliding off his waist, though you couldn't see any boxers.

"Try some ice," the clerk said cheerfully.

Jason turned with a bag of something and started past us, his lips fat and black. His cheeks were swelled up behind the sunglasses.

Jim wheeled and followed Jason out. Through the screen door, I could hear them.

"Dale do that?"

"No."

Silence then. I saw Jason looking down. And Jim with his fists on his hips and this balanced posture he gets when he's mad.

"Then what happened?"

"Nothing. Get away from me, man."

"I can have a word with your brother."

"Bad idea."

Jason swung his leg over his bike and rolled down the gravel parking lot.

The next evening, Dale came up our driveway in a black Ram Charger pickup. It was "wine thirty," as Jim calls it, about six o'clock, which is when we would open a bottle, sit, and watch the osprey try to catch one of the big trout rising in our pond out front.

The truck pulled up close to the porch, all the way to the logs Jim had staked out to mark the end of the parking pad. Dale was leaning forward in the seat like he was ready to get out, but he didn't. The window went down, and Dale stared at us, face flushed red, which with his short red hair made him look ready to burst into flames.

"Dad told me to get over here to apologize for the jewelry, so that's what I'm doing."

"You beat up your brother because he brought it back?"

"He deserved every bit he got."

"A twelve-year-old doesn't deserve a beating like that," said Jim.

"He's thirteen."

"You can't miss the point much further," said Jim.

Dale gunned the truck engine, and I watched the red dust jump away from the ground below the pipe. He was still leaning away from the seat like you would back home in July when your car's been in the sun and all you've got on is a halter or your swimsuit top. But this was Idaho in June at evening time, and it probably wasn't more than seventy degrees.

"Get out and show me your back," said Jim.

"What about it?"

"You know what it's about."

"You don't know shit," said Dale, pressing his back against the seat. "I deal with things."

Then the truck revved and lurched backward. I could see Dale leaning forward in the seat again and his eyes raised to the rearview. He kept a good watch on the driveway behind him as the truck backed out. Most young guys in trucks, they'd have swung an arm out and turned to look directly where they were driving. Maybe braced the arm on the seat. JJ always did that. I liked watching JJ learn to drive because his attention was so pure and undistractible. Dale headed down the road, and the dust rose like it was chasing him.

"Someone whipped his back," I said.

"Dad."

"You made some calls."

Jim nodded. Cops are curious people. Just because they retire doesn't mean they stop nosing into things. Jim has a network of friends that stretches all the way across the country, though most of them are in the West. Mostly retired but a few still active. And they grouse and gossip and yap and yaw like you wouldn't believe, swap information and stories and contacts and just about anything you can imagine that relates to cops. You want to know something about a guy, someone will know someone who can help. Mostly by Internet but by phone too. Jim calls it the Geezer Enforcement Network.

"Dale's father has a nice jacket because he's a nice guy," said Jim. "Aggravated assault in a local bar, pled down to disturbing the peace. Probation for assault on his wife. Ten months in county for another assault—a Vietnamese kid, student at Boise—broke his jaw with his fist. There was a child-abuse inquiry raised by the school when Dale showed up for first grade with bruises. Dale got homeschooled after that. Dad's been clean since '93. The wife sticks by her man—won't file, won't do squat. Tory and Teri Badger. Christ, what a name."

I thought about that for a second while the osprey launched himself from a tree.

"Is Tory an Aryan Brother?"

"Nobody said that."

"Clean for thirteen years," I said. "Since Jason was born. So, you could say he's trying."

Jim nodded. I did the math in my mind and knew that Jim was doing it too. Clean since 1993. That was the year JJ died. We can't even think of that year without remembering him. I'm not sure exactly what goes through Jim's mind, but I know that just the mention of the year takes him right back to that watch commander's desk on August 20, 1993. I'll bet he hears the "officer down" call with perfect clarity, every syllable and beat. Me, I think of JJ when he was seven years old, running down the sidewalk to the bus stop with his friends. Or the way he used to comb his hair straight down onto his forehead when he was a boy. To tell you the truth, sometimes I think about him for hours, all twenty-five years of him, whether somebody says "1993" or not.

That Saturday Jason came back over and split the wood. I watched him off and on from inside as he lined up the logs in the splitter and stood back as the wood cracked and fell into smaller and smaller halves. Twice he stopped and pulled a small blue notebook from the back pocket of his slipping-down jeans and scribbled something with a pen from another pocket. The three of us ate lunch on the porch even though it was getting cold. Jason didn't say much, and I could tell the lemonade stung his lips. The swelling around his eyes was down, but one was black. He was going to be a freshman come September.

"Can your dad protect you from your brother?" Jim asked out of nowhere.

"Dale's stronger now. But mostly, yeah."

Jim didn't say anything to that. After nearly forty years of being married to him, I can tell you his silences mean he doesn't believe you. And of course there were the broken lips and black eye making his case.

"If you need a place, you come stay here a night or two," he said. "Anytime."

"You'd be welcome," I said.

"Okay," he said, looking down at his sandwich.

I wanted to ask him what he wrote in the notebook, but I didn't. I have a place where I put things for safekeeping too, though it's not a physical place.

Later that night, we went to a party at Ed and Ann Logan's house on the other side of Spirit Lake. It was mostly retired SoCal cops, the old faces from Orange County and some Long Beach people Jim fell in with whom I never really got to know. I've come to like cops in general. I guess that would figure. And their wives too—we pretty much get along. There's a closedness about most cops that used to put me off until JJ died and I realized that you can't explain everything to everybody. You have to have that place inside where something can be safe. Even if it's only a thought or a memory. It's the opposite of the real world, where people die as easily as leaves fall off a tree. And the old cliché about cops believing it's them and us, well, it's absolutely true that that's what they think. Most people think that way—it's just the "thems" and the "usses" are different.

A man was stacking firewood on the Logans' deck when we got there. He was short and thick, gave us a level-eyed nod, and that was all. Later Jim and I went outside for some fresh air. The breeze was strong and cool. The guy was just finishing up the wood. He walked toward us, slapping his leather work gloves together.

"I apologize for Dale," he said. "I'm his dad. He ain't the trustworthiest kid around."

"No apology needed," said Jim. "But he's no kid."

"He swore there was nothin' missing from that bag."

"It was all there," I said.

Badger jammed the gloves down into a pocket. "Jason says you're good people. But I would appreciate it if you didn't offer him no more work. And if he comes by, if you would just send him back home."

"To get beat up?" said Jim.

"That's not an everyday occurrence," said Badger. "We keep the family business in the family."

"There's the law."

"You aren't it."

Badger had the same old-ice eyes as Dale. There was sawdust on his shirt and bits of wood stuck to his bootlaces, and he smelled like a cord of fresh-cut pine. "Stay away from my sons. Maybe you should move back to California. I'm sure they got plenty a'need for bleedin' heart know-it-alls like you."

———

WE LEFT THE party early. When we were almost home, Jim saw a truck parked off in the trees just before our driveway. He caught the shine of the grill in his headlights when we made the turn. I don't know how he saw that thing, but he still has twenty-fifteen vision for distance, so he's always seeing things that I miss. A wind had come up, so maybe it parted the trees at just the right second.

He cut the lights and stopped well away from our house. The outdoor security lights were on, and I could see the glimmer of the pond and the branches swaying. Jim reached across and drew his .380 automatic from its holster under the seat.

"We can go down the road and call the sheriff," I said.

"This is our home, Sally. I'm leaving the keys in."

"Be careful, Jim. We didn't retire up here for this."

I didn't know a person could get in and out of a truck so quietly. He walked down the driveway with the gun in his right hand and a flashlight in the other. He had that balanced walk, the one that meant he was ready for things. Jim's not a big guy, six feet, though, and still pretty solid.

Then I saw Dale backing around from the direction of the front porch, hunched over with a green gas can in one hand. Jim yelled, and Dale turned and saw him, then he dropped the can and got something out of his pocket, and a wall of flames huffed up along the house. Dale lit out around the house and disappeared.

I climbed over the console and drove the truck fast down the driveway and almost skidded on the gravel into the fire. Had to back it up, rocks flying everywhere. I got the extinguisher off its clip behind the seat and walked along the base of the house, blasting the white powder down where the gas was. A bird's nest up under an eave had caught fire, so I gave that a shot too. Could hear the chicks cheeping. I couldn't tell the sound of the extinguisher from the roaring in my ears.

After that I walked around, stamping out little hot spots on the ground and on the wall of the house. The wind was cold and damp, and it helped. My heart was pounding and my breath was caught up high in my throat and I'm not sure I could have said one word to anyone, not even Jim.

An hour later Jim came back, alone and panting. He signaled me back into our truck without a word. He put the flashlight and automatic in the console, then backed out of the driveway fast, his breath making fog on the rear window. There was sweat running down his face, and he smelled like trees and exertion.

"He'll come for his truck," Jim said.

Then he straightened onto the road and made his way to the turnoff where Dale's truck waited in the trees. We parked away from the Ram Charger, in a place where we wouldn't be too obvious.

———

WE SAT THERE until sunrise, then until seven. There were a couple of blankets and some water back in the king cab, and I'm glad we had all that. A little after seven, Dale came into view through the windshield, slogging through the forest with his arms around himself, shivering.

Jim waited until Dale saw us, then he flung himself from the truck, drawing down with his .380 and hollering, *"Police officer,"* and for Dale to stop. Dale did stop, then he turned and disappeared back into a thick stand of cottonwoods. Jim crashed in after him.

It took half an hour for him to come back. He had Dale out in front of him with his hands on his head, marching him like a POW. Their clothes were dirty and torn up. But Jim's gun was in his belt, so he must not have thought Dale was going to run for it again.

"You drive," Jim said to me. "Dale, you get in the backseat."

I looked at Jim with a question, but all he said was "Coeur d'Alene."

Nobody said a word to Coeur d'Alene. It wasn't far. Jim got on his cell when we reached the city and got the address for army recruitment.

We parked outside.

"Tell Sally what you decided to do about all this," said Jim.

"I can join the army or get arrested by your husband," said Dale. "I'm joining up."

"That's a good thing, Dale," I said.

"Name me one good thing about it."

"It'll get you out of trouble for a few years, for starters," I said.

We walked him into the recruitment office. There were flags and posters and a sergeant with a tight shirt and the best creased pants I've ever seen in my life. He was baffled by us at first, then Jim explained that we were friends of the family, and Dale had decided to join up but his mom and dad weren't able to be here for it. Which didn't explain why Dale's and Jim's clothes were dirty and more than a little torn up. The sergeant nodded. He'd seen this scene before.

"How old are you?" he asked.

"Nineteen."

"Then we've got no problems. Notta one."

There were lots of forms and questions. Dale made it clear that he was ready right then, he was ready to be signed up and go over to Iraq, try his luck on some ragheads. He tried a joke about not having to cut his hair off, and the sergeant laughed falsely.

Then the sergeant said they'd have to do a routine background check before the physical, would take about half an hour, we could come back if we wanted or sit right where we were.

So we went outside. The wind was back down and the day was warming up. Across the street was a breakfast place. The sun reflected off the window in a big orange rectangle, and you could smell the bacon and toast.

"I'm starved," said Dale.

"Me too," said Jim. "Sal? Breakfast?"

We ate. Nothing about Dale reminded me of JJ, but everything did. I hoped he'd find something over in that blood-soaked desert that he hadn't found here.

And I hoped that he'd be back to tell us what it was.

SACK o' WOE

BY JOHN HARVEY

T he street was dark and narrow, a smear of frost along the roof of the occasional parked car. Two of a possible six overhead lights had been smashed several weeks before. Recycling bins—blue, green, and gray—shared the pavement with abandoned supermarket trolleys and the detritus from a score of fast-food takeaways. Number thirty-four was toward the terrace end, the short street emptying onto a scrub of wasteland ridged with stiffened mud, puddles of brackish water covered by a thin film of ice.

January.

Tom Whitemore knocked with his gloved fist on the door of thirty-four. Paint that was flaking away, a bell that had long since ceased to work.

He was wearing blue jeans, a T-shirt and sweater, a scuffed leather jacket—the first clothes he had grabbed when the call had come through less than half an hour before.

January 27, 3:17 a.m.

Taking one step back, he raised his right leg and kicked against the door close by the lock; a second kick, wood splintered and the door sprang back.

Inside was your basic two-up, two-down house, a kitchen extension leading into the small yard at the back, bathroom above that. A strip of worn carpet in the narrow hallway, bare boards on the stairs. Bare wires that hung down, no bulb attached, from the ceiling overhead. He had been here before.

"Darren? Darren, you here?"

No answer when he called the name.

A smell that could be from a backed-up foul-water pipe or a blocked drain.

The front room was empty, odd curtains at the window, a TV set in one corner, two chairs and a sagging two-seater settee. Dust. A bundle of clothes. In the back room there were a small table and two more chairs, one with a broken back; a pile of old newspapers; the remnants of an unfinished oven-ready meal; a child's shoe.

"Darren?"

The first stair creaked a little beneath his weight.

In the front bedroom, a double mattress rested directly on the floor; several blankets, a quilt without a cover, no sheets. Half the drawers in the corner chest had been pulled open and left that way, miscellaneous items of clothing hanging down.

Before opening the door to the rear bedroom, Whitemore held his breath.

A pair of bunk beds leaned against one wall, a pumped-up Lilo mattress close by. Two tea chests, one spilling over with children's clothes, the other with toys. A plastic bowl in which cereal had hardened and congealed. A baby's bottle, rancid with yellowing milk. A used nappy, half in, half out of a pink plastic sack. A tube of sweets. A paper hat. Red and yellow building bricks. Soft toys. A plastic car. A teddy bear with a waistcoat and a bright bow tie, still new enough to have been a recent Christmas gift.

And blood.

Blood in fine tapering lines across the floor, faint splashes on the wall. Tom Whitemore pressed one hand to his forehead and closed his eyes.

———

HE HAD BEEN a member of the Public Protection Team for nearly four years: responsible, together with other police officers, probation officers, and representatives of other agencies—social services, community psychiatric care—for the supervision of violent and high-risk-of-harm sex offenders who had been released back into the community. Their task—through maintaining a close watch; pooling information; getting offenders, where applicable, into accredited programs; and assisting them in finding jobs—was to do anything and everything possible to prevent reoffending. It was often thankless and frequently frustrating—*What was that Springsteen song? Two steps up and three steps back?*—but unlike a lot of police work, it had focus, clear aims, methods, ambitions. It was possible—sometimes—to see positive results. Potentially dangerous men—they were mostly men—were neutralized, kept in check. If nothing else, there was that.

And yet his wife hated it. Hated it for the people it brought him into contact with, day after day—rapists, child abusers—the scum of the earth in her eyes, the lowest of the low. She hated it for the way it forced him to confront over and over what these people had done, what people were capable of, as if the enormities of their crimes were somehow contaminating him. Creeping into his dreams. Coming back with him into their home, like smoke caught in his hair or clinging to the fibers of his clothes. Contaminating them all.

"How much longer, Tom?" she would ask. "How much longer are you going to do this hateful bloody job?"

"Not long," he would say. "Not so much longer now."

Get out before you burn out, that was the word on the Force. Transfer to general duties, Traffic, Fraud. Yet he could never bring himself to leave, to make the move, and each morning he would set off back into that world, and each evening when he returned, no matter how late, he would go and stand in the twins' bedroom and watch them sleeping, his and Marianne's twin boys, five years old, safe and sound.

That summer they had gone to Filey as usual, two weeks of holiday, the same dubious weather, the same small hotel, the perfect curve of beach. The twins had run and splashed and fooled around on half-size body boards on the edges of the waves; they had eaten chips and ice cream, and when they were tired of playing with the big colored ball that bounced forever down toward the sea, Tom had helped them build sandcastles with an elaborate array of turrets and tunnels, while Marianne alternately read her book or dozed.

It was perfect: even the weather was forgiving, no more than a scattering of showers, a few darkening clouds, the wind from the south.

On the last evening, the twins upstairs asleep, they had sat on the small terrace overlooking the promenade and the black strip of sea. "When we get back, Tom," Marianne had said, "you've got to ask for a transfer. They'll understand. No one can do a job like that forever, not even you."

She reached for his hand, and as he turned toward her, she brought her face to his. "Tom?" Her breath on his face was warm and slightly sweet, and he felt a lurch of love run through him like a wave.

"All right," he said.

"You promise?"

"I promise."

But by the end of that summer, things had changed. There had been the bombings in London for one thing, suicide bombers on the tube; an innocent young Brazilian shot and killed after a bungled surveillance operation; suspected terrorists arrested in suburbs of Birmingham and Leeds. It was everywhere. All around. Security alerts at the local airport; rumors that spread from voice to voice, from mobile phone to mobile phone. *Don't go into the city center this Saturday. Keep well away. Stay clear.* Now it was commonplace to see: fully armed in the middle of the day, a pair of uniformed police officers strolling down past Pizza Hut and the Debenhams department store, Heckler & Koch submachine guns held low across their chests, Walther P990 pistols holstered at their hips, shoppers no longer bothering to stop and stare.

As the Home Office and Security Services continued to warn of the possibility of a new terrorist attack, the pressures on police time increased. A report from the chief inspector of constabulary noted that, in some police areas, surveillance packages intended to supervise high-risk offenders were now rarely implemented due to a lack of resources. "Whether it is counterterrorism or a sex offender," explained his deputy, "there are only a certain number of specialist officers to go round."

"You remember what you promised," Marianne said. By now it was late September, the nights drawing in.

"I can't," Tom said, slowly shaking his head. "I can't leave now."

She looked at him, her face like flint. "I can, Tom. We can. Remember that."

It hung over them after that, the threat, fracturing what had held them together for so long.

Out of necessity, Tom worked longer hours; when he did get home, tired, head buzzing, it was to find her turned away from him in the bed and flinching at his touch. At breakfast, when he put his arms around her at the sink, she shrugged him angrily away.

"Marianne, for God's sake . . ."

"What?"

"We can't go on like this."

"No?"

"No."

"Then do something about it."

"Jesus!"

"What?"

"I've already told you. A hundred times. Not now."

She pushed past him and out into the hall, slamming the door at her back. "Fuck!" Tom shouted and slammed his fist against the wall. "Fuck, fuck, fuck!" One of the twins screamed as if he'd been struck; the other knocked his plastic bowl of cereal to the floor and started to cry.

———

THE TEAM MEETING was almost over when Christine Finch—one of the probation officers, midfifties, experienced—raised her hand. "Darren Pitcher. I think we might have a problem."

Tom Whitemore sighed. "What now?"

"One of my clients, Emma Laurie, suspended sentence for dealing crack cocaine, lives up in Forest Fields. Not the brightest cherry in the bunch. She's taken up with Pitcher. Seems he's thinking of moving in."

"That's a problem?"

"She's got three kids, all under six. Two of them boys."

Whitemore shook his head. He knew Darren Pitcher's history well enough. An only child, brought up by a mother who had given birth to him when she was just sixteen, Pitcher had met his father only twice: on the first occasion, magnanimous from drink, the older man had squeezed his buttocks and slipped two five-pound notes into his trouser pocket; on the second, sober, he had blacked the boy's eye and told him to fuck off out of his sight.

A loner at school, marked out by learning difficulties, bullied; from the age of sixteen, Pitcher had drifted through a succession of low-paying jobs—cleaning, stacking supermarket shelves, hospital portering, washing cars—and several short-term relationships with women who enjoyed even less self-esteem than he.

When he was twenty-five, he was sentenced to five years' imprisonment for molesting half a dozen boys between the ages of four and seven. While in prison, in addition to numerous incidents of self-harming, he had made one attempt at suicide.

Released, he had spent the first six months in a hostel and had reported to both his probation officer and a community psychiatric nurse each week. After which time, supervision had necessarily slackened off.

"Ben?" Whitemore said, turning toward the psychiatric nurse at the end of the table. "He was one of yours."

Ben Leonard pushed a hand up through his cropped blond hair. "A family, ready-made, might be what he needs."

"The girl," Christine Finch said, "she's not strong. It's a wonder she's hung on to those kids as long as she has."

"There's a father somewhere?"

"Several."

"Contact?"

"Not really."

For a moment, Tom Whitemore closed his eyes. "The boys, they're how old?"

"Five and three. There's a little girl, eighteen months."

"And do we think, should Pitcher move in, they could be at risk?"

"I think we have to," Christine Finch said.

"Ben?"

Leonard took his time. "We've made real progress with Darren, I think. He's aware that his previous behavior was wrong.

Regrets what he's done. The last thing he wants to do is offend again. But, yes, for the sake of the kids, I'd have to say there is a risk. A small one, but a risk."

"Okay," Whitemore said. "I'll go and see him. Report back. Christine, you'll stay in touch with the girl?"

"Of course."

"Good. Let's not lose sight of this in the midst of everything else."

————

THEY SAT ON the Portland Leisure Centre steps, a wan sun showing weakly through the wreaths of cloud. Whitemore had bought two cups of pale tea from the machines inside, and they sat there on the cold, worn stone, scarcely talking as yet. Darren Pitcher was smoking a cigarette, a roll-up he had made with less than steady hands. *What was it,* Whitemore thought, *his gran had always said? Don't sit on owt cold or you'll get piles, sure as eggs is eggs.*

"Got yourself a new girlfriend, I hear," Whitemore said.

Pitcher flinched, then glanced at him from under lowered lids. He had a lean face, a few reddish spots around the mouth and chin, strangely long eyelashes that curled luxuriantly over his weak gray eyes.

"Emma? That her name?"

"She's all right."

"Of course."

Two young black men in shiny sportswear bounced past them, all muscle, on their way to the gym.

"It serious?" Whitemore asked.

"Dunno."

"What I heard, it's pretty serious. The pair of you. Heard you were thinking of moving in."

Pitcher mumbled something and drew on his cigarette.

"Sorry?" Whitemore said. "I didn't quite hear . . ."

"I said it's none of your business . . ."

"Isn't it?"

"My life, yeah? Not yours."

Whitemore swallowed a mouthful more of the lukewarm tea and turned the plastic cup upside down, shaking the last drops onto the stone. "This Emma," he said, "she's got kids. Young kids."

"So?"

"Young boys."

"That don't . . . You can't . . . That was a long time ago."

"I know, Darren. I know. But it happened, nonetheless. And it makes this our concern." For a moment, his hand rested on Pitcher's arm. "You understand?"

Pitcher's hand went to his mouth, and he bit down on his knuckle hard.

———

GREGORY BOULEVARD RAN along one side of the Forest Recreation Ground, the nearest houses, once substantial family homes, now mostly subdivided into flats, and falling, many of them, into disrepair. Beyond these, the streets grew narrower and coiled back upon themselves, the houses smaller, with front doors that opened directly out onto the street. Corner shops with bars across the windows, shutters on the doors.

Emma Laurie sat on a lopsided settee in the front room; small-featured, a straggle of hair falling down across her face, her voice rarely rising above a whisper as she spoke. *A wraith of a thing,* Whitemore thought. *Outside, a good wind would blow her away.*

The three children huddled in the corner, watching cartoons, the sound turned low. Jason, Rory, and Jade. The youngest had a runny nose, the older of the boys coughed intermittently, open-mouthed, but they were all, as yet, bright-eyed.

"He's good with them," Emma was saying, "Darren. Plays with them all the time. Takes them, you know, down to the forest. They love him, they really do. Can't wait for him to move in wi' us. Go on about it all the time. Jason especially."

"And you?" Christine Finch said. "How do you feel? About Darren moving in?"

"Be easier, won't it? Rent and that. What I get, family credit an' the rest, s'a struggle, right? But if Darren's here, I can get a job up the supermarket, afternoons. Get out a bit, 'stead of bein' all cooped up. Darren'll look after the kids. He don't mind."

———

THEY WALKED DOWN through the maze of streets to where Finch had left her car, the Park & Ride on the edge of the forest.

"What do you think?" Whitemore said.

"Ben could be right. Darren, could be the making of him."

"But if it puts those lads at risk?"

"I know, I know. But what can we do? He's been out a good while now, no sign of him reoffending."

"I still don't like it," Whitemore said.

Finch smiled wryly. "Other people's lives. We'll keep our fingers crossed. Keep as close an eye as we can."

Sometimes, Whitemore thought, *it's as if we are trying to hold the world together with good intentions and a ball of twine.*

"Give you a lift back into town?" Finch said when they reached her car. It was not yet late afternoon, and the light was already beginning to fade.

Whitemore shook his head. "It's okay. I'll catch the tram."

Back at the office, he checked his e-mails, made several calls, wrote up a brief report of the visit with Emma Laurie. He wondered if he should go and see Darren Pitcher again but decided there was little to be gained. When he finally got back home, a little after six, Marianne was buckling the twins into their seats in the back of the car.

"What's going on?"

She was flushed, a scarf at her neck. "My parents. I thought we'd go over and see them. Just for a couple of days. They haven't seen the boys in ages."

"They were over just the other weekend."

"That was a month ago. More. It is ages to them."

One of the boys was marching his dinosaur along the top of the seat in front; the other was fiddling with his straps.

"You were just going to go?" Whitemore said. "You weren't even going to wait till I got back?"

"You're not usually this early."

"So wait."

"It's a two-hour drive."

"I know how far it is."

"Tom, don't. Please."

"Don't what?"

"Make this more difficult than it is."

He read it in her eyes. Walking to the back of the car, he snapped open the boot. It was crammed with luggage, coats, shoes, toys.

"You're not just going for a couple of days, are you? This is not a couple of fucking days."

"Tom, please . . ." She raised a hand toward him, but he knocked it away.

"You're leaving, that's what you're doing . . ."

"No, I'm not."

"You're not?"

"It's just for a little while . . . A break. I need a break. So I can think."

"You need to fucking think, all right."

Whitemore snatched open the rear door and leaned inside,

seeking to unsnap the nearest boy's belt and failing in his haste. The boys themselves looked frightened and close to tears.

"Tom, don't do that! Leave it. Leave them alone."

She pulled at his shoulder and he thrust her away, so that she almost lost her footing and stumbled back. Roused by the shouting, one of the neighbors was standing halfway along his front garden path, openly staring.

"Tom, please," Marianne said. "Be reasonable."

He turned so fast, she thought he was going to strike her and she cowered back.

"Reasonable? Like this? You call this fucking reasonable?"

The neighbor had come as far as the pavement edge. "Excuse me, but is everything all right?"

"All right?" Whitemore shouted. "Yeah. Marvelous. Fucking wonderful. Now fuck off indoors and mind your own fucking business."

Both the twins were crying now: not crying, screaming.

The car door slammed as Marianne slid behind the wheel and started the engine.

"Marianne!" Whitemore shouted her name and brought down his fist hard on the roof of the car as it pulled away, red taillights blurring in the half-dark.

Whitemore stood there for several moments more, staring off into the middle distance, seeing nothing. Back in the house, he went from room to room, assessing how much she had taken, how long she might be considering staying away. Her parents lived on the coast, between Chapel St. Leonards and Sutton-on-Sea, a bungalow but with room enough for Marianne and the twins. Next year they would be at school, next year would be different, but now . . .

He looked in the fridge, but there was nothing there he fancied. A couple of cold sausages wrapped in foil. Maybe he'd make himself a sandwich later on. He snapped open a can of lager, but the taste was stale in his mouth and he poured the remainder down the sink. There was a bottle of whiskey in the cupboard, only recently opened, but he knew better than to start down that route too soon.

In the living room, he switched on the TV, flicked through the channels, switched it off again; he made a cup of tea and glanced at that day's paper, one of Marianne's magazines. Every fifteen minutes, he looked at his watch. When he thought he'd given them time enough, he phoned.

Marianne's father came on the line. Soft-spoken, understanding, calm. "I'm sorry, Tom. She doesn't want to speak to you right now. Perhaps tomorrow, tomorrow evening. She'll call you. . . . The twins? They're sleeping, fast off. Put them to bed as soon as they arrived. . . . I'll be sure to give them your love. . . . Yes, of course. Of course. . . . Good night, Tom. Good night."

Around nine, Whitemore called a taxi and went across the city to the Five Ways pub in Sherwood. In the back room, Jake McMahon and a bunch of the usual reprobates were charging through Cannonball Adderley's "Jeannine." A Duke Pearson tune, but because Whitemore had first heard it on Adderley's *Them Dirty Blues*—Cannonball on alto alongside his trumpeter brother, Nat—it was forever associated with the saxophonist in his mind.

Whitemore's father had given him the recording as a sixteenth-birthday present, when Tom's mind had been more full of T'Pau and the Pet Shop Boys, Whitney Houston and Madonna. But eventually he had given it a listen, late in his room, and something had stuck.

One of the best nights he remembered having with his father before the older man took himself off to a retirement chalet in Devon had been spent here, drinking John Smith's Bitter and listening to the band play another Adderley special, "Sack o' Woe."

Jake McMahon came over to him at the break and shook his hand. "Not seen you in a while."

Whitemore forced a smile. "You know how it is, this and that."

McMahon nodded. "Your dad, he okay?"

"Keeping pretty well."

"You'll give him my best."

"Of course."

Whitemore stayed for the second set, then called a cab from the phone alongside the bar.

———

DARREN PITCHER MOVED in with Emma Laurie and her three children. October became November, became December. Most Sundays, Whitemore drove out to his in-laws' bungalow on the coast, where the twins threw themselves at him with delight and he played rough-and-tumble with them on the beach if the cold allowed and, if not, tussled with them on the living room settee. Marianne's parents stepped around him warily, keeping their thoughts to themselves. If he tried to get Marianne off on her own, she resisted, made excuses. Conversation between them was difficult.

"When will we see you again?" she asked one evening as he was leaving.

"When are you coming home?" he asked. Christmas was less than three weeks away.

"Tom, I don't know."

"But you are coming? Coming back?"

She turned her face aside. "Don't rush me, all right?"

It was just two days later when Christine Finch phoned Whitemore in his office, the first call of the day. Emma Laurie was waiting for them, agitated, at her front door. She had come back from work to find Pitcher with Jason, the eldest of her two sons, on his lap; Jason had been sitting on a towel, naked, and Pitcher had been rubbing Vaseline between his legs.

Whitemore and Finch exchanged glances.

"Did he have a reason?" Finch asked.

"He said Jason was sore, said he'd been complaining about being sore . . ."

"And you don't believe him?"

"If he was sore, it was 'cause of what Darren was doing. You know that as well as me."

"Where is Darren now?" Whitemore said.

"I don't know. I don't care. I told him to clear out and not come back."

Whitemore found Pitcher later that morning, sitting cross-legged on the damp pavement, his back against the hoardings surrounding the Old Market Square. Rain was falling in fine slanted lines, but Pitcher either hadn't noticed or didn't care.

"Darren," Whitemore said, "come on, let's get out of this rain."

Pitcher glanced up at him and shook his head.

Coat collar up, Whitemore hunkered down beside him. "You want to tell me what happened?"

"Nothing happened."

"Emma says . . ."

"I don't give a fuck what Emma says."

"I do," Whitemore said. "I have to. But I want to know what you say too."

Pitcher was silent for several minutes, passersby stepping over his legs or grudgingly going round.

"He'd been whinging away," Pitcher said. "Jason. How the pants he was wearing were too tight. Scratching. His hand down his trousers, scratching, and I kept telling him to stop. He'd hurt himself. Make it worse. Then, when he went to the toilet, right, I told him to show me, you know, show me where it was hurting, point to it, like. And there was a bit of red there, I could see, so I said would he like me to put something on it, to make it better, and he said yes, and so . . ."

He stopped abruptly, tears in his eyes and shoulders shaking. Whitemore waited.

"I didn't do anything," Pitcher said finally. "Honest. I never touched him. Not like . . . you know, like before."

"But you could have?" Whitemore said.

Head down, Pitcher nodded.

"Darren?"

"Yes, yeah. I suppose . . . Yeah."

Still neither of them moved, and the rain continued to fall.

————

ON CHRISTMAS MORNING Whitemore rose early, scraped the ice from the windows of the secondhand Saab he'd bought not so many weeks before, loaded up the backseat with presents, and set out for the coast. When he arrived the light was only just beginning to spread, in bands of pink and yellow, across the sky. Wanting his arrival to be a surprise, he parked some houses away.

The curtains were partly drawn and he could see the lights of the Christmas tree clearly, red, blue, and green, and, as he moved across the frosted grass, he could see the twins, up already, still wearing their pajamas, tearing into the contents of their stockings, shouting excitedly as they pulled at the shiny paper and cast it aside.

When he thought they might see him, he stepped quickly away and returned to the car, loading the presents into his arms. Back at the bungalow, he placed them on the front step, up against the door, and walked away.

If he had waited, knocked on the window, rung the bell, gone inside and stayed, seen their happiness at close hand, he knew it would have been almost impossible to leave.

EMMA LAURIE APPEARED at the police station in early January, the youngest child in a buggy, the others half-hidden behind her legs. After days of endless pestering, she had allowed Pitcher back into the house, just for an hour, and then he had refused to leave. When she'd finally persuaded him to go, he had threatened to kill himself if she didn't have him back; said that he would snatch the children and take them with him; kill them all.

"It was wrong o' me, weren't it? Letting him back in. I never should've done it. I know that, I know."

"It's okay," Whitemore said. "And I wouldn't pay too much attention to what Darren said. He was angry. Upset. Times like that, people say a lot of things they don't necessarily mean."

"But if you'd seen his face . . . He meant it, he really did."

Whitemore gave her his card. "Look, my mobile number's there. If he comes round again, threatening you, anything like that, you call me, right? Straightaway. Meantime, I'll go and have a word with him. Okay?"

Emma smiled uncertainly, nodded thanks, and ushered the children away.

AFTER SPENDING TIME in various hostels and a spell sleeping rough, Pitcher, with the help of the local housing association, had found a place to rent in Sneinton. A one-room flat with a sink and small cooker in one corner and a shared bathroom and toilet on the floor below. Whitemore sat on the single chair, and Pitcher sat on the sagging bed.

"I know why you're here," Pitcher said. "It's about Emma. What I said."

"You frightened her."

"I know. I lost my temper, that's all." He shook his head.

"Being there, her an' the kids, a family, you know? An' then her chuckin' me out. You wouldn't understand. Why would you? But I felt like shit. A piece of shit. An' I meant it. What I said. Not the kids, not harmin' them. I wouldn't do that. But topping myself . . ." He looked at Whitemore despairingly. "It's what I'll do. I swear it. I will."

"Don't talk like that," Whitemore said.

"Why the hell not?"

Whitemore leaned toward him and lowered his voice. "It's hard, I know. And I do understand. Really, I do. But you have to keep going. Move on. Look—here—you've got this place, right? A flat of your own. It's a start. A new start. Look at it like that."

He went across to Pitcher and rested a hand on his shoulder, not knowing how convincing his half-truths and platitudes had been.

"Ben Leonard. You talked to him before. I'll see if I can't get him to see you again. It might help sort a few things out. Okay? But in the meantime, whatever you do, you're to keep away from Emma. Right, Darren? Emma and the children." Whitemore tightened his grip on Pitcher's shoulder before stepping clear. "Keep right away."

———

IT WAS A little more than a week later when the call came through, waking Whitemore from his sleep. The voice was brisk, professional, a triage nurse at the Queen's Medical Centre, Accident and Emergency. "We've a young woman here, Emma Laurie, she's quite badly injured. Some kind of altercation with a partner? She insisted that I contact you, I hope that's all right. Apparently she's worried about the children. Three of them?"

"Are they there with her?"

"No. At home, apparently."

"On their own?"

"I don't know. I don't think so. Maybe a neighbor? I'm afraid she's not making a lot of sense."

Whitemore dropped the phone and finished pulling on his clothes.

———

THE HOUSE WAS silent—the blood slightly tacky to the touch. One more room to go. The bathroom door was bolted from the inside, and Whitemore shouldered it free. Darren Pitcher was sitting on the toilet seat, head slumped forward toward his chest, one arm trailing over the bath, the other dangling toward the floor. Long, vertical cuts ran down the inside of both arms, almost from elbow to wrist, slicing through the horizontal scars from where he had harmed himself before. Blood had pooled along the bottom of the bath and around his feet. A Stanley knife rested on the bath's edge alongside an oval of pale green soap.

Whitemore crouched down. There was a pulse, still beating faintly, at the side of Pitcher's neck.

"Darren? Can you hear me?"

With an effort, Pitcher raised his head. "See, I did it. I said I would." A ghost of a smile lingered in his eyes.

"The children," Whitemore said. "Where are they?"

Pitcher's voice was a sour whisper in his face. "The shed. Out back. I didn't want them to see this."

As Pitcher's head slumped forward, Whitemore dialed the emergency number on his mobile phone.

Downstairs, he switched on the kitchen light; there was a box of matches lying next to the stove. Unbolting the back door, he stepped outside. The shed was no more than five feet high, roughly fashioned from odd planks of wood, the roof covered with a rime of frost. The handle was cold to the touch.

"Don't be frightened," he said, loud enough for them to hear inside. "I'm just going to open the door."

When it swung back, he ducked inside and struck a match. The three children were clinging to one another in the farthest corner, staring wide-eyed into the light.

———

DARREN PITCHER HAD lost consciousness by the time the paramedics arrived, and despite their efforts and those of the doctors at A & E, he was pronounced dead a little after six that morning. Sutured and bandaged, Emma Laurie was kept in overnight and then released. Her children had been scooped up by the Social Services Emergency Duty Team and would spend a short time in care.

Tom Whitemore drove to the embankment and stood on the pedestrian bridge across the river, staring down at the dark, glassed-over surface of the water, the pale shapes of sleeping swans, heads tucked beneath their wings. Overhead, the sky was clear and pitted with stars.

When he finally arrived home, it was near dawn.

The heating in the house had just come on.

Upstairs, in the twins' room, it felt cold nonetheless. Each bed was carefully made up, blankets folded neatly back. In case. He stood there for a long time, letting the light slowly unfold round him. The start of another day.

THE DROUGHT

BY JAMES O. BORN

The photograph of the girl hadn't changed since the first time Broward Sheriff's Office detective Ben Stoltz had looked at it three years before. She looked pretty much like she had when he walked up to her in the center of yellow crime-scene tape in a vacant lot off Sunrise Boulevard. Something about her nose and eyebrows reminded him of his own daughter, and that was really all it took. One of the things that had saved his sanity was the rise in the murder rate in Broward County, which had kept him too busy to really consider how he had failed her ever since a jogger had first discovered her body on that cool March evening. Now that things had slowed down, he had time again. Shit.

A musical ringtone shook him out of his daze as he looked at the photograph. He missed the practical and obnoxious rings that phones used to make. Sitting at the same desk he had occupied since entering the detective bureau, using the same Paper Mate pen he had used his first day in plain clothes, he wondered why the phones had undergone such an evolution. Some had a gentle, breezy electronic chime; others sounded like a tiny fire alarm. His phone had whatever was programmed into the damn thing when some pencil-necked geek had plopped it down four years before. If it weren't for the weary secretary who, tired of taking his messages, had set up his voice mail, he'd be the only one in Homicide without the precious service.

Now, staring at the files of his open cases, Stoltz wished someone would call and get him off his dead ass and doing something. He feared these slight lulls in the murder rate. The times when he might have to sit in the office and look over his mistakes. That's what he considered his open cases. Why not? If he was unable to solve them, then it was his mistake. He had failed. Aside from his deep desire to retire in Homicide, he knew what his duty was. It was to catch the assholes who killed other people. Sometimes it was more personal or more rewarding. Sometimes he just felt like the referee in some giant game in which one group shoots up another. Of the four files in front of him, three were drug related. He wanted them closed but never felt satisfied with the result. Somewhere, maybe a few years down the road, some dumbass would get picked up on a trafficking charge and give up the triggerman on a drug homicide. Or, as had happened to him several times, a gun would be recovered and traced back to the killing. Once, they had lifted some DNA off the grip of a Beretta that had led to a conviction. These were back burners.

The fourth file. Jane Doe number sixty-eight was a girl that had died around the age of twenty. Jenny's age. Except this girl wasn't a junior at the University of Central Florida. She was some lonely girl whom someone had stabbed and left in a vacant lot off Sunrise Boulevard. Still in unincorporated Broward County, about two blocks from the city limits of Sunrise. At first, his boss asked, almost pleaded, for him to say it was in the city's jurisdiction. But geography didn't lie, and neither did he. It was their case. No witnesses, no leads, no motive, and no true name for the victim. His sergeant looked like he was about to have a seizure. Then the sergeant had a stroke of genius. Suicide. Stoltz had to bring up the uncomfortable question of how someone stabbed themselves four times to commit suicide and then didn't leave a weapon near the body. His sergeant was ready. Animals had carried it off. After all, it was a vacant lot. But as the lead investigator, Stoltz refused to go with the "well-armed raccoon" theory and had carried the case for the past three years. Three years, two sergeants, nineteen cases, and one marriage ago. Felt like a lifetime.

He sensed more than saw the figure of Chuck, his partner on most cases, as he dropped into the chair next to his desk.

"Ben, what's the good word?" asked the only detective who was senior to him in the Homicide Unit.

Ben Stoltz just looked out over his cluttered desk and sighed.

"Yeah, I know. Droughts like this bring up a lot of old shit. I'm recanvassing the neighborhood where we found Cassie Brown's body." The heavyset detective looked across at the other cops at their desks. "You never see this many guys in here at once. Rumor is that they may shift some of us to other areas."

Stoltz looked up and paid attention for the first time. "Like where?"

"Dunno. Fraud is hot right now, and there's always sex crimes."

"We got nothing to worry about. We're senior."

"Ben, you and I got no juice. These young guys, they're climbers. They talk to the colonel and the sheriff. They get 'face time,' and all we do is get cases and clear 'em. We'll be the first to go. They'll tell us some bullshit like it'll do us good to see something other than corpses."

Stoltz looked around, seeing, for the first time, his competition. He had always just done his job and been left alone. Would that work in today's environment? He looked at the other detective. "You're in DROP. I didn't come on the Sheriff's Office until

I was thirty-one. I got four years, just to go into the DROP for five more." In reality, Stoltz didn't view the DROP retirement incentive as a chance to make more money but as an opportunity to stay a while longer. The Deferred Retirement Option Plan allowed a cop to collect retirement in a savings account and still work for a five-year period. The intent was to move old-timers out of the job.

Chuck loosened his tie. "Man, that would suck to finish up in another unit."

Stoltz didn't acknowledge the comment. He was distracted by his sergeant, who, at thirty-four, was nearly twenty years younger than he. The balding young man who never smiled said, "Ben, we got an officer-involved shooting."

"Where?"

"Our favorite beach town, where else?"

"The cop okay?"

"Of course. That bunch are shooters, not targets."

"Any weapon?"

"Not from the stiff. Looks like he took the cop's ASP and the cop fired twice. You two get over there. Crime Scene is on the way." He ran a bony hand through thinning blond hair. "Ben, you're the lead. I'll be along shortly."

"Got it, Sarge."

The young sergeant added, "Carla Lazaro is the assistant on it."

Stoltz gave an involuntary shudder. "She's not in the Homicide Unit."

"Public Integrity. They get police shootings. Watch your ass so she doesn't swallow you whole."

"I'm still the lead investigator. She's just an assistant state attorney."

"But she has a big mouth and bigger ego. If she called the captain and wanted you removed, she'd probably pull it off. Just watch it. She'll use a case like this for political advantage."

"I don't follow politics."

"But she does."

Stoltz nodded, not worried about whomever the state attorney had assigned to the case. He just found and repeated facts.

His partner said, "The drought breaks, good thing you're the duty detective. This'll give you some juice to stay here if things go bad." He paused and added, "Too bad the Queen of the Damned is assigned."

"She won't bother us."

"You hope." He stood and headed toward his desk. "Like I said, at least you caught a case. That'll look good during review time."

Stoltz hated to admit it, but he had already thought of that. He had his "go kit," with a tape recorder, camera, and note pads, all zipped up and ready within a minute. This was the kind of stuff that had kept him sober and sane as the last year had unfolded. Mary's leaving him, Jenny's college expenses, and Craig's Christmas revelation had shaken him out of the life he had found so comfortable. Thank God he still had Homicide.

———

HE PARKED MORE than a block away from the point of the shooting, so he could take in the scene and get his bearings before anyone noticed him and started to tell him what had happened instead of him *discovering* what had happened. He could see the outer edge of the yellow crime-scene tape coming from the convenience store one block east of the Intracoastal. The Sheriff's Office had a memo of understanding with the town that the S.O. Homicide Unit would investigate their officer-involved shootings. The previous sheriff had signed the memo, not realizing that there would be more shootings in this small beach town than in all other municipalities combined, and no one knew why. In addition, none of the suspects, five of whom were dead, had ever had a weapon. They had reached for wrenches, umbrellas, tape players—one had used a car—but none had had a gun or knife. That didn't mean the cop hadn't acted in self-defense; it just looked bad in the media. Stoltz didn't care about the media or even the reasons why there were so many shootings in the town. All he cared about was doing a good job on the investigation and finding out what had happened in this shooting. If the cop had acted incorrectly, he would note it. If the shooting was justified, he would note that too. That was his job, and the only thing he had going for him now.

As he neared the tape, he heard a voice say, "Detectivesaurus Rex, I thought you had retired."

Stoltz looked over at the forty-year-old police chief of South Fort Lauderdale Beach. He had known the chief since the guy was a patrolman and never thought he'd be a chief of police. At least not in the United States. "Hey, Howie, your man doing okay?"

"He's a little shaky. The perp wrestled with him for a good five minutes before he finally had to drop back and fire. This'll be an easy one for you."

"Will he talk to me?"

"Through the PBA attorney. Just to be safe."

"Whatever he wants."

The young chief straightened his tie and adjusted his suit coat. "You haven't changed. Still the Joe Friday look."

"The dress code is shirt and tie."

"Yeah, but short sleeves and a blue clip-on?"

"Never had a client complain."

The chief smiled. "Nice to see some things never change."

"I could say that about how your cops react to threats."

"Stoltz, you know that's not fair. Just because you never had a rough patrol zone, don't think it's not dangerous out there."

He looked around at the beach shops and the park that extended five blocks. "You call this a rough patrol zone?"

The chief ignored him. "C'mon, I'll take you to the scene."

Stoltz followed the younger man to the tape, where a female officer in a city uniform wrote down his name as he entered the scene. She looked young enough to be one of his kids. He ducked under the tape that sealed off the entire ten-car parking lot at the Beach Snack Shop. He noticed that the S.O. Crime Scene people were already photographing the area. One tech had a detailed sketch of the lot and was placing yellow markers next to the two spent .40-caliber casings on the ground in front of the store's door. Inside the brightly lit store, Stoltz saw six people leaning or sitting near the back wall, one of them a small man with a dark complexion, wearing a bright-red shirt with a badge that read BEACH SNACK SHOP.

This was what he had been trained to do and why he hadn't had a bad day in his six years with the unit. His mind seemed to understand the template to use to set down the case. Interview the witnesses, interview the cop, get the radio transmissions, talk to the dead guy's family, pull together crime scene and ballistics, throw in a few photos, and he had a case that would make sense. That was what he loved, pulling order out of chaos. That was all he had left.

He turned to find his partner next to the worried-looking chief. "Chuck, talk to the witnesses inside and get me an idea of what happened. Chief, I'll need your radio tapes and the cop's clothes and gun. You have something for him to use until we're done with the examination?"

He nodded.

"Can we use your PD for interviews and stuff? It's a lot closer than the S.O."

"No problem." He paused and then said, "Ben, you're not gonna bury this guy, are you? Albury is fairly new but a good cop."

"C'mon, Howie, you know I gotta look at this with an open mind."

"That's all I ask."

"Why would you think I wouldn't?"

"Because Carla Lazaro is waiting at the PD to sit in on interviews."

Stoltz patted the chief on the arm and said, "Don't worry, Howie. She doesn't conduct the investigation and she doesn't influence me."

"I'm just worried about her using something like this to make a name for herself."

"It'll be fine. I'm sure she won't interfere. She's just a dedicated assistant state attorney."

They both started to laugh as they moved on through the scene.

———

BEN STOLTZ FELT a sort of Zen pattern with homicide investigations. When he was on the scene of something like this, nothing else mattered. The problem he had experienced was that, when working a hot case, an activity that often took days or weeks after a body was discovered, he excluded almost everything else from his consciousness. He had missed Jenny's dance recitals and cheerleading contests, more than one anniversary, which explained his current one-bedroom apartment in the town of Davie, and would have missed Craig's sporting events if he had ever played sports. He did miss his son's slow transition from rock to punk to Goth to whatever the hell he was now, with the piercings and tattoos. That was one favor the job had done for him.

Now, he let his instincts dictate what steps to take in the case. He didn't worry about family, salary, or even Jane Doe number sixty-eight. The drought in homicides had lasted so long, he had to savor this activity of checking in with all the cogs that made an investigation run. The young woman from Crime Scene showed him where the body had fallen and where a small amount of blood had leaked onto the cement sidewalk. He tried to visualize where the body had landed. He didn't like to call them "victims" in officer-involved shootings because he cringed when he heard the TV reporters refer to them that way. It made the cop sound like a murderer even if he was doing what he had been paid to do and was protecting the public. Contrary to Hollywood lore, Stoltz had never actually seen anyone use chalk lines on a body. If the corpse had been involved in immediate violence, like a drive-by, he or she would have been rushed to the hospital so every effort could have been made to save the person. If a body was found that was days old, Crime Scene took hundreds of photographs to provide an accurate view of how the corpse was discovered and what condition it was in. Chalk lines served no purpose. At least at a homicide scene.

He stood at the door to the small store, with the bloodstain a few feet away and the two casings about ten feet beyond the blood. He tried to get a sense of what the witnesses might have seen from the door or from inside the store. He tried to imagine what the corpse saw as the cop approached him. Stoltz had to wonder why, if the dead guy saw the cop with a pistol pointed at him, he didn't drop the ASP. While the ASP expandable baton was a lethal weapon, it was no match for a Glock .40 caliber.

The lack of blood on the sidewalk probably meant good shot placement and that the guy's heart stopped before it pumped much blood. Some bloody napkins and paramedics' bandage wrappers lay next to the wall and in the lot just off the sidewalk. Someone had made an effort to save him.

Stoltz scanned the area to see all the vantage points. Inside the store, two of the female witnesses cried into paper towels.

The shooting had occurred more than an hour ago. He had a hard time understanding the lingering stress of the incident. To him, the aftermath was just an activity, like doing your wash or balancing the books. He often was mystified by the emotion that followed. At least the hysterics of witnesses who didn't know the corpse. He noticed his partner speaking to a witness off to the side, away from the others. That seemed natural to him, not emotional. Get the scene in order, then break it down. Talk to the witnesses separately so one account doesn't influence the others.

He noticed the chief of police walking toward him, accompanied by a short, bald man in casual clothes. The bald guy was young, maybe thirty-three, and had a serious look about him.

The chief said, "Ben, this is David Whist. He's the PBA attorney handling this." The Police Benevolent Association always sent a lawyer to the scene of a shooting that involved one of its dues-paying members.

He shook the younger man's small, smooth hand.

The attorney blew past all niceties. "You wanna hear our side? As a proffer, of course."

"I'd rather talk to your man."

"He's composing himself."

"And if there's a problem with the shooting, you can't testify."

"That's why we have attorneys and offer proffers of what happened, Detective."

Stoltz listened to the quick summary of the cop's encounter with an uncommunicative man who wouldn't leave the premises as the owner had ordered. The cop popped out his ASP so the man could see the extended baton, then tapped him on the leg to get him moving. The attorney emphasized it was a tap, not a strike. The man grabbed the ASP, and the two wrestled for control of the weapon. When the cop couldn't fight any longer, he released the ASP and climbed to his feet, exhausted. The officer drew his pistol and ordered the man to drop the weapon and not to come any closer. After several attempts to get the man to stop coming toward him, the cop fired twice, hitting the man in the chest. The officer applied immediate first aid and called for help.

"That's it?" asked Stoltz.

"In a nutshell."

"Can I speak to your client?"

"Absolutely."

"I'll be over to the PD in about half an hour."

———

STOLTZ TOOK A few minutes to confer with his sergeant, who had just arrived, and with his partner, who had briefly spoken to each witness and was preparing to get formal taped statements from them.

The young sergeant looked up at his two seniormost detectives. "What do ya got, Ben?"

Ben relayed the attorney's account.

The sergeant looked at Chuck without saying a word.

The heavier partner with the monogrammed shirt looked down at his pad. "The store owner called in that the dead guy wouldn't leave the premises and appeared to be ignoring the outside world. The owner said he didn't notice the cop until they started struggling outside. He said they sort of 'lay on top of each other for a long time,' until the cop stood up and shouted several times, then fired his pistol twice. The shop owner thinks it's great, because he believes it'll scare off the other homeless guys from across the Intracoastal." He looked at Stoltz and added, "The others say pretty much the same thing, except . . ."

Ben said, "Except for who?"

"The surfer-looking guy." They all turned at once and looked through the window. Stoltz immediately saw a smaller blond man, about twenty-five, in the corner, drinking a Pepsi.

"What about him?"

"He says the cop smacked the guy with the ASP in the head

for no reason, then shoved him to the ground. He also said that after only about twenty seconds, the cop stood up and shot the man without warning."

Stoltz rolled his eyes. There was always one witness who saw things differently. Now he had to find out why the guy saw events occur in a way no one else did. Often it was just the stress of the situation. Sometimes it was something else. He knew this would take some time.

"Bring him over to the PD, and we'll talk to him last."

If only he had been able to direct his family life as well as a scene, maybe he'd be anxious to wrap things up to get home now. He knew that wasn't true. He had never been anxious to leave a scene. That was his issue.

———

HE ARRIVED AT the small but professional-looking building that served as city hall in the front. The tiny police department on the side and the one-engine fire department in the back. The sun was just setting, and he felt a breeze off the ocean combined with the autumn temperature and wished he had a Windbreaker. That was the heaviest coat he owned, except for his lone suit coat, which he needed for his rare appearances in court. He shrugged off the chill and headed inside with his partner.

As he entered the main hallway, he heard, "Stoltz, good. Come here—I need to tell you something." He knew the harsh New York accent and hesitated to turn, hoping instead he was just having a stroke or his hearing had gone. He couldn't hide as his partner murmured, "Oh shit, I forgot about her."

Stoltz turned and nodded. "Carla, I need some time. I haven't even taken a statement yet."

The younger woman motioned him over, knowing that his partner would avoid joining the conversation at all costs. "Lis-

ten." She placed a hand on his shoulder and leaned in as if someone might try to intercept the conversation. "You can take your
statement, but this looks like shit."

"What does?"

"This shooting."

"Why, what did you see in it?"

"He shot someone who had only a stick."

"You mean the ASP?"

"Don't you start on that bullshit. A baton is not a threat to a
big cop like Albury."

"I disagree, but until I speak to everyone, I can't say what
exactly happened."

The prosecutor ran a hand through her richly dyed hair. Her
pretty face often fooled people until she started to speak. "Look,
this department has had a dozen shootings, and no one ever has
boo to say about it. This one is not gonna slide by while I'm assigned to it." She turned and wiped her forehead with her bare
hand, clearly exasperated. "There are already TV vans filming at
the scene. This case means something. This case can make up
for a lot of bad press."

"I thought each case was independent and we looked at the
facts." He tried to suppress his smile.

"The fact is that if we don't indict a white cop in this town for
killing a black transient, people are gonna shout."

Stoltz was ready. "Luckily the justice system isn't influenced
by bullshit like that."

By the color of her face, Stoltz knew he had hit a nerve. It
wasn't right, but this was fun.

The young prosecutor came right to the point. "If you can't
make this case, let me know and I'll get someone who can. I need
this indictment." She paused. "Besides, there is no dispute that
the cop shot the homeless guy. He has to pay for that."

"I agree, the cop has to pay."

"That's more like it."

Stoltz went on, "If the cop had no reason to shoot. Right now, it looks like he had a reason to shoot—they wrestled until he was exhausted, and then he lost a deadly weapon to the assailant." He looked up for support from his partner but saw he was alone. "Besides, it shouldn't matter if people shout. It should matter what's right."

"Cut the 'brotherhood of the badge' shit. You write it so I can present it."

"Look, Carla, I'm not looking at a brotherhood issue. I'm looking at an officer-involved shooting. Only one, not the last eleven. This one, single shooting. And if it looks clean, I'll pass it on, and if it looks like a bad shoot, I'll pass that on. But you're out of line telling me how to write it up."

She stepped back and turned her dark eyes up at him. "I'm out of line? I'm out of line? Let me tell you something, Detective. You fucking work for me, and I tell you anything I fucking want to."

In a perfectly calm voice, Stoltz said, "I work for the sheriff of Broward County, who has assigned me to the Homicide Unit to look at death investigations objectively. Until he says otherwise, that's what I'm gonna do." He turned and headed into the rear section of the building to continue his investigation before the assistant state attorney could make another comment.

———

BY ELEVEN THAT night, Stoltz had spoken to the cop, who was shaken by the incident, and to two of the witnesses, who said the fight lasted several minutes and the cop did everything short of running away before he shot the man and then applied immediate medical aid. Stoltz knew the other witnesses had corroborated that sequence of events—except for Sammy Walker, the surfer, who was waiting in a nearby room and whom Stoltz intended to question next. As he set up the recorder and waited for his partner to come back from the bathroom, Carla Lazaro stuck her head in the small room.

"You done yet?"

"One more witness."

"The surfer?"

"Yeah."

"He says it was murder."

"I still want to talk to him, if you don't mind. The others say it was justified."

The prosecutor slipped her wide but shapely frame into the room and lowered her voice. "I'm telling you, Stoltz, you write it my way or your ass will be out of Homicide so fast your clip-on tie will stay at your desk."

"Look, Carla—"

"I'm serious. The way the murder rate is going and the new blood that wants in at your unit, you'll be in Warrants or Fraud, slogging through buckets of financial records until the day you pull the plug." Her flushed face showed she was not kidding and that this had become personal. "See if you can ever figure out who killed Jane Doe number sixty-eight while working midnights at the airport."

That brought him up short. He stared at her. "What do you know about Jane?"

"I know that if you're out of the Homicide Unit, no one will ever give a shit about her. I know she cost you your wife. And I also know she won't let you fuck up here. That's why you'll do as I tell you."

Thankfully his partner walked up behind Carla with the surfer in tow.

The prosecutor took a seat and said, "I'll sit in on this interview."

ld've protested but knew it wouldn't do him any
tever you want, Carla."

r, Sammy Walker, had seen the whole thing. He re-
cou... detail how the cop had swung at the man's head and
how the officer had drawn his gun and fired before ever issuing
a warning. The whole time, the assistant state attorney nodded
her head in acknowledgment and made an occasional note. The
look on her face approached pleasure.

Stoltz felt her eyes on him every once in a while, and he met
her gaze a couple of times, sensing her satisfaction at the young
man's story. He knew she was serious about having him transferred and believed she probably had the clout. She knew just
what to threaten him with and how it would hurt.

He hadn't always felt this way about the job. Originally he
started because the benefits and retirement were much better
than those of his job as a teacher at a private school in the north
end of Fort Lauderdale. His wife had worried about the change
at first, but with his better pay and benefits, she was able to go
part-time at the bank, and she realized her husband wasn't stupid
and wouldn't take ridiculous chances. Then, after becoming a
detective, he had started to change. Slowly at first. Working a
few extra hours or bringing home reports to review. Then, as he
transferred into Homicide, the job took on more of a global effect. When he wasn't at the office, all he talked about were cases
or the guys he worked with. Now, through some slow evolution,
he had come to view not only his job as a cop but his assignment
in Homicide as who he was rather than as a part of his life. Then
Jane Doe number sixty-eight entered his life. Other than in her
resemblance to Jenny, he never knew why this young woman had
taken ahold of him, but she was almost as big a part of his life as
his own daughter. In a way, over the last three years, he had spent
more time thinking about Jane than about Jenny.

Now he listened as the surfer seemed to lay out a compelling case for believing that the cop had acted without proper cause to shoot the homeless man, who, it appeared, had lived behind a shopping plaza across the Intracoastal.

Stoltz let the young man finish everything, made a few notes, and looked up and nodded at the assistant state attorney.

She nodded back and let a slight smile cross her pretty face.

"So, Sammy," he started slowly, "have you ever been arrested?"

"What?"

"Have you ever been arrested? For anything?"

The young man hesitated, rapping his fingers on the table. "What's that got to do with anything?"

"That sounds like a 'Yes, you have been arrested.'"

He brushed back his long bangs. "Yeah, a couple of times."

"What for?"

"Why?"

"Look, Sammy, I can run a criminal history on you. I just want to know what you've been arrested for."

"Usual."

"What's the usual?"

"You know. Burglary, possession, auto theft. That sort of stuff."

"Possession of what?"

"Drugs, you know. Crack, weed, a few pharmaceuticals."

"And you live over on this side of the Intracoastal, right?"

"Yeah, with my parents, in a condo."

"And the arrests happened where?"

"Hollywood, mostly."

"Just in Hollywood?"

"And Davie, I think."

"What about here?"

"Where?"

"Here, in this town?"

"Over here? Near my folks?"

"Yes, here, near your folks."

He took a long breath and said, "Yeah, a couple of times."

"Now here's an important question, and you better tell me the truth." He looked at the young man to impart the gravity of the situation.

"What's that?"

Stoltz asked, "Did the officer you saw in the shooting ever arrest you?"

The young man hesitated and looked to the prosecutor, to whom he had obviously already spoken.

Stoltz pressed him. "C'mon, Sammy, did this officer ever arrest you?"

"Well, I, ah . . ."

"Sammy, the truth."

"Yeah."

"What for?"

"Burglary of a conveyance and possession and maybe once for shoplifting."

"Three different arrests?"

"Yeah."

"Did you talk to him today?"

"No, I don't think he ever even saw me."

"Now, before you're in real trouble, do you want to tell me what you saw today? And this time, no bullshit."

The young man slowly nodded his head and told a story a little more believable than the first one. It matched the others.

———

OUTSIDE THE ROOM, as Stoltz prepared to wrap up the on-scene investigation, the assistant state attorney approached him. "You know that doesn't change shit, Stoltz. We need an indictment on this."

"No jury would ever convict."

"That's fine, then it's the jury's fault for not convicting him, but the state attorney's office has to take action. We're gonna indict at the grand jury."

"How?"

"You know how. The standard is just probable cause, not reasonable doubt. We could indict Don Shula for loitering if we present it right."

"But if you put me, the lead detective, on the stand, I'll just tell the facts, and you're sunk."

"We've got a few weeks. You think about life in another unit. You take some time to decide if you want to answer a fucking phone, 'Stoltz, airport traffic.' Look at the Jane Doe file. You think it over, and we'll see what you say when the time comes."

Stoltz resisted drawing his small .38 and putting it to the prosecutor's head as she turned and stomped out the main door.

He did have a lot to go over.

———

THE WEEKS AFTER the shooting were filled with investigative duties: the autopsy, criminal checks on the corpse and witnesses, reviewing the 911 tapes and radio logs, going over the department's policy on the use of the ASP and the state's guidelines on the use of deadly force. The whole time, a cloud seemed to hang over Ben Stoltz as he considered his possible transfer if he didn't proceed the way Carla Lazaro had instructed him. He dreaded a transfer more than he had his divorce. He might find another wife, but he'd never get back into Homicide. He felt his ulcer start to flare up; his migraines returned worse than when Craig had introduced him to his "friend" Alex. He lay sleepless most nights, imagining life on the Fugitive Unit or the Property Crimes Unit. And he did go back to the Jane Doe number sixty-eight file more than once, getting lost in the photos of the lifeless form in a vacant lot. He wondered who missed her. How might the world be different in fifty years if she had not been treated like discarded trash? He looked at the photos and felt as strongly about her now as he had when he was on the scene.

———

HE SLOWLY STARTED to think that it didn't matter if the cop were indicted because he'd just be acquitted at trial. No one would be hurt. He wondered how he might present the facts of the case to leave open enough doubt for the grand jury to indict. It wasn't reasonable doubt. A case was indicted on majority of votes by the jurors. It would be easy. Easier than working on Road Patrol. Midnights. With Wednesday and Thursday off. He took more than one break to vomit in the small men's room on the third floor.

———

THE DAY OF his grand jury testimony, he wore his lone blue suit with the matching blue tie that the guy from Penney's had thrown in because he was a cop. He had a file with a few notes and some lab reports in case anyone asked him about them. He knew it would hinge on how long the fight was, if the officer had had any other option, and if he acted within state guidelines for use of force.

Stoltz nodded to the PBA attorney outside the grand jury room. Although Stoltz had spoken to Carla Lazaro numerous times since the shooting, always giving her reports and keeping her informed, he had been careful not to give her any clue as to what he planned to do. He dealt in facts, not feelings. Her superior tone showed that she believed she had won. He knew she felt as if she owned him. Why not? She could call his captain and complain, and he'd be moved. The S.O. needed the state attorney more than it needed him. He shuffled into the room and took a seat, and a bailiff swore him in.

He swore to tell the truth. His stomach flipped. He felt bile build in the back of his throat.

All Stoltz really remembered was the look on Carla Lazaro's face when he noted that all the witnesses had said the cop was exhausted. He threw in a fact from what he had researched: it was the longest hand-to-hand fight between a cop and a suspect in Florida history. Also that the suspect had five convictions for assault on a police officer, one of whom he had tried to choke to death. Stoltz followed up, without being asked, with how the cop applied first aid immediately.

The grand jury came back with a "no true bill" in record time.

As he stepped down from the witness stand, the look from Carla Lazaro said everything. He figured he had nothing to lose and winked at the fuming assistant state attorney, leaving the room with his integrity intact.

On the following Monday, his new phone played the theme to *Hawaii Five-O* as he picked it up and said, "Stoltz, Economic Crime, may I help you?" He jotted some notes on a check-cashing fraud and opened his first economic-crime case. He now had one case to go with the file his sergeant had allowed him to bring over from Homicide. Jane Doe number sixty-eight had her own drawer in his new desk. As he copied down some information on his first identity-theft investigation, he wondered when he'd get to her. One thing was for sure: there were no droughts in financial crime in South Florida.

DIVINE DROPLETS

BY PAULA L. WOODS

> The past is not dead. It's not even the past.
> —*William Faulkner*

D uring those anxious nights, coiled into his narrow bunk, his mind would soar along the 101, down the 405, or out on remote stretches of Pacific Coast Highway until he arrived at one of those longed-for places—with their low counters, perfectly spaced chairs, glass cases holding the glistening jewels he'd come to crave. Ruby-hued *maguro,* carnelian-colored beads of *ikura,* or *kurage* glistening like citrine ribbons—he could feel the cool flesh yielding in his mouth, washed down with a subtly flavored sake. The sensation was liberating, one of the most intense he'd ever experienced. And he had come that close to losing it all.

But this afternoon, as he hastily assembled his Japanese pens and sketchbooks, he knew with a certainty that made his nerves dance that all the pleasures he craved would once again be his. He was being released from the county jail, his case dismissed by a fair-minded judge after his defense team showed just how stupid and overzealous the police had been. *Their* stupidity, not his.

Because, in almost every aspect of his behavior, he had been remarkably clever. Clever enough to allow himself visits to only exclusive sushi bars such as Urasawa or Matsuhisa when preparing for his outings, although he'd stopped when he became aware of the pattern after the third. Later, there were the receipts from the decidedly downscale Yamashiro and the eyewitness testimony of bartenders who rang up rounds of sake he conspicuously bought for himself and anyone sitting within shouting distance in the lounge overlooking Hollywood. Even his accessories had been purchased years before, from specialized stores all over the country, always for cash and never more than one or two pieces at a time. Every contingency had been considered. There was no reason he should have been arrested.

As he was escorted to the reception area by two burly sheriff's deputies, he savored the moment, knowing in the end he was much smarter than the cops would ever be. He hadn't fallen for their subterfuge that first time they came calling. Had they asked him outright, they would have learned that he could thoroughly account for his movements on the nights in question, that they would never be able to put him anywhere near the locations where those eight girls had been found.

Yet because of his carelessness and one foolish lie, they had persisted until they trapped him. Then it was those detectives—Truesdale from the LAPD and Firestone from Simi Valley—who had interrogated him for four hours in a little room in Parker Center, their hot breath tickling his ears like the gnats one August at his mother's home in the Hamptons. He'd laughed in their faces when they tried to trick him into confessing in exchange for a reduced sentence. But he never cracked, never said one word they could use against him.

But they indicted him anyway, on two counts, although he had refused to believe the misbegotten evidence would be admitted into court. And he was right, although his certitude had to be backed up by three days of grilling the cops on the stand and a fortune in legal fees to get the evidence excluded. It pleased him to think that the trust fund his mother had so diabolically constructed to control him from the grave had been relieved of 1.3 million dollars to secure his freedom. It pleased him even more to know he was being released three days before Mother's Day.

But his vindication was anticlimactic. As opposed to the pack of reporters who had clamored outside the jail at his arrest and throughout the proceedings, their number had dwindled to only a half-dozen stalwarts willing to brave the weather for a sound bite. He stepped outside the confines of the jail—refusing the umbrella being held by Michelle Dunn, the lead attorney on his team—and tilted his head back, allowing the drizzle to caress his face. He could imagine how the shot would look on CNN—his untanned, chiseled face raised skyward, longish brown hair lifting slightly in the wind. He allowed himself to be gently led away by Dunn, selected as much for her resemblance to Tiffany Rutherford as for her skills in the courtroom. Superimposed over the shot, he could envision the words "Heir to Solange Fashion Empire Freed After Murder Charges Are Dismissed," as the camera caught him in a private moment, mouthing a prayer, his palms raised as if the raindrops whispered a heavenly communication.

He wasted little time talking to the reporters, moving swiftly into the limo that had been arranged to pick them up. "Aren't you joining me?" he asked, lowering the window as Dunn closed the door that separated them. "You worked so hard, I thought we might celebrate." He sniffed the air around her, his nostrils identifying the scent of her rage and fear, but nothing else that told him she was his. "Urasawa maybe?"

One hand to her face as if to shield her mouth from the cameras' prying eyes, Dunn leaned into the car, the smile she wore for the reporters congealing into an ugly grimace. "Our services to your mother's estate are concluded, Mr. Nolent."

He fingered the sketchbook in his lap. "I'm sorry, but you seemed to admire my work so much, I thought that you and I might—"

He reached out for his attorney's unadorned hand, which she withdrew at a speed that surprised him. "You're out of your fucking mind if you think I'd ever have anything to do with you. Good-*bye!*"

Scanning the faces of the people around her, Christophe raised the window, hoping the paparazzi hadn't captured the tense exchange. Had she forgotten who he was? With just a phone call to one of the major magazines, he could obliterate Michelle Dunn and her media-hungry partners, these so-called defenders of justice who raided his mother's estate of its assets but never shook his hand, never touched him unless it was for the cameras. But what did she matter? She and the rest of the minions his mother's money had bought were no more than servants, there to do his bidding, not the other way around.

"Let's get out of here!" he muttered to his driver through the open glass partition. As the small knot of reporters and deputies receded in the rear window, Christophe Nolent settled into the leather seats for the ride to his home in Bel-Air, knowing God was on his side.

———

A LONE FIGURE stood at the rear entrance of the county jail, collar of his suit jacket turned up against the stinging rain, wondering why God was punishing him. He'd stood for a half hour, waiting, then watched as Christophe Nolent slithered by him, had a brief conversation with one of his attorneys, then pulled off in a Bentley limo, burning rubber as if leaving the scene of a crime.

Which he was, the little shit. First crime being the murders of those women, and the second, beating the rap because his slickster attorneys had got him off on a technicality. But no one would remember it that way. All they'd remember—the cops he used to work with here and those at his current job in Simi—was that Steve Firestone had fucked up again, and now a serial killer was back on the streets.

What the hell was he supposed to do?

His former coworkers in the department would have never had Nolent on their radar if it hadn't been for him. He was the one who watched the news and pored over the LAPD bulletins on the murders of several women that Robbery-Homicide detectives believed were the work of a single killer. He was the one who reached out to Lieutenant Kenneth Stobaugh when they found Tiffany.

Tiffany Rutherford was an exotic dancer, like the other vics in the LAPD's bulletins. She worked at a club in West LA, although she lived in Simi, out in Ventura County. She was found near the entrance to a remote park at the north end of town, skin flayed from her body and chunks of flesh removed from her stomach and arms. Firestone had caught the case with his partner, Kraig Tytus, nice guy but a wuss, threw up all over the crime scene. Steve had seen much worse than that in his fifteen years as a Homicide detective in the LAPD, although he had to admit that in his ten years at Simi, there hadn't been one as brutal as this.

But rather than hold on to the sensational case and sew up that promotion to chief of the Detective Unit he'd been coveting, Steve had swallowed his pride and picked up the phone a couple of days after Tiffany was found, and called Lieutenant Stobaugh. "Just don't tell me Detective Cortez or Justice is working it from your side," he'd tried to joke with his former boss.

Stobaugh had refused to laugh about it, merely referred him to Billie Truesdale, who had been a fairly new transfer from one of the divisions into RHD when he was there but who had almost ten years on the job now. She'd shown up that afternoon wearing a boxy blazer, fitted trousers, and no makeup. Women that butch and that dark had never been Steve's type, which probably was fine with her, from what he'd heard through the grapevine.

"Mind if I look around?" she'd asked as she stood in the tiled entryway of Tiffany Rutherford's town house that day.

"Why the fuck else would I've called you?"

"Look, Firestone, I got no beef with you, okay?"

"You think Cortez and Justice feel the same way?"

"That's the past, forget about it!"

Steve felt his fists unclench and his shoulders go down an inch or two. Maybe Truesdale meant it, maybe she didn't, but at least she looked him in the eye when she said it. Maybe it was because she knew the sexual-harassment charges those bitches had filed against him were bogus, just sour grapes because he'd slept with one and not the other.

"You find anything of interest when your team went through the place?" Truesdale was asking him.

He shrugged. "For a stripper, she sure bought a lot of clothes."

"You mean for her act?"

Steve shook his head as he led her upstairs. "According to her employer, she did a straight-up thong song at the Three-Way. What I mean is, she bought a lot of professional-looking clothes, like the girls wear on those *Law & Order* shows."

The master bedroom's wenge-wood bed and expensive perfumes on the dresser hinted at a sophistication out of step with the suburban setting. The adjacent walk-in closet was jammed with skirted suits, soft blouses, and flowing dresses, tags on a full third of the garments. Truesdale pulled out a tiny knit dress with the tag still on it, in a tiger print like Steve's ex-wife used to wear and that probably would have suited the petite detective, if this dyke ever wore dresses.

"And look at all the receipts." Steve gestured to an accordion file on a desk in the corner. "Maybe her family can return the shit with the tags still on and get their money back."

Truesdale had donned a pair of gloves and started fingering through the file, making notes as she went along. "Your vic spent good money on her clothes. More for some of these outfits than I bring home in a week." She flipped through some more receipts, pausing at one near the front. "It looks like Tiffany went shopping the day she was murdered."

"No shit, Sherlock." Steve tried but couldn't keep the acid from his voice. "We've already talked to the salesladies where she bought the stuff on that receipt. They recognized her from the picture we had but didn't remember anyone with her." Steve and Tytus had used the high school graduation photo sitting on the desk, Tiffany's California-girl looks striking even then. Taken no more than three or four years before, it was more flattering than her driver's-license picture, not to mention the postmortem photo taken by the coroner, the girl's face rendered unrecognizable by the butcher who'd killed her.

Truesdale extracted a crumpled piece of paper that was wedged in a corner of the file. "You talk to the customer-service department too?"

Wondering what he'd missed, Steve could feel his shoulders stiffen. "The people working the counter that day were off when we went through," he'd lied.

"Well, I'd talk to them sooner rather than later. It looks like Tiffany paid her credit card bill the same day she went shopping. The date and amount's been recorded on the statement, right here."

Smartass Truesdale's discovery led them to the Simi Valley Town Center and a videotape of Tiffany Rutherford paying her bill in Macy's customer-service department. Just as Tiffany was leaving, a white male wearing a Kirin baseball cap was recorded bumping into her. After they exchanged a few words, he approached the counter as if to ask the clerk a question, then headed in the same direction as the victim.

"Pause it right there," Truesdale had ordered the guard in Security, where they were watching the tapes. She started fumbling through her notebook, muttering, "So *that's* what she was saying!"

"What is it?" Steve had asked.

"Mrs. Apkarian, the salesperson in the lingerie section of Bloomie's, Beverly Center, thought our seventh vic, Yustina Flores, was being followed by a white male in a baseball cap. With her accent, I thought she was saying 'Korn,' like the band, was the logo on the cap, not 'Kirin.'" She handed a police artist's drawing to Steve. "Mrs. Apkarian said he eased up on Flores like he did to your vic on the video, squeezing her forearm as he made his apology, as if sizing her up. I blew her off as being overly dramatic, but damn if I'm not watching this guy do the same thing she described!"

"She remember if he bought anything?"

"A pink flannel nightshirt with dogs on it."

Steve suddenly felt cold in the pit of his stomach. "There were pink fibers found on my vic's ankles and wrists. Was Yustina a stripper?"

"No, she was an exchange student from Argentina."

"So if it's the same guy you suspect did the strippers, then he was stepping outside his pattern with Yustina . . ."

"But went right back to it with your vic a few days later," Truesdale added. "Sounds like he's escalating."

Which made him that much more dangerous. "What else do you have?" Steve asked.

"Apkarian almost got him to sign up for a credit card, but he decided midway through filling out the application to pay cash. Left without his change."

"Probably in hot pursuit of your vic. Wonder what set him off." Steve stared at the video as if it could tell him. "Did the saleslady, by any chance, keep the application?"

It was Truesdale's turn to be embarrassed. "I didn't think to ask."

Thank God he did. A quick call to Bloomingdale's revealed that Mrs. Apkarian, assuming the man was part of the store's mystery-shopping team, had folded his change up with the application in case he returned to claim it. She dug it out from under the bill drawer to show Truesdale and Steve when they arrived an hour later.

Holding the application gingerly by the edges, Steve had known instinctively that it was bogus—the name "D. Vinedropletz" sounded completely made up, and the address the guy had given on PCH was so far up the coast, it should have been in Oregon. But there was always the hope that his prints would show up in one of the computerized systems, if he had a prior.

Because the prints were related to a murder in the LAPD's jurisdiction, Truesdale had SID, the department's Scientific Investigation Division, run them through the AFIS database. She got back a Christophe Nolent, convicted of a misdemeanor assault on a girlfriend back in the early nineties. A search of court records revealed that the charge had originally been felonious assault, but his attorneys had somehow been able to get the charges reduced and their client probation, a fine, and anger-management courses.

Christophe Nolent's name also generated a DMV photo with an address in Bel-Air. But the license, like the conviction, was more than ten years old, although a check of the property's address revealed the title was held in the name of the Solange Nolent Family Trust.

The name didn't ring a bell with Truesdale when she called Steve on Friday afternoon to share her findings, but Steve knew it well. "My ex used to buy that Solange shit all the time," he said, tapping the mother's and son's names into the "search" feature on his computer's browser. "Little dresses like the one you were looking at in Tiffany's place, expensive perfumes, and purses that cost a small fortune. I never understood the appeal, but when a woman's got to have it, what can you do?"

Truesdale was silent on the phone for a moment, although Steve could hear the sound of pages being flipped. "You know that dress was one of the things she bought the day she died."

Steve got back more than a million hits on the names search. Scanning the list, he randomly clicked on the fifth link and started reading about Solange Nolent's car collection. "My gut tells me we should pay Christophe Nolent a visit."

———

IF HE HAD followed his gut, he never would have let them in. They'd stood outside the gates in their nondescript car, peering into the surveillance camera and talking as nice as pie, so sorry to disturb your Saturday. The curly-haired man seemed clearly aware of whose Saturday he was disturbing, as he meekly identified himself as Steve Firestone of the Simi Valley Police Department and his cohort as Billie Truesdale of the LAPD's Robbery-Homicide Division. They had traced him through a credit-card application and they had taken the liberty of calling on him on a Saturday because they needed his assistance on a case they were working.

"And to give you your change," the woman named Truesdale had chimed in.

Ignoring his gut, he'd invited them in anyway, had the housekeeper set them up with green tea in the kitchen, and listened politely as the two of them rattled on about how they found him because of the saleswoman at Bloomingdale's and the change he forgot to take, and how they, these two poorly dressed cops, had been working with a task force to capture a ring of boosters who'd been ripping off stores all over the Southland for tens of thousands of dollars in merchandise.

He knew he hadn't used his real name on that application, but he went along with their little game, just to see where they were headed. "'Boosters' sounds like a group of cheerleaders." He'd tried to laugh, but the sound caught in his throat. "So you think *I'm* one of these booster people?"

Detective Truesdale gave him a mirthless smile as the other cop, Firestone, explained that they were talking to customers in all the departments the thieves hit, and something he may have seen in the store last Tuesday, no matter how small, could help them hook up these criminals. "You were in the lingerie department, correct?"

"That's right."

"You visit any other departments?"

"Just fragrances and women's accessories." When Detective Firestone raised an eyebrow, Christophe added, "I was on a mission."

Detective Truesdale shifted in her chair. "Mission?"

"Yes. I was looking for a gift."

"Do you remember anything unusual as you were shopping for this gift?" Firestone prodded. "Anything unusual the women were doing?"

"Just shopping, like women do." But Christophe remembered everything about one particular woman, down to the repellent perfume he saw her trying on in the fragrance department. Dense, cloying, artificial, his keen sense of smell identified it immediately as Chanel No. 5. His mother had told him the story about the millions of women who bought it after Marilyn Monroe claimed two drops of it were all she wore to bed. The losses his mother's company suffered in both perfume and lingerie sales had almost put her out of business all those years ago, a fact she never stopped yammering about, even on her deathbed.

"How about the woman you spoke with in Lingerie?" Detective Truesdale had prompted. "Yustina Flores? Was she doing anything unusual?"

Watching the pale Latina beauty sample and buy that hideous fragrance had aroused him then, just as thinking about it was doing now. He had imagined a girl like that would wear something evanescent, something floral and innocent. He had almost passed her by when the Chanel called out to him, taunting him. Dazed, he had followed the scent through three departments in Bloomingdale's, wanting to be certain she was the vehicle through which he'd fulfill his divine mission. Flustered, he turned away from the detectives in his kitchen and asked if this Yustina person was involved in the booster ring, needing to say something to distract himself from his growing erection.

The room was silent for a moment, then Firestone said, "You say that like she's dead, Mr. Nolent."

"I didn't intend to," Christophe replied, exhaling all at once. "I just assumed two detectives coming here on a Saturday morning wasn't just because she stole some clothes." When they didn't reply, he decided to take another tack, and made a show of racking his brain before remembering an Afro-American guy hanging around one of the racks, mumbling something as the women walked by. "Maybe he was controlling Yustina and the others."

Truesdale fixed him with an off-kilter gaze, asked if there was any reason he'd remember that particular Afro-American guy. "He called me a faggot," he'd replied, the childhood memory of his mother taunting him with the epithet adding some heat to his response.

After a few more questions about where else he shopped in the mall and how he spent the rest of the day, they seemed to be satisfied, when suddenly Truesdale asked to use his bathroom. "Too much tea," she'd explained. As the housekeeper directed her to one of the downstairs powder rooms, Christophe watched Firestone go to the sink and deposit their earthenware cups, the detective's beefy hands violating his collection of antique iron teapots and the sushi knives in the wooden block. "You have a lovely home, Mr. Nolent. I like the Japanese theme, right down to the accessories. It's, I don't know what to call it . . ."

"Peaceful? It took quite a bit of effort to transform it after Mother died." And a lot of his mother's money, which made the effort that much more enjoyable.

"Well, you've done an outstanding job, and I gotta tell you, I've seen some nice houses in my days as a detective." Firestone gazed out the window, past a jumbled collection of ceramic pots and a grove of Japanese maples that led to the garages. "Do you keep your mother's car collection on the property?"

"Some of it," he'd replied, impressed that this hick cop would have heard of it. "There are over a hundred cars, all totaled. We couldn't possibly store them all here."

Firestone wheedled out of him that there were a dozen scattered in three garages on the estate before he asked about the 44 Roadster, the one everyone wanted to see.

"Actually, my mother owned three Bugattis—a '27 Bugatti 44 she bought after her company went public and a couple of T-57 Cs she bought to celebrate her divorces." Besides the money, the cars were the only aspect of his mother's estate Christophe enjoyed, as much for the power and status they conferred on their owners as for their design or performance. And the Bugattis were the ne plus ultra of cars, like the three-hundred-dollar sushi dinners at Urasawa or the Divine Droplets, a sake the chef there kept for him that cost more than a bottle of Dom.

"I've never seen a Bugatti," the detective said wistfully. Seeing Christophe's hesitation, he pleaded, "Just a peek, man. I'll tell Detective Truesdale to wait in the car. Chicks just don't get cars the way us guys do, you know what I'm saying?"

Reluctantly, Christophe escorted Firestone to the garages, where the detective whistled at and ogled the cars like they were those murdered women, suddenly brought back to life. But twenty minutes later, he was still at it, time enough for Detective Truesdale to get tired of waiting and wander into the garage, where Firestone crouched near the 44 Roadster, admiring its pristine running board. "Christophe here—you don't mind if I call you that?—was just showing me his mother's Bugattis. Tell her about the yellow one."

Christophe began reciting the car's features and the races it had won over the years. Firestone asked him to show her the others in the adjacent garages while he went to stand under the maple trees between the house and garages to make a call. He caught up with them a few minutes later, dropping his phone into his pocket and buttoning his jacket. "I need to get back to my office," he announced. "There's been a break in the case."

Worry pricked at the nape of Christophe's neck. "So you don't need me to provide a description of the guy in the lingerie department?"

"I can come back later for that."

Truesdale cast a look at Firestone, then said, "There *is* one question you can answer for me, Mr. Nolent—who'd you buy the nightshirt for?"

"Uh . . ." The question had caught Christophe flat-footed. What should he say?

"Let's go, Detective," Firestone said.

"It was for a friend, uh, a *girl*friend's birthday."

"That's odd," Truesdale replied, consulting her notes. "The salesperson swore you said it was for your mother. But that couldn't possibly be, could it? Your mother's been dead for six years now."

Christophe suddenly felt light-headed. "I think you should both leave now."

"Let's go, Detective," Firestone repeated, flapping his hands in his jacket pockets to urge Truesdale along.

He'd gotten her into the car and her door was almost closed when she asked, "And your girlfriend's name is . . . ?"

Christophe crossed to Firestone's side of the car, as far from her prying questions as possible. "I'd rather not say."

Firestone leaned out the driver's-side window and grasped Christophe's suddenly damp hand. "If I had a girlfriend in the habit of wearing dowdy nightshirts like that saleslady showed us," he whispered, "I wouldn't say either. I'm a silk-teddy man myself."

Looking back on that interview in the days and weeks that followed, Christophe decided his wealth and breeding had made him an enemy of the two detectives, fueled their middle-class rage, and started a vendetta against him that had almost cost him his freedom. But as the Bentley pulled into Christophe's mother's, no *his,* estate, he thanked God it had all backfired, and in such a spectacular fashion that he knew they would never bother him again.

———

"I CAN UNDERSTAND your defending your client," Steve muttered as Michelle Dunn passed him on her way inside the jail, "but did you have to ruin my reputation in the process?"

Dunn shrugged, raindrops dripping off her eyelashes. "It wasn't personal, Detective. We had to get that nightshirt excluded from the evidence. Our focus groups indicated that Yustina Flores's and Tiffany Rutherford's DNA on that nightshirt were enough to get our client convicted, regardless of his family's brand-name recognition."

Steve spat on the ground in front of her. "Criminal trials are like making movies or selling cars—nobody makes a fucking move without their focus groups."

Dunn took the insult calmly. "That's why I'm getting out of defense work. Retire and open a yoga studio or something."

Tall and lean, she didn't seem old enough to retire, but he didn't give a shit about what she did from here on out. "How can you live with yourself, knowing you put a twisted fuck like Nolent back on the streets?"

She took a step toward him. "The better question is—how can you, knowing if you hadn't removed evidence from Nolent's home and tried to replant it later, he might be on his way to death row?"

As Dunn click-clacked her way back inside the jail, Steve asked himself again what the hell he was supposed to do. He'd glimpsed some strips of fabric he was pretty sure came from that nightshirt—the brown stains almost obliterating the pink fabric beneath—behind some ceramic pots near the maples in Nolent's garden, and was faced with a dilemma: should he identify the fabric right then and there, take Christophe Nolent in, only to have him claim they belonged to his gardener or his driver? Nolent was a smart guy. Smart enough to have an alibi prepared for every moment of his morning, noon, and night on the day Yustina Flores was murdered, as he would, Steve knew, for that of Tiffany Rutherford and any of the other murders they might accuse him with. And if Steve had left those scraps of nightshirt behind, how long would it take for Nolent to destroy them after the way Truesdale went after him on the girlfriend lie? Faster than Truesdale could get a search warrant signed and be back at the house to discover them, that was for damn sure.

So he knew he'd done the right thing—stuffed the fabric into his inside jacket pocket and got the hell out of there. It was a bit trickier convincing Truesdale to file a request for a search warrant, finally having to lie and tell her he'd seen but not touched the evidence they were seeking that would hook up this pervert for good.

How could he have known that Nolent's housekeeper had seen him remove the fabric from the pots and then replace it hours later when they officially searched the premises? Or that Michelle Dunn would hire a private investigator to dig into his background, dredging up the ten-year-old sexual-harassment beef brought by those bitches he worked with in RHD, or that the stories would surface of how he'd tried to get them both out of the way when things got a little messy? And if he'd set up his own partners, Dunn's argument had gone, what would he do to show up the department that had dumped him all those years ago?

It was gone now—his reputation, his chance of a promotion, maybe even his job with the Simi PD—all because some trust-fund baby knew the right attorney to hire. He was just about to call his second ex-wife when Michelle Dunn emerged from the jail, a black leather sketchbook clutched in her hand. "Where you headed now?" she asked.

"To a bar somewhere to drown my troubles. Or at least teach them how to swim."

"That's a good one." She dropped the sketchbook she was holding at Steve's feet as she opened her umbrella against the intensifying rain. "Oops! Menopause can make a woman as clumsy and forgetful as a teenage girl. Here I was, opening my umbrella, and I dropped one of the sketchbooks Christophe doodled in during the trial."

Steve stared at her for just a moment before scooping it up. Ornate three-color ink drawings seemed to spill from its pages, scenes from the courtroom, Truesdale defiant and Steve sitting stone-eyed under cross-examination. Little dresses danced across the next two pages, and square bottles spilled drops of what looked like blood. He flipped to another page to find mountain peaks rising above a Japanese inn, the lake beside it offering up sushi from the bodies of fish and mermaidlike creatures that looked disturbingly like Yustina Flores and Tiffany Rutherford.

"The DA did the right thing, going after my client for two of the eight murders," she whispered. "They were the strongest cases, but they weren't the only ones."

"What are you suggesting?"

She pointed at the sketchbook. "Maybe you can make it right with this."

"Why would you do this?" he said softly. "You could get disbarred!"

"As I said, I'm getting out of the game. You, on the other hand, are still in it. You still care." She gave his arm a friendly squeeze. "And if this doesn't help, you can always waylay him at Urasawa for a little talk. A little birdie told me he'll be there celebrating later tonight."

"Thanks, Ms. Dunn."

"Michelle."

"Okay, Michelle. I don't know what to say."

"Just get him off the streets."

SERIAL KILLER

BY JON L. BREEN

P arking the unmarked squad car in a space reserved for the president of North End Community College, Detective Berwanger said to his partner, "I always wanted to do this." Detective Foley resisted pointing out that it was an empty gesture: they knew the president was on vacation in Hawaii.

It was a cool early-fall evening, half an hour before night classes were scheduled to begin, and the campus was relatively quiet. Entering the administration building, the two plainclothesmen reported to the evening director's office, where a pretty Latina student assistant sat behind the counter. She looked up from what appeared to be a math textbook and smiled. "Can I help you, gentlemen?"

Berwanger showed his identification. "Yes, ma'am. I'm Detective Berwanger, city police. This is my partner, Detective Foley."

Her eyes widened. "I've heard of you."

"Yes, ma'am. Lots of people have. I wonder if you could help us find someone."

"A suspect, Detective?"

The two cops exchanged poker-faced glances. "For now, ma'am, let's just say somebody we need to find. It's just routine. Nothing to be alarmed about."

"Of course I'd like to help you," the student said. "Can you describe this person?"

"Yes, ma'am. He's a male Caucasian, about six-four, weighs maybe two eighty. Looks like an interior lineman that's let himself go a bit, but still not someone you'd want to mess with. He commonly has what I can only call a menacing demeanor. Usually shabbily dressed, maybe in an old sweatshirt and jeans. If he's wearing a short-sleeved shirt, you'll notice some elaborate tattoos on his biceps. Marine Corps haircut, stubbly unshaven look, just about always has an unfriendly scowl on his face."

The young woman shivered. "Sounds scary."

"Yes, ma'am. Have you seen him?"

"He's standing right behind you."

Berwanger turned to see Foley shaking hands with Moe Gustavson, who had briefly shed his scowl for a wide smile.

"How do you put up with this guy?" Gustavson demanded of Foley. "Detective Berwanger, you're going to get in trouble one of these days, harassing female students."

Looking hurt, Berwanger asked, "Was I harassing you, ma'am?"

"No, Detective," she said. "Are you under arrest, Mr. Gustavson? Should I postpone your class?"

Gustavson threw up his hands in mock exasperation. "Very funny. And here I was, trying to protect your honor. Can't I get any respect in this place at all? Fellas, this young woman is Lourdes Ramirez, one of my most promising students. She'll make a writer if she can learn to write dialogue and set a scene in less than ten pages. If her desk relief shows up, you'll see her in the front row in half an hour."

"I'm glad I came, then," said Foley.

"Quit harassing female students, Foley," his partner grumbled. "So you want to be a mystery writer, Ms. Ramirez?"

"I hope to, yes."

"Just like your teacher here, huh?"

She grinned impishly. "Well, maybe not just like him, no."

"She's a little too violent and profane for my taste," Gustavson explained. "And I think she writes her, uh, romantic scenes the way she does just to make me blush." Under a feminine pseudonym, Gustavson wrote cozy mysteries, with a caterer and her cat in featured roles.

Berwanger and Foley had been visiting Gustavson's mystery-writing class for several years. It was one of their favorite stops on a demanding schedule of appearances before community groups.

As they walked with Gustavson down the corridor to the classroom, Berwanger asked, "Anybody repeating the course?" Creative-writing classes could be taken more than once for credit.

"A few familiar faces, sure. So you'll have to come up with some fresh material."

"That's no problem," Foley said.

"We're still working cops, you know," Berwanger said. They were in such demand as speakers, it was a struggle to resist a full-time public-relations assignment.

The class was well attended as always, with more than twenty of the thirtysome desks occupied. The students represented a variety of ages, from teens to sixties, and an even wider range of talents, but they were united in their enthusiasm. Most were dressed student-shabby, a look that fit in perfectly with their instructor's casual appearance. Others, who obviously had come straight from work, had on office wear.

Lourdes Ramirez sat in the front row, with male attendants on her left and right who paid closer attention to her than to the two cops, at least until Berwanger and Foley got into their more dramatic war stories. The anecdotes about domestic murders, drug killings, neighborly disputes, armed robberies, and gang wars were well polished and constantly replenished, and their tidbits about ballistics, jurisdictional issues, and crime-scene procedures kept the students' pens and laptops busy. As usual, Berwanger did most of the talking, with Foley demonstrating the equipment—sidearms, handcuffs, weapon-weight flashlight—and throwing in the occasional one-liner from the sidelines. After about forty-five minutes, Berwanger asked the class for questions.

A hand in the second row shot up immediately. "Have you guys ever gone after a serial killer?"

Berwanger glanced at his partner with a humorous smirk and said, "These mystery writers love their serial killers, don't they, Foley? Can't they come up with something more original?"

"That wasn't the question, though," Foley pointed out.

"Right, it wasn't. Well, you have to understand that serial killers get attention way out of proportion to their numbers. I mean, from the TV news and the paperback racks, you'd think there was one on every corner. Most Homicide detectives like ourselves go through a whole career without ever getting a crack at a serial killer. And I, for one, am thankful."

Berwanger scanned the room as if looking for another question, but his partner said, "There was one, though."

Berwanger said, "What? A serial killer?"

"Aren't you forgetting about . . . ?"

"Oh, you mean . . . ?"

"Yeah, that one."

"They don't want to hear about that," Berwanger said, but a murmur from the class contradicted him. Scowling at his audience, he said, "And even if you do want to hear about it, I'm not sure I want to tell you about it. Why should we encourage the creation of more serial killers, real or fictional, right, Foley?"

"Come on, Detective," said a good-natured voice from an

older student in the back row. They recognized him as a police buff who often hung around the station, asking research questions. "You have to tell us now."

"I'm afraid he's right, Berwanger," Foley said. "We're obligated."

Berwanger sighed in resignation. "Well, I guess it was kind of interesting at that. And unique in its way. But it means you have to go to work, Foley." He told the class, "My partner fancies himself an actor. He's not really all that good, and I'm not all that much better"—Foley made a face—"so you'll have to use your imagination while we do a little scene for you. You want some time to get into character, Foley?"

Foley twitched his shoulders, made a few faces, and looked at Berwanger with an intent stare. "Ready if you are," he said.

"My partner, the Method actor," Berwanger said. "Now you'll have to use your imagination here. Close your eyes if it'll help. It's early morning on the bank of a big man-made lake in a city park. Cool morning, very pleasant, just after sunup. This lake is home to all kinds of aquatic birds. See them? Ducks, geese, coots, pigeons, seagulls. Occasionally, you might even see pelicans passing through, especially if the lake's just been stocked with fish. There's an island with some high trees in the middle of the lake, and there are usually a few cormorants perched on the branches, spreading their wings to dry them. Sometimes, when the cormorants go fishing, the pelicans will watch them, looking for guidance. That pair with a red ring around their necks are Egyptian geese, and that blue-beaked guy is an American wigeon. In this little scene we're about to reenact for you, I'm a guy we'll call George. Foley isn't here yet, but when he turns up, he'll be a guy named Fred. They don't know each other. George likes to come here mornings and feed the birds." Berwanger reached his right hand into an imaginary bag and made a tossing motion. "Notice how they all congregate at the edge of the lake, competing for the bread crumbs George throws to them. George thinks he's alone, but then Fred turns up."

Foley walked across the front of the classroom and stood next to Berwanger.

FRED WATCHES GEORGE for a while, looking as if he's debating with himself whether he should speak. Finally he says, "Feeding the birds, huh?"

"You got it, pal," George says, mildly sarcastic. "I'm feeding the birds."

"Don't think I've seen you around before. My name's Fred."

"George." He says it kind of grudgingly, not really wanting to strike up a conversation.

"Glad to know you, George." Fred pauses a few beats, then says, "You really shouldn't do that, you know."

"I shouldn't do what?"

"Feed the birds."

"They like it."

"Well, yeah, sure they like it. But they're birds. They are not the best judge of what's good for them. We're people. We should have more sense." Fred keeps his comments casual, as if determined to stay reasonable, keep it friendly. "Haven't you seen the signs saying 'Don't Feed the Birds'? They're all over the place."

"I don't take those seriously."

"Well, George, don't take this the wrong way, but you should. There are good reasons for those signs. Lots of reasons."

George looks at Fred scornfully. "Enlighten me," he says with heavy sarcasm.

"To begin with, feeding the birds gets them too dependent on humans. They're wild creatures. They shouldn't rely on people for handouts."

"Look, buddy, you see how many birds there are on this lake?

And there's just one of me. Giving a few of them a little treat isn't going to make them dependent on people. And even if it did, that's the nature of urban birds in city parks. I'm sorry if it bothers you, but you need to get over it."

"No, really, it's more serious than you think. Some of these are migratory birds."

"Yeah? So?"

"If free meals discourage them from migrating, they'll just stay here, and that makes for all kinds of problems."

"Why? It's a big lake."

"To begin with, if there's overpopulation of birds, the ones that don't migrate will compete with the native birds for natural resources. That can lead to the spread of bird diseases. Like duck viral enteritis, fowl cholera, and botulism."

George looks at Fred suspiciously. "What are you, some kind of veterinarian or zoologist or something?"

"No," Fred says with a modest laugh, "but there's a big sign over there that lists the diseases and also tells why people shouldn't feed the birds. You should read it sometime."

"Look, buddy, you get your kicks memorizing bird diseases and I'll get mine feeding the birds and we'll both be happy, okay?"

"The birds won't be happy. The migratory waterfowl that come through here, when they do migrate—"

"I thought your point was they won't migrate."

"Maybe some of them won't. But some of them will, and if they do and they're sick, they can carry the diseases to other areas that haven't been infected up to now."

"If they can fly away, how sick can they be?"

"They could be carrying the disease but not showing any symptoms yet. Another thing is, when you've got bird overpopulation, you get interbreeding of species. They have genetically altered offspring who often can't fly. The result is more nonmigration, more overpopulation."

"Okay, pal, you've said your piece. I don't agree with you, but I've listened to you politely. Now have a nice day, and let me get on with feeding my friends here, okay?"

Fred's left eye begins to twitch nervously, and staying low-key appears to be an effort. "You think they're your friends, huh? What you're doing isn't very friendly. The friendly thing is to let wild birds be wild birds." Fred swallows hard, takes a deep breath, and presses ahead. "Another thing. What you're feeding them. Bread crumbs. It's not good for them. If they load up on stuff with no nutritional value, they'll get malnourished. It'll kill them eventually."

"Urban folklore. The occasional bread crumb isn't going to kill them."

"If you don't care about the welfare of the birds, your so-called friends, think about it from a selfish human point of view. Birds can be noisy, and the more of them there are, the more noise pollution they create."

"Doesn't bother me. I don't live on the lake. I just visit."

"What about this, then? These ducks and geese graze on the shrubbery and lawns. If there are too many of them, they could eat everything down to its roots. That would really mess up the landscaping in this beautiful park we all enjoy so much. And don't forget, oversocialized birds can get aggressive. These geese, for example. They've been known to attack people. You don't want too many of them around."

"I'll take my chances," George says blandly.

Fred shakes his head. He looks thoughtful, as if searching his mind for one last argument that might move George. Finally he says, "Do you fish?"

"No, I don't believe in fishing. Hunting either."

Fred grows more agitated. He raises his voice slightly, though trying to restrain himself. "That is just so . . . so ironic. Then the fish are your friends too? Like the birds?"

As Fred gets more exercised, George looks amused. "I wouldn't put it that way. I just don't like the idea of fishing, that's all."

"It might interest you to know, George, that each and every one of the geese on this lake produces one pound of feces per day. That can lead to unpleasant odors for us but to even worse effects on the fish. It lowers oxygen levels, and that can be deadly to all aquatic life. And speaking of feces, ever heard of salmonella? A real public health hazard, right? It can come from duck feces. And do you want even more droppings on the picnic tables than there are now?"

"Oh. Okay. And if I don't feed the birds bread crumbs, they won't shit?"

Fred takes another deep breath. There is now a fanatical gleam in his eye. He appears to be a man losing control. "You may not fish on this lake, George, but others do. If birds get too friendly with people, they'll wind up getting hooks caught in their beaks, or they can get tangled up in the fishing lines. That's a terrible way for one of your so-called friends to die, don't you think? What you're doing is no good for anybody, people or birds or fish or anybody. You're ruining the whole ecology. You really gotta stop."

"And are you going to make me stop?" George says, still more amused than anything.

"I didn't come here looking for any trouble. But there's nobody around but you and me, and I probably could make you stop if I wanted to."

"So now you're threatening me?"

"I'm not threatening anybody. Just giving you some advice."

"Well, take your advice and get outta here. I was enjoying the morning—calm, serene, feeding the birds, communing with my fellow creatures—and you're ruining it for me. Get lost."

"This is a public park. I can go where I want and say what I want and do what I want."

"You can, huh?"

"Yeah, I can!" Fred starts waving his arms and yelling, frightening the birds, making them scatter.

George has had enough. He reaches into his pocket, pulls out a handgun, and fires point-blank at Fred, who clutches his chest and falls dead at the edge of the lake. George looks down at him lying there for a moment, then resumes feeding the birds.

———

"You can get up now, Foley," Berwanger said. His partner regained his feet, and both bowed as the class applauded.

Lourdes Ramirez said, "That was great. But wouldn't it have been even more effective if you'd pulled your real gun on Detective Foley instead of just pointing your finger and yelling 'Bang'?"

"They would have gotten me fired if they had," Moe Gustavson said from the back of the room.

Berwanger nodded. "Can't make it so realistic we give somebody a heart attack."

"Man, but that was so awesome," said a young man in the back row. "I thought Fred was the serial killer. I was sure he was going to off George for feeding the birds. You really do a good fanatical nutcase, Detective Foley."

"It's not such a stretch for him," said Berwanger.

"I feel kind of sorry for George," said a serious-looking girl in the second row. Several of her classmates groaned, as if they'd heard off-the-wall points of view from her before. "No, really. I mean, in his mind, he was doing something good and generous for the birds. He thought of them as his friends. He was saving them from hunger. And along comes this guy, Fred, who tries to stop him. He listened to him, pretty politely really, until Fred started to chase the birds away. Then George just did what he needed to do to keep helping the birds. I mean, not that it was right, not that it was sane or anything, but he could keep feeding the birds, you know?"

"Wouldn't the gunshot have scared them off more than a guy waving his arms and yelling?" a male student said reasonably, and she appeared deflated.

"But, man, this is really totally awesome," said one of the young men bookending Lourdes Ramirez. "Really cool. Like, I mean, not that I'm in favor of murder or anything like that, but just imagine. This guy, George, becomes a serial killer. He feeds birds in remote places with nobody else around, and if anybody shows up to object, he blows them away. I mean, that is just too cool, you know?"

Moe Gustavson asked, "How many people did George kill before he was caught?"

Berwanger looked surprised at the question. "Just the one."

"Just the one?" Lourdes echoed, looking outraged.

"Sure," Berwanger said mildly. "Some other people heard the shot. He fled, but we got a good description of him. We picked him up that same day, matched his gun to the slug found in the victim, made the case in court real easy. His lawyer tried to get him off on an insanity plea but got nowhere. He's in prison now, and will be for a long time."

"Is he working with birds there?" asked the serious girl in the second row. "Like the Birdman of Alcatraz?"

"No idea," Berwanger said.

"Wait a minute!" Lourdes protested. "I feel totally cheated."

"Never enough blood and gore to satisfy Lourdes," Gustavson said.

"That's not the point, Mr. Gustavson," she said. "Detectives, you said he was a serial killer. If he killed only one guy, how could you call him a serial killer?"

Berwanger and Foley looked at each other for a moment. Then Foley said, "But what about all those birds he killed?"

A CERTAIN RECOLLECTION

BY JOHN BUENTELLO

H e woke to the sound of sirens filling his ears. He called to his partner, Darby, who was not there, and then to his wife, who must have left for work as usual in the darkness of the early morning. Brenda worked at the bakery just down the street, three blocks from the house they had lived in for thirty years. Or had they been here longer? He fumbled out of the sheets, listening to the sirens, wishing Brenda was here to help shake him awake. He'd always been a heavy sleeper. Maybe that came from so many long hours driving to crime scenes and making out reports, sifting through all the evidence, interviewing witnesses and grilling suspects, looking for a clue to whatever case he and Darby had been assigned to.

The clock on the nightstand said it was three in the morning, and there was a chill in the air from the September winds that had been blowing through the city for days. He wondered why Brenda hadn't turned on the heat before she left. Probably trying to save pennies again. They'd been saving for a vacation, three, no four, years now. So far they hadn't saved much. Not enough to get away to—where was it she wanted to go again? She had

wanted to relax a little. *Someplace with water and a beach,* he thought. *The Cayman Islands?*

He shook his head to clear it and reached for his trousers, which lay hanging over the chair by the door. Flipping on the light, he pulled a shirt from a hanger in the closet. It was wrinkled. He frowned as he slipped it on. Brenda usually didn't miss things like that. It wouldn't look professional to report for duty in a wrinkled shirt, even if it was early in the morning. He skipped the tie and grabbed a dark jacket from the back of the closet. It smelled of mothballs.

He turned to the nightstand, where he always put his badge and gun before going to sleep. He reached for the drawer and saw that there was no drawer to reach for. What was going on? Maybe Brenda had bought a new nightstand. He'd been working lots of overtime, at least it felt like it, and she'd had to run the household on her own this year. But then he always worked overtime. He searched around the edge of the bed on both sides. Maybe she had put his badge and gun in the lockbox they kept under the pile of old clothes in the closet. He looked, sifting through pairs of men's shoes, stacks of shirts still in their wrappers, and behind a clutter of umbrellas. No lockbox. No pile of old clothes. Brenda must have been doing some cleaning.

A part of his memory suddenly recalled where he'd stashed his old badge: in the pocket of his overcoat. He slipped the coat on and fished around in the pockets. There it was. He stared at the badge, thinking it didn't feel right that it was tucked away in a pocket way back in the closet. He should be carrying it with him always. But what about his new badge? The one they'd given him to replace the old one. Where was it now? He'd have to ask Brenda later what she did with it. Slipping on his shoes, he pushed the badge back into a side pocket and left the room. The sirens were fading now.

He followed the dying sounds out his front door. Sunlight was

just beginning to mark the sky with bands of pink and purple and gold. He stood on his lawn, his shoes untied and wet from the morning dew, trying to track the sounds. Somewhere to the south. He reached into his pants pocket for his keys as he opened the door to the sedan parked by the curb. No keys. He searched his coat pockets. Nothing but the badge there. As he slid into the driver's seat, he wondered where his keys had gone. Then he saw them stuck in the ignition. He shook his head and started the car, looking out at the beams of his headlights as they shined down the road. Which way had the sound come from again? South. He turned the car around and headed down the road toward the crime scene.

It took a bit of driving to find it. Finally, after circling back and forth down endless blocks, he saw the bubble lights of the police cruisers parked ahead of him. Lots of people were milling around. Many seemed to be just passersby, but a few were in their robes or pajamas. He hoped Darby had cordoned off the area. Lots of patrol cops trying to corral a crowd of onlookers and witnesses meant evidence was likely being tramped over or destroyed. They'd have to sift through what the crowd had left behind as well as any traces left by the criminal they were looking for. That was a sloppy way to investigate a crime scene.

He saw that one of the cops was questioning someone by the open back door of a patrol car. Probably a witness. Someone he would need to talk to as soon as possible.

He parked his car behind the last cruiser on the scene and stepped out into the chilly air. The sky was beginning to brighten. Daybreak was coming. That was good. You lost too many things in the dark. Too many things you couldn't get back. He glanced around and spied an irregular shape beneath a sheet farther up the hill from where the cars were parked. A couple of plainclothes policemen were standing over it. He could see that the ME had arrived and was taking preliminary measurements

around the body. He couldn't see Darby anywhere. Maybe his partner had missed the call. He'd have to tell one of the men standing around—what were they called? Officers, that was it. He'd have to have an officer call Darby at the precinct and get him over here. Or was Darby at home in bed now with his wife? Did Darby have a wife? He'd have made the call himself, but he saw that his radio was somehow missing from his car.

The officers were busy keeping the curious passersby away from the scene and talking to potential witnesses. One patrolman was laying flares across the road while another redirected traffic. The second officer watched him with a wary eye as he walked away from his car and tramped slowly up the hill toward the body and the two detectives. He waved and fished out his badge, flashing it in the patrolman's direction. The officer nodded and went back to motioning to cars.

The detectives had stepped away from the body and were comparing notes at the top of the grassy hill. They stopped talking when they saw him approach. He stopped in front of the sheet and showed them his badge, then bent down with an effort and lifted the edge of the cloth. The girl who lay there on the wet grass couldn't have been more than sixteen. She had long brown hair with red streaks in it, and her face was round and smooth and delicate, like a doll's. He thought she looked a little like his daughter. Karen, no, it was Shannon, wasn't it? Shannon had always reminded him of one of those porcelain dolls. Her skin was so clean and smooth, like glass. He'd been afraid to hold her when she first was handed to him in the hospital. Shannon, no, no, Karen, had looked at him with big round eyes. *Blue,* he thought when he stared back at her and smiled. They were blue. He stared down and wondered what color this girl's eyes were.

"Excuse me, Detective?"

The girl had been stabbed in the stomach. There didn't seem to be any other marks on her. There wasn't much blood, but he figured it might have seeped into the soft ground beneath her. He looked around for bloody footprints but didn't see any. There were no stains on the grass leading away from the body. Perhaps the perp had killed her somewhere else and dumped her body here. He doubted it. This little hill was a popular place for young lovers to meet. There was a park nearby, and plenty of trees to hide it from the main road. Maybe they had known each other. Well enough for the killer to get close enough to stab her without a struggle and run off before anyone could see him.

"Detective?"

He bent down further and saw a small piece of thread near her left arm. It was small, very small. He didn't pick it up. He'd leave that for forensics, but noted that it was two-tone, red and blue together. It looked like the kind of thick thread that he pulled regularly from the sweaters that his wife—Brenda, was it?—always made for him. He could have used one of those sweaters now. He smelled something now too. Something lingering in the air. It was almost like cigarette smoke, but not quite. This was a bit heavier than cigarette smoke, even those high-tar brands some of the older men smoked. He thought maybe a cigar, one of those smelly little ones he'd seen the teenagers and twenty-somethings smoking on the streets these days. Or was that back when he was just a young patrolman himself? No, they hadn't been available back then, had they? He stared down at the girl again and sighed.

"Lieutenant, can I speak with you please?"

He stood up, expecting that they would give him all the information they had and let him and Darby get on with the job of finding the killer. He looked around, studying the grass, the sidewalk below, and the street. There were lots of people still hanging around. He wondered if one of them might be the killer. Sometimes they hung around to see what the police were able to figure out. They feared being caught by something they left behind. Sometimes their guilt prevented them from keeping away. There were no signs of a struggle. He was sure of it. If the girl was killed here, then she knew her attacker, probably a boyfriend. Had they argued? About what?

He'd have to interview her parents eventually, break the bad news to them about the loss of their daughter. He always hated that part of the job. He'd ask about her dating habits, find out if they knew of any jealous or possessive boyfriends. Boys, men, could be like that. He remembered not letting his daughter, whatever her name was, date until she was seventeen. At least not the kind of dating that amounted to anything serious. There had been plenty of arguments on that subject. He recalled fighting with both his daughter and his wife over it. Or had it been over something else? Did he and Brenda ever really fight over anything? His daughter and he had. Hadn't they? No, their relationship had been good. She had married and done all right, hadn't she? He stood there on the grass and tried to recall if she had ever married at all.

"Lieutenant, can you tell me what precinct you're with?" One of the detectives took him by the arm and pulled him away from the body. The edge of the sheet fluttered from his fingers and settled back over the girl. The ME probably wanted to take a look at her. Collect whatever evidence he could before taking her down to the morgue. He should tell them about the thread and the cigar smell he'd noticed.

"Can I see your badge again?" the other detective asked him.

He handed his badge over, scanning the area to see if Darby had arrived yet. Hadn't one of the patrolmen called Darby? He'd given them the order to ring his partner, hadn't he? He looked around for Brenda—no, not his wife, not her this time, for his partner. He looked at the faces of the milling crowd. People shifted on the street, craning to get a look, whispering to one another and pointing up the hill. Something caught his attention.

Was it Darby? He searched the faces of the crowd more earnestly now. No, it was something else. Not Darby. Darby was back at the house, or at the station, wasn't he? He examined eyes, expressions, arms and legs moving in the crowd. He wasn't sure what he was looking at, but he knew it was important.

"This badge belong to you?" one of the detectives asked him. The other was walking down the hill toward one of the patrol cars. He watched the detective reach in through the front window and speak into the radio. Maybe he was talking to Darby, telling him his partner was already on the crime scene.

"Are you supposed to be here?" the other detective asked him.

He didn't answer. He looked back at the crowd. More eyes, faces, legs, bodies, floating in the darkness before him. Something was out there, just beyond his vision, just at the nearest edge of his memory. He looked back at the body of the girl beneath the sheet. The end of the sheet hadn't covered her outstretched hand when it came out of his grasp, and he stood and stared at the tiny, delicately thin fingers splayed out on the grass. God, was that his daughter under there? Shannon, dead? He felt his chest tighten. Something cold crawled into the center of his stomach. Had Karen been killed by that boy who always came around the house? What was his name? Roger? No, that was her husband's name. Had he been the one who kept coming around? Why would Roger have wanted to kill his daughter? They'd had cookouts together once a month, long ago, hadn't they? Was it so long ago? He took a step toward the body, but the detective took hold of his arm and didn't let go.

"That's a retired badge," the other detective said, jogging back up the hill from the patrol car. He stopped next to his partner and leaned close to whisper. "Don't be too hard on the guy," he told the other detective. "He ain't right."

"He's a detective?"

The other man nodded. "Was. Retired twelve years ago."

There was no time to retire. A criminal was getting away with murder. He pulled his arm from the detective and stood staring into the faces of the crowd. Eyes and mouths flashed at him in the dark. He thought he saw his wife's face, Brenda, or Karen, or something. He knew her face. At least parts of it. He stood and tried to pull the pieces of her together in his mind. And where was his daughter? She had to be somewhere below, didn't she, with her husband, Larry, or Roger. Had she married twice? Then he saw someone he recognized. A face in the crowd with the right arms, the right clothes. That was Darby, wasn't it? His partner was the one moving slowly through the crowd. No, not Darby, but someone else he was looking for.

"It's not his fault," the detective who'd been speaking to Darby on the radio said. "Dispatch says he was retired because he was diagnosed with Alzheimer's."

"Alzheimer's? How did he get here?"

"He's been pulled in before for showing up at disturbances, especially late at night. The sirens seem to be a trigger for it. He doesn't know any better. Dispatch said his daughter is aware of the problem. She thinks he needs to be in a nursing home, or something like that."

"Well, one thing I know is he doesn't belong at a murder scene," the other man replied. "Get him out of here, make sure he gets home. Tell his daughter to come get him. Tell her that she needs to bring her father home."

"She lives in another state, according to dispatch," the detective said.

"Well then, call a nursing home and have him carted away. And keep that badge away from him. He flashes that in the wrong place at the wrong time, and he's going to get himself or somebody else killed."

The first detective put a gentle hand on his arm as he was

still searching the crowd. He turned and looked at the man. He wasn't the one. He wasn't wearing a sweater. He was in a coat and tie. White shirt, black coat. No cigar smell on him. He pulled himself free and pointed down at the crowd below.

"He's down there, just to the left at the end of the block, standing by the hedge."

"Come on, now," the detective told him, trying to take hold of him again. "We have to get you home. Your wife must be worried."

"Dead," he told the man, not taking his eyes from the crowd, from the man at the edge of the block. "She's dead."

Who was dead? Brenda? How could she be dead? Hadn't he just left her back at home in bed? No, she had already been off to work. She was off to work overtime every day, trying to save, like he was, trying to save until the overtime became too much to take. No, not Brenda, not dead, not now. That was years ago. Long ago and buried. The girl on the hill under the sheet with the doll-like face just like his daughter's was dead, now, tonight, and he had a job to do. Even without Darby there to help him. Even without Brenda to live somewhere there in the back of his brain.

"Is there anyone we can call for you?" the detective asked, holding him.

He used his free hand to point into the crowd. "There, see the teenager moving along the sidewalk at the edge of the block? The one in the blue-and-red sweater?"

"Come along, now."

"He's smoking a cigar, a little thin one. Can't you see the ember burning at the edge of his mouth? Can't you smell the smoke around the body? Cigar smoke, like those smelly things the kids like. There's a thread by her right arm there, no, her left. Can't you see him down there?"

"God, he's right." The other detective, who had bent down

to examine the body again, held a small piece of thread in his gloved fingers. He looked at it in the beam of a flashlight and then stared at his partner. "Is there a guy down there like that?"

The other detective pulled his walkie-talkie from his belt and spoke into it. Two patrolmen looked up. They spoke back to the detective and sighted in on the teenager moving faster down the street. They moved away from the hill and started toward him. The young man bolted then, churning his legs and arms to get away, but the patrolmen drew their guns and ordered the suspect to stop. The kid skidded to a stop. His breath came out in frosty chokes. They were on him in a heartbeat. He watched them lie him down, cuff him, and drag him to his feet. The patrolmen took him to one of the cars by the curb.

The detective who'd been bending over the body took off down the hill. The young man was crying and shouting by the time he got to him. "I didn't mean to do it!" he cried as he was stuffed into the back of the patrol car. The detective got in the passenger seat in front of him.

He watched as the car drove off. Turning back to the body, he wondered if Brenda would be here soon to help take care of Shannon. He didn't think he could do it on his own. How could he possibly bury his own wife? No, his daughter, wasn't it? Then he remembered that it wasn't Shannon, or Karen, underneath the sheet. She was away at college, wasn't she? Or was she married now? Who was this dead girl, then?

The other detective came over to him and handed back his badge. He took it and looked at the bright shield nestled in its black case. He was glad the other detective had found it. Had he accidentally dropped it while he was examining the crime scene?

"You did a pretty good job here tonight," the detective told him.

He nodded. "That's the job we're supposed to do."

The detective smiled. "I guess you're right. Hey, would you like a ride home?"

He looked down to where he had parked his car. He could drive home all right. He'd gotten here, hadn't he? He'd solved the case too. They'd found the killer. The girl's parents could at least have that. Darby was with the killer now, probably getting a full confession from him. No, he could drive all right. But as he stood there staring at his car, thinking he should get home before Brenda worried about him and called the station, he thought he could use some help from the detective after all.

"I'll be all right driving," he told the other man. "But could you tell me where it is exactly that I live?" He stared at the badge in his hand again. It was bright and heavy and felt as if it belonged there. "For the life of me, I can't seem to remember."

A CHANGE IN HIS HEART

BY JACK FREDRICKSON

Detective Edrow Fluett leaned the aluminum shovel carefully against the shingle siding, brushed snow off one boot, then the other. It was a laugh; the snow was inside his galoshes. They were as old as the siding, and just as cracked. Better he should have shuffled up and down the driveway a few times, scooped up snow with the gaps in his boots, instead of risking a heart attack, shoveling.

He eased open the kitchen door, lowered himself to sit at the top of the basement stairs. Blanche's snoring came through the ceiling, steady and righteous, but a nickel bouncing in the next block or, God forbid, a drop falling from his galoshes, could jerk her awake, angry, in an instant.

He bent to pull off his right boot. Too hard; his foot popped out with a sudden, loud sucking sound, like he'd freed it from a swamp. Out too came water, puddling onto Blanche's linoleum.

He held his breath, strained to listen. Upstairs, she slept on.

Every winter, he told her there was no more fixing the boots, showed her the patches curling away like shriveling corn plasters. But every winter, she refused to hear, turned back to the television, telling him he should use better glue.

Slower this time, he pulled off the other boot, peeled off his drenched socks. His naked feet were gray and wrinkly, ghost prunes. Carrying the dripping boots and socks, he padded down the stairs, made wet footprints of flat arches as he crossed the cold concrete. He set the boots by the floor drain, the socks atop the pile of laundry, crept back up the stairs to the kitchen.

The slow, steady engine of Blanche's snoring continued above his head.

Gently, he separated two paper towels from the roll on the wall. Blanche had fits when he used them for the floor, but he'd forgotten to bring up the sponge mop, and his frozen feet were in no mood for another walk down to the basement. So long as he remembered to take the towels out, hide them in the neighbor's trash, she might not know.

He dropped the towels on the puddle by the door. In an instant, they were drenched. Two sheets wasn't enough, but there was no sense risking a third. Blanche was known to keep track of the sheets on the roll. He bent to pick them up, cupping one in each hand, like melting snowballs. With luck, the floor would dry and he'd be gone before she came downstairs.

"Edrow," Blanche screamed, firing his name like a cannon shot through the floor.

Splat, splat, the soaked paper snowballs hit the linoleum, loud enough to hear upstairs. "It's barely six o'clock," he yelled, hurrying to pick them up, as though she could see through the floor. "Go back to sleep."

"You made it impossible with that ruckus, shoveling."

No. She'd heard him taking the paper towels, here-a-penny, there-a-penny, from the roll. "There's a foot of snow, wet like fresh cement. Heart-attack snow," he shouted, hustling to set the dripping wads in the sink.

He just had to remember to take them with him when he left for work.

"Couldn't you have pushed the snow instead of scraping it so loudly?" she shrieked.

"Lucky for you that damned snowblower hasn't started for ten years. That would have really been loud."

"I told you, you got to drain the gas from it every spring."

"You told me to buy that blower from the bandit at the Closeout Hut. Piece of crap. It doesn't even have a name on it."

"Don't leave boots by the back stairs."

"They're in the garbage, draining," he shouted, pleased by his wit. "I'm buying new ones, fifty-dollar ones."

"Glue," she screamed.

"No more glue," he yelled.

There was silence, maybe a whole minute's worth, and then the bedsprings groaned. "The Closeout Hut ran an ad for boots. Seven ninety-five."

Her voice had lost a decibel, maybe two. His feet were winning. He pressed. "Their stuff is crap," he shouted to the plaster.

The bedsprings groaned again. "Don't slam the door," she yelled.

———

JERZY SAT AT his desk in the crammed second-floor storeroom, looking down at the cars inching through the blizzard. "We're going to sell boots today," Reggie had said that morning, laughing, cupping his hand to catch a few flakes as he dropped into the Seville. And, like always, he'd been right. Downstairs, the old plank sales floor vibrated from all the shoppers, stomping in like cattle being led to trucks on their way to becoming meat. They'd started coming, just like Reggie had said, right as Jerzy taped the banner in the window: BOOTS, $7.95. Fake, fur-lined, vinyl boots, they looked a nice deep blue under the Closeout Hut's low-watt fluorescents. In direct sun, Jerzy knew, they would be purple. But there would be no sun today; just snow, dirty clumps of it, big as squashed marbles, falling all over the little town just west of Chicago.

Jerzy would be glad when those boots were gone. Slitting open the shrink-wrapped cartons that morning, spreading the boots on the big tables, had set the place to stinking of mildew and smoke so bad that Jerzy had to pinch his nose. The boots had been in a fire. Reggie had smiled, the day's never-lit cigar already wet in his mouth, and told him to turn on the overhead fans. No one would notice fans turning on a thirty-degree day, Reggie had said, so long as they thought they were getting a great deal. And from what Jerzy could hear coming from downstairs, Reggie had sure been right about that too. Mixed in with the stomping feet and the babushkas chattering in Polish came the chirpity sound of Reggie humming along with the ringing of the old mechanical cash register. Nobody was saying "fire" in Polish, English, or anything else.

Squinting to see through the snow as Jerzy drove them in, Reggie said it was providence that made him buy the half-truckload of fire-sale boots at 78.4 cents a pair. Jerzy didn't know providence from apples, but he knew Reggie. Making the old building rumble like some sort of goofity machine, those boots were walking out the door at $7.95 a pair. Reggie had reason to hum.

And when Reggie was happy, Jerzy was happy. Reggie treated him well, took care of everything. Jerzy had worked for Reggie since he dropped out of high school, twelve years now, contented all the time. Except for Agnes, of course. But Reggie had helped him with that too. Jerzy was grateful. He lived rent-free in the basement of Reggie's house, had a color television and only a two-block walk to the food store for the frozen dinners he microwaved. He'd even saved five thousand dollars. Not much, maybe, for working twelve years, but like Reggie always told him, for what did he need money, with all his needs satisfied?

And regrets? Besides Agnes, he didn't have any, and that was better than most of the people he saw on television. On TV, everybody seemed to be regretting everything.

Jerzy turned from the window, back to the sales-tax forms on his desk. Reggie had been right, for sure. They were going to sell boots today.

———

DRIVING IN, DETECTIVE Edrow Fluett got stopped by a traffic accident. He pulled his bubble out of the glove box, stuck it, flashing, on the roof, and radioed Queenie for uniforms. She told him he had to work it himself until the tow drivers got there. She said even the captain was out, working the snow. "And the chief?" Edrow asked, flipping a finger out his open window at a minivan pilot who had stopped to gawk. The chief was at city hall—Queenie laughed—working the mayor, telling him everything was under control.

In no town on the planet did detectives work a traffic accident. No town, that is, save one—the turdweasel burg, stuck like a boil on the west side of Chicago, where his wife grew up.

Edrow got out into the slush, hustled the drivers of the damaged cars—whiners both—to the sidewalk, and stepped back into the center of the highway. And for two hours, he stood in salt-melted snow, waving his arms, screaming into his cell phone for tow trucks, and dodging half-witted drivers. By the time the tow jockeys did arrive—junior turdweasels, both of them full of pimples—his shoes were sodden lumps of pulp, refrigerating the arthritis in his feet.

He headed for his car, eager for the blast of the heater on his toes. But the accident drivers, each a victim, each a liar, were not done. From the sidewalk, they shrieked at him for making them wait outside in the blizzard for their cars to be towed. Edrow stopped the traffic, motioned them to his car in the center of the highway, and, above the blaring horns, told them to report to the station within twenty-four hours so he could ticket them for failing to avoid an accident, driving too fast for conditions, and another dozen charges he had yet to consider. That set them to more yelling, until he raised his arm to restart the traffic. That sent them running for the sidewalk, and Edrow got in his car and drove away.

Now, at his desk, Edrow was watching his shoes change shape on the radiator. Twenty-four ninety-five, Blanche had paid for them, at a place off the interstate where she got lightbulbs. He'd tried polishing them, but like just about everything in Edrow's life, they never had softened up.

And now they were bubbling up little tumors.

"Edrow?" Queenie buzzed his phone.

"I'm not going out. I'm watching my shoes dissolve on the radiator."

"Got a report of a break-in at Mart's Gas Mart."

"I'm a detective."

"Yeah, and I'm a queen. I told them you're on your way."

He put on his bubbling shoes, drove into the blizzard.

The break-in was to the men's room.

"I'm standing here, in soaked shoes, because somebody busted into your washroom?" Edrow bent to examine the outside doorknob.

"I need a report for the insurance," Mart, the turdweasel, said.

Edrow stepped inside, took in the taped-shut heat vent, the black streaks in the sink, and the mildew dots on the walls. He stepped out. "Maybe somebody broke in with a hose, to clean it."

"Ha-ha. The report."

"There's no marks on the door."

"I need the report to collect."

"Be at the station tomorrow. I'm going to write you up for attempted insurance fraud, filing a false police report, and other violations I've got to look up codes for."

Driving back, heat vents pointed full at his frozen feet, he checked his cell phone for messages. There was only one, from Blanche. "Seven ninety-five," she'd said, "not a penny more."

He took it as a victory. She hadn't changed her mind, carped about glue instead of new boots. He swung over to Main Street, parked in a handicapped space in front of the Closeout Hut. The red letters on the sign were bright, even through the blizzard: BOOTS, $7.95. Crap for sure, but better than glue. He got out.

———

"YOU AWAKE UP there?" Reggie shouted from downstairs. Jerzy knew Reg didn't like to come up much, because at 380, stairs made Reggie's heart beat funny. But, jeez, if the guy climbed a few more stairs, he could lose that weight, and then his heart wouldn't beat so funny.

"More boots, Jerzy," Reggie yelled.

Down below, the sales floor went silent as the babushkas paused like the piranhas in the pet store when the clerk was about to drop the dead goldfish.

"Okay, Reg," Jerzy shouted back, getting up and clumping loudly across the floor. Reggie liked to hear people being purposeful.

There were only four of the big cartons left, each holding twenty-four pairs of boots. Reggie would be mad. Instead of being happy, selling half a truckload of boots at ten times what he'd paid, all he would think of would be the half he didn't buy, the boots he didn't sell because he'd run out. It wouldn't be a happy ride home.

Jerzy dragged the boxes to the landing, knelt to look over the railing. Down below, the Closeout Hut was jammed with even more shoppers than the time Reggie had dumped those microwave ovens that had been missing UL labels. Jerzy did a quick count, each finger being ten people. There were nearly fifty—

babushkas, mostly, but also businessmen in suits, young shop-girls wearing lots of makeup—all of them pushing around the tables, grabbing at the boots. It was going to be impossible to empty the boxes without catching some elbows.

———

THROUGH THE WINDOW, Detective Edrow Fluett saw Hell—a mob of babushkas in black wool, pawing at tables like they were scratching for gold. He turned, started to walk away, but stopped. As soon as he got to the station, maybe within only a minute of setting the remains of his shoes on the radiator, Queenie would catch something else that would send him back into the storm. Another bogus broken lock or a fender bender; the storm was bringing on a frenzy of turdweasel pain. He looked down at his shoes, half-buried in the slush on the sidewalk. They wouldn't last the day. He turned around and went in.

The place smelled of wet wool, babushka sweat, and . . . an old fire. And there was a draft. No, not a draft, a wind. Edrow looked up. The bandit had the ceiling fans running. For the fire stink. For shame.

Edrow never flashed his button unless the job demanded. But that day, the job demanded. He could be called, at any instant, to chase crime into the snow. And for that, he needed dry feet. He held up his badge, pushed his way through the mob to the fat guy behind the cash register. He remembered him from the snowblower, the bandit.

"Jerzy," the fat man yelled.

———

JERZY SAW SUICIDE down on the sales floor. "What say I just cut the tops off the boxes, skip the tables?" he shouted from the top of the stairs.

Reggie turned away from an old guy to look up. Slither-sucking his cigar from the right to the left side of his thick lips, he shook his head.

"Why not, Reg?"

"I ain't paying you to think, Jerzy," he yelled up. "I'm paying you to do. The boots go on the tables. And Jerzy?"

"Yeah, Reg?"

"First, find a men's size eleven for my friend the detective, here."

"I wear a size nine," Reggie's friend the detective called up.

"Eleven, Jerzy; they're running a little small," Reggie shouted, slither-sucking his cigar back to its rightful right-hand side.

Jerzy busted the tapes on the boxes, making his arms windmills, pushing through the stinky boots. Reggie liked to see hustle, always the hustle. He found a men's eleven and ran them down.

―――――

THE KID POUNDING down the stairs like the roof was on fire wasn't really a kid, Edrow realized. He was a big, hulking young man in his late twenties. But he had a kid's expectant look on his face, like a beagle's, waiting for a coo and a scratch. The fat guy ignored it, grabbed the boots, and handed them to Edrow with a slight bow, like he was presenting Cinderella's slippers. The young man's face fell. *He should have learned by now,* Edrow thought. *Thanks were hens' teeth, especially in this turdweasel town.*

"Your size and color, sir," the fat man said, making a joke.

Edrow made his own joke. Glancing up at the fans whirling overhead, he gave the boots a long sniff to let the fat guy know he wasn't being fooled by the tornado blowing through the store. The boots stank, but they'd be dry. Edrow handed the bandit one of the two fifties he kept hidden in his wallet.

"Call it eight even." The fat man smiled around his limp cigar, a big shot giving away a few pennies of the state's sales tax. He put the fifty in his right pants pocket, already bulging, made the change, two twenties, two singles, out of his left. It wasn't Edrow's concern if the bandit never rang the register; Edrow wasn't the Illinois Department of Revenue, chasing sales-tax cheats. It was a turdweasel town.

Edrow turned to push through the babushkas.

"Spell me for a minute, Jerzy," Edrow heard the fat man say behind him. "I gotta make a pit stop."

Outside, Detective Edrow Fluett stopped to look through the window. Jerzy was pulling a big carton through a swarm of old women. Farther back, the fat man was pulling himself up the stairs by the handrail like he was dragging cement. It was painful, watching him. He must have weighed four hundred pounds.

———

REGGIE NORMALLY WAITED until the end of the day for the pit stop, so as not to make the climb twice, but as the older man started pulling himself up the stairs, Jerzy saw that his pants pockets were already packed solid. Lots of babushkas that morning, buying two, three pairs of boots. That meant lots of fifties. Reggie thought Jerzy was too stupid to know about the hidey-place under the chair mat. But Jerzy was the one who mopped the floor. And Jerzy was the one who brought the deposits to the bank, deposits that never had fifties. Jerzy knew. He just never said anything.

Fifteen minutes later, the toilet flushed, which could have been just for fooling, and Reggie thumped down the stairs, for sure his pockets, and maybe his body, emptied. Jerzy ran back up, in a hurry to wash the stink of fire off his hands.

But as he crossed the storeroom, he saw that Reggie's chair mat was bumped up in the middle. Reggie hadn't put the floorboard back right.

Jerzy stopped, but kept clumping his feet on the floor. Even above the babushkas, a part of Reggie would be listening to make sure Jerzy was being purposeful, crossing the floor to get right back to work. Jerzy thought about fixing the board, but maybe Reggie had left it that way as a test to find out if Jerzy knew about the hidey-place. Best to leave it alone, he decided, and clumped to the bathroom to wash his hands.

At his desk, he kicked off his shoes and tried again to work on the sales-tax form. It didn't require much, just recopying the numbers Reggie had already penciled on a photocopy, then signing "Jerzy Wosnowski, President" on it. It was capital B Boring, copying all those numbers, and it took forever. Jerzy once asked, since Reggie always did the calculations to begin with, why he didn't just sign the form himself instead of making Jerzy recopy everything. "You're the president, Jerzy. You have to sign the official documents," Reggie had said, and that had made Jerzy feel good, being trusted to sign important documents.

But that snowy, gray afternoon, feeling good about responsibilities wasn't enough to stop the boring, and Jerzy's eyes kept wanting to look at that bump in the chair mat. What if Reggie hadn't left the board cocked up on purpose? He'd think Jerzy was being a nosy neighbor. Reggie hated nosy neighbors.

Jerzy had never really wondered what was in the hidey-hole, figuring it was only a day or two's worth of the fifties Reggie grabbed before they hit the cash register. And, for sure, Jerzy had never thought seriously of looking. Reggie had the ears of a cat. He could hear from downstairs whenever Jerzy crossed the room, moving inventory or going to the can.

Except on a day like today, when there was too much racket from the babushkas.

Jerzy stared at the bump in the mat and decided it wasn't obvious enough to be a trap. Reggie had just been in too much of a hurry. Best to leave it alone.

Except when Reggie came up after they closed the store

for desk time—that's what Reggie called it, "desk time"—he would see the board sticking up and would think Jerzy had been snooping.

Jerzy crossed the floor in his socks, careful to stay off the squeaky boards. Downstairs, the babushkas shouted, the cash register rang, and Reggie hummed.

Jerzy moved the chair, then the mat, and got down on his knees. For a minute, he paused. He had to lift the secret board anyway, to put it right. It wouldn't be snooping, just glancing.

He pulled up the board. And stopped his breath.

The space between the joists was crammed with bundles of money, each an inch thick. He pulled one out. They were fifties, rubber-banded together. Jerzy counted the bills. Two hundred. He made the numbers on his fingers. Each bundle contained ten thousand dollars. There were twenty-six bundles jammed in the narrow place. Two hundred sixty thousand dollars. Jeez Louise. He put the bundle back. He didn't want to know about that much money.

But as he reached to set the floorboard back, he saw the two white envelopes scrunched next to the money. The closest one was addressed to Jerzy and was from the State of Illinois Department of Revenue. He picked it up, took out the letter inside. It was dated two weeks before and said "Third Notice" in scary dark letters, followed by a bunch of words about an audit of sales-tax returns, discrepancies, and liability for prosecution. "Discrepancies," "prosecution" . . . the words beat loud around him, like he was inside a dinosaur heart. They were bad words.

He reached for the second envelope. Thank God this one was not from the State of Illinois. It was blank except for his first name written in pencil. There was something about the handwriting . . .

Then he knew. His hands shook as he pulled out the slip of notepaper.

"Dear Jerzy," Agnes wrote. "I'm not going to call the store anymore. Reggie always tells me you'll call back, but you never do. So for the last time, come with me to technical college in Milwaukee. My aunt says you can live in her house too. You have to be brave. Agnes."

He dropped the letter, squeezed his goofity hands together to make them stop shaking. She must have left it with Reggie just before she went to Milwaukee, ten months ago. About a month before she'd been killed by a bus.

Reggie, you son of a bitch.

––––

IN THE CAR, outside the courthouse, Detective Edrow Fluett held his stocking feet under the heater vent for a blessed last few minutes. On the floor next to him, the blistered tan leather on his lightbulb-store shoes looked like butterscotch pudding, bubbling and puckering in midboil. He pulled on his new boots. The vinyl was rigid and didn't want to bend. But the boots were dry.

He walked, stiff-legged in his unyielding boots, into the courthouse. He had to testify against a burglar he'd arrested six times. With luck, this time they'd put him away, flush another turdweasel from the turdweasel town.

––––

REGGIE, YOU SON of a bitch.

Reggie hadn't liked Agnes. "Don't throw your life away on a broad, Jerzy," Reggie had said. "You're the president of the Close-out Hut." And because Reggie was always right, Jerzy had listened. He told himself he didn't even know Agnes that well. She worked at the drugstore a few blocks over, and they gave each other silly greeting cards and had Cokes a couple of times at lunch was all. But he'd gotten to thinking about her all the time, and then she went away, and he figured she'd left him behind, like her job at the drugstore. He never figured she cared enough to be calling or to leave a note. "She doesn't need you anymore, Jerzy," Reggie had said when Agnes left. "She had a change in her heart."

Reggie, you son of a bitch.

Jerzy forced away the sound of Agnes's voice, the way she smiled. He picked up the letter from the state. "Discrepancies," "prosecution." They were coming after him, Jerzy—Jerzy the president—the one who signed the sales-tax returns that didn't tell about those fifties under the floor.

And Jerzy understood: Reggie could never have let him go off with Agnes; he needed him like the pet-store lady needed the little goldfish, something to toss to the piranhas.

Reggie, you son of a bitch.

———

"WHAT'S THAT SMELL?" Robison, the sergeant, blathered, loud as always, as he tossed his jacket on the pile on the coat tree.

"What smell?" Queenie said, like she didn't know.

"Smells like a fire in here." Robison, ever the turdweasel, wrinkled his nose toward Detective Edrow Fluett. "Edrow, you been on fire?"

Edrow stuck a foot out past his desk. "Eight bucks."

"They're purple."

Edrow looked down at his feet. Sure as shit, the boots were purple. But worse, the drops the boots had left on the tile floor were purple too. The boots were running, purple, like ink.

"Turdweasel," Edrow said.

———

"JERZY, YOU ALIVE up there, boy?" Reggie called from downstairs.

Jerzy was still on the floor, squeezing Agnes's letter. All afternoon, he'd been trying to feel her in the paper. But she was gone. He looked up. Outside, the sky was black. It must be time to go to the bank. He put the letters back, replaced the floorboard, and slid back the chair mat, not much caring if Reggie heard him. He grabbed the zippered bag and went down.

"Your eyes are all watery," Reggie said when Jerzy got to the bottom of the stairs.

"I'm getting a cold," Jerzy said, pulling his coat off the rack.

Reggie looked at him funny but nodded as he emptied the cash register into the zippered bag. The store was almost empty now. Only a few stray boots, size mismatches, lay on the tables. Jerzy pulled on his orange knit hat (one of their top closeouts— *Wonder how many secret fifties that had got?*) and went out the door.

On the sidewalk, he saw the purple in the snow where the boots had bled in the slush. He wanted to kick at it, kick at the lies.

"Heard you were selling boots today, Jerzy," the teller, a nice girl who reminded him of Agnes, said when he got to the bank.

Today she looked so much like Agnes he had to look away.

"Jerzy, you all right?" she asked when he didn't answer.

"Lots of boots today," Jerzy said.

"So how come no fifties, Jerzy?" Always she kidded him about there being no fifties.

Because that son of a bitch Reggie stashes them in the floor, he wanted to yell, *right next to the letters he steals before people can read them.* But he didn't yell. He just took the receipt and left.

————

DETECTIVE EDROW FLUETT walked to his car, grateful that it was dark and people couldn't see the purple footprints he was making in the snow. His feet were cold from the hard vinyl. When he got home, he was going to leave the boots in the middle of the kitchen floor, dripping purple, so Blanche could see what eight bucks bought at the Closeout Hut.

But as he put the key in the ignition, he remembered what he hadn't remembered earlier. He'd forgotten to take the two soaked paper towels out of the sink. Advantage lost. Hell was coming.

———

"WATCH IT, JERZY!" Reggie shouted.

Jerzy hit the brakes, let the semitrailer pull ahead. The whole ride, he'd been seeing Agnes, dead Agnes, outside the windshield wipers, instead of the highway. And now he'd almost slammed into the back end of a truck.

He squeezed the steering wheel. "Who owns the Closeout Hut, Reggie?" he asked.

"What the hell kind of question is that?" Reggie said, shifting his bulk but still staring straight ahead for more trucks.

"I mean, because you're the owner, Reg, you're the guy who's responsible?"

"I should have bought the whole truckload," Reggie said around his limp cigar. The entire car smelled dead from that wet cigar.

Jerzy wanted so bad to scream at the fat face. But he didn't; he kept his eyes on the taillights of the truck in front and spoke easy. "So why am I the president?"

"I could have sold another half-truck," Reggie said.

Jerzy let it go. He didn't need the bastard to tell him why Jerzy was president. Besides, more important thoughts were crowding into his head.

As they pulled in the driveway, Reggie rubbed his chest. "I

think I'll take a rest tomorrow, let you go in alone. Business will be slow."

If his insides hadn't been scrunching, Jerzy would have made a laugh. Slow, baloney. The Closeout Hut was going to be packed tomorrow with people angry as wasps about dissolving purple and stinky fire smells and the mildew they'd seen on their socks. Tomorrow was going to be as bad as the day after Reggie unloaded those tiny tin microwaves. Then, there'd been so many people lugging back the bitty ovens, they'd lined up outside, banging on the glass, yelling about radiation leaks from the loose-fitting doors. That day too, Reggie had stayed home, "taking a rest," leaving it to Jerzy to point to the ALL SALES FINAL signs and tell the babushkas there was no cash in the register.

But this time it would be okay. In fact, after thinking all afternoon, Jerzy had decided he needed Reggie to stay away. And to make sure, Jerzy had pointed to the purple splotches in the snow as they walked out to Reggie's Seville. Reggie kept moving like he didn't see and pulled at the door to the car. But Jerzy knew he saw.

———

DETECTIVE EDROW FLUETT lined up the blistered shoes and the dripping boots just inside the kitchen door.

"You get a raise, so we can afford to pay for paper towels to do what a sponge mop does for free?" Blanche carped through the television noise as he passed through the front room on his way to the stairs. He said nothing, went up to sit on the edge of the bed. He peeled off his wet black socks.

"Shit," he said. His feet were purple, like he'd spent the day soaking them in wine.

That fat turdweasel was going to hear from him tomorrow.

———

BECAUSE JERZY WASN'T allowed to drive the Seville unless Reggie was in it, he had to leave at six thirty the next morning. He didn't mind. It had stopped snowing. And he needed the walk, train ride, and second walk to go over the plan. Reggie always said planning made perfect. That day, Jerzy needed perfect.

He got to the Hut at eight, taped the new banner in the window just as the first of yesterday's customers, a short babushka, marched up. She was holding two pairs of boots by their laces, like they were fish stinking on a string. Her face was mad. But when she saw the banner, she stopped. And she smiled.

———

"I'LL BE DAMNED," Detective Edrow Fluett said in front of the Closeout Hut. At first he thought it had to be a stunt, something the bandit had schemed to screw his customers. But the happy babushka faces coming out the door told him otherwise. And when he got up to the cash register, the hulking man-kid took care of him so quickly Edrow didn't think to open his mouth, and he left there knowing he should have brought that no-name snowblower back years ago, instead of leaving it to rust in his garage. He shook his head. His years on the job were making him see too many turdweasels.

He whistled all the way across town, to the sporting-goods store.

———

THE NEXT MORNING, after shouting Jerzy's name a hundred times, Reggie thumped down the basement stairs. "What the hell, Jerzy?" he yelled through the door, huffing and puffing like the Big Bad Wolf. "The Seville's not out, warming up."

Reggie's TV had been blasting those goofty real-life shows the previous evening when Jerzy got home, the signal he didn't want to talk. It was okay. Jerzy was tired. He'd stayed downtown, had soup and a grilled cheese at the diner he used to go to with Agnes for Cokes. A couple of people in there nodded and smiled at him. They'd been in the store earlier.

Jerzy spent the night sitting on his wood chair. He hadn't even tried to sleep.

"I'm sick, Reg," he said now, from inside his room. "I been throwing up. You gotta go in alone today."

"What the hell, Jerzy?" Reggie gulped in air from the other side of the door. "With my heart, you know I don't like to drive."

"Call a cab, Reg."

"That's money."

Jerzy made a cough, then another because the first one sounded so good.

Reggie huffed some more. "Any problems yesterday?"

"Everything got took care of." Jerzy made another cough.

Jerzy watched the doorknob, afraid Reggie would come in to sit to catch his breath. But after a couple of long minutes, the breathing on the other side slowed, and Reggie hauled himself up the basement stairs. The back door slammed, and five minutes after that, the Seville pulled out of the driveway.

———

DETECTIVE EDROW FLUETT took the call that morning because the uniforms were out making sure all the wrecks from the snow had been towed. This one, he didn't mind. His feet were dry and warm, and he figured one good turn deserves another.

———

UPSTAIRS, REGGIE'S PHONE started ringing at noon, and then every half hour after, but Reggie always locked his door. So Jerzy stayed at the table, except when he had to go to the bathroom, to practice.

———

That evening, Detective Edrow Fluett's headlamps swept across the white stone and orange brick of the newer ranch as he pulled into the driveway. He'd gotten the address from the call list they had of business owners. The house was dark. But he'd get out anyway, to try the side door. His feet were warm and dry.

But first he called Blanche. "You were right. There's no need to spend more than eight bucks for boots."

He listened, and smiled. Sometimes, both had to give.

———

Jerzy knew the Seville's engine. The headlights outside didn't belong to it. He sat in the dark for what seemed like hours, until at last the back doorbell rang.

He stomped up the basement stairs to sound purposeful. Switching on the outside light, he opened the door.

The man in the dark raincoat looked surprised. "Jerzy Wosnowski?"

Jerzy recognized the old man from the first time with Reggie, and from yesterday, when he'd come back.

The man held up a police badge bigger than the ones the TV guys had. "Mind if I come in?"

Jerzy held the door open.

———

The kid — the man — had startled him, appearing like a ghost in the sudden light. "You always keep the lights off?" Detective Edrow Fluett asked as he stepped inside and stomped his feet on the rug.

"I been asleep. I didn't feel too good today."

Convenient, Edrow thought.

The kid-man surprised him again, started down the stairs. *Sweet Jesus,* Edrow thought. *Reggie keeps Jerzy in the basement, in the dark, like a gerbil.*

———

JERZY SWITCHED ON the light in his room. All the time he'd lived in Reggie's basement, he'd never had a visitor except for Reggie, and that was hardly ever, because of all the stairs. But that didn't mean Jerzy hadn't planned how to be polite. He slid out the one chair for the policeman and went to stand next to the refrigerator.

———

DETECTIVE EDROW FLUETT sat down. Sales-tax forms were scattered on the table. "Working from home?"

The hulking young man nodded. "Making sure I kept all the worksheets. Just because I'm the president doesn't mean anything. Reggie figures the numbers; I just copy."

Kid-man was talking in riddles. "What?"

"You could test the forms, like they do on TV," Jerzy said. "It's Reggie's handwriting. And his fingerprints are on them, for more proof. I just copied. Ask Reggie; I didn't know about the letters." Jerzy stepped to the table, handed him what looked like an audit notice.

The hulk thought Edrow was from the Department of Revenue. Worse, the hulk needed Reggie alive, to answer to the state.

Edrow put the audit notice down. "Listen," he said, "I'm afraid I got some bad news for you."

———

"WE FOUND REGGIE Loomis dead in your store today." The cop was looking right into Jerzy's eyes, like they were windows and he could see through to the middle of Jerzy's brain.

Jerzy dropped his eyes, noticed the policeman was wearing new boots, nice ones with rubber on the bottoms and tan leather on the tops, the kind hunting guys wore. Jerzy raised his head, made his mouth tremble, like he'd done in the mirror every time he had to go into the bathroom. "He was robbed?"

The policeman's eyes didn't blink. Reggie always said looking somebody right in the eyes made them trust you. Jerzy concentrated on the policeman's eyes, but it was hard because they didn't blink.

"Heart attack," the policeman said. "Must have happened first thing. A woman passing by saw the front door wide open and called us."

"At least nobody killed him," Jerzy said, looking at the wall above the cop's head.

———

"Not a robber, anyway," Detective Edrow Fluett said.

The kid-man said nothing, kept looking above Edrow's head. His face was blank, but maybe that was shock.

"I found him dead on the stairs," Edrow said.

"He didn't like those stairs on account of his weight," Jerzy said to the wall.

"That bothers me," Edrow said.

"Me too. I kept telling him, 'Reggie, you gotta pull off those pounds.'"

"I meant that he died on the stairs. The coat rack's on the first floor."

"I don't get it," Jerzy said.

Edrow stood up so the hulk would have to look at his eyes. "Why would Reggie go charging up, still with his coat on, if he didn't like the stairs?"

"To use the bathroom," Jerzy said.

"With his coat still on and buttoned up?"

"You got to go, you got to go," Jerzy said.

"We looked around upstairs, found a loose floorboard," Detective Edrow Fluett said.

————

JERZY FURROWED HIS brow like the people on TV when they didn't understand something. "I don't know about a floorboard."

"I'm thinking it was a hiding place, except there was nothing in it." The cop's eyes were hot on Jerzy's face, but they didn't blink.

"I don't know about a floorboard," Jerzy said again, still with his brow furrowed. It was beginning to hurt, but he could hold it a while longer.

"I'm thinking when Reggie first arrived, he saw something right away that made him go charging up the stairs." The cop reached into the pocket of his trench coat and pulled out a crumpled roll of paper. "Something that made him forget about shutting the front door, something that made him race upstairs, to check under that floorboard."

"But you said nothing looked like a robbery," Jerzy said. He relaxed his forehead. He was doing fine.

————

"NOT A REGULAR kind of robbery." Detective Edrow Fluett tapped the crumpled roll of paper against Jerzy's chest. "This was in Reggie's hand. He must have ripped it off the window when he ran in." He slipped off the rubber band and unrolled the first few inches for Jerzy to see.

"I make banners for the window," the kid-man said.

"Like this one yesterday? Huge red letters saying fifty bucks back for each pair of returned boots?"

"Reggie didn't know those boots were junk until he sold most of them. He said we would give fifty bucks back to anyone re-turning a pair. He said they'd buy from us forever if we did that."

"That cheap bastard said fifty dollars back on an eight-dollar purchase?"

The kid-man nodded.

"So, all those smelly boots piled on the tables by the front window where someone coming in would see them first thing . . . ?"

"Yesterday I took back just about every pair Reggie sold. Even yours."

Edrow glanced down at his new fifty-dollar boots. "Fifty bucks back. I couldn't believe it," he said, looking up.

"Reggie said it would make you want to shop us again and again and again."

"Reggie was a real son of a bitch," Edrow said.

Jerzy shrugged.

Detective Edrow Fluett turned toward the door, but then he stopped.

———

THE COP HAD a slight smile on his face, and Jerzy was sure he was seeing into the center of his brain, where Jerzy kept the truth.

But the cop just smiled wider. "What about all those signs on the wall: 'All Sales Final'?"

Jerzy felt he could afford a little smile of his own.

"Reggie had a change in his heart."

THE HERALD

BY LESLIE GLASS

The two deaths occurred sometime in the early morning, in the parking lot of the public boat ramp off Fruitville and Route 41, also known as the North Trail. The bodies were discovered by a homeless man who'd spent the night at the Goodwill facility on 10th Street a few blocks from the bay and who was prowling the waterfront in search of some peace and quiet. He saw blood on the driver's-side window of a Ford truck and wandered over to investigate. He viewed the bodies from both sides of the vehicle and checked the doors before threading back through the traffic on the North Trail to the Chevron station on the other side, where he told the attendant to call the police. Then he took off.

———

On Wednesday, the hump day of the week, Paradise Major Case detective Alfie Rose had not been expecting any excitement beyond his juvie mission, which got him up before he liked seeing the light of day. He'd gotten an early call from Roy Sultan, an officer responding to an attempted break-in who knew Rose was familiar with the would-be perpetrator involved. Bleary-eyed, Alfie hurried out to confront Jeff Burt, a tattooed kid he wanted to save from the system. That's how he happened to be on Bee Ridge in the parking lot of Persnickety Cat, talking alternatives with a boy who could go either way. Drink and dope his way into a flying leap off the Skyway Bridge, or face up to the human fucking condition and get his ass back in school. It was seven a.m., and there was still time. Sometimes, Alfie saw himself through a camera's eye and thought, *This is my life.* Unmarried cop, in a car with a kid who looked like something out of an eighties punk band, hoping to do a tiny bit of good for someone who needed a little extra help.

Alfie pulled into the Dunkin' Donuts parking lot and bought two glazed donuts and some coffee while Jeff remained silent. Then he set out the alternatives for Jeff in a matter-of-fact voice that was far calmer than he felt. No kid in free-fall really thinks he's going to end up in a body bag, and Alfie wanted to get that across in a measured sort of way while eating something he knew might clog up his arteries and kill him down the road. He'd sung the same old tune to Jeff before to no good effect, so he felt a powerful sneeze of rage coming on at the early hour and at his inability to be truly useful. Just like his dog, Alfie registered his negative feelings through his nose. But it wasn't just the kid and the morning that were bothering his sinuses.

It was spring in Paradise, and the air was filled with all kinds of shit. There weren't supposed to be seasons in Florida, but seasonal changes occurred there nonetheless, Alfie had learned in his first year. Before the hurricane phase officially began, a mammoth rebirth of plants big and small started in March and dragged on right through June. Sometimes in the morning Alfie's car, parked in a carport, would be green or yellow or red with pollen that had blown in during the night and covered everything like sandstorms in the desert. The stuff coming out of the trees could choke a horse.

Come on, speak to me. Alfie started drumming his fingers on his thigh. Jeff had to say something. That was the rule. He wouldn't let the kid's silent, guilty, hangdog, shoot-me-in-the-head expression end the discussion. Silence only signaled a postponement of the inevitable—another incident to follow. Shit, Alfie didn't have all day. He resisted the urge to glance at his watch.

Never mind what Jeff had been planning for his morning, or how the fifteen-year-old had talked himself into the rightness of what he'd been doing—Alfie didn't want him back in an orange suit, in front of a judge who wouldn't be as understanding the third time in two months. It was hardly a major case, but he was taking the time. Also Alfie liked the boy's clueless mom, Sharon.

Alfred Rose had been in the cops up north, then in the military. He'd seen war, and after he came home, he drifted to Florida for the weather and joined the Paradise PD, where until recently he'd been a detective in Vehicular Homicide. Six months ago, he'd pulled Jeff out of the car wreck that killed his dad. The two had been on their way to a father/son golf tournament out at Foxfire Country Club near I-75 when they'd been broadsided by a pool-cleaning truck driven by an illegal alien without a license.

The fatal car wreck was the kind of case Alfie had worked for the last three years, every single one a catastrophe. In the Burt family tragedy, the driver of the truck had been drunk at the time of the accident. Despite evidence to the contrary, the owner of the vehicle claimed it was stolen and he'd never seen the guy before. As for Jeff and his dad, the father/son golfing team had been a good one, and they'd been hoping to win that day. It was a real nasty case, and neither Jeff nor Sharon was doing well.

Still, if Alfie hadn't had a promotion, his connection to the family would have ended there. A few months later, however, Alfie was promoted to the Major Case Squad, and Jeff started crossing his path as a juvie, breaking into shops, looking for cash to buy dope. He sported Goth tattoos and dyed black hair, and didn't look as if he had enough to eat. Alcohol and dope were one thing, but Goth didn't go down well in Paradise. The grieving Sharon didn't get the role of parenting a kid on a suicide ride, and Alfie knew he was going to have to talk to her about wising up and getting some help. Court-ordered rehab was what he had in mind.

When Jeff refused to say much more than the fact that he was sorry, Alfie broke down again, gave the boy his strongest "Come to Jesus" talk, then drove him to Riverview High School and watched him melt—as much as a Goth at Riverview could melt—into a crowd of pretty preppy-looking kids. Jeff entered what Alfie thought was the right building and didn't look back, so Alfie hoped he might stay. It didn't change his mind about the six-month program, though. His box squawked, and he answered.

"What you got, Matilda?" he said.

She told him, and he turned north on Tuttle. All the Major Case detectives in the department, including his partner, a tough female former New York cop named Betty Mudd, happened to be at a law-enforcement conference in Vegas. So he caught the call. His expression tightened as he considered the complications that were sure to come with this one. Murder was not exactly a welcome tourist in Paradise.

At 7:38, after season, it was only a six-minute drive up the Trail to the public boat ramp. By the time Alfie got there, three units had already secured the area and a coast guard chopper circled above, as if someone might be making an escape by sea. No civilian cars were sitting in the parking lot, but Patrick Pride of the *Herald Tribune* was parked as close as he could get. As soon as Alfie got out of his car, Pat rushed over to block his progress.

"Alfie, old buddy, what's the story?" If he got one step closer, he'd be treading on the detective's snakeskin cowboy boots.

All the annoyance that had been building up since before dawn finally exploded out of Alfie. He sneezed loudly. Patrick Pride wasn't his buddy, and nobody else in the department was Pride's buddy either. The young man was in his first newspaper job—maybe first *job* ever, and he was a real dickhead when it came to getting his stories straight. This guy wasn't about the facts, and the pisser was that nobody at the paper cared about his tactics. The crime beat at the *Herald* was the lowest rung of the ladder, from which the most inexperienced newcomers started the climb. Alfie only just refrained from elbowing the youngster in the chest. "You're the reporter, you tell me," he said as he pushed past him.

"Looks like a murder-suicide." Undaunted by the reception, Pat trotted along beside him.

"Don't make it up as you go along like last time, buddy," Alfie warned him, trying to make an impression. "It matters."

"He did her and then himself. You want to tell me who they are?" Patrick Pride wasn't a good match for his name. He was short and soft in the belly, didn't look as if he had to shave more than once a week. His shirt hung out, and he wasn't wearing socks. He didn't smell as if he'd bathed too recently either. He was twenty-one, maybe, just old enough to buy a drink.

"Come on," he wheedled, a wart that wouldn't go away. His notebook was out, and already a page was full of scribbles.

Alfie glanced at it, then over at the officers guarding the scene. He could see blood on the truck window but not the mess that was inside. Crime Scene hadn't arrived yet, and it looked as if no one had disturbed the bodies by searching for IDs. "Beat it," he said, "and don't speculate."

"Come on," Pat protested.

"I mean it. Don't make any more trouble with your fictions," Alfie said.

"I don't write fiction." He spit the word out with contempt. "Just do my job, same as you."

"Yeah." Alfie sneezed again. "Someday I'll show you how," he said, and left him there, writing something. Later, Alfie thought he should have grabbed that notebook and given Pat a real verbal kick in the ass. But it seemed he wasn't that good at lecturing on Wednesdays. In any case, his eyes had already focused on that bloody window, and he wasn't thinking about anything else.

The bodies were in the cab of a Ford truck, with the logo BLACKWOLF CONSTRUCTION on the doors. A man and a woman. Young, not more than thirty or so. A few years younger than Alfie. To the left of the parking lot was a boccie court, where Italians in white shorts and shirts played on Sunday. Straight on was the bay, where the sailboats from City Island held their races on Friday afternoons. People used the boat ramp for the sleek go-fast boats and for fishing runabouts. Except for the bloody truck and the police cars, it was deserted now. Nothing to the right except swamp and then low buildings and businesses, and then the wall of condos marching north up the Trail toward the airport. It was not brightly lit at night. He was thinking witnesses. Who might have seen something?

The officers stepped back as Alfie took his look. First thing he noticed was the pistol in the hand of the male deceased. What up north they called a "Saturday night special." Nothing fancy, just something to get the job done. The bullet had not entered his head cleanly and had made a mess of his face, which had probably been good-looking enough in life. Alfie speculated that he might have been a novice shooter and hadn't held the gun steady when it went off. He might have aimed at his heart, his neck, or the side of his head, and missed them all. Or else he'd tried to shoot in the air and missed that too. A saliva test would show if he'd ever put the barrel in his mouth. The doors were locked, and he'd been knocked back against his window, but maybe, somehow, he hadn't done himself. Those were Alfie's first thoughts.

In another life, up north, Alfie had seen an autopsy of an apparent suicide. Everyone thought the man had jumped off the terrace of his apartment until the ME found a bullet in his brain. The entry wound had been in his mouth, and he couldn't have jumped after he was already dead, now could he? Alfie had learned back then never to assume. In any case, the bullet in this DOA's face went where not even a suicidal person would want a bullet to go, and the man might even have lived a little while in agony, with the car doors locked and a dead girl no help beside him. There was plenty of blood to support that conjecture.

The dead woman, by contrast, was leaning against the passenger door with a clean hit from the driver's side—bullet in the heart, probably. She seemed to have been taken by surprise. Her mouth gaped, as if she hadn't expected the evening to end this way. Or the morning to begin this way, either one. She was a pretty blonde; what else could she be in Paradise? Alfie had to admit that it looked like a boyfriend/girlfriend thing after all. Homicide-suicide, just like Pat Pride had said. Open-and-shut case. All it needed was a few weeks of paperwork to clear the case. He tapped his boot tip to get on with it.

CSI came eventually, the chopper dipped away, and deconstruction of the scene began. It looked like what it looked like, and the girl's name was Lydia Florence Dale. Lydia Dale's driver's license and twelve credit cards were in her purse by her feet. She was thirty-two. The male DOA had no ID on him, but they guessed he was the owner of the truck. Alfie wondered where the guy's wallet was. Lost it? Left it on a motel bedside table? Someone lifted it at a bar? He ran a check of the license plate and came up with a name.

REED LUSTFIELD LIKED to leave home early, sometimes as early as five o'clock. His wife, Julie, wasn't always out of bed when he left. What was the point? He was a good-looking guy, and she'd been proud of him when they married a decade ago. He'd built her this house, down in North Port, a tidy three/four bedroom because they'd expected to have a bunch of kids right away. But it didn't happen. Turned out, she was okay in the reproduction department, but Reed had a problem. Handsome hulk as he was—as healthy as he looked—his sperm turned out to be sparse and lazy. It came as a shock. With the knowledge, he lost his sex drive. Ten years into the marriage, the two of them were still trying to figure out what to do with the devastating information. Julie knew that Reed would have been able to deal with a flaw in *her* much better than one in himself. He'd shut down. Now she was thirty-three and didn't jump out of bed to fill his lunch bucket so often anymore.

Reed was busy building two mansions up in Panther Ridge, where the lots were three acres or more, and it took forty-five minutes to get there. He didn't build houses like theirs anymore, homes where people could live comfortably. Now his houses were so large that it was a major commitment just to go down to the kitchen for a cup of coffee. Half-mile walk through a maze of rooms and down a couple of flights of stairs. Each house was filled with brass hardware and marble bathrooms and granite kitchens and acres of travertine floors. They took forever to get done, and each project was a protracted migraine headache for Reed. Suffice it to say, he was gone a lot, managing an army of subs who couldn't speak English.

Julie suspected he was avoiding her for another reason too. He didn't like the negativity of their situation. And sometimes she just thought his absence was due to Lydia, his so-called book-keeper, more like soul mate. Julie had been feeling sick about her life for a couple of years and hadn't decided yet what to do about it. Except for the "having her man in jail" part, she thought of herself as a country song. She was alone a lot while he was drinking beer and hanging out somewhere else. She guessed the rest of it.

Today, for some reason, she was up in the dark, pulling on her jeans and following Reed into the garage, where he'd gone without stopping for coffee in the kitchen.

"Reed?" She didn't even know what her question was. *Do you love me? Do you hate me? Should we get a divorce? Hey, say something.* But it was almost too late to start asking the deep questions. She could see it in his face . . . when she saw his face. These days, he wasn't doing much looking at her.

"Hey, baby," he said without turning around.

When she saw what he was doing, she stopped short. Reed was loading his fishing gear into his truck. Two rods, the nets, and the bait cooler. The tackle box. Life jackets, again two. It made her think of *Brokeback Mountain*, a movie she'd hated. The word "gay" popped into her head, and she almost choked on it.

"You going fishing?" She didn't get the question out. She stopped because Reed would think it was a stupid question. He didn't like her stating the obvious. Like, they couldn't have children, so how about making another plan? He didn't like that at all.

She could see he was going fishing. But why and with whom? Confused, she looked back into the kitchen, where the clock on the microwave said it was 5:45 a.m. Last she knew, it was Wednesday. Was he getting the boat down from the boat high-rise it lived on and going out fishing in the middle of the week when there were all those headaches at Panther Ridge to deal with? She just couldn't speak up and make the query. Funny thing about men: they could make a girl feel like doggy doo just for asking a simple question. Reed hadn't told her last night he was going fishing. He didn't tell her now when she was standing there, watching him load up the truck. He was a Republican, real secretive, and just didn't like to tell.

"Have a nice day," she said finally, and went back into the house.

"You too, babe," he replied.

———

THE POLICE CHIEF showed up, and Alfie talked with him. He was a big, heavy guy with a gray crew cut who'd been in the department since the town was half its size. Chief Hogle had hired Alfie, and the two got along okay.

"Don't let anything out until we inform the families," Hogle warned in a soft voice. Comcast and the local ABC affliliate were only a few blocks away on 10th Street. There'd be coverage. Alfie nodded. He didn't have to be told procedure.

"'Specially not that dickhead at the *Herald*—what's his name?"

"Pride."

"Yeah. Okay, you know what to do." He got back in his car, his uniform already damp from the spring humidity, and headed in to headquarters.

Alfie left the scene soon after, before the bodies were bagged. The two criminologists already had a scenario in mind. No motive yet, of course, but it seemed clear enough to them that no third party could have contributed to the deaths of the two individuals in the truck. There was no mystery here, just a sad outcome of an encounter gone wrong. All they had to do was inform the families and figure out why.

By noon the Ford truck in question had been brought into a warehouse for examination, and Alfie was up in Bradenton doing what he liked least in the world to do. He was knocking on the door where Lydia Dale had lived, looking for a family member to notify about her death. No answer from inside, so he nosed around, asking information from the neighbors in the other units in the complex. Pretty much everyone was out at work at that time of day, but the two oldsters who lived in units kitty-corner to hers said she came from Ocala, worked early and came back late, a real nice girl. Kept to herself. No boyfriend that anyone knew. Her car was not in the space marked for her unit. Alfie figured she must have met him somewhere, maybe the place where his wallet disappeared. Eventually a janitor opened the door of Lydia's unit for him.

Right about this time, Alfie missed his partner, Mudd, but would never in a million years admit it. He called her Muddy. Betty Mudd was older than he, quite a few pounds heavier too, and she might have been a man in drag for all he knew. The woman had balls. She came from New York, the city, and didn't miss much. Alfie sneezed and hit the light, then scratched an eyebrow at the dead girl's neat little pink unit. Doll-size chairs and sofa. Little round table outside what must optimistically have been called a kitchen. From her taste, the vic could have been fifteen.

Alfie snapped on thin gloves, took a breath, and sneezed again before digging in. He was looking for names of next of kin, photos, date book, meds: pretty much the story of the dead woman's life, and he went at it slowly. He found a phone book with the names he was looking for, pay stubs that showed she'd worked for Blackwolf. There were also photos of her and a bunch of smiling people in Blackwolf T-shirts at what looked like a Rotary bowling tournament. Alfie was debating about getting on the road and driving up to Ocala to talk to Lydia's mom when his cell phone vibrated in his pocket.

The chief screamed in his ear, "Where the hell are you, Rose?"

"Up in Bradenton. At Lydia Dale's house."

"Well, get the hell back here."

"What's up?"

"That fucking Pride went down to North Port to get a story from Lustfield's wife. She's hysterical on the phone."

"I'm there," Alfie said, bagging the Rotary photographs and the phone book.

———

JULIE DIDN'T KNOW what the man was up to. He was kind of a geeky-looking guy, photographing the outside of her home as if for *House & Garden*. Ha-ha. Or as if he were from *Homes & Land,* and her place were about to go on the market. Briefly, she considered the possibility. Who knew what Reed might be up to? Maybe one of those new houses in Panther Ridge was for her. No chance of that—they were worth millions. She watched the guy with the camera for a moment, readying herself to go out there and burst his bubble. The place was not for sale. People did the weirdest things. His being out there with the camera reminded her of the time, a few years back, when a sniper appeared outside her weaving room. She'd seen him through the sliders that led to the patio and pool area, and did a double take as she was setting up her loom for gossamer scarves. The man, wearing fatigues and army boots, appeared to be dancing with an AK-47 right near the lake and the dock. He spun that rifle around and then stopped, raising the barrel up at her, in the house. Back then, the Lustfields' was the first finished building in the subdivision, so there weren't any neighbors to rally for help. Julie had watched him for a moment, strangely calm. She knew he couldn't see her behind the sun blind she'd bought for the window to keep the deadly UVs out but let the light in. She'd stood there just long enough to know he was a mental case—just another Florida Cracker with a gun, living in a world all his own. She'd called the police, and when the entire department arrived in four squad cars and got out with their guns drawn, her sniper indignantly explained he was after the bobcat that ate his "daawg." They set him right, telling him he couldn't kill a bobcat even if it ate his mother.

Julie wasn't afraid of Crackers, so she went outside. "You're on private property," she told the geek with the camera.

"What are you going to do about it?" he challenged.

Huh? Her jaw dropped at the rude tone of voice, and he snapped a picture. That made her really mad. "What do you think you're doing?" she demanded, waving her hand at the camera.

He took another picture.

"Hey, cut that out." She started to go after him. He took that angry picture too.

"Did you know about your husband and Lydia Dale?" he asked, camera in her face.

Huh? Flash. She blinked.

"They were having an affair, but she wanted to end it, so he shot her."

"What!" A shriek came out of Julie's mouth before she even knew she was making a sound. *What, Reed shot Lydia?* "What?" Her heart was pounding. She could hardly breathe, the words hit her so hard. *Reed? Shot Lydia?*

"Who are you?" she screamed. "What are you doing here?"

"I'm Pat Pride. I tracked your address from the license plate on the truck at the scene of the crime. Sorry to startle you. I just wanted your reaction for the *Herald*," he said as if this were an everyday thing for him. "Do you have any comment?"

"Comment? You want me to comment?" She took a step, and her ankle twisted. She fell to her knees, speechless at the request for a comment. This was worse than the sniper, worse than the silence all these months. She gasped for air, and the reporter just stood there. *What the freaking Jesus is this?* Julie had been around a long time, had heard a lot of stories about girls and boys and the fights they got in. But she'd never heard anything like this.

Reed shot Lydia? No way. He wouldn't have. She didn't know she was sitting on the ground, tears flowing and shaking her head. Reed loved Lydia more than anyone in the world.

"Hey, I'm sorry. Want a cup of coffee? I didn't mean to shock you."

This brought Julie back. Everything inside her that had gone limp started tightening up again. *He didn't want to startle her?* She was back on her feet, going for him. "You're with the who?"

"The *Herald.*"

"How do you know this?" she demanded.

"I heard it on the police radio. I went out there to the scene, boat ramp in Paradise." He backed away as her face screwed up with puzzlement.

"Paradise?"

He nodded. "I saw them. They were both dead. Looks like he killed her and then shot himself. I'm sorry, ma'am," he said. "Do you have any comment for me now?"

"Hell no, you son of a bitch." She went into the house, slammed the door, and called Paradise Police.

————

ALFIE GOT DOWN to North Port a little more than an hour later. The picture of what had gone down the night before was still clear as mud. He had a lot of questions and no answers. All they knew was that Lydia hadn't come home from work the night before; her mail from yesterday was still in the box. They had a BOLO out for her car and a name for the registered owner of the truck but no definite ID on the shooter. He rang the doorbell.

"Alfred Rose, Paradise Police," Alfie said, showing his badge. "Can I come in?"

The door opened slowly. Julie Lustfield had soft pale hair down to her shoulders that should have been mousy but somehow wasn't, stunned gray eyes, and jeans that showed off a good figure. No hint of a smile, but no fear either. "I'm Julie Lustfield. Is it him?" she said faintly.

"Mrs. Lustfield, when was the last time you talked to your husband?"

"He went fishing this morning," she said.

"What time?"

"He left before six, about five forty-five." Her serious eyes held that stunned look of people in denial. *He can't be dead, I just saw him a few hours ago.* "I saw him load up the truck. Just tell me, is it him?"

"Does your husband have a gun?"

Her eyes skittered around. "Yes. Some rifles. I think there's one in the truck."

"How about handguns?"

She shook her head. "He just uses them for hunting."

"What does he hunt?"

She shook her head again. "He got a coral snake once, right out here. For God's sake, tell me. Is it him?"

"He didn't have a wallet on him. And his face is pretty messed up. We're still checking." It sounded so lame that he couldn't tell her for sure one way or the other.

They stood there in the doorway. Her eyes filled with tears. "That reporter said he killed Lydia and himself. I don't think it's possible."

"You want to sit down and tell me about it?" Alfie said.

"They knew each other since birth," she said disparagingly. "We only met in high school."

"Uh-huh." Alfie wasn't sure what that had to do with it. "Were they seeing each other?"

"Well, sure, they saw each other every day. She was the book-keeper. They were on the phone all the time."

"I mean, did they have a personal relationship?"

"They had a very serious personal relationship." Her lips twitched in a tiny smile.

"A physical relationship?"

"Yes. She was his sister. Well, stepsister, not blood. Reed wouldn't kill anybody, but he certainly wouldn't kill kin."

"Oh," Alfie said. Sometimes they can surprise you. *Okay, the rifle had not been discovered in the truck, but maybe Reed had a handgun his wife didn't know about.*

"Mrs. Lustfield, do you know any reason why your husband might kill either his sister or himself?"

She shook her head, then her shoulders lifted just a little.

"What was that thought?" Alfie asked.

"I don't know. He hasn't exactly been confiding in me lately."

"You've been having problems?"

"I wouldn't call it 'problems.' He just hasn't been here much. He came in late last night, left early this morning. I knew he and Lyd hung out a lot. But . . . lovers? They wouldn't do that." The words had a hollow ring.

Alfie sneezed. You never knew. He asked her for a photo of her husband. She got up suddenly and went into the other room. When she came back, she had a new expression on her face, his wallet in her hand, and a photo of him and her on a fishing boat. Alfie studied the likeness in the snapshot first. The man in the photo had the same blond hair, same sort of build as the dead man, but to Alfie the wallet seemed to clinch it.

"He leave his wallet home often?" Alfie asked.

Julie shook her head. "This is the first time." Then she held out something else, her husband's cell phone. Alfie's intake of breath came at the same time her face cracked wide open. "He wouldn't go out on the water without his cell."

Of course he wouldn't. Alfie frowned but not at what the husband did. Julie was the kind of heartbreaker he went for. No one could tell him why. He didn't know. Similar to Sharon, Jeff's mother. Both girls about his age, down on their emotional luck, with things getting worse and worse, and they hadn't a clue how to dig out. Julie's plight tugged at him so much, he felt a sneeze coming on. Husband was a cheat, but she loved him anyway. And shit, nobody wanted to lose a husband to a homicide-suicide. He flashed back to Pride coming here this morning to get her reaction. Held back the sneeze of rage at that cowardly act.

"Do you have a family member or a friend who can come and stay with you?" Alfie murmured.

"It's him, isn't it?" she said.

"You could confirm that by identifying the body. We need a family member."

She shook her head. "He has brothers, a mother, people up in Bradenton. They can do it."

Ah, problems with the in-laws. Alfie nodded, got those names, and told her he'd get back to her later.

The sneeze came on the way to the car. It was a big one and somehow brought on a whole bunch of new questions about the sister. Men kill their girlfriends, but they don't often kill sisters they hang out with. Something about a sister—no matter how much you hate her, you don't shoot her in the heart the way you want to. Alfie's throat itched too. That itch reminded him that things aren't always the way they seem. Jumping to conclusions was the one thing you should never do in police work.

It started with the sister and went to the gun. Julie said her husband didn't keep a handgun, but there was a rifle in his truck. There was no rifle in the truck parked by the boat ramp. And no boat either. Where was the boat? Alfie drove to High and Dry, the marine storage where Julie said Lustfield kept his boat.

Pete Mulvey, an old geezer from another era, wearing a wife-beater and cutoffs, told him, "Yeah, Reed come by this mornin' and took out the boat."

"You saw him go out?"

"Oh, yeah. He was going south down to Naples to look at some property from the water."

"Anybody with him?" Alfie asked.

"Some dude. I didn't get a real good look at him. Seemed like a city feller."

Alfie snorted. "City feller" had another meaning down here. He went back to the parking lot and slapped his forehead when he easily located a second Blackwolf truck. He called the chief.

"It's Rose."

"What you got?" Hogle said.

"Looks like Reed Lustfield's on a fishing trip down to Naples today."

"No shit." Hogle grunted.

Got him. "The company has more than one truck."

Silence on the other end.

If they had a few more people on the job, they could have figured that out a whole lot sooner. 'Course, they were working three towns out of their jurisdiction. "Lydia Dale is his sister," Alfie added.

"Any way you can reach Lustfield?"

"He left his cell phone and wallet home, but I'll see what I can do."

Alfie called some of the numbers Julie had given him. Second call, he got a name for the Blackwolf foreman who usually drove the second Ford truck, the one with the license plate of the death truck in Paradise. Name Everett, another high school contact. Just before sunset, the coast guard located Lustfield's Grady-White just down the coast at a marina in Punta Gorda, where Lustfield had stopped for gas and a grouper sandwich.

It had been a long day, but Alfie wanted to make things right with Julie before he headed north to Paradise, where it now looked like an old story dating from high school had played out in one final rejection. Lydia had said no to a deadly suitor for the very last time. This kind of thing should never have happened in Paradise, but a lot of things should never happen.

Alfie turned into the subdivision where Julie lived. He'd been too busy to call during the investigation. But now he wanted to apologize for what Pride had done—getting the shooter/suicide wrong and devastating her needlessly. For all he knew Lustfield wasn't having an affair at all. All these things were in Alfie's head. He wanted to be a good cop and erase that look of horror Julie Lustfield had when she found her husband's wallet and cell phone—the suicide message that wasn't.

And then, as he cruised closer to the house, he saw the lights on and heard the stereo blasting an eighties house-party song: "Dance to the Music." Inside, Julie's friends were doing just that. Alfie got out of the car, puzzled by the party scene clearly visible through the living room picture window. He started up the front walk, saw the chips and dip on the coffee table and the drinks flowing, and slowly realized that Julie had done what he'd told her to do. She'd called her friends to be with her in her time of mourning. *It's him*, she'd said, but he'd read her wrong. She'd spoken with relief, not sorrow. He shook his head. Maybe in all these hours, no one had called to tell her different.

Alfie turned around and got back in his car, where he sat in the dark, drumming his fingers to the beat. Funny how the two men both left their wallets home on the same day. What was the meaning in that? When the song finally changed, he picked up his cell and placed the call. The phone inside the Lustfield house rang and rang. None of the revelers stopped to pick up. When voice mail finally beeped, Alfie left a message for Julie: Lustfield had been located alive on his Grady-White down by Punta Gorda and was on his way home. At least he could tell himself he warned her.

SUCH A LUCKY, PRETTY GIRL

BY PERSIA WALKER

I was fifteen when my stepfather died. I don't remember much about it. The doctors said I didn't want to. "Selective amnesia," they called it. Whatever it was, I thanked God for it. For years, I managed to put that time out of my mind. For years, everything was fine.

Until the Snow case.

They still talk about Chrissie Snow on West 86th Street. They still whisper about how she looked coming down, like a doll, with her T-shirt billowing out and her hair trailing behind her. She didn't claw at the air or put out her hands in any desperate attempt to stave off the inevitable.

She simply came down. Fast.

It was three o'clock on an icy Saturday afternoon in mid-January. My partner and I caught the call. Chrissie was still warm when we got there.

Even sprawled on a sidewalk, in a pool of blood, she was lovely, with a mass of soft bronze hair and ebony eyelashes that beat any they sell over the counter. She couldn't have been much more than sixteen—seventeen, at most. She wore a pastel-pink T-shirt with strawberry-colored bows dotting the collar, light-blue jeans, and pale-blue socks. She was on her stomach, her hair fanned out, blood trickling from her ears, her right leg bent at an impossible angle. Stab wounds punctured her chest. Her right hand gripped a panel of curtain. The left side of her face was crushed, but her right eye was good, and it was open. She moved her lips, struggling to speak or breathe, but nothing came out—nothing but a bubble of blood.

Seconds later, her struggle was over.

Such a pretty girl, said an inner voice. The words chilled my soul.

We were standing before an old tenement from the early 1900s. Six floors up, I could see an open window, and a curtain flapping in the breeze.

The emergency medical team declared the girl dead at the scene. The uniforms held back rubberneckers and questioned those on the street. Ellis Bates of the Crime Scene Unit photographed and measured the scene and the body. My partner and I checked her for ID.

Lee went through her pockets. "Found something," he said, and pulled a note from her back pocket. "It's got the name of a hotel. Very expensive, very first-class. You'll recognize it."

When I saw it, I did.

The place was swanky, all right. Nothing you'd think a kid could've afforded on her own.

Lee and I joined Bates in going into the building. The lock on the front door was broken, and so was the one on the inner door. Stylish, it wasn't, but the place was a rare haven in Manhattan for low-income, rent-stabilized tenants. A narrow, creaking elevator took us up in a jerky ride. We got off on the sixth floor and walked down a narrow, funky hallway, counting doors till we came to the one that seemed right.

It was unlocked.

We entered the apartment to a gust of frigid air. It was a two-bedroom that looked as though it had been cut off of a neighboring unit. The kitchen wasn't much more than a sliver. The place was austere, devoid of knickknacks. It was immaculate, with the precise cleanliness of an institution.

The apartment ran along the front of the building. I went from room to room, checking the windows. Those in the kitchen, living room, and bathroom were fine; the one in the bedroom was not. There were the gaping window and the flapping curtain I'd seen from the street. Dark-red dots spattered the wall next to the window and the hardwood floor.

A school ID card lay on her desk. It gave her name and birthday. She was all of fifteen years old.

It was not the room of a typical teenager. There was nothing of the sweet jumble of jeans, sweaters, sneakers, photos, posters, stuffed animals, and heart-shaped makeup kits of my niece's room. Nothing personal here. Nothing childish. There was something very adult about this place, something that said this little girl had put her toys away a long time ago.

Such a lucky girl, whispered that inner voice. I rubbed my temples and tried to repress a shudder.

Bates gestured to the window. "She didn't go easy, but I don't think she fought either—didn't have time. Probably taken by surprise." He nodded toward the blood on the walls. "Looks like she was driven back and then fell . . . or was pushed. Of course, it'll be a few days before we know if the blood is hers."

A search warrant was obtained. Lee and I walked the scene, beginning with her bedroom. He went through her desk. I checked the night table, looked under her pillow, her mattress, her bed, all the usual places. Bates continued his work, systematically checking for trace evidence, fingerprints, a weapon, etc. Lee left to check the roof, and a minute later a uniform ducked in to say, "We got a guy here, says he's the father."

"Bring him in," I said.

He was in his late forties, had short gray hair and thick bags under pale-blue eyes.

"I'm Detective Stone." I flashed my shield.

"What happened here? Who are you people? Where's my daughter? Where's my Chrissie? Downstairs, they said . . . They tried to tell me that . . ."

I stepped outside into the hallway. There's no way to sweeten bitter news. I've found that it's better not to try. He put a fist to his mouth to stifle a groan.

"Mr. Snow, we need to know where you were when it happened."

He was mute with shock.

"Mr. Snow?"

"Downtown," he whispered. "I wanted to buy her a sweater. I didn't see anything I liked, so I came back and . . . I don't believe this. It can't be real."

Lee returned and answered my unspoken question with a shake of his head. Nothing on the roof.

"Mr. Snow, why don't we step inside?" I led him into his own kitchen. He sat hunched at the table. Lee followed and leaned against the countertop, and I continued the questioning. We got a description and explained that we'd have to seal the apartment.

"When can I see her?" he asked. "Downstairs, they wouldn't let me. They . . ."

"You can see her later, sir." I watched that sink in, then asked, "Where's Chrissie's mother?"

"We're divorced."

"You got custody?"

"No. Chrissie and her mother fought all the time, and that man Angela married . . . Chrissie hated him." He clasped his hands to control their trembling. "Chrissie moved here only last September." A bittersweet smile touched his lips. "She said she was going to take care of me. Can you imagine? She was a child, but she was going to take care of Papa."

Papa will take care of us if we take care of him. Just give him what he needs, and we'll be fine.

"How'd her mother feel about her moving here?"

The sweetness left his smile, leaving it bitter. "She was against it."

"Did anything happen to precipitate Chrissie's moving in with you?"

"No. I would've taken her sooner, but . . . I was in prison."

Lee and I exchanged looks.

"When did you get out?" I asked.

"In August. I told Chrissie to wait until I got settled and found a job. But she wouldn't."

"How's it been?"

"Rough. I can't find work."

"What do you do?"

"Bookkeeper."

"What'd you get sent up for?"

"Embezzlement."

Well, that explained that.

I asked him about enemies. Did Chrissie have any?

Snow blinked to hold his tears. "Why would anyone hurt her? She was a great kid." He put a hand over his eyes and sobbed.

"We'd like you to take a look at her room, sir. Tell us if anything's out of place," I said.

"Sure," he whispered, and dragged himself to his feet.

Bates was still at work. He glanced at the father and gave a polite nod, then kept on working, dusting for prints.

"Mr. Snow, did Chrissie keep a diary?" Lee asked.

"I don't know."

"You never seen her scribbling in something?" I asked. "When I was a kid, all my girlfriends kept diaries."

"Did you?" Lee asked me.

"No . . . but I was a tomboy. So what about it, Mr. Snow? Did she have one?"

"I told you, I don't know. She was more of a computer person." He nodded toward the PC and webcam on Chrissie's desk.

"Maybe she had a blog," I said. "One of those online diaries. My niece has three of them."

"How things change," Lee said. "When I was growing up, a girl would kill you if she caught you reading her private stuff. Now, they put it out there for the world to see."

"It's called 'hidden in plain view.'" To Snow: "We're going to have to take the computer."

He nodded.

"This thing's pretty expensive," Lee said. "And the cam's not cheap either. Mr. Snow, how could you afford this if you don't have a job?"

"Angela married a rich man. Chrissie had the computer when she moved in. She has a friend—Claire. They were always working on it."

"That reminds me," I said. "We'll need the names of her friends."

"Other than Claire, try Abigail and Susan. I don't have their numbers, but they go to Chrissie's school. The teachers'll know."

We found Chrissie's cell phone in her backpack. Numbers for Abigail Dixon, Susan Bradford, and Claire Wilkerson were on her speed dial.

———

IT WAS EARLY evening when we went to the Dixons' Upper West Side condominium. By then, we'd knocked on every door in the Snows' building and gone up and down their street, checking every business, looking for witnesses. We'd stopped by the hotel too and showed Chrissie's picture around. Nobody knew anything.

The Dixons had a palatial living room, with floor-to-ceiling windows that overlooked Riverside Drive. Their multimillion-dollar layout was a far cry from the Snows' tiny low-end rental.

Abigail was sixteen, tall and curvaceous, with dark, watchful eyes and even, white teeth that flashed when she spoke. Also sixteen, Susan was similar in build, but neither were her eyes as dark nor was her smile as bright as Abigail's. Both favored plucked eyebrows, crimson lipstick, and crimson fingernail polish. The hair, the makeup, the nails: all perfect.

Claire was another story. She was flat-chested, narrow-hipped, and makeup-free, with wire-rimmed eyeglasses and frizzy red hair. Her fingernails were bitten to the quick and her eyes were puffy from crying.

Abigail's mother hovered in the background, every now and then disappearing into the kitchen, where she was baking muffins.

"Did Chrissie seem worried to you?" I asked the girls. "Or frightened?"

They exchanged looks. Abigail answered, "We don't think so."

"Did she mention being threatened by anyone? A boyfriend, maybe?" Lee asked.

Claire started to speak but stopped at a look from Abigail.

"Yes?" I prodded.

Claire bit her lip and looked away.

Abigail's mother spoke up. "Girls, please, if there's anything you know, then you sh—"

"We don't know anything, Mom, so just stay out of it."

Abigail's mother blushed, glanced down, and did as her child had told her to. She piped down and backed out of the room. Lee's face expressed my thought: *Who is in charge here?*

I was about to press the matter when my pager beeped.

———

MICHAEL SHIN IS a thin, wiry man, with excellent instincts and a conscientious work ethic. He had just finished the autopsy when Lee and I entered.

"Such a beautiful child." Shin stripped off his gloves and dropped them into a bin. "Come on, I'll buy you coffee and give you a rundown."

We followed him down the corridor to the staff kitchen.

"Three stab wounds to the chest," Shin said. "A thin, flat instrument. Smooth-edged. The tip broke off in one wound. And the wounds match the tears in the clothing. I also found traces of condom use, foreign pubic hairs, and epidermal cells."

"Rape?" I asked.

"There was no tearing or bruising. I'd say it wasn't the first time."

"A boyfriend? The father?" Lee suggested.

"Get a DNA sample and we'll see."

We paused at the kitchen entrance.

"She'd eaten about three hours earlier—pasta with meat sauce—and she must've had a snack soon after. Looks like brownies."

Shin took three cups from a cabinet and poured coffee. Someone had made a fresh pot.

"There's milk and sugar." He pointed to the stocked countertop. "Feel free."

Lee and I took our coffee black.

"Anything else?" I asked.

"She'd been drinking."

"Beer?" Lee asked.

"No, wine."

Lee frowned. "A fifteen-year-old who drank wine?"

"Maybe it was there because wine is used to make the sauce," I said.

Shin shook his head. "Her stomach contained more than could be explained by that. And it wasn't just any merlot," he added, "but a rather fine one."

We checked back with the hotel: room service did indeed serve pasta with meat sauce but no brownies. We asked the manager to check the records. Who had ordered the Pasta Bolognese?

———

THE NEXT DAY, we went to see Snow. The apartment had been sealed, and Snow had slept overnight in a men's shelter. He was rumpled, unshaven, and wearing the same clothes. He reeked of whiskey but was steady on his feet. He waved us in. Bates came along.

"We need a DNA sample," I explained. "Just to keep our records straight."

He cooperated. Bates took a mouth swab and packed it away. The moment Bates left, Lee asked Snow whether Chrissie had a boyfriend.

"What does it matter?" Snow went behind the open kitchen counter and returned with three glasses and a bottle of vodka. "Have a drink with me, won't you? Help me toast my little girl."

"We'd love to," Lee said, "but that's not our way."

"What is?"

"To find out what happened."

Snow gave a grunt. "You want to know what happened? I'll tell you."

Lee glanced at me. We were thinking the same thing: *This*

jack is going to confess. It was written all over him—the need to spill.

"Two days ago, when she was alive, I told her she might as well be dead. That life was shitty and she should go before she realized it." Snow poured himself a double shot and tossed it back. He stared at his empty glass. "I'm ashamed," he said. "I've ruined everything." He looked up, his bloodshot eyes leaking tears. "And now, all I can manage to do is get drunk."

I'll admit it: I felt a moment of disappointment.

"Help us," Lee said. "Tell us, did she have a boyfriend?"

"Yes, that was your question, wasn't it? No. To my knowledge, no. Why?"

"Did she drink or use drugs—of any kind?" I asked.

"Why? Did you find out something?"

"We're just trying to form a picture," Lee said.

"No. She didn't use drugs. Didn't drink. She was a good girl, a normal kid—with normal dreams."

"Like what?" Lee asked.

Snow gave a whisper of a smile. "She wanted to be a doctor, work with kids . . . but drugs? That wasn't one of her problems."

"What was?" I asked.

"Her mother . . . and her stepfather: she hated them."

———

CHRISSIE'S MOTHER HAD a Park Avenue address that looked as expensive as it sounded: doormen in gold braid, marbled entryway, massive floral arrangements, thickly carpeted corridors—the whole nine yards.

"Wonder what happened to make Chrissie give all this up," Lee murmured.

"Whatever it was, it must've been pretty bad."

Rich wood paneling, beautiful antiques, Chinese watercolors,

Tiffany lamps, and gilded mirrors. The apartment fit in too—as did the mistress of the house.

Angela Snow was the proper lady in Chanel, with her heavy eighteen-karat-gold charm bracelet, her legs crossed at the ankles, and every hair in place. She jabbed out her cigarette in a heavy crystal ashtray.

"I should've known better than to send her to him. I should've known he wouldn't take care of her. When can I have her back?"

"Soon," Lee said.

"The fall . . . did it mess up her face?"

She couldn't be serious. It was the shock talking.

"Mrs. Snow—" Lee began.

"O'Donnell," she corrected. "I'm now Mrs. O'Donnell, Mrs. John O'Donnell."

"As in Assemblyman O'Donnell?"

"Yes," she said with pride. "So I do hope you'll show discretion. No one's connected John with this mess so far. We would like it to stay that way."

Maybe it wasn't shock. Maybe she was that cold.

"Mrs. O'Donnell," Lee said, "did Chrissie have a boyfriend? An older man, perhaps?" Wine. Expensive hotel. We were thinking an established man with money.

"I wouldn't know. She and I had no contact after she moved out."

"And why did she leave?" I asked.

She lifted her chin. "Chrissie felt sorry for her father. He was coming out of prison. She didn't want him to be alone."

"We've heard that she didn't get along with your husband," I said.

"He told you that, didn't he?"

"Is it true?" Lee asked.

She hesitated. "Chrissie was difficult. She . . . said things."

"What kinds of things?" I asked.

"Nothing worth repeating."

"Mrs. O'Don—"

"I won't repeat those lies. Not now, not ever."

Inside my head, I could hear a young girl pleading. *Mama, can I talk to you? Talk to you right now?*

"We'd like to speak with your husband," Lee was saying.

"He can't help you. He doesn't know anything."

Mama, can I talk to you? He hurt me—hurt me real bad—and I can't stand the pain.

"How long have you two been married?" I asked.

"Five years."

"We need to talk to him," Lee said.

Another chin lift. "Well, you can't. He's in Albany. He won't be back for a couple of days."

"Have him call us when he's in." Lee gave her his card.

———

THE HOTEL MANAGER had phoned in the names of guests who'd ordered the Pasta Bolognese that Saturday and the time they'd ordered it. The list had nineteen names. One of them was "Jake" O'Donnell.

"Coincidence?"

Lee's smile was grim. "What do you think?"

I picked up the phone and dialed the Park Avenue number. "Mrs. O'Donnell? Detective Stone here. Have you spoken to your husband yet?"

"I told you—"

"I strongly suggest you get him on the phone . . . now."

"Detec—"

"Let me put it like this: it's better you call than me."

A worried silence.

"All right. He'll be back by tomorrow evening. I'll make sure of it."

"You do that."

———

OUR SHIFT OVER, we stopped at McKinley's bar on 17th Street. Lee ordered whiskey and soda. I usually did too, but that night I took it straight. Lee noticed.

"You okay?"

"I'm fine."

He played with his stirrer. "It's always lousy when it involves a kid."

"I'm handling it."

"You don't look like it. You look like shit . . . beautiful shit, but shit."

"Thanks."

He's the only one I'd let talk to me like that, and he knew it. We'd grown up around Cathedral Parkway on the Upper West Side. Now it's up-and-coming. Back then it was Cocaine Central. After my stepfather died, I moved away, and Lee and I lost contact. Years later, I looked up and there he was, at the academy. We'd been partners ever since.

"Look," he said, "I remember what happened with your stepfather—"

"Don't go there."

"All I'm saying—"

"I said—"

"—is that if you want to talk about it, I'm here. That's all. I'm here."

But it hurts. It hurts so bad. And the blood . . .

Hush, child.

But—

You let him do what he's got to do, 'cause he's our bread and butter.

The mirror behind the bar reflected my image. Lee was right. I did look like shit. I turned away and pressed my glass against my cheek. It felt cool and refreshing.

"Sometimes, I feel like I'm a ghost, you know? Sometimes, I wonder who really died that night. Him or me?"

"That's crazy."

"I've been hearing things, Lee. Don't tell the captain, but I've been hearing my mother's voice. Haven't thought of her in years. Don't know if she's alive or dead. But ever since we caught this case, she's been whispering to me."

"What's she saying?"

"Same things she used to say, to get me to cooperate." I set the glass down. "You think I'm crazy?"

"No."

"Got any advice?"

"Tell her to leave you alone. Next time she says something, tell her to get the hell outta your head and leave you the fuck alone."

"That's it?"

"That's it."

I thought about it. He was right.

Get the fuck outta my head, Mama. It sounded fine to me.

———

MONDAY AFTERNOON, ABIGAIL and Susan sat behind a table on the sidewalk around the corner from their school, near Central Park. They had two large sliced cakes—one chocolate, one strawberry—plus an array of brownies and cupcakes. A big sign next to them read: BAKE SALE TO BENEFIT CHRISSIE'S FAMILY.

Crumpled dollar bills and assorted change half-filled an upended water-fountain jar on the table.

"Looks like you're doing a brisk business," Lee said.

"Yeah," Susan said. "We're doing pretty well."

"Where's Claire?" I asked.

Something ugly flitted across Abigail's face. Susan started to speak, but Abigail put a staying hand on her wrist, and the girl snapped her mouth shut.

"Claire's not part of this," Abigail said, flashing an extrabright smile. "Says she's got too much work to do."

Lee raised an eyebrow. "Even for a good cause like this?"

Abigail shrugged. "You know how it is: different people, different priorities." Another false smile. "So, how's your investigation going?"

"We have more questions," Lee said.

"Sure. We're always ready to help."

"I see that." I glanced at the grip on Susan's wrist.

Abigail colored and withdrew the hand; Susan rubbed the spot as though she'd been freed from shackles.

"Maybe we could speak to each of you separately." I raised a hand before Abigail could object. "That way, the table will stay manned. You won't miss any donations, and no one can walk away with the jar."

She didn't like it, but she couldn't argue. She gave Susan a warning look, stepped away from the table, and turned to me.

"What is it?"

"Did Chrissie ever mention an older guy?"

Abigail set her jaw.

"Look," I said, "if you don't give me a straight answer, we'll be having a conversation at the station with your mother."

She tried to look brave. Folding her arms across her chest, she said, "You have no right to threaten me."

"Sweetie, we have the right to threaten anyone with cause—and you're giving us cause. Now, did Chrissie ever mention an older man?"

"Yeah," she said resentfully. "Her stepfather."

"They were having problems?"

"You could say that. He started raping her when she was ten."

Mama, can I talk to you? Talk to you right now?

Pressure started building at the back of my skull. "Did she tell anyone?"

"She tried. But her mother didn't care."

"You mean, her mother didn't know."

"What're you, deaf? Her mother knew but didn't care. All she cares about is being Mrs. Big Shot. She even tried to stop Chrissie from moving in with her dad. She was scared Mr. Big Shot would leave her."

"Why should Chrissie's moving—"

Again that irritated superior look.

"Don't you get it? Having sex with Chrissie was part of the deal. That's how her mother got that guy to marry her."

It always hurts the first time, child. Just let him do what he's got to do, 'cause he's our bread and butter.

JIMMY WATTS IN forensics had left us a message to stop by. He was at his desk, working on a ham-and-tomato sandwich. Watts weighed more than two hundred pounds, but in the eight years I'd known him, I'd never seen him eat a large meal.

He waved to us, dabbed his mouth with a tissue, and got up. We followed him as he lumbered past shelves of confiscated equipment in stages of disassembly. Chrissie's computer and webcam were on a table by themselves.

"She had a sweet hookup," he said. "Surprisingly good security for a teenage girl. Simple but effective."

"But you could bypass it, right?" I asked.

"Oh, sure. I'm logged in now. I just let it sleep until you came."

He sat down, touched a key, and the dark computer screen lit up. He double-clicked one of the icons littering the screen. A browser window opened.

"Look at this."

Lee and I leaned forward. We were viewing a blog. It was called "Selling the Pink."

"Does that mean what I think it means?" I asked.

" 'Fraid so."

Lee and I scanned the entries. The teenage author was running her own porn site. She'd started an earlier one with three friends—"Amber," "Chloe," and "Elektra"—but then decided to go off on her own. The decision sparked a feud, and she was still reeling from it.

But the fight with her friends/business partners wasn't the focus of her most recent entry—or even her deepest concern. She was worried about a man, someone she called "Mr. Big Shot."

"We got him," Lee whispered. "The stepfather. It's him."

A link from the blog led us to stills from archived footage.

"That poor kid," Lee said.

"Poor, she was not," said Watts. "She was raking it in. So far, I've found two online accounts—one's got one hundred fifty thou and the other's got thirty-five."

You're such a pretty girl. Such a lucky, pretty girl. Men'll always give you what you want when you're such a pretty girl.

I gave myself an inner shake. *Go away*, I said inwardly, but the words had no strength.

"She was going to surprise her father," Watts was saying, "help him open a new business and send herself to college."

"Any sense of how long she was at it?" I asked.

"I'd say about two and a half years."

So she'd started when she was thirteen.

"What about the e-mails?" Lee asked.

Watts's fingers danced across the keyboard, and another window opened up. "You'll find this interesting." A few more clicks with the mouse, and rows of messages flowed down the screen.

The e-mails were furious and taut. They spoke of broken promises and angry betrayals. Most were from Amber, who spoke for Chloe and Elektra.

"Can you print them out?" I asked.

"Already did. Printouts are on my desk. But wait," Watts said. "You guys are gonna love this."

He double-clicked another icon. Chrissie's mail program opened up.

"She left all her messages on the server—all except these. These, she downloaded."

A ream of messages opened up, all from Mr. Big Shot. He was obsessed with her. She didn't want to see him again, but he wouldn't take no for an answer. The clincher came when he threatened her father:

"I can make sure he's sent back," he wrote. "I can and I will."

A date was set. It was the day she died.

———

THAT EVENING, AFTER pouring myself a generous shot of Johnnie Walker, I turned on my computer and found the first entry on Chrissie's blog. It described how, days earlier, she'd set up a webcam and posted information on a Web directory, hoping to find friends. She'd gotten her first contact within minutes. It was another girl, she thought, but as they chatted, she sensed that something was wrong. Eventually, the "girl" admitted to being a guy. Chrissie started to sign off, but the man was friendly, apologetic. He was witty and flattering—and ready with gifts. Within hours, she'd "met" others just like him.

One evening, one of her digital admirers said he was feeling blue. How could she cheer him up? she asked. Looking at her made him feel good, he said. He loved looking at her. If she wanted to be kind, all she had to do was raise her blouse and let him see her. He'd pay her "fifty bucks for three glorious minutes." He'd pay it into her online account. It was like cash in the hand. She didn't have an account? He'd help her open one.

It wasn't as though she didn't know what he was after. It wasn't as if she didn't sense where his request might lead. It was the money and sense of power his asking gave her—that and a feeling of despair. Was this kind of attention the only kind she could hope for? If so, then why not make the best of it? According to her blog, she was suffering at her stepfather's hands nightly. She couldn't fight him. But here, she had the power to say no and the right to exact payment when she said yes. Here, the men couldn't even touch her. They could only watch her, long for her—and only for as long as she let them.

Chrissie said she had more than a thousand "fans" who made monthly "donations" for her performances. They advised her on the best camera and software to use. They even paid for it, having suggested that she set up a "wish list" on online stores. She could ask for anything she wanted, they said. She could list DVDs, CDs, clothes, jewelry, computer hardware—anything. They would pay for it, and the stores would deliver while keeping her address secret.

It was a hell of a ride, and Chrissie was holding on tight. But it wasn't all fun and games. She battled fear and self-loathing. Certain men were terrifying. One wrote that he wanted to possess her. Many pressed her to meet them, but she refused—all except one.

Enough. I drained the last drop of whiskey, turned off the computer, and went to bed, but I couldn't sleep. I kept thinking about her, trapped with her stepfather, and about another girl I'd known, likewise trapped.

Mama, can I talk to you? I can't take the pain.

Shush, it always hurts the first time, child.

Stop him, Mama. Stop him, 'cause I won't let him near me again.

I thought about the day my stepfather died. For years, all I could remember was what they told me: that my mother heard me screaming, rushed into my room, and found him on me. He was dead, bleeding like a stuck pig, and I was under him, holding the knife. That's all. Simple.

I didn't serve a day in jail. I didn't live another day with my mother either. The court forgave me. She didn't. I'd killed her man, taken her livelihood. She left town and never looked back. I decided to do the same. That was that. Simple.

Until Chrissie.

Around midnight, Shin called. "The wine was definitely a merlot. It matches a bottle from the hotel. Also, you remember I said she ate brownies?"

"Now that you mention it . . . what about them?"

"Ever heard of bud brownies?"

Brownies made with pot. "You telling me she was high?"

"As the wind blows."

———

O'DONNELL MET US at the door with a brandy in hand. His tie was loosened and his jacket tossed across a chair. He looked stressed. Good. Chrissie's mother was nowhere in sight. Even better.

"Look, I'm stunned," he said, "but guys, c'mon. I had nothing to do with it."

"Let's sit down," I said.

He glanced at his watch. "I have to get back tonight. You shouldn't have sent for me. We could've talked on the phone."

"I don't think so."

"Fine. Let's get this over with."

Lee and I made a show of consulting our notes.

"We know," I said, "that you met Chrissie at a hotel on Saturday, that you had sex with her and bought her lunch."

"Preposterous."

I eyeballed him. "Think about it."

"There's nothing to think about. I was in Albany. I've been there since Friday."

I was tired and short-tempered after a bad night. "Mr. O'Donnell, the hot-and-heavy e-mails on Chrissie's hard drive will tell us they came from you. Your credit cards will tell us where you stayed and when. DNA taken from Chrissie's body will tell us that it came from you. Now, do you really want us to go to all that trouble? Trust me, sir. If you make it hard for us, we'll make it hard for you."

He broke out in a sweat. "You're bluffing."

"Try me."

He ran a hand through his thick silver hair, sorting options, finding none. "All right. But I left her at the hotel—alive. And I loved her. I never would've hurt her."

I felt cold inside, cold enough to kill without batting an eyelash.

"You're sick," Lee told him. "You know that, right?"

"I had nothing to do with her death."

"She threatened to reveal you," Lee said. "You had to shut her up."

O'Donnell licked his lips. "Listen, I was nowhere near her when she died. I can prove it. I usually take a train to Albany, but I was late, so I flew instead. The flight was at four. I have the boarding pass."

"Let me see it," I said.

He dug it out of his wallet and handed it over.

The pass was legit. I showed it to Lee.

"You're not off the hook," I said.

"But I've proved—"

"You're going to jail," Lee said. "For child abuse and rape."

"You're crazy."

"When we're finished with you, you'll wish we were."

Back in the car, Lee scratched his temple. "That SOB. He wasn't just our main suspect. He was our only one."

"It's time we had a meeting," I said.

"With who?"

"Elektra."

———

I MADE THE calls from the car. She was at the station when we got there. I expected to see her mother too, but the girl was alone.

"I sort of expected to hear from you," she said.

"Why?"

"Abigail and Susan said they'd seen you. I figured you'd want to see me too."

I ushered her into a small soundproof room with a desk, three chairs, and walls that were bare, except for a one-way mirror. I pointed to the metal fold-up chair set in the narrow space between the desk and the mirror. The room was claustrophobic, the chair uncomfortable. They were meant to be. She sat on the edge of the chair and eyed the mirror.

"Is anyone watching?" she asked.

"Where's your mom? I thought you'd bring her."

She gave me an indecipherable look, then said, "She's busy."

"I'll call her."

"No, please. She doesn't need to come here." Panic edged her voice. She pushed her glasses back up on her nose. "Was it the e-mails or the blog?"

"Both."

She grew paler. "Can this be kept from my mother?"

"Clear this up now, and she'll never be the wiser."

She worried her lip.

"At least you were never on camera," I added.

"Abigail wouldn't let me. I'm just a geek, so I could only do the technical stuff."

"Whose idea was it?"

"Abby's. She found out that Chrissie had this porn site and told her that if she didn't let her in on it, she'd tell."

"Only it didn't work out the way Abigail planned, did it?"

Again, she shook her head. "Abby's pretty, but not like Chrissie. Chrissie's the one the guys wanted to see. Chrissie said she was bringing in all the money. She didn't see why she had to split so much of it with us. So she went back to having her own site and took the best-paying guys with her. Abigail and Susan were left with the crazies, the guys who wanted weird stuff. They got angry."

"How angry?"

A pause. "Very."

There was a knock on the door. It was Lee: time for a talk with Amber and Chloe.

"I'll be right back," I said, and stepped outside.

"They're in one and two," Lee said.

"Parents come?"

"The girls refused to have 'em."

They were old enough. They had that right.

"Dumb choice," I said. "But thank God they made it."

———

SUSAN HAD BACKED her chair into a corner, so her back was against the wall. She was hugging herself and chewing on a lock of hair.

"Hi, Susan," I said.

"Hi." Her voice was barely a whisper.

I had a folder thick with papers and labeled with her name. I slapped it on the desk, and she cringed. Lee leaned against the wall. I perched on the edge of the desk and regarded her with concern. She averted her eyes.

"So, I guess you know why you're here," I said. "I can understand why you didn't bring your mother."

She licked her lips.

"Susan, we know about the porn sites and we know that you were there, in Chrissie's room, when it happened."

Her eyes widened. "No—"

"We know that you and Abigail gave Chrissie pot-laced brownies. That you baked them in Abigail's kitchen and told Chrissie they were a peace present."

"But—"

"We know that once Chrissie was high, you and Abigail stabbed her and pushed her out the window."

"No! I would've never hurt Chrissie. I—"

"You were just angry at her because she was being selfish. You guys had worked just as hard as she had. It wasn't fair that she should end up with the best-paying customers, right?"

"But—"

"I should tell you that Claire's in the other room." I paused. "And she's told us everything."

She was frantic. "But she—no! It didn't happen that way. I swear it!"

"Then what did happen?"

She looked down. "I . . . I can't talk about it. Abigail said—"

"Abigail said to lie to us, didn't she?"

She didn't answer.

"Susan, it's time for me to read you your rights."

"Does this mean I'm under arrest?"

I didn't answer, just pulled out a card bearing Miranda and read it to her. I looked at her and shook my head. "It's a shame."

"What?" she asked, her eyes sparkling with tears.

"I'd like to believe you didn't kill Chrissie. But the evidence says you did. And unless you speak up, you're going down for it."

She opened her mouth to speak, but I held up my hand.

"Too late," I said. "I can't hear another word you have to say — not unless . . ." I handed her the card and the pen. "Initial it and we can hear your side of it."

She hesitated, and then, tears rolling down her cheeks, she scratched her initials.

"We didn't kill her." She sniffed. "I swear we didn't."

"We can prov—"

"We did give her the brownies. But we really meant to make up with her."

Lee and I maintained a cynical silence.

She looked from me to him, wide-eyed and terrified. "Please! You've got to believe me!"

"Susan, I'm trying to help you. Don't bullshit me."

She swallowed and gave in to a shudder but didn't speak.

"Okay. If that's the way it's going to be, then . . ." I spoke to Lee and pointed to Susan. "Take her out."

She blanched. "Wha—?"

He laid a heavy hand on her shoulder. "Let's go."

"No!" She twisted around. "Please! I'll tell you what I know."

"I don't have time to waste," I said.

"I'm not going to jail for her. I want this to be over. I want it to stop!"

She covered her face with her hands and burst into terrified sobs.

———

ABIGAIL EXAMINED ONE expensively manicured fingernail.

"So," I said. "Whose idea was it?"

"I don't know what you're talking about. Am I under arrest?"

"Should you be?"

Abigail pushed her chair back and stood up. "I'm leaving. You can't—"

"Girlfriend, we can do this hard or we can do it easy. You talk to me alone or with your parents. Either way, you will talk."

She thought about it, lifted her chin, and flopped back down in the chair. "What do you want?"

"The truth."

She narrowed her eyes. "Did I tell you that my daddy's a lawyer? He eats people like you for breakfast."

"Well, he's about to get a bad case of indigestion, and you're the reason why."

She started to retort but thought better of it.

"We already have you on the porn," I said. "And now we're going to get you for murder. We know how you did it and why. Best of all, we have proof: the brownies that made Chrissie so dizzy she couldn't fight you, and witnesses who saw you leaving the apartment."

Lee came in and handed me a file with Abigail's name written prominently on it, and three typed sheets of paper laid atop it. He glanced at Abigail, who gave him a knowing look and ran the tip of her tongue along her lower lip. He laughed at her, and she flushed. He started out, then turned back.

"Take some advice," he told her. "My partner here, she's not interested in giving you another chance. Me, I think it's only fair to tell you that Claire's already cut a deal. She's hung you out to dry."

I held up the three sheets. "It's all here."

"She said that I . . . ?" Abigail's mouth dropped open. "That little bitch! That crazy little bitch!" She sat up. "Now, you listen to me . . ."

———

"Her mother should be here," Lee said.

I agreed.

We glanced through the wired glass pane in the door. She'd taken out a small fingernail file, the handle ornate, not something you'd expect a girl too shy to wear makeup or stylish clothes to have.

The tip was broken.

I went in. "What an unusual file."

"Chrissie gave it to me."

"No, she didn't."

She went very still. "You've been speaking to Abigail, haven't you? Why do you believe her? She's a liar."

"So are you."

What color she had drained from her face.

"But it doesn't matter," I continued. "The nail file won't lie."

For a long moment, she forgot to breathe. Then, hands trembling, she continued to file her nails. "So what's next?"

"We've called your mother."

"She doesn't care."

"I'm reading you your rights."

"Don't bother."

I took out the card. "You have the right—"

"Don't. Bother."

Carefully, she stored the file in her backpack. "Am I supposed to sign something? Let's get this over with."

"The file: why didn't you get rid of it?"

"Because it was Chrissie's. It's pretty . . . like she was." Her voice was calm, her tone rational. "It was their fault. Chrissie's and Abigail's. They made it happen. They wanted it. Maybe not Susan—but Abigail definitely."

"She actually asked you to kill Chrissie?"

"No, but she said Chrissie was a problem and that we had to find a solution. I thought . . ." A quaver crept into her voice. "I thought that if I did this, then maybe Abigail would help me. Show me how to do my hair and fingernails. Help me be pretty." A pause. "I've always wanted to be pretty."

She swallowed. "So after Chrissie came back from seeing her stepfather, we took some brownies over. Abigail and Susan left. I told Chrissie I had to talk to her. I thought it would be easy, you know, to get her to open the window . . . and then come up behind her. But she turned around. I had to do something. The nail file was there."

She drew a deep breath. "And then, when I told Abigail, she said she didn't want to have anything more to do with me. She said . . ." Her voice dropped. "She said I was crazy."

Lee and I exchanged glances.

"But why didn't you ask Chrissie to give you a makeover?"

"She refused to. She said I was lucky . . . lucky to be ugly. Can you imagine?" Angry tears sparkled in her eyes. "That's when I did it. I pushed her . . . pushed her out the window, so I wouldn't have to see her pretty face anymore."

The image of Chrissie's face, crushed and contorted by agony but still lovely as she lay broken on the sidewalk, came to mind. The sound of her last breath whispered in my ear. Then came another voice, soft and malevolent.

Such a lucky, pretty girl—

Yeah, dead lucky.

———

THAT NIGHT, AT McKinley's, Lee said, "The memories, they're coming back, aren't they?"

I nodded. My mother's screams, the police, the social workers, the decision not to prosecute her for letting her husband do what he did and the judge's decision to set me free—it was all there.

"But it's okay," I said. "No need to worry."

"No?"

My image in the mirror returned my gaze. I smiled, it smiled back, and it hit me that this was no ghost but a reflection of the living.

"My mother always told me I was lucky. For once, she was right. I am lucky. I survived."

FRIDAY NIGHT LUCK

BY EDWARD D. HOCH

It happened on a Friday, which had always been a bad day for Will Blackstone. Ever since college, he'd had a habit of relaxing at week's end with a few drinks or a joint. It had lost him a pretty good job and more than one girlfriend. Sadie Murray was finally interested enough to stick by him, and it was she who got him the job at Techno-Bio, a firm whose specialty was cleaning up the remains at particularly messy crime scenes.

He liked the work, and it brought him into contact with a number of city detectives. One night over coffee, after a double-suicide cleanup, a detective named Tim Press told him he'd make a good cop. "I passed the exam once but didn't make the cut," Will told him.

"Why don't you volunteer a few hours with the police auxiliary?" Press suggested. "We got two men in our squad started out as auxiliary cops. It looks good on your record, gives you an in."

It sounded worth a try. Soon Will was putting in ten hours a week as an auxiliary, wearing a basic uniform and badge that were impressive even if they didn't quite look like the real thing.

Santos, head of the clean-up crew, kidded him about it. "You big Dick Tracy guy now!"

"Hardly! They've got me on park patrol. Last weekend I stopped some kids from throwing stones at the ducks."

He'd been on the auxiliary force for three months, working Friday evenings and weekends in addition to his regular job. Sadie was pleased that he'd stuck with it and that he was thinking again about taking the police department exam. "You passed it last time, Will," she told him. "And you've done well with the auxiliary. That should help."

It would have helped, if it hadn't been for that damned Friday. It was toward the end of the summer, on one of those rainy August weekends that seem to tell you autumn is just around the corner. No one came to the park on evenings like this. Sitting in his car, he'd found a half-smoked joint in his jacket pocket and decided to finish it. He'd just lit up when his supervisor came by.

Will tried to palm the joint, but its odor lingered in the car. "What's that I smell, Blackstone?" the supervisor asked. He was a grizzly old man named Cranston who went by the rule book.

"I . . . I guess I—"

"Are you smoking pot while on duty?"

"I had maybe one puff."

"That's one too many. You know the rules. Finish your shift tonight and then turn in your badge. You're finished with the auxiliaries."

"Yes, sir." He flicked the butt out the car window into a puddle.

———

WILL DIDN'T TELL Sadie about the incident right away. He just said he was off for the weekend because they were overstaffed. He simply didn't go in the next day and didn't turn in the silver badge he'd come to admire. He kept it in his pocket when he went to work on Monday, half-thinking Cranston would be on the phone at any moment, demanding its return. But the police auxiliary was a volunteer organization and more loosely managed than the Force itself. The week passed without his hearing a thing.

That Saturday night he told Sadie Murray he'd quit the police auxiliary. "Why?" she asked. "I thought you wanted to get on the Force someday."

"I did, I still do. But there are other ways to go about it. This way wasn't getting me anywhere, and it was keeping us apart on weekends."

"Your career is the important thing right now, Will. You don't want to spend your life scraping brains off wallpaper."

He was sorry he'd told her about some of Techno-Bio's messier jobs. "I won't be there forever," he promised.

But the following Monday he was back again, working with Santos and the rest of the crew on an uptown apartment where an elderly woman and all her cats had passed away without notice several weeks earlier. Usually the routine was about the same. They entered the home or apartment dressed in biohazard suits until they could establish the extent of the cleanup. With luck, it might be confined to a tile bathroom, where the job was relatively easy.

The next few days passed uneventfully. The police auxiliary still hadn't asked for their badge back, and the cleanups were messy but manageable. It was on another Friday—that damned day!—when the crew reached a Chestnut Street loft and found a nightmare of blood and guts covering the walls and floor.

"What happened here?" Santos asked the detective in charge. It was Sergeant Rafferty, and they all knew him.

"A mess is what happened, and we still haven't straightened it all out," Rafferty told them. "We had one body, a known drug dealer named Hashid, shot several times. But there's a large quantity of blood from a second person whose body wasn't found, as much as two or three quarts. The medical examiner doubts he could have left this loft alive after losing half the blood in his body."

After he'd gone and the crew got to work, Santos said, "It is too much blood here. I feel death."

"He could have had a friend who carried him away," Will suggested.

"No elevator. Steep stairs and no blood on them. Why bother if he's dead or dying?"

"His identity may implicate others."

"Ha! Dick Tracy!" They'd been working most of the day on the loft, scrubbing and spraying, when Sergeant Rafferty returned, this time with the loft's owner, Carlos Palmeto, a stocky man of about fifty who'd recently made a name for himself by converting a couple of loft buildings into upscale apartments for the gentry. His pale features were not particularly Hispanic, despite his name. As he walked through the areas they'd already scrubbed, running his fingers over some surfaces like an inspector general, Will felt that he was more interested in welcoming his next tenant than in mourning the past one. "Hashid was a loser from the start," he told the detective. "More money than brains. I should have figured there were drugs involved."

"Your statement says you were at the doctor's about the time of the killing."

The landlord nodded. "Near as I can tell. I have to see Doc Soloman twice a week for a phlebotomy. I stopped by here after the doctor's and found this mess."

"We've identified the other man through his DNA. We keep a file on convicted felons now. His name is Gutman, Samuel Gutman. Do you know him?"

Palmeto shook his head. "A lot of these people I know by sight, but the name means nothing to me." He shifted his large frame as if trying to get comfortable in his leather jacket. "What was his felony?"

"He stole a large quantity of prescription drugs five years ago from a nursing home where he worked. He served fifteen months and was on probation for a year. Right now he's missing from his apartment, and I expect we'll find his body sooner or later."

After Palmeto and the detective left, the Techno-Bio crew finished the cleanup. They were in the final phase, checking out the bathroom, when Will peered beneath the old claw-foot tub and spotted something the police had missed. It was a little black address book leaning against the black tile that circled the bottom of the wall. He wasn't surprised that they'd missed it, if they even bothered to look beneath the tub.

The wisest thing would have been to turn the address book over to Sergeant Rafferty or Santos. But he might not see Rafferty again for a month or more, and Santos would only kid him about being Dick Tracy. He slipped it into his pocket and said nothing. Later, at his apartment, he opened it and glanced through the names and addresses. Apparently it had belonged to Hashid, the man who'd rented the loft and died there. Will flipped to the G page and found several crossed-out addresses and phone numbers for Samuel Gutman, the man who was missing. The only number not crossed out was marked "cell." He took a chance and punched in the number on his own cell phone. He heard a blast of music he vaguely recognized, plus the sound of male and female voices. "What's up?" a man's voice asked.

"Is this Gutman?" Will asked.

The voice didn't answer, and after a few seconds the connection was broken. To Will's ear, the music sounded like a jazz combo called the Lucky Spots who played at an East Side club named Schuster's.

SADIE WAS OFF with some girlfriends that night, and he decided there was no harm in checking Schuster's. He occasionally dropped in there anyway, and there was a good chance he could spot the man with Gutman's cell phone. Before he left the apartment, he pocketed the police auxiliary badge that he'd failed to turn in. Maybe it would come in handy, and if he held his thumb over the word "Auxiliary," it looked fairly authentic.

Schuster's was always crowded on a Friday evening, when young (and not so young) singles were drawn there from the nearby office buildings. Will could hear the jazzy sounds of the Lucky Spots before he was through the door, and he was certain that that was the music he'd heard on the cell phone. The bar was crowded, three-deep in some spots, with every table taken. He managed to get close enough to order a beer, glancing around for someone he knew. Finally he stood against one wall, out of the flow of traffic, and tried to spot the man he sought. It occurred to Will that the man might have departed in the time it took for him to get there. He reached into his pocket for the cell phone and entered six of the seven numbers on Gutman's phone. Then he made his way into the thick of the crowd, about halfway to the bandstand. Moving between the booths and the tables, he pressed the final number on his cell phone.

Even with the noise, he heard it ring, about ten feet behind him in one of the booths. He casually turned in that direction, leaving the phone in his pocket. A young woman with a reddish-brown ponytail held the phone to her ear and tried to get a response. "Hello? Is anyone there?" Finally she muttered something he couldn't catch and returned the phone to her purse. She was seated with two men, but neither of them had claimed the cell phone. Still, it was a man who had answered earlier.

After another twenty minutes, the men finished their beers

and stood up to leave. Will feared that she might leave with them, but she didn't. One, a balding man quite a bit older than she, said, "Good night, Glenda."

She remained alone in the booth, and Will walked over. "Mind if I join you?" he asked, holding up his beer. "There are no free tables."

"All right," she replied, barely glancing in his direction. Instead she took a cigarette from her purse and started to light it.

He slid into the booth. "There's no smoking here," he reminded her.

She looked up and studied his face, her eyes just a bit blurry from drink. "What are you, a cop?"

"That's right." He showed her the badge, carefully covering the "Auxiliary" part.

"Christ, I sure get all the winners! Am I under arrest?"

"Not as long as you don't light that cigarette."

She squinted at him. "Are you here for business or pleasure?"

"Business at the moment. You're Glenda, right?"

"That's me."

"Got a last name? I'm Will Blackstone."

"Glenda Briggs. What do you want, Will Blackstone?"

He shifted in the booth, thinking she'd have a nice smile if it wasn't for a chipped tooth on the right side. "I'm looking for Samuel Gutman. I think you know him."

She shook her head. "Never heard of him."

"You have his cell phone in your purse."

Her eyes widened with something like fear. "I don't—"

"Just tell me the truth, and nothing will happen to you."

She considered the possibilities. Finally she said, "A man I was drinking with earlier gave it to me. It rang while he had it and he answered, but then he hung up and gave me the phone. He said I could make calls with it but couldn't receive any."

"What's his name?"

"Gus something. I don't know his last name."

"You're sure it was Gus and not Gut, short for Gutman?"

"I don't know," she admitted.

"What did he look like?"

"Ordinary-looking, nothing special."

Will was suddenly aware that he had no idea what the dead or missing Samuel Gutman looked like. "Where can I reach you if I have more questions?"

"I can give you this cell phone number."

"I already have that," he said. "How about your home phone?"

"I . . . I'm staying with someone right now. You couldn't call me there."

"Can I meet you here tomorrow night? Around seven?"

"I guess so," she conceded.

"Good. I'll be looking for you, Glenda. Don't let me down."

————

ON SATURDAY MORNING, Sadie appeared at his place before ten o'clock, as she often did on weekends. They'd been a couple for nearly a year, and he knew she was good for him. But this Saturday, he saw at once that something was wrong. Her usual sunny face was clouded over, and she didn't even have a morning kiss for him. "What's the matter?" he asked.

She brushed the dark hair back from her eyes. "Will, one of my girlfriends called to say she saw you in Schuster's last night with another woman."

Talk about his Friday night luck! Now he'd have to tell her everything. "It's just a misunderstanding. I didn't even know the girl. I was just questioning her."

"About what? How much she charges?"

"My God, what do you think I am? Don't you trust me by now? I was questioning her about a murder."

"You do detective work for Techno-Bio now?"

"No, it's . . . Look, when I quit the police auxiliary, I never turned in my badge. I still have it. I've been following up on a supposed double murder."

"You're impersonating a police officer?"

"Not really. I just wanted to get some information out of this woman."

"Will, that's a criminal offense! Are you trying to get yourself arrested?"

He told her the whole story then, about how he'd found the overlooked address book while cleaning the bathroom at the loft. And ringing the missing man's cell phone number only to hear Schuster's familiar jazz combo. Then ringing it again to spot this woman, Glenda Briggs, with the phone. "I'm meeting her tonight, just for a few minutes," he admitted. "I need to get a picture of Gutman that she might be able to identify."

Sadie sighed in exasperation. "Look, call that detective you're friendly with, Tim Press. Tell him the whole story. And turn in that badge before you get in real trouble!"

"Sadie—"

"Will you do that for me?"

"I'll call him Monday morning," he promised.

"Not Monday. Today!"

"All right." He went to the phone, figuring there was a better-than-even chance Press would be off duty on a Saturday morning.

But the familiar voice answered, "Detective Press, Homicide."

"Tim, this is Will Blackstone. How are you doing?"

"Fine, Will. What can I do for you?" The words were friendly enough, but there might have been a certain coolness to his voice.

"Could I come see you this morning? It's a long story, but I'll make it short."

"Come on down. I should be here till noon unless we get a call."

He hung up and told Sadie he was on his way to meet Tim Press. She smiled and kissed him. "Now you're being sensible."

Will remembered Sadie's words when he sat across the desk from Press in the squad room, but he also remembered the badge in his pocket and his scheduled meeting with Glenda Briggs that evening. He simply could not abandon the case when he might be on the verge of uncovering important information.

"What can I do for you, Will?" the detective asked.

"You know I work on cleanups at Techno-Bio. This week we've been cleaning up a loft following what appears to be a double homicide, only there was just one body found."

Tim Press nodded. "Sergeant Rafferty's case. We've talked about it."

"He told me the DNA identified the second victim as a convicted felon named Samuel Gutman. I may have a lead on whether he's dead or alive, but I need a mug shot for a witness to identify."

Tim Press frowned. "You got any information, you should turn it over to Sergeant Rafferty."

"I will as soon as I'm sure of it. I just need a mug shot of him."

"Look, Will, I think you've got great potential if you don't screw up." He looked away and then back again. "Cranston tells me he fired your ass from the auxiliary for smoking pot on duty."

"That was a terrible mistake. It'll never happen again."

Press sighed and went over to the next desk to rummage through a case folder. He found a mug shot and ran it through their copy machine. "You got one more chance, Will, that's all. If you find out anything, you call me or Rafferty at once. Don't go playing cop on your own."

Will looked at the copy of the mug shot. It showed a white

man with black hair and a beard. Without the hair, there was no telling what he looked like. "This is Gutman?"

"That's what he looked like when he was arrested five years ago."

Will put it in his pocket. "Thanks, Detective." He left the squad room without mentioning the badge in his pocket. He could only hope that when Glenda Briggs saw the photo, it might trigger a memory.

That evening he arrived at Schuster's at quarter to seven, to be certain of not missing her. The place was already filling up, with one group of diners waiting for a table. He ordered a beer and stood at the bar. By five after seven she hadn't appeared, and he had a chilly feeling that she'd never intended to. But he had to give her a half hour, at least. It was ten after seven when he heard the ambulance siren approaching down the street. A customer came in to say that a woman had been hit by a car.

Will left his beer and hurried outside. He could see the flashing red lights in the next block, where a crowd had already gathered. He fought his way through until a police officer stopped him. "What happened here?" he asked.

"Hit-and-run driver. Step back, please."

He caught just a glimpse of her bloodied face before the ambulance technician shook his head and pulled the sheet over it. Her lips were pulled back in a final grimace of pain, and he could see that chipped tooth on the right side. Glenda Briggs wouldn't be meeting him tonight.

———

ON SUNDAY HE told Sadie about it, because there was no concealing his state of agitation over the woman's death. "I showed her the badge, let her think I was a detective, and now she's dead because of it."

"Don't be foolish, Will. Traffic accidents happen in this city every day. Have you told Detective Press about it?"

"Not yet. I need a few more days. That woman—I dreamed about her last night."

"Maybe if I went away, you'd start dreaming of me."

"Sadie, please—"

"Will, you've got to snap out of this. You're not a real detective, and you never will be, at the rate you're going. Forget about that woman, turn in the badge, and get on with your life."

Sadie was right—traffic accidents happened every day. Glenda Briggs's death rated only a couple of paragraphs on an inside page. She'd been thirty-one years old and a medical technician, and police were seeking leads on the vehicle that killed her. Something clicked in Will's memory. The missing Samuel Gutman had gone to prison for stealing drugs from a nursing home where he worked. Was it possible that Glenda had worked at the same place and met him there?

On Monday after work, he decided to research Gutman's past. He couldn't go back to Tim Press for more information without revealing his connection with the dead woman, so he went instead to the public library, winding through microfilms of five-year-old daily papers until he found the article on Gutman's conviction. He'd been employed at the Shady Lark Nursing Home in one of the suburbs. During Tuesday's lunch hour, Will changed into a suit and tie, telling Santos he might be a bit late getting back.

He drove out to Shady Lark, a sprawling single-story building that housed about fifty patients. He showed his badge and asked to see the administrator. After a brief wait, he was ushered into an office, where a man in a white coat was going over some spreadsheets. "I'm Frank Caster. What can I do for you, Detective?" he asked.

"I'm working on a case involving Samuel Gutman, an employee of yours who was convicted five years ago of stealing drugs."

The man nodded. "That was before my time here, but I know the details."

"Right now we're investigating the death of a medical technician named Glenda Briggs. I need to know if she was ever employed here by you, as a nurse, as a technician, or in any other capacity. Especially if she was employed while Samuel Gutman was working here."

Caster went to a file drawer and flipped through a number of folders. "Well, she wasn't here while he was. I'll check before and after."

"I'd appreciate it."

Caster completed the computer search with a shake of his head. "No one named Glenda Briggs ever worked here. I even checked for any Glendas, thinking Briggs could be a married name. But we've had no Glendas at all here. I guess it's not too common a name anymore."

"Thanks for checking," Will said, hiding his disappointment.

He always saw Sadie on Wednesdays, and against his better judgment, he again started talking about the investigation. "I thought that was over, Will. You promised me—"

"I know. But I can't help feeling I'm responsible for her death. I think Gutman is still alive. I think he answered the cell phone at Schuster's when I called his number. Then he gave the phone to Glenda to get rid of it. Later, when I traced it to her and questioned her, she lied about it. She said she was staying with someone, and I'm betting that someone was Gutman. When she told him a detective had traced the phone to her, he panicked. She was on her way to meet me last Saturday when he ran her down with his car."

"If he lost all that blood in the shooting, how could he be out drinking at Schuster's just a few days later?"

It was a good question, and he didn't have the answer. It's just that nothing else seemed to make sense. He was sorry he'd brought it up, and glad when the conversation shifted to other topics. It was only when he took her home after midnight that she said, "Forget that badge, Will. You're not a cop. Leave it to them."

On Thursday afternoon, he and Santos were working together in a West Side garage that had been used by a religious cult for the ritual slaughter of animals. "I would prefer a good clean gunshot victim to this," Santos complained. "Isn't that right, Dick Tracy?"

"I don't like it any better than you do."

They were wearing gloves and biohazard suits, but somehow, in digging up the animal remains, a hidden razor blade sliced through the arm of Santos's suit. It wasn't a deep cut, but he was bleeding, and Will worried about an infection. "You'd better see a doctor," he said. "I'll finish up here."

"Hell, leave it till tomorrow. We're only a block from Dr. Soloman's office. That might be easier than going to emergency for a little thing like this."

"I'll go with you," Will said. It seemed the least he could do.

They waited in the office for nearly an hour before the doctor could squeeze Santos in between other patients. Finally he came out with a small bandage and some pills to fight possible infection. "How you feeling?" Will asked.

"I'm fine. Let's go have a beer."

"Can you drink with that medication?"

Santos snorted. "I'll drink first, before I start taking it."

Will didn't want to go to Schuster's, so he steered them to a nearby neighborhood bar. Over beers, he said, "We'll have to finish that job tomorrow."

"There's not much left, so long as we avoid razor blades."

He touched the bandage on his arm. "That Soloman is pretty good."

Will took a sip of beer. "I've never been to him."

"You know that woman who was killed by the hit-and-run? She worked in his office. They're all pretty broken up about it."

"Really?" Will downed the rest of his beer and said, "I've got to get going. See you in the morning."

But he didn't go anywhere. He spent an hour walking alone. This time he knew he could break the case, if only he could fit all the pieces together.

———

THEY FINISHED THE garage job early Friday afternoon, and Santos went off to see what was on tap for Monday. Will phoned Sadie to tell her he couldn't see her till later. "There's something I have to do first."

"Are you still trying to play detective, Will?"

"I'm not playing. I think I've solved this case. I have to go back up to the loft where Hashid was killed."

"If you won't stop this right now, I'm calling Detective Press," she told him. "Maybe he can knock some sense into you." She hung up before he could reply.

He made his way across town to the loft on Chestnut Street. From the road, he could see lights and assumed that Palmeto's people were sprucing up the place for the next tenant. He made his way up the two flights of stairs to the apartment. A painter was just leaving with his brushes and cans, and Carlos Palmeto himself was giving the job a final inspection.

"Hello," he said when he saw Will. "You're one of Santos's crew, aren't you?"

"That's right. Will Blackstone. I helped clean up after the murders."

"Terrible thing! It might take me a year to rent this place again."

Will moved a few steps closer. "I've taken a special interest in this case, especially since Glenda Briggs was killed."

Palmeto frowned. "Is that a name I should know?"

"Let me tell you a story. A man named Samuel Gutman is convicted of stealing drugs from a nursing home and sent off to prison. When he gets out, he decides to start a new life and is quite successful at it, probably using a name off a cemetery tombstone to get a social security card and other false identification. But his former life still exists. He needs to kill off his former self, and he hits upon an ingenious method of doing just that. He wants Hashid out of here anyway because of his drug dealing, so he kills him and splashes around a couple of quarts of his own blood, knowing the police would have a DNA match to identify him. His Gutman identity vanishes completely, and the police are satisfied he's dead even though they don't have a body."

"How would he get a couple of quarts of his own blood without killing himself?" Palmeto asked.

"Simple. He goes to the doctor's office twice a week for a phlebotomy, removing a pint of blood each time because it contains too much iron. The procedure is performed by a nurse technician named Glenda Briggs, who gives him the blood instead of disposing of it in the usual manner. When I discovered she worked for your doctor, the whole thing fell into place."

"You think you can prove a crazy story like that?"

"Of course I can. The blood at the murder scene will show a high concentration of iron, and your DNA will identify you as Samuel Gutman. You never looked Hispanic in the first place. The doctor's record will show that Glenda Briggs performed your phlebotomy twice a week. And I suspect the police will find evidence on your car linking it to her hit-and-run death. Once she told you I'd traced the cell phone to her, you had to kill her before she talked to me again."

"She said it was a detective who questioned her, and she was scared she'd be sent to prison."

Will showed his badge. "I'm taking you in, Gutman. Maybe Hashid deserved to die, but not Glenda Briggs."

He nodded. "I'll get my jacket."

It's as easy as that, Will thought. He never saw the gun until Gutman fired and he felt the bullet tear into his chest.

———

HE DIDN'T KNOW how long he'd been unconscious. He awoke in a hospital room, with Tim Press and Sadie at his side. "You're going to be all right," Sadie assured him.

"She phoned to tell me you were going to the loft," Press said. "I was coming up the stairs when I heard the shot. I got him before he could finish you off."

"That badge—"

"We'll talk about that later."

Sadie touched his arm where an IV tube was attached. "The doctor says the bullet went right through without hitting a vital organ. He says you were awfully lucky."

Will tried to smile. "Maybe my Friday night luck is changing at last."

THE FOOL

BY LAURIE R. KING

S ergeant Mendez, there's some nutcase on line two. Can you figure out what he wants?"

Bonita Mendez did not reply, so deep in the maddening details of the Rivas/Escobedo case that she didn't notice the uniformed officer in her doorway. For the twentieth time that morning, she read the note: *8:35 p.m., March 2, Mrs. Claudia Padilla (821 Pacific Circle) hears a bang and, a few minutes later, a car accelerating.* She picked up the second page, torn from her notebook, to read: *8:49 p.m., 911 call. Young, panicky voice reporting shooting at 814 Pacific Circle (cell phone/Mrs. Adriana Torres/used by daughter, Jasmina, 13).* Stuck on to this page were two Post-it notes with related information: *Jasmina (Mina) says phone was lost the week before (phone records requested).* Then, added the day before: *Calls thru March 1 match usual pattern—ask?* The two pages lay on either side of the laconic *Patrol car arr 9:04—Gloria Rivas (16) babysitter 814 Pacific, doa/gsw.*

"Sergeant Mendez?"

It was shaping up to be one of those cases, the kind that brought you in on your days off and sat at the front of your mind when three a.m. came around on the bedside clock. *What haven't I seen?* Sixteen-year-old babysitter Gloria Rivas, dead on arrival, of a gunshot wound to the neck. Twelve-year-old Enrique Escobedo, her charge, missing. Here on Sergeant Mendez's desk, a sheet of lined paper with a series of apparently random notes: *Friends of EE absent March 3 incl. Jasmina Torres, Ernesto Garcia, Todd Stevens, Crystal Pihalak, Gilberto Oliveras.* The name "Jasmina Torres" is underlined, simply because it has come up twice. *11:14 p.m., Joseph "Taco" Alvarez $500 Shell ATM at the Shell station north of town—gas, gone.* In translation, this means that local gangbanger Taco Alvarez withdrew money from the Shell station ATM, filled his tank with the same ATM card, and drove off into the night. This note was included because Mendez learned from two witnesses that Taco had threatened Gloria Rivas not only because she had refused to go out with him but because she was going out with his younger brother, and she had further compounded her insult by talking the brother into not going through with the gang initiation he was supposed to face.

The entrance of Taco Alvarez onto the scene had reduced the uncomfortable possibility that Enrique—twelve, a good student, with no record—had shot his babysitter and fled.

"Um, Sergeant Mendez? The telephone?"

Sergeant Mendez knew the name Taco Alvarez; she'd even arrested him once for tagging, back when he was a smart-mouthed fifteen-year-old headed toward his own gang initiation. She wasn't surprised that he'd shot someone or that he'd successfully fallen off the map—Taco had a brain. What did surprise her was that he'd apparently snatched up Gloria's charge, Enrique, as a hostage.

"Sergeant?"

"What?"

"There's some wackjob on line two. I hung up on him once, but he called back. I thought maybe you could tell what he wants."

Mendez stared at him for a moment, then flicked her eyes to the phone that lay half-buried by the Post-its, notebook pages, refolded California maps, and scraps of paper that covered her desk. The phone's light was blinking, which meant the caller was safely on hold and couldn't have overheard Danny Scarlotti's insulting remark: it had happened before. She scowled at the uniformed boy in the doorway. "Why give it to me?" she asked, although as she said it, she knew it was a stupid question. She was the only detective dumb enough, or obsessed enough, to hang around the station on a Saturday morning.

"Because you're here," Scarlotti answered, sounding like a teenager—although he had enough sense not to roll his eyes while he was in the room with her. She wondered if uniforms were this casual in a big-city police department or if it was just her.

"I'm busy. And Paul's the one on call today. Can't you figure out how to transfer it to him?" She looked down at the stray scrap of paper in her hand, on which she'd noted: *March 2, p.m., Mrs. Escobedo hysterical; March 3, phoned five times; March 4, not answering phone.*

"Well, he's at his daughter's tournament today, and I sort of thought . . ." Scarlotti's voice trailed off, and Mendez knew that the answer was no, he couldn't figure out how to transfer the call. She sighed, knowing she was going to regret this, wondering why on earth they'd hired a kid who couldn't speak Spanish and therefore interpreted the language as a lunatic's ravings.

"Sergeant Mendez," she snapped, in English, to see if she could unsettle the caller, maybe make whoever it was just hang up.

Instead, the voice that came into her ear was real English—the kind from England, like you heard on the television, and not the hard-edged regional accents either. A man; an older man; a voice deep and oddly melodic, as if its owner were reciting on a stage.

"What am I? An infant crying in the night," it said. Then it stopped.

Her head snapped up and her eyes grew wide, then narrowed. Danny boy's diagnosis of "nutcase" might not be far off. "Sir, you have reached the Rio Linda Police Department. Do you have a crime to report?"

"Man's hand is not able to taste, his tongue to conceive, nor his heart to report, what my dream was."

It was what her English teacher would have called a non sequitur, and what most people would call lunatic ramblings, but something in his voice, some pressing intelligence, kept her from hanging up the phone and going back to her fruitless perusal of the material related to the death of Gloria Rivas and the disappearance of Enrique Escobedo. "I'm sorry, sir, I don't understand what you're trying to tell me."

"Words are like leaves; and where they most abound, much fruit of sense beneath is rarely found."

She pinched her fingertips hard into the inner corners of her tired eyes. When did she last have a solid eight hours? The Rivas/Escobedo case had crashed down on them on the second, and it was now the fifteenth, with no arrest and no sign of the boy. Going on two weeks of gathering evidence; interviewing family, friends, and neighbors; getting alone with one after another of Gloria's high school friends and trying to find a wedge to drive under those blank walls. Long, fruitless conversations with the police of Chiapas, where Taco Alvarez was from and therefore where he might be headed, and of Oaxaca, where the Escobedos had lived before they came north in the seventies. Dead ends for the murder, a complete puzzle for the boy's disappearance, the weight of it settling heavily on all their shoulders. *Hang up on this guy, Mendez. You'd do everyone a lot more good if you went home and got some sleep.* But the caller's voice had none of the slurred consonants of drink or the edginess of drugs. His brief statements, though nonsensical (and now rhyming), did not resemble the ravings of any lunatic Sergeant Mendez had met. He sounded polite and calm. Determined, almost. Maybe the English accent was deceiving her, but he sounded like a professor, one trying to deliver a particularly challenging lesson. Okay, see how he dealt with a bright student.

"Well, sir, you called me. If you want me to pick up the fruit of sense, you'll have to drop it where I can find it."

"Truth can never be told so as to be understood."

"Yeah, ain't that the pits? So, if you can't tell me the truth, why are you calling?"

"For now we see through a glass, darkly, but then face-to-face."

This, anyway, was something she recognized, although what First Corinthians had to do with anything, she hadn't a clue. "Sir, if you want to discuss the Bible, why don't you go down to St. Patrick's and have a nice chat with Father—"

The man broke in, his voice forceful as he repeated his first words: "An infant crying in the night."

Detective Bonita Mendez sat and thought about that for a minute. "Are you telling me that a child is in danger?"

The voice boomed into her ear, rotund with approval: "It needs a very clever woman to manage a fool!"

Something about that final word set off a tiny twitch in the back of Sergeant Mendez's mind, a pulse of recognition, or apprehension. But a tiny twitch was all, little more than a faint aroma in the air, and it was gone. She looped back to her own beginnings: "I think you ought to come into the department and tell me all about it, sir."

"So near, and yet so far." He sounded wistful.

She looked at the number on the display, saw it was local in both area code and prefix, and knew he couldn't be too far away. Maybe he was disabled somehow. Other than mentally, that is.

"You want me to come to you?"

"Come before his presence with singing."

She hoped this didn't indicate that her caller thought of himself as God; she really didn't have time to get involved with a psychiatric hold. The paperwork alone would sink her little boat. Damn it, she wasn't even on call today. "So where are you located?"

"Absent thee from felicity awhile, and in this harsh world draw thy breath in pain, to tell my story."

Her cop's mind snagged for a moment on the word "pain" before it moved on to the possibility that "tell my story" might be where the man's emphasis lay. "I'm sorry, sir, I don't think . . ." She stopped, only half-hearing the sounds coming down the line: the faint crackle; the build and fade of a diesel engine in the background; the voice of a child giving forth a long, unintelligible Spanish monologue. When she was a child, not much older than the owner of that piping voice, she'd had an aunt who lost both sons to a drunk driver and who responded to her agony by joining a church. The aunt's church was one of those that lived and breathed the Bible, that consulted Proverbs and Job for advice and to make sense of daily life, that referenced any decision, from ethical action to what to have for breakfast, by summoning a verse. Some verses were strikingly apt—the Bible is, after all, a large and diverse book—but for other references, meaning was stretched past the snapping point, leaving the aunt and her audience staring at one another, dumbfounded. Rather as she felt with this man on the telephone, in fact. "Are you by any chance talking about Felicia? The elementary school?"

"My library was dukedom large enough," he responded, with faint stress on the second word.

"You're at the Felicia library?"

"I give you a wise and understanding heart," the Englishman said, in an approving voice that made her feel oddly warm.

"Okay, it'll take me maybe fifteen, twenty minutes to get there. Will you wait for me?"

The phone went dead, which she guessed meant *yes*.

She sat for a minute, tapping her middle fingernail on the desk, wondering what the hell she'd just been listening to. There remained the tiny, faraway sense of familiarity in the back of her mind, but for the life of her, she couldn't tease it forward. Something years back and not here, but an echo . . . The Bible, snippets of poetry, Shakespeare—she'd caught both *Hamlet* and *The Tempest* there—it was an odd conversational form, to be sure. But conversation it appeared to be, albeit of a convoluted and inadequate style. She felt a stir of interest at this welcome distraction from frustration—and then caught herself.

She had to be careful. This thespian-voiced Englishman could be some honest-to-God nutcase setting a trap for a cop. A small backwater town like Rio Linda might not shelter as many purely vicious individuals as a big city, but that didn't rule viciousness out.

When in doubt, take backup.

And always be in doubt.

Mendez closed the Escobedo file on her computer and hunted down the location of the number the Englishman had been calling from. Yes, a public phone, located at the little Felicia Public Library, as he'd said. Or sort of said.

She shut down the computer and began shoveling the stray papers back into their file. "Scarlotti!" she shouted.

"Yeah?" came the formal answer.

"Yes, Sergeant Mendez," she muttered, locking up her desk.

"What?"

"Nothing. Who's on patrol down in Felicia?"

"What, you mean now?"

She looked at him from the doorway where she was standing, adjusting her gun for comfort.

"Yes, I mean now," she told him.

"Um, let me see." He pawed through the mess before him, came up with the right piece of paper, and read from it. "Torres and Wong."

"Patch me through to them, will you?"

It took him only two tries to do so, and when she had Jaime Torres on the line, she asked if the two patrolmen could swing by the front of the library in fifteen minutes, just to provide a little backup, in case.

There was a pause before the puzzled voice responded, "That's where we are now."

"What, at the library? Why?"

"Someone called in a report of a suspected terrorist in Arab robes hanging around out front."

"An Arab terrorist? In *Felicia*, for God's sake? Hey—I don't suppose it's a guy with an English accent?"

"Don't know about the accent. We just pulled up, but there's an older white-haired male sitting on the bench near the phones. He's got a knapsack on the ground next to him, but I'd have to say he looks more like a monk than an Arab. Doesn't have a turban or anything."

"Look, would you mind not approaching him until I get there? Unless he's actively causing problems, that is. I'm just at the station."

"Sure, he's just sitting there, looking pretty harmless. You want us to watch him from the car or from the café across the street? There's a clear line of surveillance from there."

"Why don't you go ahead and take your break, sit where you can keep an eye on him? I'll be there in twelve minutes if I make both signals."

"Take your time. Wong's got the prostrate trouble—he's happy to piss for a while."

The line cut off but not before she heard the beginnings of an outraged partner's voice. She smiled, figuring that Wong had no "prostrate trouble" at all but that Torres had heard that Detective Mendez was unattached again, and was pulling his unmarried partner's leg.

The Felicia library was a tiny building with a few thousand books, two computer terminals, and one part-time librarian. It survived on the goodwill of a small army of largely Hispanic volunteers and had to argue its budget to the city almost every year. But since the Felicia District of Rio Linda, surrounded by fields of strawberries and lettuce, was the kind of neighborhood where few houses had computers (or books, for that matter), and the only other forms of entertainment in walking distance were the roadside bar a mile south and the dusty general store/café across from the library, it made the Felicia Public Library the place to go for homework, after-school gatherings, job searches, ESL classes, and visiting-nurse clinics. It also made for some great numbers to show the state auditors, and the low-income patrons had justified a regular trickle of state and federal grants. Without a doubt, the people here adored the place and kept it both busy and spotless.

Which might explain why some concerned patron had called in a stranger hanging around the public phone out front. As Mendez pulled into the pitted surface of the small parking area, a young mother and her two young kids were coming out the door, and all three patrons gave the man a wary look. He lifted one hand, two fingers pointing skyward like a benediction; when the woman came down the steps, she was smiling.

Mendez got out of her car and could understand why the woman had smiled. The figure in the brown robe—which was no more Arab than the shirt and khaki pants she was wearing—resembled a tall, thin, brown-clad Father Christmas, down to the twinkle in his eye. There was, as Torres had told her, a battered blue nylon backpack tucked under the front edge of the bench, and a walking stick, tall as a man, leaning against the far armrest. His skin was weathered, although he was clearly Anglo. A pair of nearly white running shoes peeked out from the hem of his robe.

The man saw her, and he made her instantly for a cop, but he watched her watching him with no indication of the wary or defiant manner that brought a cop's reflexes to attention. She half-turned to look over her shoulder, wondering if Torres and Wong had been paying as much attention as the skinny Father Christmas had.

In perhaps thirty seconds, the two uniforms came out of the onetime garage that was now plastered with neatly painted signs advertising STRONG HOT COFFEE, BREAKFAST BURRITOS ALL DAY, and MENUDO THURSDAYS. The two men hitched up their heavy belts as they crossed the deserted side street, not needing to look for traffic. They joined her at the car, taking their eyes off the man for only the brief moment necessary to greet her.

Torres, she had known for years, and she'd met Wong (who couldn't have been more than thirty, further marks against the prostate story) a couple of times, although she'd never worked with him.

"He's just been sitting there," Torres told her. "Occasionally says hi to someone going in or out, but otherwise just cooling it."

"Okay, I don't think there'll be a problem here, you might as well go back to work."

"We'll hang on for a minute," Torres said firmly. Jaime Torres was a few years older than she was, and she'd been friends with his sister in high school: this was a brotherly thing. She wouldn't even try to argue him out of it.

"Okay," she agreed, and led the way up the library's walk.

The bearded monk rose as she approached, not like a wary suspect but like her maternal grandfather, who'd been incapable of sitting when a lady entered the room. The resemblance ended there: her grandfather had been shaped by a lifetime of work in the fields, but even if he'd lived a life of leisure, he wouldn't have been much more than five and a half feet. This man was well over six feet and of a willowy build that wasn't far from gaunt, creating hollows in the cheeks above his beard. She figured him for a homeless man, what with being a stranger in the area and carrying that worn knapsack, but if so, he was a very clean and tidy homeless man. He reminded her of a portrait of a saint in church school.

"Sir, I believe you called the police department?" she said.

"When constabulary duty's to be done," he replied, one eyelid drooping infinitesimally in a near wink.

"Could we have your name, sir?" she asked.

Instead of answering, his right hand went toward the side of the brown robe, where a pocket might be; instantly, both men at her side leaped forward to seize him, yanking his arms around and making him stagger back with a grimace of pain.

"Wait, wait!" she told them. "Don't hurt him. Sir, do you have any weapons in your pocket? Anything sharp?"

He shook his head.

"Do we have your permission to check for ourselves?"

He nodded.

"Would you please lean with both arms against the back of that bench? Let him go," she told the two uniforms.

The old man turned and leaned his arms onto the bench, automatically spreading his feet apart as he did so: he'd been patted down before. Then again, anyone who looked like this would have been picked up regularly, no matter his behavior.

His pockets, accessible through slits in the seams of the brown robe, held no gun or knife. Some coins, a pencil stub and folded sheets of paper, and a nearly flat wallet. She held out his wallet to him. "Is this what you were after?" she asked.

In answer, he took it from her and opened the billfold portion. There was no money that she could see, but he took out a piece of folded newspaper and offered it to her.

"You want us to look at his pack?" Torres asked her.

She met the brown eyes above her. "Sir, do you mind if we take a look at your belongings?"

"What's mine is yours, and what is yours is mine," the monk said, extending one hand in a sweeping gesture toward the beat-up rucksack on the ground. Torres picked it up and unbuckled the top, while Mendez picked apart the ancient folded square of newspaper.

It was the upper half of a front page, seven-year-old *San Francisco Chronicle*. In the center was a photograph showing four people, standing in conversation.

Although the page was all but worn through on its fold lines, she recognized the figure with the white hair, the dark robe, and the long walking stick with the knob on top that was currently leaning against the end of the bench—in the grainy newsprint, the stick was tucked against his shoulder as he leaned forward to listen to a dark-haired woman not much taller than Mendez herself. To the woman's left stood the familiar image of a black man wearing a dashing hat who could be only the then mayor of San Francisco. Next to the man in the robe was the fourth figure, a middle-aged man whose face was vaguely familiar.

When she read the caption, she realized why:

"Mayor Willie Brown and Inspectors Martinelli and Hawkin of the SFPD talk with the self-styled 'Brother Erasmus' at the funeral of homeless woman Beatrice Jankowski on Saturday, St. Mary's Cathedral."

Hawkin, she knew that name. And Martinelli—they'd been involved with a couple of cases that got a lot of press.

The faint bell of memory rang slightly louder. Hadn't one of those cases been something extremely quirky to do with the homeless population of San Francisco? A murder case in which a sort of patron saint of the homeless population had played a part? One Brother Erasmus?

She opened her mouth to ask him about it, but suddenly Torres exclaimed and thrust out the object in his hand. It was a small, thick leather-bound book with onionskin pages, closely printed in some heavy writing.

"Arabic!" he exclaimed. "And it's got notes to himself in the same language!"

For a moment, just an instant, it crossed Mendez's mind that there might be a terrorist cell here in Rio Linda, the world's least likely place. She shot a glance at the accused man's face, but the old bearded man had one white eyebrow raised in a look that was more quizzical than guilty. Of course, it was possible that terrorists had now started enrolling in acting school . . .

"Let me see that," she said. Torres gave her the book and transferred his hand to the butt of his gun, flipping off the snap to be ready when the old man reached for the trigger of his vest bomb. She opened the book and immediately shook her head—she had no idea what the words said, but she'd watched enough television news to know what she was looking at.

"This isn't Arabic, Torres, it's Hebrew. And for heaven's sake, take your hand off your weapon."

"Hebrew?"

"Sure, it's all square and boxy—Arabic is all curves and curlicues. Haven't you ever noticed the banners and signs on the news?"

"So . . . what? A Jewish terrorist?"

"This is a Bible," she said. "No, look, don't bother going through the rest of his pack. I know who this is. You're Brother Erasmus, aren't you?" she asked.

"A muddled fool, full of lucid intervals." His smile was like a beatitude as he held out his hand to her.

"Er, right," she said.

She gave him her hand and felt it wrapped in a smooth, strong, warm grip that again evoked her grandfather, who had grasped the wooden handle of a hoe until the last day of a long life. But this man's fingers were long and thin and considerably less bashed about, and reminded her of that Dürer engraving of praying hands that used to be so popular when she was growing up. "Sergeant Bonita Mendez," she told him.

He held her hand a moment, then let her go.

"Thanks, Torres, you and Wong can get back on patrol. I'm fine here."

Reluctantly, and not without protest, the two patrol officers separated themselves from the library forecourt and returned to their car. Watching the two men swagger off, Mendez regretted, not for the first time, that a uniformed officer's equipment belt encouraged such a gait.

She turned to the man at her side and said, "Sir, I'm going to need to make some phone calls. Do you mind coming with me to the station house? You could have a cup of coffee or something," she added, lest he think of it as an arrest.

He stretched out a long arm for the rucksack Torres had abandoned, half-searched, on the bench, retrieved the carved staff, and walked beside her to the unmarked she'd driven there.

She put him in the front, threading the staff over the seat back, and pulled out of the library parking lot. Neither of them spoke on the drive into town, although it was not an uncomfortable silence, merely restful. At the station, she helped him get his walking stick out and led him inside.

"Sir, I'm going to put you in an interview room for a few minutes, and I'll be with you as soon as I've made my calls. Is there anything you need? Coffee, soft drink, something to eat?"

"I am glad I was not born before tea," the old man remarked.

"Tea? I'll see what we can do. Officer Scarlotti, would you please make a cup of tea for the gentleman in Interview Room One?"

"Tea?"

"Yes, there are some bags in the cabinet. And take him the milk and sugar, in case he wants them."

"Milk and sugar?"

"And offer him the package of cookies," she added, and closed the door before he could repeat that as well.

It took four calls to track down Inspector Kate Martinelli of the San Francisco Police Department, but eventually Mendez reached her at home. A woman answered; a child was talking in the background; Martinelli came on the line; and the background noise cut off.

Mendez began to explain: odd phone call; enigmatic remarks; the caller tracked to a local library; seemed to match the identity of the man known as Brother Erasmus; and she wondered—

"Our Holy Fool is there? In Rio Linda?" the detective interrupted.

"Apparently."

"Good Lord, I've often wondered what happened to the old man. How is he?"

"He looks fine. Thin but healthy."

"If I wasn't in the middle of ten things, I'd be tempted to drive down and say hello. Tell him hi from me, would you?"

The affection in Martinelli's voice was not the usual reaction of a Homicide detective to a witness and onetime suspect, Mendez reflected.

"I wanted to ask you about him, whether you'd say he was reliable, but it sounds like you've already answered my question."

"I don't know about reliable, since Erasmus might well have his own agenda, but I'd say he's the most honest man you'll meet."

"If you can figure out what he's saying," Mendez said.

"Does he still talk that way? Everything in quotes?"

"Are those all quotes?"

"That's how he talked then. It took us forever to figure out what he was trying to say."

"Why does he talk that way?"

Martinelli was silent for a moment, then said, "He would probably call it penance for his sins. He lost his family, years ago back in England, in a way he felt responsible for. Personally, I thought he was trying to keep his mind so busy, he didn't have energy left over for his own thoughts. He is actually able to speak directly, in his own words—he finally did when he was helping us with our case—but it seemed to be very hard on him. I think you'll find that, if you listen carefully, his meaning becomes clear. Have you figured out what he's after?"

"What do you mean?"

"You said he called you and said something about an 'infant crying in the night.' Has he suggested yet how he can help you?"

"You think he knows something about one of my cases?"

"People open up to him, even the most unlikely people." Something about the way the detective said this made it sound like an admission. "And if he didn't know anything, why would he have called? Do you have a case involving a child?"

Mendez was silent, picturing the abandoned bedroom of twelve-year-old Enrique Escobedo: neatly made bed, rock poster on the wall and a Lego spaceship below it, bulletin board pinned with drawings of friends and celebrities, dozens of science-fiction books on the shelf unit. "I might."

"Well, he had some reason to come to you. You might start there."

Mendez thanked her, repeated the promise to pass her greeting on to the old man, and hung up. She then phoned the priest at the Catholic church downtown—not her own parish priest, but she knew him. He knew immediately whom she was talking about.

"The kids call him St. Francis, because he has a way of coaxing birds into eating from his hand. He's been at Mass a few times over the past few weeks. I'm not sure where he lives or how he supports himself, although I've seen people slip him money, and they often bring him something to eat."

"Elijah's ravens," she commented.

"Exactly. Nice fellow, odd, but a calming influence. There was a scuffle in the food line one day, and he stepped forward and put his hands on the two men's shoulders, and they calmed right down. What's more, he had them eating lunch together afterward, talking up a storm while he sat with them and nodded."

"Have you talked with him?"

"Don't know if I'd call it talking *with* him, but I've sat and talked to him several times myself. Very restful kind of fellow. Knows his Bible better than I do."

"But you'd say he's a trustworthy sort?"

The priest did not hesitate. "I'd say he's a saint of God."

When she hung up, she sat tapping the desk for a while, then returned to the interrogation room. When she glanced through the door's small window, she could see the old man, long hands tucked together in his lap, gazing in silent contemplation at his staff, which was leaned in the corner. She turned the knob and stuck her head inside.

"I need some lunch. You want to join me?"

He rose and picked up his knapsack and staff, and followed her out of the station.

They walked down the street to the take-out burrito stand, which was doing brisk business with an assortment of children in soccer uniforms, the playing fields being just two blocks away. They waited their turn, the old man ordered by laying a finger on the vegetarian option, and two minutes later they had their fragrant meals before them on one of the stand's heavily scarred wooden picnic tables. She peeled back the paper and bit in; Erasmus was of the fork-and-knife school, taking a fastidious surgical approach to the object with his plastic utensils. His staff lay stretched out on top of a low concrete-block wall, and for the first time, she noticed that the fist-size swelling at the top was not an amorphous knob of wood but a heavily worn carving. Studying it, she realized that when it was new, it must have resembled its owner—beard, flowing hair, hawklike nose. She smiled.

"I spoke with Inspector Martinelli in San Francisco," she said.

"Subtle and profound female," he murmured.

"Yeah, she seemed to admire you as well, and asked me to say hello. She also said that you might have some information regarding an active case. That it might be the reason you called."

He put his fork down and reached through the pocket-slit of his robe, pulling out a folded scrap of newsprint that was considerably fresher than the one she had found in his wallet earlier. He laid it in front of her, resuming his fork as she picked up the clipping.

The Escobedo boy's grinning school picture looked out at her.

She knew what the article said without having to look—she felt by now that the words had been carved on her heart. It had been published on March 9, one week after Enrique Escobedo had vanished from his house, and his babysitter, Gloria Rivas, had been gunned down on the front walkway of the home. When the article was written, Rio Linda was still quivering with apprehension; they were now coming up on the two-week anniversary, and Detective Bonita Mendez hadn't slept an eight-hour night in thirteen days.

"You have information about this?" she demanded.

He frowned at the rice and beans spilling out of their wrapper, and she could see him decide on an appropriate quote. "Nothing is so firmly believed as what is least known." The stress placed on the final word suggested the direction of his meaning.

"Look, sir, can't we just drop this whole quotation business? This isn't a game."

He raised an eyebrow in sympathy and said, "The rules of the game are what we call the laws of nature. The player on the other side is hidden from us." He chewed a mouthful, watching her intently. She propped her head in her palms and shut her eyes.

"You're telling me that you don't actually have any direct knowledge that could lead me to Enrique Escobedo," she said. "You have only guesses, except that I have to jump through hoops to try to figure out what you mean, when I'm so tired that even if you were talking sense, I'd have problems sorting it out. I have to say, if you're trying to help, I wish you wouldn't. You're wasting time that I don't have."

She felt his touch then, the dry firmness of his skin as his fingers wrapped around hers, gently pulling her hand from her face. She looked into his eyes, dark into dark, and saw her torment reflected there.

"To every thing there is a season," he stated, as if the words had never been said before. "A time to weep, and a time to laugh. A time to keep silence, and a time to speak. There is a time for many words, and there is also a time for sleep. A little sleep, a little slumber, a little folding of the hands to sleep." The repetition of the word alone was soporific; Mendez wanted to lay her head onto her arms right there on the picnic table. "Take up thy bed. And if we do meet again, why, we shall smile."

"You're telling me to go home and have a nap." His eyes crinkled: *Yes*. "You're probably right. But you haven't told me what you wanted me to know, about Enrique Escobedo."

"Those that have eyes to see, let them see."

"Do you have any idea how irritating this is?" she snapped.

"The discourse of fools is irksome," he agreed.

"So why do you do it?"

The crooked smile he gave her was filled with apology and empathy. He said, "He wrapped himself in quotations—as a beggar would enfold himself in the purple of emperors."

"There's nothing wrong with a beggar's rags," she told him.

But Brother Erasmus merely said, "Like him that travels, I return again." He set the tip of his first finger against the table: *Here*. Then he spread both hands out on the dented wood, all fingers outstretched except the thumb of his left hand, tucked under the palm.

"You want me to meet you back here at nine o'clock?" she interpreted. "Tonight?"

By way of answer, he folded the paper around his half-eaten burrito, tucked it and the plastic fork and knife into his knapsack, and walked away, his staff beating a syncopation to his steps. The carved head was pointing backward; it seemed to watch her as it rose and fell.

She shook her head to get the ridiculous notion out of her mind. But in one thing, the man was surely right: she did need some rest if she wasn't to be utterly useless. She phoned the station and told Scarlotti that she was going home and wasn't to be disturbed for anything short of a catastrophe. Inevitably, he wanted to know what she meant by "catastrophe," but she slapped her phone shut and tossed her debris in the trash.

She drove home, fed the cat, kicked off her shoes, and crawled into bed, pulling the covers up over her head. And although she expected perhaps twenty minutes of fitful rest, Bonita Mendez slept like a babe in its mother's arms, her dreams filled with the warm brown eyes of wise old men.

When she woke, it was dark, and the bedside clock told her it was nearly seven. She fried up some eggs, onions, and jalapeños, wrapping them in some of the tortillas her mother had made, topped with her sister's fiery homemade salsa. Rested, fed, and warm inside, she then took a long, hot shower, washed her hair, dressed in plain clothes with a jacket to cover her gun, and went by the station in the vain hope that something—anything—had come to light in the case. There was nothing.

Mendez had no intention of meeting the old man. It was ridiculous, to waste her time listening to his colorful but meaningless talk, when she could be out reinterviewing the friends of Gloria Rivas she'd suspected hadn't told her everything they knew, or—. That reminded her. She called the Torres number, got Jasmina's mother again, and was told that no, Mina wasn't home that day. She had been in earlier and went out again with friends to a movie. Did Sergeant Mendez have Mina's new cell phone number? Yes, Sergeant Mendez had it, and now tried it, but the phone was either turned off or in one of the county's numerous dead zones.

Mendez looked at the clock again: 8:52. *Oh, hell, why not?*

When she turned down the alleyway near the burrito stand, it appeared empty, until the old man stepped out of the shadows, a swirl of dark robes and a gleaming staff. He pulled open the car door, slid the stick inside with the ease of long habit, tucked himself into the passenger seat, and had the door shut again before the car had settled into stillness.

"Where are we going?" she asked, reaching up to flick on the overhead light.

He held out a scrap of paper, a torn-off section of the local AAA map, showing Rio Linda and the outlying countryside. Near the upper right corner, twelve miles or so from the center of town, was a penciled circle.

"You want me to go here?" she asked, tapping the circle.

In response, he pulled his seat belt around him.

She put the car into gear and drove off.

She didn't have to check his map again—one thing Bonita Mendez knew, it was this valley. She had been born in the Rio Linda community hospital, had attended schools here, had gone to college just over the range of coastal hills, and had come home, after a brief fling with the bright lights of the Bay Area, to work and live. She'd learned how to drive on the roads near the map's circle, remote farm lanes where a beginner could learn the intricacies of the stick shift without endangering the driving public; she'd patrolled there when she began at the police department; and she'd helped dismantle a meth lab a little farther along the road, five years later. Before that, she remembered, the INS had raided a farmworkers' camp, carved into the hills by undocumented workers desperate to save every dollar to send to their families back home.

It was dark out there, miles from any streetlamp. When she let the car slow, the last house had been nearly a mile before; the last car they'd passed, ten minutes before. Even the headlights behind them had turned off at the final junction, when they'd left the main road.

"Okay?" she said, making it a question.

The old man's hand moved into the glow from the dashboard, one long finger pointing straight ahead. She gave the car some gas, and in a hundred yards, when his finger shifted to the right, she steered down a gravel track between fields.

They went on that way for about a mile in all, gravel giving way to dirt, then ruts. Eventually, his hand came up, and she stopped.

She would've had to stop even without the signal, because she had reached the end of the road. The fields on either side came to an end at a creek with a cliff on the other side, thrust up by an underground fault line. Her headlights illuminated a dirt turnaround and a wall of greenery. The camp of illegals had been very near here, as she remembered—the men had used the creek for water, the hills for shelter, and the trees for concealment. In the end, it had been the smell of the cook fire that had given them away.

Just as the smell of smoke as she got out of the car gave this encampment away.

She had her hand on the weapon at her side, easing the car

door shut with the hand that held the big Maglite. The old man, however, had no such urge to silence, and before she could stop him, he had slammed his door with a bang that could be heard for a mile.

The very air seemed to wince. Her companion walked toward the turnaround and spoke over his shoulder. *"Venga."*

She was already moving before the implications of his command struck her. Unless he'd come up with a very short quotation from some Spanish book, he had just addressed her directly. She trotted after him, switching on her flashlight as they plunged into a shadow of a space between some bushes.

Yes, there was a creek here, with stones laid across it to ensure dry feet. And yes, the smell of wood smoke grew, as did signs of human occupation—a pair of folding chairs that looked as if they'd literally fallen off the back of a truck, with duct tape and a stick holding one leg together; a full black garbage bag with its neck tied shut; a heap of empty plastic gallon-size milk jugs. *At least the place doesn't reek like a toilet,* she thought, grateful that she wasn't picking up disgusting substances on her shoes.

The ground under their feet began to rise, and Mendez thought they were coming near the sandstone cliff in which the illegals had carved their dwellings. The trees grew thin, the path more defined, and suddenly Erasmus came to a halt before her.

"Hola, niños," he called. *"'Stoy aquí con mi amiga. Permiso?"*

There followed a long and tense silence, during which Mendez's fingers worked at the strap on her gun, and then an answer: *"Vengan."*

She nearly dropped the flashlight in surprise: the voice was indeed that of a child, although she'd thought Erasmus had used the word as a priest would have: *"my children."* She took her hand off her gun and warily followed the shifting outline of his robes.

A barrier had been constructed, jutting out of the sandstone cliff in an L-shaped wall made of splintered pallets, tree branches, and a sheet of warped plywood with tire tracks down its length, the whole held together with duct tape and twine. Just past the end of the patchwork barrier stood the smoking circle of a burned-down campfire; around its back lay the entrance to a cave dwelling, one that either had gone unnoticed when the previous lot had been destroyed or else had been carved anew. Light came from within, and the hiss of burning propane. Erasmus started forward, but she held his shoulder and pushed past him, peering cautiously at the hole hidden by the barrier. Her hand on her weapon again, she peered inside.

The cave's three occupants, adolescents all, were standing in an apprehensive half-circle, separated from the adult intruders by an upended plastic milk crate draped with a square of cloth that had once been a pajama shirt. The girl on the right, tallest of the three, was Jasmina Torres. The boy on the left, small and dark, was Ernesto Garcia, a friend of Enrique Escobedo's whom she'd interviewed along with two or three dozen other middle school students.

The boy in the middle, clothes dirty but chin up, was Enrique Escobedo himself.

The woman in Mendez wanted to vault the plastic crate and seize the boy in ecstatic relief, then turn on the other two and deliver a tongue-lashing they would not recover from fast. She wanted to dance and sing and yank out her cell phone to tell all the world he was safe, but the cop in her nailed her boots to the ground and sent her eyes traveling across the contents of the cave, to keep the kids dangling. It was, she had to admit, dry, neat, and surprisingly well equipped. Half a dozen of the plastic milk jugs, filled with water, were stacked against the wall, along with a plastic storage bin showing the gaudy wrappers of packaged food within. A stack of neatly folded bedding—a wool blanket, a mover's pad, and a sleeping bag patched with duct tape—leaned against the storage bin, with a second propane camp light. Thought had gone into the hideout, and care—most kids would have dumped a pile of charcoal in the middle of the cave and lit it, suffocating to death by morning.

Mendez studied the impromptu tablecloth and wondered if it had been put there, and the cave tidied, just to impress her. A demonstration of their responsible behavior, perhaps.

Not going to work.

"You guys having fun here?" she said in a hard voice. "You playing at Peter Pan or something? The city's spent a fortune looking for you, half of us haven't slept in two weeks because we've been searching for your body, and your family is going nuts." At the last accusation, the boy's defiance hardened, and he glanced past her shoulder at the old man. His lack of guilt confirmed a suspicion.

"Your mother *knew,* didn't she? That you hadn't been kidnapped. That's why she stopped phoning me every couple of hours, two days after you disappeared."

"Mina told her," the boy confirmed, gesturing at the girl. "I didn't want her to worry."

At that, Mendez lost it. "Why the hell didn't you come to the police?" she shouted. "Why are you hiding out—"

Click, as the penny dropped.

"You saw it, didn't you? You saw Gloria die, and you're afraid her killer will come after you." It really wasn't much of a leap of inspiration—this sort of thing happened all the time, in a community dominated by gangs, where one crime, or even an accident, could lead to an escalation of violence and retribution until eventually the police managed to wrap official hands around it all and smother it.

The boy nodded. His defiance suddenly melted away, and he looked small and scared. Mendez sighed, rubbed at her face, and decided to start over again.

"Okay, let's sit down and talk about this."

The three kids looked hugely relieved and settled onto their dusty pads. Mendez took the camp light off the table and put it on the ground, pulling the table back toward the entrance as a chair. She glanced around to see what the old man would sit on, but he was not there—leaving the police to their work, or maybe just a recognition that the cave would be stifling with one more body in it. Or perhaps he had some kind of Zorro complex, so that when his job was done, he would fade into the night.

"Digame," she said. The boy was so eager to do so, his words tumbled in a rush of Spanish and English, with his friends contributing the occasional comment or clarification.

The first thing he wanted Mendez to know was that Gloria hadn't really been his babysitter, although his mother paid her for staying with him when she was working nights. He was twelve and didn't need a babysitter. But Gloria's family was large and she was serious about getting into college, and she could work more easily in the silence of the Escobedo house, so they all pretended she was a babysitter.

Mendez blinked at the boy's sense of priorities but decided to let him tell it as he wanted. She nodded solemnly, and he went on.

"So anyway, a little after eight, Gloria got this phone call on her cell. She got all funny when she heard who was on the line and took the phone outside so I wouldn't hear, but she didn't talk for long and wouldn't tell me who it was. Then a little while later I was upstairs, getting ready for bed, and I heard this knock on the door, and I looked down from the window and there was this guy there, and I figured it was the same guy who'd called."

"Why did you think that?"

"Well, she was angry when she saw him, and she wouldn't let him in, and they went out in the yard and talked for a while, angry but in low voices."

"Did you know him?"

"I'd seen him around once or twice. He's big in one of the gangs, or at least that's what someone told me. They call him Taco."

"Go ahead."

"Like I said, I couldn't hear what they were talking about, not without opening the window and hanging out of it, but it looked like he wanted her to do something, and she wouldn't. After a while, he got really angry and he hit her—not with his fist, with his hand, like a slap, but he knocked her back, and I was going to go down and make him stop, but he turned and walked away. But Gloria went after him and grabbed his arm just before he got to the car, and then he turned around really fast and I heard this *bang,* and Gloria fell. It took me a minute to realize what had happened, and I just stared at Gloria lying there and this Taco guy looking down at her. It was . . . I kept waiting for her to stand up, you know?"

The boy's stricken expression, the tears in his eyes, were strong reminders of the first time Mendez had seen a dead person, the unreality of it. She nodded again, with no humor this time.

"And then he looked up and he saw me in the window. He started running toward the house, and I could see the gun in his hand then, and I got the hell out of there."

"How?"

"Out the window. You can climb out onto the porch roof and down the whatchacallit, the trellis, but I sort of shot off the roof and hit the ground and ran. I was down the street before I heard his car take off, but I was afraid to go home again. I mean, I saw him, and he's got a lot of friends."

"So what did you do?"

"I sneaked down to Mina's house, and she gave me her phone, and she and 'Nesto and I hid out at her house until morning. 'Nesto

had a cousin who'd lived down in these caves for a while, before La
Migra deported him, but he said there wasn't anyone using them
right now, so we figured I could hide out here until you guys had
arrested Taco."

"That was your plan?"

"If I led you to Taco, his homeys would come after me, maybe
even my mom. But I thought that if everyone knew you couldn't
find me, they wouldn't go blaming me when Taco got arrested."

In the backward logic of the gang world, it made sense. "So
why did you have Brother Erasmus bring me here?"

Enrique's defiant look wavered, and his gaze dropped. "I realized
I was just thinking about me. Me and my mom. But then Erasmo
asked about Gloria, and so I told him about her and how she was
really nice and she really wanted to go to college and all, and when
I was telling him about her, I began to think that I wasn't being
much of a friend to her. I have a responsibility to her too."

The trio across from Sergeant Mendez seemed to sit a little
straighter, either shouldering their responsibility or squaring off
for the firing squad. Two twelve-year-old boys and a girl who'd
just turned thirteen, facing her as if prepared for the fate she
would march them to.

Must've been some conversation with that old man, she
thought.

"Thank you for being willing to come forward," she said. "It
would have saved us all a lot of grief if you'd called me ten days
ago, but you've done so now, and that lets me get on with *my* responsibility, which at the moment includes protecting you." For a
second, just a flash, she felt a powerful urge to stand up and walk
away, to leave these kids to the safety of their hideout, far from
vengeful gangbangers and the inadequacy of the legal system.
But she couldn't do that—they were lucky they hadn't run into
some adult animal out here before now. Or been inside when an
earthquake collapsed the cave. Time to bring them home.

She told them to gather their things, a process that consisted of picking up two already full backpacks and standing expectantly. She stuck the flashlight in her belt and exchanged it for one of the propane lamps, running her eyes across the sanctuary. *How much of the organization had the girl been responsible for?* she wondered. Young Jasmina showed signs of becoming a formidable woman. Mendez was smiling to herself when she ducked her head through the entrance of the cave, but the moment she was out, standing between the sandstone cliff and the wood-and-duct-tape wall, she heard a noise that wiped away any thought of a smile, a sound that froze the blood in her veins and made her hands shoot out to block the children behind her.

"Back!" she ordered. "Get back!"

A shotgun, racking its shell into place.

She was blind, with the lamp in her left hand dazzling her sight of the darkness beyond, but she knew that sound, oh yes, and although it set her guts to crawling and the impulse to fling herself to the ground was almost more than she could resist, she was not about to let these three children walk into it.

The kids hesitated in confusion, then to her relief she felt them retreat, back into the dark and inadequate depths of the cave. She kept her hands outstretched, her face and chest crawling with the anticipation of the deadly blast. It couldn't have been more than thirty feet away, no one could miss at that range, but if she turned her left side toward the gun, she might live long enough to get out her weapon and take him down as he climbed past her into the cave. She straightened slowly, leaving her hands out but shifting a fraction to the right as she moved.

"I want the kid," said the voice from the night.

"You don't want those kids. They're just vagrants camping out here. I'd suggest you leave before my partner arrives."

"You don't have a partner. You left the station by yourself."

Which was true, although he'd missed her brief stop to take on Brother Erasmus. It was also worrying. "You've been following me?"

"Just the last couple of nights. One of my boys heard you were on to the kid. He was right."

"Those were your headlights I saw behind me, on the road."

"Didn't need to follow you closer. I could see where you were coming. Now, get out of the way."

"I can't do that," she said. "And whoever you are and whatever you've done, you really don't want to shoot a police officer." If he thought she had no idea who he was, he might possibly be more inclined to back off, leaving Enrique for another day.

She heard a step, then another, and braced herself for action—throwing the lamp, dropping to the ground, or just dying, she didn't know.

Then came a sound that didn't fit: a patter of rainfall on a dry night, off to the side. She knew it had to be Erasmus and drew breath to shout a warning, but before the words could leave her mouth, there was a scuffle and a thump beneath a sudden exclamation. Then came the huge noise that she had been dreading and the brilliant flash that lit up the hillside.

What seemed a long time later, Mendez lifted her head off the ground. She was blind. And half-deaf, but over the ringing in her ears she could make out a high-pitched noise, a chorus of noises—screams—the kids, in the cave! She scrambled to her feet, vaguely grateful that she could move, that she hadn't been cut in half by the shotgun blast. She staggered, crashing into something that gave way and bit at her hand: the pallet wall. She reached out more cautiously, then remembered the flashlight on her belt. She yanked it out and thumbed it on, and over the noise in her ears, the screaming voices seemed to diminish slightly.

Two steps took her to the cave entrance, and a quick sweep of the light showed the three kids wrapped in one another's arms against the back wall, terrified but unharmed. Ernesto was the only one still screaming, his eyes tight shut, but the other two blinked against the light, and the girl's mouth moved in speech: no blood, no shooter.

Mendez ducked back out the door, shining the beam along the path: nearly collapsed patchwork wall, smashed propane lamp, near-dead fire circle, path along the cliffs, a pair of feet.

Taco Alvarez lay stretched out with his feet toward the cave, blood on his forehead, hands empty of weaponry, one hand beginning to stir. The beam continued on and came to another pair of feet, white sneakers beneath a dark-brown robe.

Brother Erasmus stood, wooden staff in one hand, shotgun in the other. He blinked when the beam hit his eyes, but the smile on his face was beatific.

"Was he alone?" she asked. First things first.

"Alone, alone, all, all alone."

She took the gun from him, peeled the shells out of it, and laid the empty weapon to one side. As she knelt to slap the handcuffs onto the groaning Taco Alvarez, the old man went past her to the entrance of the cave. When she looked up, all three children were wrapped around him like limpets on a rock, weeping.

Her cell phone, of course, couldn't get a signal.

She was not about to leave these three kids out here while she went to summon help, and she was loath to put them into a car with their would-be murderer. In the end, she left Taco, cursing in two languages and with his feet bound by lengths of duct tape, in the gentle care of Brother Erasmus.

"I'll send someone as soon as I get in range of a cell tower. You sure you'll be okay with him? I could just leave him tied to a tree."

"Bright star, would I were steadfast as thou art . . . watching, with eternal lids apart."

"I don't think it'll be anywhere near an eternity. Maybe twenty minutes, half an hour."

By way of answer, he placed his hand on her shoulder and smiled down on her.

She glanced around at the children, who had passed through the terror phase and were now beginning to talk madly about the adventure, words tumbling over themselves. She looked back at him and said, "Thank you. He'd have shot me for sure. I should have been more cautious, coming here."

"There is no fool like an old fool," he said, as if to excuse her.

She laughed. "You're right there. The last thing he could've expected was an old man with a cudgel."

"Every inch that is not fool is rogue," he said, his eyes sparkling.

"Well, I thank God for that. Okay, I'd better get these kids home. I'll see you at the station."

He merely smiled and leaned on his staff. She gathered up Enrique and his pair of protectors, got them across the creek dry-footed and into the car.

When she turned back, she saw Erasmus still standing there, outlined by the glow from the second propane lamp. "I met a fool in the forest," she murmured, as a line from one of the summer Shakespeare productions percolated into her mind, "a motley fool."

She got a signal for her phone two miles from the cave and called in her report. As she made her calls, she was dimly aware that the kids had moved on from reliving the moment of the gun going off to speculation about Erasmus. Enrique thought he was a hero in disguise. Ernesto wondered if he'd just dyed his hair and painted lines, to make himself look old. But Mina, with the superiority of age and the wisdom of her sex, said he was an angel, and that shut both the boys up until they reached the station.

Bonita Mendez thought all three might be right.

Of course, she could never be sure, because when the police arrived at the turnaround and followed the light to the thoroughly trussed Taco Alvarez, Brother Erasmus was no longer there.

BURYING MR. HENRY

BY POLLY NELSON

They lifted my rag-wrapped body off the top of a munitions wagon and left me in Stratford County, Kansas, where I remained unconscious for the better part of two months due to infection, pain, and an excess of laudanum. Eventually the leg wound healed over and my addiction came under control. My aversion to the battleground remained, however; so when Stratford asked me to serve as part-time marshal, I was quick to raise my saber-scarred right hand. Thus ended my part in the great War Between the States.

I was still young in 1864 and I believed that, except for a slight limp, the personal effects of the war were over for me. But as most career lawmen will tell you, at least once in a lifetime some case will come along that offers you an education, and if you're lucky it will touch your head, your heart, and your gut in equal measure. For me, such a case involved the burying of Mr. Henry: an event that came to represent everything I'd observed about the War Between the States and about the myriad odd effects it had on those who survived it—especially those made less by their exposure to that war. Many wished they could simply forget, transform, and become somebody else. A few of us succeeded, even if only for a short while.

I had never considered becoming a lawman, but it turned out to be a good decision for me. The only talents I'd developed during the war were a knack with a Colt firearm and—I like to think—a level head when it concerned my fellow man. Before the conflict began, my family had paid my ticket into the territory, so that I could cast a vote on whether Kansas would enter the Union as a free or slave state. Dear God, that the issue of slavery could have been resolved so simply. Anyway, coming out of my somnolence that painful November, I realized that I could hardly face the thought of returning to clerk in my father's office.

I considered the possibilities, and it took me no more than a few days, maybe a week or two, before I decided that I could probably pass as a local. What might have been a temporary job as marshal grew into my permanent position. At my retirement in June of 1893, I had served in that capacity for twenty-nine years. The day I started, my constituents numbered just over sixty, but toward the end I had close to twelve thousand people under my jurisdiction.

In 1864, Stratford was pretty much unsettled, like any of a dozen other cow towns growing up around an assortment of settlers who came from as close as Illinois and as far as the steppes of Russia. Most of the older men had fought along the Missouri line, and most of them wanted never to see fighting again.

It looked to be an easy job, even during cattle-drive season, when the town might swell from sixty to a hundred fifty. I had an affinity for those young boys driving cattle for weeks on end. Many of them had no idea how to settle down because, even as young as twelve and thirteen, they had been forced to take up arms for one side or the other and fight for survival. It wasn't so much that they couldn't recover from the experience as it was that they'd had no chance to experience a life worth recovering. And so they had to be protected, lest they stumble inadvertently beyond gambling and minor crimes into a shoot-out at dawn where death didn't matter; they'd already seen too much of it. For them, the world remained a great lawless universe, and my job was to give them rules to live by—at least within the Stratford city limits.

That uneasy balance shifted when the Kansas Pacific Railroad came through about a half-mile west of downtown. Even before those tracks could be tested, the permanent population of Stratford swelled to three thousand people. In addition to the cowboys and the settlers, I began to deal with railroad workers, buffalo hunters, Mexican vaqueros, former slaves hoping to stake a claim for freedom, ex-soldiers still battling over abolition, and even some wealthy Easterners looking for adventure, come to see what all the hoopla was about. I had to deputize Arlen Dexter to help me keep order.

Arlen played a very important role in the Mr. Henry case: first, because he was my part-time deputy, and second, because he was Stratford's full-time undertaker. We never spoke about it, but I'm pretty sure Arlen saw no service in the war. Plenty of red-blooded Americans lost themselves in the territories until the war was over, and—some may not recall—plenty of red-skinned Americans found themselves on the front lines, defending both sides of the slavery issue. For the most part, the nondrinking community members avoided the topic of who fought where, when, and why, lest bloody Kansas should begin to hemorrhage again.

I never really cared much for Arlen. He had a limited sense of humor and was way too fussy about clothing for my sensibility. He had a tendency to evaluate people based on the way they looked. And if a handsome young cowboy died, Arlen also had a tendency to show up a few weeks later in the same clothes that the cowboy had expired in. Still, while he might not have been the most scrupulous undertaker, he was a very good deputy. He was always prompt to the scene when there'd been a shoot-out. After all, it was in his best interest both as deputy and as undertaker to claim the victims. Somebody had to arrange for those burials.

If no kin came forward, the town would pay pauper's fees, but Arlen was diligent about finding family, even months after the last rites. More times than not, Arlen would shame some relative into paying for the coffin and decent black suit that the undertaker said he'd provided the corpse, claiming that, come Judgment Day, every rising soul had a right to look decently saved. This was still in the days when the soul's salvation meant something to those who considered the West to be God's gift to the white man.

I often had a suspicion that Arlen's clients went out of this world wearing only the suit they'd worn coming into it, except when the family lived close enough to attend the services. Even then, I suspect that Arlen's decent black suit had been altered to fit the frame of more than one back-shot drunken cowboy.

Arlen had an eerie sense about people, both living and dead. Sometimes he would be looking out the office window and see seven or eight young boys coming in to unwind from a long cattle drive, some of them still wearing butternut-dyed Confederacy pants. For those especially, Arlen would jot notes about suit measurements. I came to appreciate how sensible Arlen's observations could be: anyone crossing the Missouri line still wearing Confederate colors would very likely drink himself into first a shouting and then a shooting match. Arlen's foresight still didn't sit well with me.

The other annoying thing about Arlen was his feeling toward women. Generally speaking, he didn't like them. Nor they, him. Of course, this led him to hold very little regard for the institution of marriage. That fact came to play an important part in the Mr. Henry case. Until Mr. Henry, I was under the impression that Arlen had never enjoyed the company of a woman who wasn't paid for the interaction.

Arlen's distaste meant that I had to handle all the disappearing-wife cases. I might get two or three of those in a year, more if the winter had been exceptionally long or the summer unusually hot.

The summer of 1866 was a scorcher. Whatever corn made it to full growth was cooked on the stalk, and since farmers couldn't sell it to buy anything else, that's all some people had to eat. Corn, both on the cob and off. Corn bread, corn mash, corn gruel, corn grits, corn pudding, corn dumplings, and, for the really special occasion, corn cakes.

I remember about the corn because when the emaciated Esau Bandler first walked into my office, the thought came to mind that he must have known a pretty steady diet of corn. His skin had that bleached-through color, and his hair looked to be the texture of thinned-out silks. He moved with an air of stoic resolve, passing through our door in the summer heat, wearing a Union greatcoat scarred with rips and tears like a map of warring nations across his constricted back.

I didn't pick him for a disappearing-wife case, but Arlen did. Arlen usually left the office when some abandoned husband came in, and Esau had hardly begun his speech before Arlen was gone. Arlen had no patience. I could hardly ever help in those cases, but I'd always let the man talk. Although I stayed off the stuff myself, I usually kept a bottle of medicinal whiskey in my drawer to help these stricken men tell their tales. If the wife had been gone for more than a month, there was a good chance the husband hadn't spoken to another human being in the past six weeks.

Most abandoned-husband stories ran pretty much to type,

depending on the age of the disappearing wife. Six to eleven children if she was over thirty, often with one or two recently buried. Some women could get through the death and burial well enough, but they couldn't seem to bear watching the hot prairie wind blow their children's mounded graves away like last year's crop gone to seed.

If the wife was originally from somewhere like Ohio or Kentucky, the husband stood a good chance of getting her back. I never heard any of them say as much, but often all those women needed was a look at some real trees and a few nights' sleep in a bed raised off the floor. The women always came back for their children, even if they disagreed with their husbands on slavery issues.

Arlen hated hearing the husbands' stories. Most likely added to his permanent sour on marriage. He'd also handled one too many birthing deaths. Probably the nicest thing he ever said about women was that if he had ever found himself in the unfortunate circumstance of being born one, he would have gone straight to the nearest convent. Odd, because the only time Arlen Dexter ever spent close to God was at the grave. And the only tenet he religiously held was one against hard liquor. He had been a drunk in his early years and had sworn never to touch the stuff again. He couldn't even keep that faith because I personally gave him another drink, all because of Mr. Henry and Esau Bandler.

In 1862, Mr. Esau Bandler left his wife and four children homesteading on 320 wheat-seeded acres in northeast Kansas and rode south to join the frontiersmen fighting in the War Between the States, in an area where Kansas lost more men than did any other state in the Union.

Jump ahead to 1865, the war ending and Esau riding back home to his wife and family. Except that when he got home, there was nothing there. No wife, no children, no house, and no crops. Some men would have toughed it out and gone about the business of rebuilding their lives. Not Esau. By the time he got to me, he had already tracked down some neighbors who had gone into longhorn punching in north Texas. They were able to tell him what had happened to his children: cholera.

Nobody knew anything about the wife except that she had done her best by the children, and when the time came, she was the one who dug the graves, sold the animals, and lit the house afire. After that, she disappeared. A thinking man would have written her off as long gone. A gentle one would have hoped her happily settled somewhere else. Only one man in ten thousand would believe he could find her again and that, if found, she would still be available to him. Esau was that one in ten thousand. A man who had taken unto himself a wife.

By the time Esau had finished the telling of his personal tale of woe, there was only one man I could think of who might be able to help him: Mr. Henry.

I think I've mentioned that Stratford in 1866 was beginning to grow, and we could offer some accommodations. We had a hotel with four single rooms and two doubles. Ole Johansen's Outfitting Store and Walter Goddard's Barbershop were both standing then. So was Sokolov's Dry Goods, and he took the post in there too. And of course there were the five saloons, two gambling houses, and one dance hall butting one another on down the wrong side of Main Street.

The best of those establishments was the Stratford House, next door to my office. You could buy a drink there and a decent meal and a reasonably lenient woman if you wanted. In most of my disappearing-wife cases, I would suggest that the bereaved husband get himself one, two, or all three items, depending on how hungry and hurt he looked at the time. But Esau Bandler didn't seem like the kind who would enjoy any of those things, as badly as he might need them all.

That's what led me to think of Mr. Henry.

Actually, I met Mr. Henry through Arlen Dexter. Mr. Henry had an uncommon tolerance for the neediness of the human beings who found their way through the open gates of his hundred-acre ranch. And Arlen found his way there often, although the trip took sixteen miles, both ways. Mr. Henry's women would clean and mend whatever clothing Arlen might have recently acquired, and whenever he rode back to town, the hammered-tin badge on his chest would sit polished and straight.

I wouldn't say that Mr. Henry and I were friends, but I liked him. He was a small man who carried himself well, and he always seemed to have the respect of the women who worked for him. It wasn't a place to go for immoral women, although occasionally one of the bordello gals from town would get fed up or old or wise, and usually Mr. Henry would let her try working his piece of the countryside. Most of the women there seemed to make ends meet by serving hot food spread out on cottonwood tables. They offered up some choice provisions: eggs and butter, vegetables, and the occasional buffalo steak. Their chairs were overturned laundry tubs that they'd used to scrub clothing early of a morning.

To all outward appearances, Mr. Henry was a fine, upstanding man. In fact, one time in the early years, a woman stumbled into my office who had been horsewhipped across the face. Doc patched her up, and I took her out to Mr. Henry, who put her in a room off the kitchen and taught her to cook. That's another disappearing-wife tale, but you can be sure her husband got no direction from me.

So the story on Mr. Henry was that he might at any given time have between two and twenty women living with him. Not the kind of high-stepping fancies that the saloon and dance hall carried. His women were the kind who could have been your sister, if you had a sister who'd known a streak of bad luck. More than a few were women whose husbands failed to return from the war, or returned so damaged that they forgot their wives were on the good side. I should have considered that before I sent Esau into their welcoming fold.

Mr. Henry's general clientele were mostly older men, many of them looking for a wife, a night away from home, or just some friendly conversation. And surprisingly, it turned out that what a lot of those wild young cowboys from town really wanted, or wanted soon after the drunk wore off, was a good meal, a clean shirt, and a kind woman's touch. So long as they behaved, Mr. Henry made room for them too. He had one boy staying with him for several months, cleaning up around the barn, talking to the women, learning to get over that fear of loud noises in the night.

I stayed there once or twice myself over the years, and I never found it to be anything but a clean and decent and honestly run affair. Mr. Henry's was one of the few places that allowed the emigrant railroad workers to visit, although he made it clear in any language that he could and would shoot a gun in defense of his women.

When Mr. Henry lost a woman, it was usually because he had married her off to some widower out in the hinterlands. If the woman wanted to go, the man would give Mr. Henry whatever he could in exchange. Sometimes money, sometimes labor. Mr. Henry had some of the best produce to be gotten in the whole of Kansas, what with the cattle drivers, the farmers, the railroaders, and the women themselves coming back to visit.

So, looking into the cold religious fervor of Esau Bandler's prairie-blue eyes, I figured that Mr. Bandler needed a dose of what Mr. Henry's place could offer. I walked him through the door and across the splinter-board sidewalk to where I could draw a proper map in the dry dust that then formed Stratford's Main Street.

Bandler had been gone an hour when Arlen came back to the office. I told him what he'd missed by way of Esau's story, and when I finished by saying Esau should be renewing his soul at Mr. Henry's by now, Arlen bet me we hadn't seen the last of Esau Bandler. I remember joking about how maybe I'd sent him to the wrong kind of house; since maybe his was the wife who'd joined the convent. Arlen said no, but not joking back. A wife running from Esau wouldn't join a convent because living with Esau himself would be closer to the wrath of God than most women could ever abide.

If it wasn't the next day, then it must have been the day after. One of Mr. Henry's women rode in to tell us there'd been trouble and asked if Arlen could come back to the ranch with her. I told Arlen to stay—I'd take this one. That's when the woman broke down enough to tell us that Mr. Henry had been shot dead and they wanted both him and Esau Bandler to have a proper burial in the Stratford Cemetery. No blown-away grave for their Mr. Henry.

Ordinarily either Arlen or I tried to stay within shooting distance of Main Street, but the day Mr. Henry died, we left the cowpokes and the card sharks to fend for themselves while we rode the sixteen miles to Mr. Henry's place.

It was one of those unforgiving hot, dry days with too much sun and too little shade. I remember thinking, as we bowed to pass through the open doorway into Mr. Henry's personal quarters, just how low Esau Bandler must have had to stoop to gain access. It was a sparse room, with two of its sod-caked walls canted to one side. The remaining walls stood relatively straight, being propped up by additional structures that were added over the years: a kitchen wing and a large space where the women slept around the perimeter, while leaving an open area in the center. The complex of rooms smelled heavily of burnt buffalo dung, which the women scoured from the plains in summer and stockpiled in winter. Mr. Henry's two windows were covered with an oiled paper that contributed to the smoky air of mystery within his private space.

He was dead, all right. Shot neat and clean through the chest. Right beside him lay Esau Bandler, who had turned the gun on himself after firing it into the heart of Mr. Henry. There wasn't much for me to do, nor for Arlen either. Mr. Henry's women all told the same story and they had already bathed and dressed both bodies in what looked to be matching black suits. Only thing left was to bury the pair.

I helped Arlen load the two of them into his burial wagon, and since the women had already said whatever words they'd wanted over Mr. Henry, I rode alongside them to the cemetery and then returned to see if the longhorns had left the town in a standing condition.

Fortunately it worked out to be a quiet afternoon. I sat by the window in my office and meditated on how little I actually knew about Mr. Henry. Stratford had grown dramatically in the past two years, but looking out on the facades along Main Street, I saw that the real nature of the buildings behind them was barely disguised by the gaudy signs designed to draw in the miscellany who passed our way. If even the buildings had something to hide, then why not Mr. Henry? At first it occurred to me that Esau Bandler might have proposed something unacceptable to one of the women. Maybe he enjoyed inflicting pain. He didn't look like a man who readily accepted no for an answer. But to kill for a yes? That didn't explain why he shot Mr. Henry.

Maybe those two had some unfinished business left over from the battlefield. God knows I had experienced a few tense moments myself, in the fear that some newcomer to town might remember seeing me at the shooting end of a Confederate rifle. I tossed this off as unlikely; neither of them talked enough to confirm any suspicions on that score.

A religious problem? Perhaps Mr. Henry belonged to that religious sect that felt themselves entitled to marry all those women at his ranch. It wouldn't be the first time some counterbelieving zealot like Esau Bandler decided to save womankind from a life of multiple wifehood.

Where in hell was Arlen? I sank back in my chair and nodded to the passing gamblers, with their finely groomed handlebar mustaches, cultivated to camouflage lips that might quiver while bluffing at the table. A pair of prospectors passed, wearing full beards: those two should be so lucky as to have something to hide.

By the time Arlen had finished the undertaking half of his job and come back to the deputy half, I'd run through a half-dozen other whys and wherefores on Esau Bandler that I wanted to try on him.

But all Arlen wanted was a drink.

He came through the door with a bundle under his arm, threw it onto the chair by the window, and waited while I unlocked my drawer and poured him a whiskey. Alcohol does funny things to a man who's been an abuser but hasn't tasted it for years. Arlen sank like a two-day drunk.

"I probably never told you this before," he said, "but I had a wife once. She was a good woman, strong and fine and courageous. She made a better man than I did, and one day after I'd drunk half a gallon of cheap sugar rye, I got on a horse and rode until I hit the Kansas border. I hardly ever think of her anymore."

"Doesn't surprise me, Arlen," I said. "I'm sure there are lots of men out there who have left a woman behind. Most of them manage to find someone else." I wanted Arlen to feel good enough to talk but not so good that he couldn't. I poured him a second glass of whiskey and capped the bottle. "What about Mr. Henry, Arlen?"

Arlen tossed down his second helping and pushed the empty back to my side of the table. "Something else I probably never told you is that I rustle the clothes off dead bodies."

I knew about that, of course, but at the time it seemed to be one of his lesser sins. It certainly wasn't a topic I wanted him to elaborate on at that moment. "Arlen, what about Mr. Henry?"

Arlen indicated his empty glass and waited until I poured him another. I held on to the glass until he shrugged and picked up his bundle. Finishing off this third drink, Arlen opened the bundle and laid four pieces of fabric out neatly across the floor. "Maybe you didn't have time to notice the fine jacket and the fine pair of trousers Mr. Henry was laid out in. And this other set here, equally fine, came from the corpse of Mr. Esau Bandler. I mean, what undertaker in his right mind could cover clothes as fine as these with ashes and dust and corn-poor Kansas sod?"

"I guess not you, Arlen."

"I guess not me, but I certainly will next time." Arlen indicated his glass again.

After no more than a second's thought, I set a container for myself next to his. "I'm losing patience, Arlen. Pretty soon you're going to kill another half-gallon of whiskey. Tell me what you know about Mr. Henry and Esau Bandler."

"I know I should have planted those two, side by side and fully dressed, just the way Mr. Henry's women and the good Lord intended it."

"Why, Arlen?" At the sight of Arlen's puckered face, I poured myself another round.

"Because then tonight I wouldn't have to go to sleep knowing that Mr. Henry, without his clothes on, was Esau Bandler's wife."

I just sat there as Arlen picked up my bottle and put it under his left arm. "You mean . . ."

"I mean that when Mr. Bandler's children died, Mr. Bandler's wife decided that she had had enough of what mankind and nature had thrown her way, and she set out to become someone else."

I had nothing to say.

"You know what I've learned from this?" Arlen reached across his chest and unhooked that deputy-marshal star from the side of his vest. "I've learned that a person's secrets—a person's past—ought to be respected whether living or dead."

I remember feeling the effects of the liquor—similar to those I'd known when tapering off from the laudanum. I don't know if I told him I agreed. I don't even know if it took me a few moments to realize my agreement. The next thing I became aware of was watching Arlen Dexter walk out the door, across the boardwalk, and out into the street, where he unhitched the horse from his burying wagon, cinched up a saddle, and then rode slowly out into the world to become somebody else.

I don't know why Arlen and I were shocked. It was no secret that a man could ride throughout the open plains and become anything he had the mind and the courage to be. Many of us had passed out of the nightmare of the War Between the States covering our wounds in whatever fashion might ensure survival. Who was I to cast that first stone? After all, would those kindly soldiers dressed in abolitionist blue have dropped me off behind Union lines if I'd been dressed in the Confederate brown of my own affiliation?

I don't know how long it took me. Days, maybe. No more than a week or two. But I was always thinking. Finally, after I considered all the possibilities, it seemed to me that if the men could do it, why not the women? I do know that I got up one morning shortly thereafter, saddled up my own horse, and rode out to Mr. Henry's place to see how I might help them begin anew. It turned out to be a good decision for me.

OATHS, OHANA, AND EVERYTHING

BY DIANA HANSEN-YOUNG

J ames Lopaka let out his belt two notches. Discreetly. Quietly. But nothing slipped past Auntie's eye.

She rose to her feet, whisked away his empty calabash, and replaced it with another helping of poi. "You too thin, James," she said, adding more laulaus, ripe mangoes, and a square of coconut pudding. "You cannot do a good job when you so thin." Her muumuu blossomed around her ample figure as she lowered herself gracefully onto the woven mat. She waggled a finger. "No one respect a skinny hapa police officer."

James dipped two fingers into the poi. That was the last notch on his belt. If he kept eating, he would have to remove it altogether. How would it look to have slipping-down pants? Never mind that his belt held his holster, which held his gun, and what was a police officer of the Republic of Hawaii to do without a gun? He sighed and reached for the pudding. Maybe by tomorrow night, after the seven-mile ride back to Honolulu, he would be able to fit his belt. Meanwhile, he was home, and although the occasion was sad and did not call for a celebration, he was going to enjoy Auntie's food.

James was slicing his third mango when the dogs set to barking in the yard. Chickens squawked. James set down the mango knife, unfolded his 241-pound body, and walked to the door of Auntie's pili-grass shack. His little brother, Richard, slid off his lathered roan and staggered toward the house, kicking his way through panicked fowl.

Richard's voice was slurred and angry. The smell of liquor rolled off him. "Mary's at Bolo's. Again, godfunnit." He pushed past James.

"Watch your mouth." Auntie's face was grim.

"I kill him already," Richard said.

"No pidgin English in this house."

Richard kicked at the stack of empty calabashes waiting to be washed. Koa bowls rolled across the hard-packed red-dirt floor. "You hear me, Auntie? Bolo's."

"Take off your boots," Auntie said, and started to cry.

"I kill him. Dead." Richard grabbed the mango knife from the mat. "I swear."

James grabbed Richard's wrist and twisted, and his little brother dropped the knife onto the swept dirt floor. James planted his bare foot over the handle. "Who told you?"

"Silva got a phone call." Silva was the Portuguese owner of the Homestead Store down the road, next to the Ewa stop on the Oahu Railway. Last year, when the train company ran the phone wire from Honolulu, Silva took the opportunity to hook up a line to his store. No one in Ewa said anything to the company about Silva's free line. Everyone shared the phone. "I stopped for a drink. Silva told me."

"Who was it from?"

"A woman," he said. "A lady."

Auntie rose from her cross-legged position. "One more time, James. Go and get her one more time. Please."

"How many times is 'one more time'?" James had retrieved Mary many times from Bolo's. She promised to stay. They took turns sitting through her shaking and moaning, and when her head came clear, it would happen again. And again. James felt the familiar anger in his shoulders. "How many times is 'one . . . more . . . time'?"

"No more 'one more time.'" Richard scooped up the mango knife. "*Pau* already."

"Give me the knife."

"You gonna arrest me?"

"I made an oath."

Richard kicked James in the shin and punched him in his stomach, one-two, right into the tight belt. James doubled over, and Richard lurched out the door.

"Boys, for the love of God, we're *ohana*," Auntie said, running after Richard, who was looking for his roan. He found the horse ripping into the grass by the outhouse. He was in the saddle when Auntie reached for the reins.

"Pray instead, Auntie," he said. He kicked, and the startled roan skittered through the poultry.

James's stomach hurt like hell. He sat on the bench by the door and picked up his boots from the neat row of slippers. He tried to pull them on quickly, but his belly was in the way. He stomped his feet into the boots. They stuck. He hobbled to the horse pen. Popolo was feasting on elephant grass. She would not take the bit. Richard put two fingers into the side of her mouth and rubbed her gums. She flattened her ears and opened her teeth. A gob of green slobber rolled out and onto James's shirt and badge.

In the distance, James could see Richard on his roan, riding away faster than James could get Popolo saddled. Auntie brought out an armful of banana leaf–wrapped packets of food. "I'm sorry you have to go so soon."

"I'm sorry too," James said, unpinning his slobber-covered badge. He stuffed it in his pants pocket while Auntie stuffed food into his saddlebag.

"I thought you would be here two days."

"I thought so too." James had told his supervisor, Wong, that his mother was sick, and thus he must go to the country for two days. Wong knew the truth, of course, and so did his Chinese partner, Kam, and the Filipinos and Japanese: no officer with Hawaiian blood would report to work on August 14, 1898.

How could he get up in the saddle with his belt so tight? Enough already. He unbuckled his belt, wrapped it around his holster and gun, and tucked them next to Auntie's packets. Auntie promptly put in three ripe mangoes and closed the latch.

"I'll cook more food when you bring Mary home."

James stroked her waist-length gray hair. "I have to hurry now to catch that brother of mine."

"*A hui hou,*" she said. Until we meet again.

Popolo trotted sullenly down the road. The sun was low over the Waianae Mountains. Shadows of pandani and palm trees fractured the blinding light that covered the Ewa Plain. Richard had a head start. But Richard was drunk, and his roan was tired. With any luck, James would find his brother sleeping beside the road.

He turned in the saddle. Auntie stood in front of her pili-grass house and waved. James lifted his hand in response. He reined left, riding toward Honolulu, the setting sun at his back.

————

A FULL MOON was high over Diamond Head by the time James pushed his exhausted pony through Iwilei, where some of the rickety plantation houses had red lanterns on the porch. He scanned the roads for any sign of Richard. Nothing.

Worried, he urged Popolo into the familiar Hotel Street district. Three years ago, James and his partner, a short, chubby Chinese man named Bo Sau Kam, had been accepted into a police force that was rapidly expanding under the marshal's office. Both twenty-three, both rookies, they were assigned to Hotel Street and south Chinatown, and had been there ever since.

They knew every business, bar, and back room. They were on a first-name basis with merchants and ladies of the night. They moved the troublemakers along rather than arresting them. Sometimes they sent for a relative to fetch their drunken kin. Young men who dabbled in petty theft were returned to the harsh justice of their parents. They sent sailors back to ships and men to their wives and tourists to their hotels. Rarely did they bring anyone into the station house on Bethel Street. They had established an easy balance of commerce and peace, and in return, every meal was free, and new clothes stayed on uncollected tabs.

James looked in the alley behind Tongg Dry Goods. No Richard. *Maybe it is time for a new belt with more holes,* he thought. Popolo stumbled. James dismounted and led her down Hotel Street, lit, as usual, with torches and gas and an occasional electric bulb. James thought it had a merry look, like Christmas scenes in books. He realized that the street was nearly empty. Here and there, a few sailors wandered in and out of seedy bars: the Shanghai, Black Pearl, Paradise. What was going on?

He stopped in front of the Hawaii Bank, where he had borrowed money to buy his one-room bungalow in Papakōlea, the Hawaiian community on the slope of Punchbowl Crater. As a police officer, he had a salary, and with credit, he could make the monthly payments. Nonlandowners could not vote, which meant most Hawaiians. To buy the house, he had to use his whole name—James Huntington Lopaka. The bank manager wrote "white" for race and left off his last name. As James Huntington, his mortgage would not be a problem. The manager smiled, and James left, his cheeks red with shame that he had had to disavow his Hawaiian part. But the pride in owning land outweighed the shame. *Give to get,* he thought. *How could a Hawaiian get ahead if he did not own a piece of his own land?*

The bank had a new poster in the window. A Negro woman in a hula skirt (although James wasn't sure of that, as he'd never met a real Negro woman) was in the arms of a white man in a business suit. The red, white, and blue caption read MARRIED AT LAST!

Was that the haole view of the annexation of Hawaii? James wanted to drive his hand through the window, rip out the poster, and throw it into the dirt. *Move along, James. You have bigger fish to fry. Besides, you made an oath when you got your badge.*

Fifty feet away, two groups of sailors squared off. On one side, a half-dozen haole boys with sandy hair; on the other, two Filipinos, recruits from the Spanish-American War. They all wore the caps of the USS *Philadelphia,* anchored in the harbor. They were all drunk.

James sighed. He reached for his holster and then remembered it was on his belt, in the saddlebag. Where was his badge? *Pocket,* he thought, fumbling for the tin octagon embossed with the coat of arms of the Republic.

"Hey, Flips." The haole boys had mainland accents.

The Filipinos stepped forward. "Who you calling Flips?"

The groups joined in combat. "Let's move them along, Popolo," James said. He pulled his pony directly into the melee. She doled out a few kicks, and the sailors fell back, swearing and cursing.

The two Filipinos had taken the worst pounding. Blood streamed from broken noses. The Filipinos picked up their hats and limped down the street, but the white boys weren't through.

"You Hawaiians like Flips better than haoles. Is that right, *kanaka?*"

James held up his badge. The drum beat in his head, but his voice was soft. "Honolulu police, boys. Move along."

"Honolulu police tonight, but tomorrow, you *kanakas* are gonna be American." A freckle-faced sailor tossed a red, white, and blue carnation lei at James. It fell in front of Popolo. She put her head down and ate it. The sailors saw the look in James's eye and moved down the street.

James pinned his badge back on his green-stained shirt. He wanted to kick the sailors as they walked away. *Oath,* James thought. When his anger boiled up, he reminded himself that he had made an oath on a Bible when he got his badge: *Ua mau ke ea o ka ʻaina I ka pono.* The life of the land is perpetuated in righteousness.

James imagined all the things he would have done to the sailors had he not made the oath. Deep in thought, he nearly missed the ramshackle bar at the end of the street: the Western. The roof sagged from termites. Timbers propped up the second-story porch. The building was rotten, like its owner.

He heard voices and glass-clinking. He looped Popolo's reins around a timber and walked in. The glass-clinking stopped. "Where's Bolo?"

"Not here, *bruddah.*" Kimo, the bartender, was Hawaiian. Kimo's wife was sick, and Bolo paid well, but Kimo was *ohana.* He raised his eyes toward the second floor.

The yard behind the building was bright with moonlight. Popolo's ears went forward. Richard had tied his roan under the banyan tree. James tied Popolo's reins to the saddle and let her go. She trotted to the roan.

A wooden staircase led up to the back porch. The risers and

railings were all hammajang, sticking out this way and that. James started up the stairway. He put his hand on his gun, but there was no gun—it was still in the saddlebag, holster and belt. Never mind the gun; he had to find Richard.

A broken spindle snagged his pants. Without his belt, his pants started to slip down over his *okole*. He yanked at them. He heard them rip. Cursing quietly, he walked up the last four steps and turned the corner, and there was Richard, sprawled on the landing.

James forgot about the pants rip. He knelt and heard ragged breathing. Passed out, not dead. James left him and walked toward the closed door. Was Mary inside? If so, how would he get both of them home?

James turned the knob, pushed the door open, and stepped into a cloud of smoke. Coals glowed at the end of the hookahs. He smelled unwashed bodies, sex, and urine under the opium and hashish. Patrons smoked or lay in berths that lined the walls. A woman raised her head and offered him her pipe. "You don't have to pay me." She giggled. "Paradise is free."

He pawed through tangled clothing until he recognized long black hair fanning out on stained sheets. Mary? He rolled her over. His little sister's head lolled to one side. Her ribs protruded below slack breasts. Her breath was foul, her lips caked with dry spittle, but she was alive. James pulled her away from her male companion, who flailed his arms at James. James put a boot to the man's face. Something cracked.

He hoisted Mary over his shoulder and headed for the door. Where had she been? How long had she been back in Honolulu, in this opium parlor, on his beat, under his nose?

Bolo, in cowboy hat and boots, blocked the doorway. His deformed left hand was tucked into a pocket. "Put her down, Lopaka," he said, his voice thick with phlegm.

"Move along, Bolo."

"I pay you plenty."

"You pay me nothing."

Bolo spat mucus. "I pay your boss at Bethel Street to leave me alone."

James was ashamed that Wong had taken money. "I owe you nothing."

"Put her back. She's working off a tab."

James tightened his grip on Mary and prepared to hit Bolo, but as he stepped forward, Bolo sagged against the doorframe and slid to the ground. Behind him, James saw his little brother, Richard, pull the mango knife out of Bolo's back, roll him over, and slit his throat. Blood sprayed everywhere.

Richard looked at James. "You found Mary? Good. I found Bolo."

He ran. Carrying Mary, James stepped over Bolo's body, unable to avoid the bloody spray. He followed Richard, who was oh, so light on his feet, the feet that were leaving prints in blood on each step. James looked down. Bolo's blood covered his pants and boots, and his footprints covered Richard's.

James ran after Richard. "You killed him."

Richard reached the roan. "You gonna arrest me?"

"I made an oath."

"He deserved to die."

Richard lifted Mary from James's shoulder. Together, they placed her facedown over Popolo's saddle. James unpinned his badge again, put it in his pants pocket, took off his green-stained shirt and arranged it over Mary's naked back and buttocks.

"Got a tie-down?" Richard said.

James opened the saddlebag and reached in for his belt, holster, and gun, now covered with mashed mango. He stuck the gun and holster in his waistband and wiped off the belt. Together they passed it around Mary's waist and buckled her to the saddle horn.

When they were through, James took out his gun and pointed it at Richard. "I have to arrest you."

"You're not gonna shoot me." Richard seemed amused.

James considered. Even if he could get Richard to take the gun seriously, there was the practical problem of taking Mary home and Richard to the station. Besides, he couldn't get up in the saddle without help, with Mary lying there, while holding the gun and reins. On the other hand, his brother killed a white man, and James was involved. *Ohana?* Oath? Could he sort it out later? "Hold this, and help me up," he said. He handed the gun to Richard, who pointed it at James.

"You won't shoot me," James said.

"We're going different directions, big brother."

On the porch, a woman screamed. Shouts came from the bar. Men ran up the stairs. James hauled himself up on the back of the saddle. Mary was wedged in under his ample belly. Popolo groaned.

James held out his hand to Richard. "Move along if you want, but give me the gun."

Richard handed the gun to James, who jammed it into his waistband and kicked Popolo into a sullen canter across the yard. Hotel Street was empty except for the two Filipino soldiers sitting on a hitching rail. They stared at James as he rode past. What was the Hawaiian officer doing with a half-naked woman on his saddle, long black hair fanning over bloody boots?

Behind him, he heard shouting. Were the men from the bar following? Just then, he saw the mango knife in his mind's eye, lying next to Bolo. For the love of God, no one had picked it up.

He heard more shouting and looked back. It was his little brother, Richard, on the roan.

THEY LED THE horses for the last little way before James's bungalow. Here, houses were set far back from the road, partially hidden by banana patches and papaya trees. A dog barked. Here and there, a curtain opened and closed.

"They see us," Richard said.

And no one would say anything about the Lopaka brothers bringing Mary home.

They carried her into the tiny room and laid her on the bed. James covered her with the breadfruit-pattern quilt that hung over the koa rocking chair. Emma, his natural mother, had made it when she was the housekeeper and common-law wife of his natural father. On James's fourteenth birthday, his father asked Emma to leave the Waikiki house because his new bride was arriving from San Francisco. Emma took the quilt and her three children and went to stay with her auntie Leimomi. One afternoon, while the children ate laulaus in the pili-grass house, Emma sat under the mango tree, drank kerosene, and died. Auntie was childless, and in the Hawaiian tradition, James, Richard, and Mary became her *hanai* children.

Richard drew fresh water from the cistern and started a fire in the outdoor pit. They changed, and James carried the bloody clothes and boots out to the shed. He gave the horses timothy grass and water, and then, in the moonlight, rubbed gun oil into the boots and saddles, scrubbing in circles until the blood blended into the leather. Satisfied, he put on his boots and dropped the bloody clothes into the outhouse, using a stick to push them down into the muck.

He was carrying Richard's boots to the house when he became aware of someone standing in the shadows. He smelled pikake and fresh-washed hair and lilac starch. He stood absolutely still.

She stepped into the moonlight. She had on a dark cloth cloak and a black lace scarf, draped over her head like those of Spanish women he had seen in books. Her voice had a faint pidgin lilt under a cultured British accent.

"James?"

Who was she? What did she want? How could he have been so engrossed that he had missed her arrival? And where was his gun? Inside the house, with his belt and holster. His badge? James groaned. It was inside the pocket of the bloody jeans he had just thrown into the outhouse. *For the love of God,* he thought, *I will have to retrieve my badge.*

It was at that moment he recognized her, remembering memories all at once, the four of them running through the parlor, which was against the rules, breaking the blue-and-white Chinese vase and dropping the pieces down the outhouse, where the man who brought the lime discovered them. No swimming or surfing for a week as punishment, but they still sneaked out to play with the peacocks on the lawn of Ainahau, the estate that really belonged to her, Princess Victoria Kaiulani, and not to her father, Archibald Cleghorn, who was James's neighbor and best friend of his natural father.

She had grown tall and slim. A blue ribbon held her long black hair away from her face. Under her simple blue muumuu, her feet were bare and dusty.

"Vicky?" he said.

"Yes."

They hugged each other, and twelve years melted away.

———

VICKY DID NOT flinch or ask questions when she saw Mary on the bed and the gun on the table. James needed to retrieve his badge before things got worse in the outhouse. He left Vicky washing Mary with water that Richard heated.

James stripped to his knickers, smiling. He moved the lime bucket and opened the trapdoor. He used the stick to fish out his pants. He smiled as he wrapped his hand in oilcloth, retrieved his badge, and returned the clothes. He could not remember being so happy as he dropped the badge into a tin pot to boil and washed his hands with Lava soap.

Inside, Mary was scrubbed clean, her hair braided and bound with Vicky's blue ribbon and her body wrapped in Vicky's cloak. The quilt was back on the rocking chair. *It is like old times,* James thought, *with the four of them together.* After his father sent them away, James kept track of Vicky in the newspapers: her education in England, her visit to the White House to plead against annexation, her unhappy return home. All that was in the past.

Inside, James set out his Hilo Saloon Pilot crackers and made strong Chinese tea. Vicky dipped dainty fingers into Auntie's poi and ate four of her laulaus and two sweet potatoes. They talked of old times. Remember the day Vicky and Mary took the canoe without permission, and James and Richard had to paddle out past the reef on their longboards to bring them in? Remember riding the trolley to Tongg's to spend James's birthday dime on hard candy? Remember the book about Indians and blood oaths? And remember, behind the banyan tree, when they drew blood and pressed fingers together and swore a sacred oath of allegiance?

"One day, you were gone," Vicky said. James told her about Emma. Vicky cried, and then they could no longer speak of the past.

James went out to get his badge. He dumped it onto the grass. It cooled, and he put it into his pocket. When he walked back into the house, he saw Vicky as if for the first time: her Scottish heritage in her cheekbones and her Hawaiian heritage in her dark eyes. She was an adult woman and a princess with sadness in her eyes. She was the last hope of the monarchy, and in a few hours there would be no Hawaiian throne for her to inherit.

Vicky patted James's empty chair. James knew he would now hear what she had to say.

"Auntie Liliu asked me to come."

James was surprised. It may be "Auntie Liliu" to Vicky, but "Auntie Liliu" was Queen Liliuokalani to her subjects. The queen was secluded in Iolani Palace tonight, sitting vigil for the death of her kingdom. How did she even know James existed?

"Are you going to the annexation ceremony?" asked Vicky.

"Of course not."

Richard slammed the table. "No real Hawaiian would go."

"Auntie Liliu and I will not attend," Vicky said. "But she has asked that you be there."

James did not hesitate. "No," he said. Say no to the queen? "No."

Sobering up had not diminished Richard's anger. "Don't ask him to go."

"By our blood oath," she said, "I'm asking you to go."

How would it look for James to be the only Hawaiian at the ceremony? Consider the shame of standing at attention while their flag was lowered and presented to the new haole governor. It would hang over his desk, a symbol of subjugation for the world to see.

Auntie Liliu did not want the last flag of Hawaii to become a wall hanging. She wanted an officer of Hawaiian blood to accept the lowered flag and switch it for a new one. The real flag would rest in honor in the secret caves behind the Ewa Plain, next to the bones of Kamehameha the Great, until it could fly again over a free Hawaii. The governor would have the flag-without-a-meaning.

But no Hawaiian officer planned to be present. She sent for the roster of officers' names, studied them, and asked: Who has knowledge of these men?

"I saw your name," Vicky said. "I told Auntie that if I found you, you would honor your blood oath to me."

James's head was swimming in oaths. *Too many oaths,* he thought. They were pulling him into pieces.

"I went to the station. Your partner said you went to Ewa to your family, all except Mary, who had disappeared. I used the coconut wireless"—and here she smiled—"and found Mary. I called Silva and left a message. I knew you would return immediately." She stared steadily at James. "I'm glad you found her."

She knows about Bolo, he thought, *and Bolo is irrelevant.* Vicky had given Mary back. Even if there had been no blood oath, he owed Vicky.

"Where's the new flag?"

"I left it with Kam." Vicky looked at Mary. "Go ask your father to send Mary to San Francisco, to a clinic. It's her only chance."

Richard exploded. "Never. Never." He punched the wall of James's bungalow, one-two, until the windows rattled in their frames. "Rather Mary die than ask my father, the bastard, may he rot in Hell."

"The *Celtic* sails in the morning," she said. "It's your father's ship." She pointed a slender finger at Richard. "Little brother goes with Mary." Vicky walked to the window and pulled aside the rice-bag curtain. Outside, there was a small trap with a single horse and driver.

James's head swam with questions. When had the carriage arrived? How had he not heard it? How had Vicky known to leave the new flag with Kam before she saw him? How had she found Mary so fast? How could he ask his father when he had sworn an oath to himself that he would never speak to him again? What would happen to Mary if she didn't go to San Francisco? To Richard? And when they found the knife, what would happen to him?

His calves tingled, but it wasn't out of anger or shame. It was the same feeling he had had once on his longboard, when he had paddled out beyond the reef and the biggest wave he had ever seen rolled toward him, and he had realized there was no way to outrun it. The only way to survive was to catch it and ride it in to shore, before it caught him and smashed him into the rocks.

Mary lay on the bed. Richard sat in the corner, knuckles bloody and raw.

"Don't ask your father," Vicky said. "Tell him."

———

JAMES ACCEPTED VICKY's offer of a ride to Bethel Street. Before he could go to his father, he needed to talk to Kam. How could he and Kam make sure James would stand in the honor guard by the flag? What happened with Bolo?

Squeezed into the small carriage beside Vicky, James was acutely aware of her as a woman. He tried to make himself small, but they were touching anyway. Wisps of her hair fluttered across his cheek, sending tingling to lips, and lower.

"Here," James said, a block away from the station. The driver stopped. "What do I do with the real flag?"

"You'll know." Vicky kissed him on the cheek. "*A hui hou,* James."

———

THE STATION HOUSE buzzed with activity. His partner, Kam, was writing down the names of the patrons at Bolo's, who were now slouched against the wall or on the floor. Kam signaled James to leave, but it was too late. Wong, his superior, blocked his path. "Someone killed Bolo."

James made his voice all innocent. "Who?"

Wong studied James. He looked down at his newly oiled boots, up at his combed hair, his fresh clothes, shined badge, belt, holster, and gun. "No good witnesses yet." He pursed his lips. "I thought you were up in Ewa."

"I was," James said. He couldn't think of any plausible reason why he had come back to Honolulu except the truth, which he certainly wasn't going to tell Wong.

"Where's your brother?"

"Still in Ewa."

"Yeah? Where's your sister?"

"Who knows?" James shrugged. "I'm not my family's keeper."

Kam's voice was loud. "Can I get some help over here?"

"Stick around," Wong said.

———

JAMES HELPED KAM write down names. Still doped up, no one recognized James except for the paradise-is-free woman, who mumbled something. Kam whispered in her ear, and she shut her mouth.

Wong came out of his office, carrying a lantern and a flask. "No one saw anything?"

"These guys saw something." There was a commotion at the door. Saito and Beppu, Japanese officers, dragged in two hand-cuffed sailors, the Filipinos from Hotel Street. They had new cuts, and their eyes were puffed and bruised.

"You recognize anyone, boy?" Wong prodded one of them with his foot.

The sailor looked at James. "Was a guy on a yellow horse," he said. "Small guy. Chinese, I think."

Saito kicked him. "You said Hawaiian."

"Not Hawaiian," the other sailor said. "Maybe Japanese. Short, like you. Japanese."

Beppu and Saito punched them until Wong told the officers

to get the Filipinos out of there. Beppu pointed a gun at their heads and laughed when they ran. Saito and Beppu left for the bar across the street. The third shift arrived, and Wong took his lantern and flask and went to the outhouse.

James told Kam everything. Kam insisted that he go with James to see his natural father. James said no, but Kam said he was his partner, and what were partners for? Neither could think of a way to switch the flags.

Wong returned, smelling of outhouse. He carried an oil-paper package, which he unwrapped. It was Auntie's mango knife, crusted in blood. "Ever seen this before?"

"No," James said. In the name of God, how would he keep track of all the lies?

"I think you've seen it," Wong said, "because I think you were there when your brother killed Bolo."

James made his voice lower than Wong's. "Bolo said he paid you plenty."

Wong flushed. "The only one who can prove that is Bolo."

"Good he's dead then," Kam said.

There was a long silence. Wong raised his voice and slapped James on the back. "Now that you're here, boy, you may as well work tomorrow." He grinned with spite. "Someone with Hawaiian blood should be there when your flag comes down."

Kam winked at James and shouted at Wong, "You can't ask him to do that!"

James took the cue. "I won't," he said.

"In fact, you take down the flag and give it to the governor. Kind of on behalf of all Hawaiians."

"No," James said.

Kam shook his head sadly. "You gotta do what he says, James. He's the boss."

"That's right, boy," Wong said. "You be here at noon. And when they raise the Stars and Stripes, maybe you should think about which side of the bread your butter is on. Now get out of here."

———

KAM SADDLED HIS own pony, and James helped himself to Wong's horse. They trotted toward Diamond Head. The moon was low in the sky; there was little time before the *Celtic* put out to sea, and now it was imperative that Mary and Richard be on that ship.

The ornate Victorian house of Jameson P. Huntington was smaller than James remembered. He knocked politely. Nothing happened.

Kam pounded and shouted, "Honolulu police! Open up."

Huntington answered the door. He had thrown a silk jacket over striped pajamas. He looked at James and Kam, then motioned for them to follow.

James looked at the back of his father's head—the thick white hair, the pink ears—and hatred welled up in him. He wished he could stick the mango knife into that silk-covered back. He tasted bile. Why him? Why did he have to ask his father for help? Why was it all on his shoulders? Oaths, *ohana,* and everything?

James looked around the study, with its rich rugs and polished table. Sailing timetables were spread on the table, along with a handwritten note. James could see the signature: Jefferson Blackwell. He and Huntington ran the Committee of Safety, a clandestine group of businessmen who had plotted for more than a decade to seize Hawaii and bring it under American law.

When the queen had drafted a new constitution that gave more rights to native Hawaiians, they saw their control slipping and intensified their drive for annexation. The queen went to Washington and convinced the president that annexation was wrong. But his successor, McKinley, believed in Manifest Destiny. Besides, he wanted the harbor for his ships, now fighting the Spanish-American War in Manila. There was fear that Japan would claim the harbor; military interests coincided with financial interests. In July, the ship that sailed into the harbor spelled out the bad news in black flags: annexation. The Committee of Safety had finally prevailed. The monarchy was gone. And James Huntington had been the driving force behind the committee.

"You look like your mother, James," he said.

A pale, bleached woman in a pink dressing gown opened the door. "Jameson, is everything okay?"

"Go back to bed." Huntington was curt. The woman closed the door.

James stared at his father. How could he ask anything of this man who had killed his mother as sure as if he had poured the kerosene down her throat? James could think of nothing to say.

Kam jumped in. "Mary and Richard are in trouble. Mary has . . . given of herself to support her addiction," he said. "Your son just murdered the man who gave her opium."

"Their weakness of character is not my concern." Huntington's face turned red. "Did you come here to tell me the sordid details of my bastard children?"

James grabbed the front of the silk gown and punched his father, one-two, straight into his soft belly. *See how it feels?* Huntington fell to his knees, and James slapped the sides of his head with open palms, one-two, until Kam pulled him away.

"I did plenty for my children," Huntington said. He touched his ear and looked surprised to see that his hand came away bloody. "They lived well in this house." He looked at James. "Your mother understood that I never intended to marry her."

"Did she?" James's voice was thick with anger.

"I did plenty for you. I got you a loan for your house. I got you your job on the Force."

James heard drumming in his ears. "I got my job on my own," he said.

Huntington laughed. "I would have done the same for your brother and sister, if they had even tried to better themselves."

"How could they begin to better themselves, after what you did?"

"Because they're half white," Huntington said. "My haole blood runs in your veins."

James turned away so his father would not see his tears. *Oh, the shame of crying,* James thought, *crying in front of the man you hate.*

Once again, his partner came to his rescue. "Mary needs a clinic, and Richard needs to leave Honolulu. They need to be on the *Celtic,* and they need your help in San Francisco."

Huntington said nothing. What had Vicky said? *Don't ask him, tell him.*

James faced his father. "I was there. I saw Richard kill Bolo," he said. "I'll tell what I saw. I don't care to keep the job you got for me. I don't care to keep the house you got for me. I don't care if I'm arrested. But I think you care that today, everyone will be talking about your son, James Huntington Lopaka, accomplice to murder."

————

HUNTINGTON USED HIS telephone to call his shipping office on the pier. He had his agent deliver a message to the *Celtic's* captain. He had a sleepy stablehand harness up the trap. James and Kam tied their horses to the back and drove the trap at high speed to the bungalow, where Mary had not moved and where Richard was asleep on the floor.

They carried Mary outside and woke Richard. He refused to go. "I'd rather hang for murder than take help from him."

"You keep your pride while our *ohana* goes down? So selfish." James pushed Richard toward the door. "We're going to move along, little brother."

James squeezed into the trap next to Richard and Mary. Kam rode his horse and led Wong's. They trotted, then cantered, toward the pier, aware of the sun rising behind them, over the Koolaus.

On the dock, the *Celtic* was ready to go. The captain and shipping agent stood next to one lowered gangplank. The captain looked at Mary and called for help. Two sailors carried her up the gangplank. Vicky's blue ribbon fell from her braid, which started to unravel. The last James saw of Mary was her long black hair, fanning.

Kam handed the trap to Huntington's agent. James picked up the ribbon from the dock and walked with Richard to the gangplank.

"Take care of the roan," Richard said. His voice was unsteady.

"Take care of your little sister." James put the ribbon in his pocket.

———

EXCITEMENT CHARGED THE air inside the station. James and Kam walked in together, and everyone fell silent.

"You have ten minutes to get dressed," Wong said. He arranged his epaulets. "We're marching to the palace together." He lowered his voice. "Where the hell's my horse?"

"In back," James said.

They donned the dress uniforms reserved for ceremonies. The blue pants matched the jacket with the motto on the pocket: THE LIFE OF THE LAND IS PERPETUATED IN RIGHTEOUSNESS.

James picked up the folded flag. How was he going to carry it without being seen? *The belt,* he thought. *The belt.* He tucked the flag smooth against his belly and buckled his belt, still on the last notch but tighter with the flag inside.

ALONG KING STREET, clusters of haoles waved American flags.
There were no Hawaiians. They were inside shuttered windows,
hung with black crepe.

The stand on the grounds of Iolani Palace was decorated with
red, white, and blue bunting. Spectators took their seats. How
was he going to switch flags with everyone looking on? Wong
pushed James to the front, next to the flagpole. His face burned
with shame. The only other Hawaiians besides himself were in
the Royal Hawaiian Band, which began to play "Hawaii Ponoi."

Wong nudged him. James stepped forward and pulled the
ropes. The Hawaiian flag began to lower. A squall of rain wet
the flag. The band played. Kam stepped forward to help James
fold the flag, and then it was in his hand.

The Royal Hawaiian Band stopped playing. The audience
gasped as they threw their instruments on the ground and
walked away.

An American soldier stepped forward, clipped the American flag
to the pole, and ran it up. Guns from the USS *Philadelphia* boomed
in the harbor as the Stars and Stripes flew high above Iolani Palace.

All eyes were on the American flag. Kam nudged him and
yanked the new flag out from James's belt. James shoved the real
flag inside. The guns fell silent, and James walked slowly toward
the new governor, carrying the new flag, feeling the dampness of
the real one against his skin.

His natural father, Huntington, stood next to the governor.
He smiled at James as if to mock James's Hawaiian blood, having to take down the Hawaiian flag. It was a smirk, really. James
met his father's eyes coldly, without emotion, as he handed the
new governor the new flag.

It was done.

THEY FOUGHT THEIR way through the drunken officers in the station. An elderly Hawaiian man, standing by the door, stepped in front of James.

"Take the flag to your auntie," he said, and walked away.

"*A hui hou,*" Kam said, and also started to walk away.

"You might as well see it to the end," James said.

James reborrowed Wong's horse while Kam resaddled his own mare. They rode toward the great Ewa Plain and did not stop until they reached the foot of Auntie's road.

Kam reined up his horse. He reached inside his own belt and pulled out the oil-paper packet. He handed it to James, who opened it. Inside was the bloody mango knife, which they buried under a pandanus tree.

CHICKENS CLUCKED AND scattered as they rode into the yard. Auntie came running and embraced them both, tears in her eyes.

"They're on the *Celtic*," James said.

"I know," Auntie said. "We talk later."

Three very old *kupunas* sat on the outside bench, next to the row of shoes. James handed the flag to the oldest. They nodded their farewell and set off walking toward the black caves above the Ewa Plain.

"They already ate," Auntie said, herding James and Kam into the pili-grass house.

Inside, they ate laulaus and sweet potatoes. James unbuckled his belt *(Oh, what a wonderful feeling)* and then took it off altogether. He tried to be discreet, but nothing slipped past Auntie's eye.

She rose to her feet, whisked away their empty calabashes,

and refilled them with poi. "You're too thin, boys," she said. She waggled a finger. "A skinny Chinaman? A skinny hapa? Officers like that don't get respect."

She brought out four more squares of coconut pudding, then placed a new mango knife next to the plate of fruit. "Will you slice the mangoes, James?"

And he did.

THE PRICE OF LOVE

BY PETER ROBINSON

Tommy found the badge on the third day of his summer holiday at Blackpool, the first holiday without his father. The sun had come out that morning, and he was playing on the crowded beach with his mother, who sat in her striped deck chair, smoking Consulate, reading *Nova* magazine, and keeping an eye on him. Not that he needed an eye kept on him. Tommy was thirteen now and quite capable of going off alone to amuse himself. But his mother had a thing about water, so she never let him near the sea alone. Uncle Arthur had gone to the amusements on the North Pier, where he liked to play the one-armed bandits.

The breeze from the gray Irish Sea was chilly, but Tommy bravely wore his new swimming trunks. He even dipped his toes in the water before running back, squealing, to warm them in the sand. It was then that he felt something sharp prick his big toe. Treasure? He scooped away the sand carefully with his hands while no one was looking. Slowly he pulled out the object by its edge and dusted off the sand with his free hand. It was shaped like a silver shield with a flat top and seven points. At its center was a circle, with METROPOLITAN POLICE curved around the top and bottom of the initials ER. On its top were a crown and a tiny cross. The silver glinted in the sunlight.

Tommy's breath caught in his throat. This was exactly the sign he had been waiting for ever since his father died. It was the same type of badge he had worn on his uniform. Tommy remembered how proud his dad had sounded when he spoke of it. He even let Tommy touch it and told him what ER meant: *Elizabeth Regina*. It was Latin, his father had explained, for the queen. "That's our queen, Tommy," he had said proudly. And the cross on top, he went on, symbolized the Church of England. When Tommy held the warm badge there on the beach, he could feel his father's presence in it.

Tommy decided not to tell anyone. They might make him hand it in somewhere, or just take it off him. Uncle Arthur was always doing that. When Tommy found an old tennis ball in the street, Uncle Arthur said it might have been chewed by a dog and have germs on it, so he threw it in the fire. Then there was the toy cap gun with the broken hammer he found on the recreation ground—"It's no good if it's broken, is it?" Uncle Arthur said, and out it went. But this time Uncle Arthur wasn't going to get his hands on Tommy's treasure. While his mother was reading her magazine, Tommy went over to his small pile of clothes and slipped the badge in his trouser pocket.

"What are you doing, Tommy?"

He started. It was his mother. "Just looking for my handkerchief," he said, the first thing he could think of.

"What do you want a handkerchief for?"

"The water was cold," Tommy said. "I'm sniffling." He managed to fake a sniffle to prove it.

But his mother's attention had already returned to her magazine. She never did talk to him for very long these days, didn't seem much interested in how he was doing at school (badly) or how he was feeling in general (awful). Sometimes it was a blessing, because it made it easier for Tommy to live undisturbed in his own elaborate secret world, but sometimes he felt he would like it if she just smiled at him, touched his arm, and asked him how he was doing. He'd say he was fine. He wouldn't even tell her the truth because she would get bored if she had to listen to his catalog of woes. His mother had always got bored easily.

This time her lack of interest was a blessing. He managed to get the badge in his pocket without her or anyone else seeing it. He felt official now. No longer was he just playing at being a special agent. Now that he had his badge, he had serious standards to uphold, like his father had always said. And he would start his new role by keeping a close eye on Uncle Arthur.

———

Uncle Arthur wasn't his real uncle. Tommy's mother was an only child, like Tommy himself. It was three months after his father's funeral when she had first introduced them. She said that Uncle Arthur was an old friend she had known many years ago, and they had just met again by chance on Kensington High Street. Wasn't that a wonderful coincidence? She had been so lonely since his father had died. Uncle Arthur was fun and made her laugh again. She was sure that Tommy would like him. But Tommy didn't. And he was certain he had seen Uncle Arthur before, while his father was still alive, but he didn't say anything.

It was also because of Uncle Arthur that they moved from London to Leeds, although Tommy's mother said it was because London was becoming too expensive. Tommy had never found it easy to make friends, and up north it was even worse. People made fun of his accent and picked fights with him in the school yard, and a lot of the time he couldn't even understand what they were saying. He couldn't understand the teachers either, which was why the standard of his schoolwork slipped.

Once they had moved, Uncle Arthur, who traveled a lot for

his job but lived in Leeds, became a fixture at their new house whenever he was in town, and some evenings he and Tommy's mother would go off dancing, to the pictures, or to the pub and leave Tommy home alone. He liked that because he could play his records and smoke a cigarette in the back garden. Once, he had even drunk some of Uncle Arthur's vodka and replaced it with water. He didn't know if Uncle Arthur ever guessed, but he never said anything. Uncle Arthur had just bought his mother a brand-new television too, so Tommy sometimes just sat eating cheese-and-onion crisps, drinking pop, and watching *Danger Man* or *The Saint*.

What he didn't like was when they stopped in. Then they were always whispering or going up to his mother's room to talk, so that he couldn't hear what they were saying. But they were still in the house, and even though they were ignoring him, he couldn't do whatever he wanted or even watch what he wanted on television. Uncle Arthur never hit him or anything—his mother wouldn't stand for that—but Tommy could tell sometimes that he wanted to. Mostly he took no interest whatsoever. For all Uncle Arthur cared, Tommy might as well have not existed. But he did.

Everyone said Tommy's mother was pretty. Tommy couldn't really see it himself, because she was his mother, after all. He thought that Denise Clark at school was pretty. He wanted to go out with her. And Marianne Faithfull, whom he'd seen on *Top of the Pops*. But she was too old for him, and she was famous. People said he was young for his years and knew nothing about girls. All he knew was that he definitely *liked* girls. He felt something funny happen to him when he saw Denise Clark walking down the street in her little gray school skirt, white blouse, and maroon V-neck jumper, but he didn't know what it was, and apart from kissing, which he knew about, and touching breasts, which someone had told him about at school, he didn't really know what you were supposed to do with a girl when she was charitable enough to let you go out with her.

Tommy's mother didn't look at all like Denise Clark or Marianne Faithfull, but she wore more modern and more fashionable clothes than the other women on the street. She had beautiful long blond hair over her shoulders and pale flawless skin, and she put on her pink lipstick, black mascara, and blue eye shadow every day, even if she was only stopping in or going to the shops. Tommy thought some of the women on the street were jealous because she was so pretty and nicely dressed.

Not long after they had moved, he overheard two of their neighbors saying that his mother was full of "London airs and graces" and "no better than she ought to be." He didn't know what that meant, but he could tell by the way they said it that it wasn't meant as a compliment. Then they said something else he didn't understand about a dress she had worn when his father was only four months in his grave, and they made tut-tutting sounds. That made Tommy angry. He came out of his hiding place and stood in front of them, red-faced, and told them they shouldn't talk like that about his mother and father. That took the wind out of their sails.

Every night before he went to sleep, Tommy prayed that Uncle Arthur would go away and never come back again. But he always did. He seemed to stop at the house late every night, and sometimes Tommy didn't hear him leave until it was almost time to get up for school. What they found to talk about all night, he had no idea, though he knew that Uncle Arthur had a bed made up in the spare room, so that he could sleep there if he wanted. Even when Uncle Arthur wasn't around, Tommy's mother seemed distant and distracted, and she lost her patience with him very quickly.

One thing Tommy noticed within a few weeks of Uncle Arthur's visits to the new house was that his father's photograph—the one in full uniform he had been so proud of—went mysteriously missing from the mantelpiece. He asked his mother about it, but all she said was that it was time to move on and leave her widow's weeds behind. Sometimes he thought he would never understand the things grown-ups said.

———

WHEN TOMMY GOT back to his room at the boardinghouse, he took the badge out of his pocket and held it in his palm. Yes, he could feel his father's power in it. Then he took out the creased newspaper cutting he always carried with him and read it for the hundredth time:

Police Constable Shot Dead

Biggest Haul Since the Great Train Robbery, Authorities Say

A police constable accompanying a van carrying more than one million pounds was shot dead yesterday in a daring broad-daylight raid on the A226 outside Swanscombe. PC Brian Burford was on special assignment at the time. The robbers fled the scene, and police are interested in talking to anyone who might have seen a blue Vauxhall Victor in the general area that day. Since the Great Train Robbery on 8 August, 1963, police officers have routinely accompanied large amounts of cash. . . .

Tommy knew the whole thing by heart, of course, about the police looking for five men and thinking it must have been an inside job, but he always read the end over and over again: "PC Burford leaves behind a wife and a young son." *Leaves behind.* They made it sound as if it were his father's fault, when he had just been doing his job. " 'It is one of the saddest burdens of the badge of office to break the news that a police officer has been killed in the line of duty,' said Deputy Chief Constable Graham

Brown. 'Thank God this burden remains such a rarity in our country.' "

Tommy fingered his badge again. *Burden of the badge of office*. Well, he knew what that felt like now. He made sure no one was around and went to the toilet. There, he took some toilet paper, wet it under the tap, and used it to clean off his badge, drying it carefully with a towel. There were still a few grains of sand caught in the pattern of lines that radiated outward, and it looked as if it were tarnished a bit around the edges. He decided that he needed some sort of wallet to keep it in, and he had enough pocket money to buy one. Uncle Arthur was still at the pier, and his mother was having a lie-down, having "caught too much sun," so he told her he was going for a walk and headed for the shops.

———

TOMMY WENT INTO the first gift shop he saw and found a plastic wallet just the right size. He could keep his badge safe in there, and when he opened it, people would be able to see it. That would be important if he had to make an arrest or take someone in for questioning. He counted out the coins and paid the shopkeeper, then put the wallet in his back pocket and walked outside. The shop next door had racks of used paperback books outside. Uncle Arthur didn't approve of used books—"Never know where they've been"—but Tommy didn't care about that. He had become good at hiding things. He bought *The Saint in New York,* which he hadn't read yet and had been looking for for ages.

The sun was still shining, so Tommy crossed over to the broad promenade that ran beside the sands and the sea. There was a lot of traffic on the front, and he had to be careful. His mother would have gone spare if she had known he hadn't looked for a zebra crossing but had dodged between the cars. Someone honked a horn at him. He thought of flashing his badge but decided against it. He would use it only when he really had to.

He walked along the prom, letting his hand trail on the warm metal railing. He liked to watch the waves roll in and to listen to them as they broke on the shore. There were still hundreds of people on the beach, some of them braving the sea, most just sitting in deck chairs—the men in shirtsleeves and braces reading newspapers, knotted hankies covering their heads; the women sleeping, wearing floppy hats with the brims shading their faces. Children screamed and jumped, made elaborate sand castles. A humpbacked man led the donkeys slowly along their marked track, excited riders whooping as they rode, pretending to be cowboys.

Then Tommy saw Uncle Arthur and froze.

HE WAS WEARING his dark-blue trousers and matching blazer with the gold buttons, a small straw hat perched on his head. *He needs a haircut,* Tommy thought, looking at where the strands of dark hair curled out from under the straw. It wasn't as if he were young enough to wear his hair long like the Beatles. He was probably at least as old as Tommy's mother. As Uncle Arthur walked along with the crowds, he looked around furtively, licking his lips from time to time, and Tommy hardly even needed the magic of his badge to know that he was up to something. Tommy leaned over the railing and looked out to sea, where a distant tanker trailed smoke, and waited until Uncle Arthur had passed by. As he did so, Tommy slipped his hand into his pocket and fingered the wallet that held his badge, feeling its power.

He could see Uncle Arthur's straw hat easily enough as he followed him through the crowds along the prom toward the Central Pier. Luckily, there were plenty of people walking in both directions, and there was no way Uncle Arthur could spot

Tommy, even if he turned around suddenly. It was as if the badge had even given him extra power to be invisible.

Shortly before Chapel Street, Uncle Arthur checked the traffic and dashed across the road. Tommy was near some lights, and luckily they turned red, so he was able to keep up. There were just as many people on the other side because of all the shops and bingo halls and amusement arcades, so it was easy to slip unseen into the crowds again.

The problems started when Uncle Arthur got into the back-streets, where there weren't as many people. He didn't look behind him, so Tommy thought he would probably be okay, but he kept his distance and stopped every now and then to look in a shop window. Soon, though, there were no shops except for the occasional newsagent's and bookie's, with maybe a café or a run-down pub on a street corner. Tommy started to get increasingly worried that he would be seen. What would Uncle Arthur do then? It didn't bear thinking about. He put his hand in his pocket and fingered the badge. It gave him courage. Occasionally, he crossed the street and followed from the other side. There were still a few people, including families with children carrying buckets and spades, heading for the beach, so he didn't stick out like a sore thumb.

Finally, just when Tommy thought he would have to give up because the streets were getting too narrow and empty, Uncle Arthur disappeared into a pub called the Golden Trumpet. That was an unforeseen development. Tommy was too young to enter a pub, and even if he did, he would certainly be noticed. He looked at the James Bond wristwatch he had got for his thirteenth birthday. It was quarter to three. The pubs closed for the afternoon at three. That wasn't too long to wait. He walked up to the front and tried to glance in the windows, but they were covered with smoked glass, so he couldn't see a thing.

There was a small café about twenty yards down the street,

from which he could easily keep an eye on the pub door. Tommy went in and ordered a glass of milk and a sticky bun, which he took over to the table near the window, and watched the pub as he drank and ate. A few seedy-looking people came and went, but there was no sign of Uncle Arthur. Finally, at about ten past three, out he came with two other men. They stood in the street, talking, faces close together, standing back and laughing when anyone else walked past, as if they were telling a joke. Then, as if at a prearranged signal, they all walked off in different directions. Tommy didn't think he needed to follow Uncle Arthur anymore, as he was clearly heading back in the direction of the boardinghouse. And he was carrying a small holdall that he hadn't had with him before he went into the pub.

———

"WHERE DO YOU think you've been?"

Tommy's mother was sitting in the lounge when he got back to the boardinghouse. Uncle Arthur was with her, reading the afternoon paper. He didn't look up.

"Just walking," said Tommy.

"Where?"

"Along the front." Tommy was terrified that Uncle Arthur might have seen him and told his mother, and that she was trying to catch him out in a lie.

"I've told you not to go near the sea when I'm not with you," she said.

"I didn't go near the sea," Tommy said, relieved. "All the time I was on the prom, I was behind the railing."

"Are you certain?"

"Yes, Mummy. Honest. Cross my heart." At least he could swear to that without fear of hellfire and damnation. When he had been on the prom, he *had* been behind the railing at the top of the high seawall, far away from the sea.

"All right, then," she said. "Mrs. Newbiggin will be serving dinner soon, so go up and wash your hands like a good boy. Your uncle Arthur had a nice win on the horses this afternoon, so we'll be going out to the Tower Ballroom to celebrate after. You'll be all right here on your own, reading or watching television, won't you?"

Tommy said he would be all right alone. But it wasn't watching television that he had in mind, or reading *The Saint in New York*.

———

THE BOARDINGHOUSE WAS quiet after dinner. When they had cleared the table, Mrs. Newbiggin and her husband disappeared into their own living quarters, most of the younger guests went out, and only the two old women who were always there sat in the lounge, knitting and watching television. Tommy went up to his room and lay on his bed, reading, until he was certain his mother and Uncle Arthur hadn't forgotten something they would have to come back for, then he snapped into action.

Ever since he had been little, he'd had a knack for opening locks, and the one on Uncle Arthur's door gave little resistance. In fact, the same key that opened his own door opened Uncle Arthur's. He wondered if the other guests knew it was that easy. Once he stood on the threshold, he'd a moment of fear, but he touched the badge in his trouser pocket for luck and went inside, closing the door softly behind him.

Uncle Arthur's room was a mirror image of his own, with a tall wardrobe, single bed, chair, chest of drawers, and small washstand and towel. The flower-patterned wallpaper was peeling off at a damp patch where it met the ceiling, and Tommy could see the silhouettes of dead flies in the inverted lamp shade. The wooden bed frame was scratched, and the pink candlewick bedspread had a dark stain near the bottom. The ashtray on the

bedside table was overflowing with crushed-out filter-tipped cig-
arettes. The narrow window, which looked out on the Newbiggins' backyard, where the dustbins and the outhouse were, was
covered in grime and cobwebs. It was open about an inch, and
the net curtains fluttered in the breeze.

First, Tommy looked under the bed. He found nothing there
but dust and an old sock. Next, he went through the chest of
drawers, which contained only Uncle Arthur's clean underwear,
a shaving kit, aspirin, and some items he didn't recognize. He assumed they were grown-ups' things. The top of the wardrobe, for
which Tommy had to enlist the aid of the rickety chair, proved
to be a waste of time too. The only place remaining was inside
the wardrobe itself. The key was missing, but it was even easier
to open a wardrobe than a door. Uncle Arthur's shirts, trousers,
and jackets hung from the rail, and below them was his open
suitcase, containing a few pairs of dirty socks and underpants.
No holdall.

Just before he closed the wardrobe door, Tommy had an idea
and lifted up the suitcase. Underneath it lay the holdall.

He reached in, pulled it out, and put it on the bed. It was
a little heavy, but it didn't make any noise when he moved it.
There was no lock, and the zipper slid open smoothly when he
pulled the tab. At first, he couldn't see what was inside, then he
noticed something wrapped in brown paper. He lifted it out and
opened it carefully. Inside was a gun. Tommy didn't know what
kind of gun, but it was heavier than any cap gun he had ever
owned, so he assumed it was a real one. He was careful not to
touch it. He knew all about fingerprints. He wrapped it up and
put it back. Then he noticed that it was lying on a bed of what he
had thought was paper, but when he reached in and pulled out
a wad, he saw it was money. Five-pound notes. He didn't know
how much there was, and he wasn't going to count it. He had
discovered enough for one evening. Carefully, he put everything

back as it was. What he had to work out next was what he was going to do about it.

———

THAT NIGHT, AS Tommy lay in bed unable to sleep, he heard hushed voices in his mother's room. He didn't like to eavesdrop on her, but given what he had just found in Uncle Arthur's room, he felt he had to.

It was almost impossible to hear what they were saying, and he managed to catch only a few fragments.

"Can't . . . money here . . . wait," he heard Uncle Arthur say, and missed the next bit. Then he heard what sounded like "Year . . . Jigger says Brazil," and after a pause, ". . . the kid?" Next, his mother's voice said, ". . . grandparents." He missed what Uncle Arthur said next but distinctly heard his mother say, ". . . have to, won't they?"

Tommy wondered what they meant. Was Uncle Arthur planning a robbery or had he already committed one? He certainly had a lot of money. Tommy remembered the three men talking outside the pub. One of them must have given Uncle Arthur the holdall. What for? Did it represent the proceeds or the means? Were Uncle Arthur and his mother going to run away to Brazil and leave him with his grandparents? He didn't believe she would do that.

The bedsprings creaked, and he thought he heard a muffled cry from the next room. His mother obviously couldn't sleep. Was she crying about his father? Then, much later, when he was finally falling asleep himself, he heard her door close and footsteps pass by his room, as if someone were walking on tiptoe.

———

THE NEXT DAY at breakfast, his mother and Uncle Arthur didn't have very much to say. Both of them looked tired, and his mother had applied an extra bit of makeup to try to hide the dark pouches under her eyes. Uncle Arthur's hair stuck up in places, and he needed a shave. The two old ladies looked at them sternly and clucked.

"Stupid old bags," muttered Uncle Arthur.

"Now, now," said Tommy's mother. "Be nice, Arthur. Don't draw attention to yourself."

The conversation he had overheard last night still worried Tommy as he ate his bacon and eggs. They had definitely mentioned the money. Was his mother about to get involved in something criminal? Was it Uncle Arthur who was going to involve her? If that was so, he had to stop it before it happened, or she would go to jail. The money and the gun were in Uncle Arthur's room, after all, and his mother could deny that she knew anything about them. Tommy had heard his mother insisting before they came away that they would each have a room. Uncle Arthur hadn't liked the idea because it would cost more money, but he had no choice. Tommy knew what it was like when his mother had made up her mind.

The bag and gun would have Uncle Arthur's fingerprints all over them. Tommy was certain Uncle Arthur must have handled the bag and the items in it after he had picked them up at the pub, if only to check that everything was there. But his mother would have had no reason to touch them or even see them, and Tommy himself had been careful when he lifted and opened the bag.

"Pass the sauce," said Uncle Arthur. "What are we doing today?"

Tommy passed the HP Sauce. "Why don't we go up the Tower?" Tommy said.

"I don't like heights," said Uncle Arthur.

"I'll go by myself, then."

"No, you won't," said his mother, who seemed as concerned about heights as she was about water.

"Well, what *can* we do, then?" Tommy asked. "I don't mind just looking at the shops by myself."

"Like a bloody woman, you are, with your shops," said Uncle Arthur.

Tommy had meant bookshops and record shops. He was still looking for a used copy of *Dr. No* and hoping that the new Beatles single "Help!" would be released any day now, even though he would have to wait until he got home to listen to it. But he wasn't planning on going to the shops, anyway, so there was no sense in making an issue of it. "I might go to the Pleasure Beach as well," he said, looking at Uncle Arthur. "Can you give me some money to go on the rides?"

Uncle Arthur looked as if he were going to say no, then he sighed, swore, and dug his hand in his pocket. He gave Tommy two ten-shilling notes, which was a lot of money. He could buy *Dr. No* and "Help!" *and* go on rides with that much, and still have change for an ice cream, but he wasn't sure that he should spend it, because he didn't know where it had come from. "Cor," he said. "Thanks, Arthur."

"It's Uncle Arthur to you," said his mother.

"Yeah, remember that," said Uncle Arthur. "Show a bit of respect for your elders and betters. And don't spend it all on candy floss and toffee apples."

"What about you?" Tommy asked. "Where are you going?"

"Dunno," said Uncle Arthur. "You, Maddy?"

"You know I hate being called that," his mother said. Her name, Tommy knew, was Madeleine, and she didn't like it being shortened.

"Sorry," said Uncle Arthur with a cheeky grin.

"Do you know, I wouldn't mind taking the tram all the way along the seafront to the end of the line and back," she said, then giggled. "Isn't that silly?"

"Not at all," said Uncle Arthur. "That sounds like a lot of fun. Give me a few minutes. I've just got to get a shave first."

"And comb your hair," said Tommy's mother.

"Now, don't be a nag," said Uncle Arthur, wagging his finger. "Maybe we'll see if we can call in at one of them there travel agents too, while we're out."

"Arthur!" Tommy's mother looked alarmed.

"What? Oh, don't worry." He got up and tousled Tommy's hair. "I'm off for a shave, then. You'll have to do that yourself one day, you know," he said, rubbing his dark stubble against Tommy's cheek.

Tommy pulled away. "I know," he said. "Can I go now? I've finished my breakfast."

"We'll all go," said his mother. And they went up to their rooms. Tommy took a handkerchief from his little suitcase and put it in his pocket, because he really was starting to sniffle a bit now, made sure he had his badge and the money Uncle Arthur had given him, then went back into the corridor. Uncle Arthur was standing there, waiting and whistling, freshly shaven, hair still sticking up. For a moment, Tommy felt a shiver of fear ripple up his spine. Had Uncle Arthur realized that someone had been in his room and rummaged through his stuff, found the money and the gun?

Uncle Arthur grinned. "Women," he said, gesturing with his thumb toward Tommy's mother's door. "One day you'll know all about them."

"Sure. One day I'll know everything," muttered Tommy. He pulled his handkerchief from his pocket to blow his nose, and it snagged on the plastic wallet, sending his badge flying to the floor.

"What's this, then?" said Uncle Arthur, bending down to pick it up.

"Give me it back!" said Tommy, panicking, reaching out for the wallet.

But Uncle Arthur raised his arm high, out of Tommy's reach. "I said, what have we got here?"

"It's nothing," Tommy said. "It's mine. Give it to me."

"Mind your manners."

"Please."

Uncle Arthur opened the wallet, looked at the badge, and looked at Tommy. "A police badge," he said. "Like father, like son, eh? Is that it?"

"I told you it was mine," Tommy said, desperately snatching. "You leave it alone."

But Uncle Arthur had pulled the badge out of its transparent-plastic covering. "It's not real, you know," he said.

"Yes, it is," Tommy said. "Give us it back."

"It's made of plastic," said Uncle Arthur. "Where did you get it?"

"I found it. On the beach. Give it to me."

"I told you, it's just plastic," said Uncle Arthur. And to prove his point, he dropped the badge on the floor and stepped on it. The badge splintered under his foot. "See?"

At that moment, Tommy's mother came out of her room, ready to go. "What's happening?" she said, seeing Tommy practically in tears.

"Nothing," said Uncle Arthur, stepping toward the stairs. He gave Tommy a warning look. "Is there, lad? Let's go, love. Our carriage awaits." He laughed.

Tommy's mother gave a nervous giggle, then bent and pecked Tommy on the cheek. He felt her soft hair touch his face and smelled her perfume. It made him feel dizzy. He held back his tears. "You'll be all right, son?" She hadn't seen the splintered badge, and he didn't want her to. It might bring back too many painful memories for her.

He nodded. "You go," he said. "Have a good time."

"See you later." His mother gave a little wave and tripped down the stairs after Uncle Arthur. Tommy looked down at the floor. The badge was in four pieces on the lino. He bent and carefully picked them up. Maybe he could mend it, stick it together somehow, but it would never be the same. This was a bad sign. With tears in his eyes, he put the pieces back in the plastic wallet, returned it to his pocket, and followed his mother and Uncle Arthur outside to make sure they got on the tram before he went to do what he had to do.

———

"YOU READY YET, Tommy?"

"Just a minute, Phil," Detective Chief Inspector Thomas Burford shouted over his shoulder at DI Craven. He was walking on the beach—the hard, wet sand where the waves licked in and almost washed over his shoes—and DI Craven, his designated driver, was waiting patiently on the prom. Tommy's stomach was churning, the way it always did before a big event, and today, 13 July, 2006, he was about to receive a Police Bravery Award.

If it had been one of his men, he would have called it folly, not bravery. He had thrown himself at a man holding a hostage at gunpoint, convinced in his bones, in his every instinct, that he could disarm the man before he hurt the hostage. He had succeeded, receiving for his troubles only a flesh wound on his shoulder and a ringing in his ears that lasted three days. And the bravery award. At his rank, he shouldn't even have been at the hostage-taking scene—he should have been in a cubicle, catching up on paperwork or giving orders over the police radio—but paperwork had always bored him, and he sought out excitement whenever he had the chance. Now he walked with the salt spray blowing through his hair, trying to control his churning bowels just because he had to stand up in front of a crowd and say a few words.

Tommy did what he usually did on such occasions and took the old plastic wallet out of his pocket as he stood and faced the gray waves. The wallet was cracked and faded with time, and there was a tear reaching almost halfway up the central crease. Inside, behind the transparent cover, was a police badge made out of plastic. It had been broken once and was stuck together with glue and Sellotape. Most of the silver had worn off over the years, and it was now black in places. The crown and cross had broken off the top, but the words were still clearly visible in the central circle: METROPOLITAN POLICE curved around ER. *Elizabeth Regina.* "Our queen," as his father had once said so proudly.

In the opposite side of the wallet was a yellowed newspaper clipping from July 1965, forty-one years ago. It flapped in the breeze, and Tommy made sure he held on to it tightly as he read the familiar words:

Schoolboy Foils Robbers

A thirteen-year-old schoolboy's sense of honor and duty led to the arrest of Arthur Leslie Marsden in the murder of PC Brian Burford during the course of a payroll robbery last August. Five other men and one woman were also arrested and charged in the swoop, based on evidence and information given by the boy at a Blackpool police station. Also arrested were Madeleine Burford, widow of the deceased constable, named as Marsden's lover and source of inside information; Len Fraser, driver of the getaway car; John Jarrow . . .

Tommy knew it by heart, all the names, all the details. He also remembered the day he had walked into the police station, showed his badge to the officer at the front desk, and told him all about the contents of Uncle Arthur's holdall. It had taken a while, a bit of explaining, but in the end the desk sergeant had let him in, and the plainclothes detectives had shown a great deal of interest in what he had to say. They accompanied him to the boardinghouse and found the holdall in its hiding place. After that, they soon established that the gun was the same one used to shoot his father. The gang had been lying low, waiting for the heat to die down before daring to use any large quantities of the money—a year, they had agreed—and they had been too stupid to get rid of the gun. The only fingerprints on it were Uncle Arthur's, and the five hundred pounds it was resting on was just a little spending money to be going on with.

The one thing the newspaper article didn't report was that the "boy" was Tommy Burford, only son of Brian and Madeleine Burford. That came out later, of course, at the trial, but at the time, the authorities had done everything within their power to keep his name out of it. Every time he read the story over again, Tommy's heart broke just a little more. Throwing himself at gunmen, tackling gangs armed with hammers and chains, and challenging rich and powerful criminals never came close to making the pain go away; it took the edge off for only a short while, until the adrenaline wore off.

His *mother*. Christ, he had never known. Never even suspected. She had been only twenty-nine at the time, for crying out loud, not much more than a girl herself, married too young to a man she didn't love—for the sake of their forthcoming child—and bored with her life. She wanted romance and all the nice things his father couldn't give her on a policeman's wage, the life she saw portrayed on posters, in magazines, at the pictures, and on television, and Arthur Marsden had walked into her life and offered them all, for a price.

Of course Tommy's father had talked about his job. He had been excited about being chosen for the special assignment and had told both his wife and his son all about it. How was Tommy to know that his mother had passed on the information to Marsden, who was already her lover, and that he and his gang had done the rest? Tommy knew he had seen her with Uncle Arthur before his father's death, and he wished he had said something. Too late now.

Whether the murder of Tommy's father had ever been part of the master plan or was simply an unforeseen necessity, nobody ever found out. Uncle Arthur and Tommy's mother never admitted anything at the trial. But Tommy remembered the look his mother gave him that day when he came back to the Newbiggins' boardinghouse with the two plainclothes policemen. She came out of the lounge as they entered the hall, and it was as if she knew immediately what had happened, that it was all over. She gave Tommy a look of such deep and infinite sadness, loss, and defeat that he knew he would take it with him to his grave.

"Tom, we'd better hurry up or we'll be late!" called DI Craven from the prom.

"Coming," said Tom. He folded up the newspaper clipping and put it away. Then, brushing his hands across his eyes, which had started watering in the salt wind, he turned away from the sea and walked toward the waiting car, thinking how right they had all been back then, when they said he was young for his age and knew nothing about girls.

CONTACT AND COVER

BY GREG RUCKA

When it was my turn, it was a son of a bitch coming at my head with a bottle of Widmer Brothers Drop Top Amber Ale while two of his drunken friends cheered him on.

The drunk swung from the outside, sidearm style, like he was throwing a slider at the plate. If he'd been swinging it like a bat, I'd have been able to step back and out of the way. But the guy went with the changeup and at the last second released the bottle from his hand. It hit me just below the left eye, high on the cheek, shooting pain through the bone and bursting light through my head.

I didn't drop. I staggered, but I did not drop, no matter what Morrison told his buddies later. I fell back against the car, sure, and I could hear the drunk calling me a bitch, and it sounded like he was at the bottom of a nearby well when he did it. My vision was spinning out of control, beer somehow up my nose and down my shirt all at once. I needed a hand on the spotlight to keep from going down, but in the end, I kept my feet.

Which turned out to be a very good thing, because when I finally found my vision again, what I was seeing was the drunk with a fresh bottle, this one unopened, winding up for another pitch. I lurched out of the way, shouting for Morrison to back me up. Even though I was slow and sluggish, the drunk was worse because he was a drunk. The shot missed, the bottle exploding against the side of my cruiser.

The drunk's friends had stopped cheering, maybe realizing that they'd graduated from drunk and disorderly to assaulting a police officer. I was swearing at both Morrison and the drunk, but the drunk was the only one answering me. Apparently, I reminded him of his ex-wife. He didn't like her very much either.

My stick was still on my belt, along with all my other non-lethals, but I just reached out and met the back of his neck with one hand, and the back of his right knee with my foot. He didn't know I was coming, and the takedown worked just the way it was supposed to. He hit the parking lot hard, and it didn't do his face any good, I guess, but then he hadn't done mine any either.

Then I had my cuffs on him, shouting at Morrison to please, in the name of God and all that was holy, give me some fucking cover.

————

THE EMTs MADE me go to the hospital. By the time I'd been x-rayed and told that, yes, I probably had the concussion I thought I had, and made it back to the North Precinct, the third shift was just short of changing. I got out of uniform and showered the stink of the beer off me, put on my regular clothes, and went in search of an open desk to do my write-up. Halfway down the hall, I ran into Morrison coming out of the men's locker room.

"What the hell was that?" I asked him.

"Thought you could handle it." Morrison shrugged, something he liked to do because it showed the world that he had broad shoulders. "Big dyke like you, I figured you were all over it."

"It's called 'contact and cover,' you asshole." I stressed the word "cover" and not the word "asshole." "Remember how that works? One officer makes contact, the other officer provides cover. You were supposed to provide me cover."

Morrison rolled his eyes. "Don't be such a baby, Hoffman. So you got a little wet, a little knocked around. I know half a dozen guys who take it worse every night, they don't complain."

"Then you know half a dozen guys with fractured skulls. He should never have gotten that second throw. You were doing your job, he wouldn't have."

"You should hear yourself," Morrison said, moving past me. "Everybody's fault but your own."

"You were my cover, damn it!"

He was walking away then, and without looking back at me, he said, "If you can't handle it, Hoffman, you shouldn't be on the job."

———

I WAS TWO days off, and by the afternoon of the second day, the bruise on my cheek had blossomed fully, the headache had gone away and I'd reached out to both Jen Schaeffer and Sophie Gault. They were each willing to get together, but it took another day to arrange everything with the shifts we were all working, so it wasn't until the end of the week that the three of us were actually able to meet.

We got together at Mother's for breakfast. Sophie arrived last, because she'd just come off shift in the North and had to change and fight the morning traffic back to downtown. We'd just had the first rain since July, and after two months of good weather, it always seemed that everyone in Portland forgot how to drive on wet roads.

"Jesus, Tracy," Sophie said when she saw my face. "You could at least put a base down over it or something."

"Doesn't embarrass me, why should it embarrass you?" I asked her, but I knew the reason. Of the three of us, Sophie was by far the prettiest, and working hard to stay that way. Patrol makes the best of us expand, and despite my best efforts, I'd added at least ten pounds to my frame in the two years I'd been an officer with the Portland Police Bureau. I liked to think I carried it well and that I was the only one who noticed. I also liked to believe that one day the U.S.A. men's team would win the World Cup, so I had pretty much accepted that I lived part of my life in denial.

I waited until all of us had ordered and the first round of coffee had been poured before raising the topic of Morrison.

"Told you," Jen said. "Didn't I tell you? He's a bully with a badge."

"He's more than that," I said. "Bullies with badges, they're everywhere. Bullies with badges, they honor the contract, Jen."

"C'mon," Sophie said. "You're talking like he wouldn't have stepped in. He's a pig, but he wouldn't have let you go down."

"That's what's bothering me. Until now, I thought there was a limit. But that second throw, Sophie, that one could have really fucked me up. It was a full bottle with a drunk's strength behind it. That had connected, it would have cracked my skull, no question."

Sophie stirred her coffee, frowning. Jen was staring past me, at the morning traffic on Stark. She was the smallest of the three of us, and the youngest at twenty-five. When Morrison had done it to her, she'd ended up wrestling alone with a guy twice her weight in the middle of Interstate. As she'd told it to me, Morrison had deliberately delayed moving to assist, just stood by his car, watching the show, until things had escalated so much he'd used his pepper spray to break it up, hitting Jen with a hefty dose in the process. She'd been blinded for several minutes, unable to see and unable to function. When she'd complained that Morrison could have, say, used his hands instead of his spray, his response had been vintage.

"Next time, baby, hold your breath," he'd told her.

She'd gone to the sergeant with it, tried to actually lodge a complaint, but nothing had come of it.

"He claimed he couldn't get to me sooner because of the traffic," Jen had said. "Three in the goddamn morning at Interstate and Ainsworth, there *was* no goddamn traffic."

It embarrassed me that, like Sophie had just done, I'd diminished it, thinking—if not saying—that Jen was overstating what had happened. We were all police, after all. That didn't make us special, maybe it didn't even make us different, but it did make us united. You could hate your fellow officer, but in the end, he was still your fellow officer, and that meant you could count on him for cover, and he knew he could count on you.

That was how it was supposed to work.

"I don't know," Sophie said, after the server had brought our breakfasts. "I mean, maybe you're both right, but . . . if we put it through channels, that might make things worse. I'm not even a year and a half in right now, and Jen's just come off her probationary period, Tracy. He's got three more years on you, he's got friends downtown. They'll give him the heads-up."

"That domestic you had where he was supposed to back you up," I said. "You remember what you told me? You remember what he did?"

Sophie poked a piece of her honeydew. "Of course I remember. He left me alone with the husband and the wife and went to look for the kids."

"And?" Jen asked.

Sophie sighed, conceding. "And they did what domestics do, and when I went to put the cuffs on the husband, the wife came at me, and then I was dealing with both of them together."

"That's not quite how you told it to me," I said. "The way you told it to me, you went to put the cuffs on the husband, and as soon as you did, the wife throws a punch. You want to tell her the rest?"

Sophie took another stab at her melon, her mouth going tight. "I turn to deal with the wife, the husband pounds me into the wall face-first. He starts punching at me, mostly in the back. Morrison came back before it got totally out of control, used his stick to get the guy off me. I was wearing my vest, so it wasn't as bad as it could have been, but for a couple of seconds there I was more than a little scared."

"The son of a bitch could have taken your gun, Sophie." I looked to Jen. "And she's sugarcoating the beating. She was out for four days on a medical as a result of it, she had to overnight in the hospital before they were sure her insides were still doing everything they were supposed to."

"How big's this residence that Morrison doesn't come running when he hears you hit the wall?" Jen asked.

"It was a two-bedroom in Kenton," Sophie said.

"So where were the kids? In the backyard?"

Sophie gave up pretending to eat her melon, dropped the fork onto the plate with a clatter.

"There were no kids," I told Jen. "There wasn't even any evidence that there had ever *been* kids there. He just stood there and watched it, Jen, same as he did to you, same as he did to me."

"Okay, fine," Sophie said. "So what do you want to do, Tracy? You want to write a letter to the chief? You want to send it to HRD?"

"That's exactly what I want to do," I said. "I want to write a letter, and I want to list what's happened to each of us, three separate incidents and the half-dozen other cases of his bullshit we all know about. There's a pattern of behavior here, Sophie, you can't ignore it, and it's going to get worse. Morrison has a problem with women, and it's beyond the standard sexist bullshit. He thinks we shouldn't be on the job, and he thinks we can't take care of ourselves, and so he goes out of the way to prove it by hanging us out to dry."

"It's not just with women on the job," Jen said. "It's with women. I've never heard any of the working girls have a nice thing to say about him."

"Maybe because he doesn't tip," Sophie said, trying to smile.

"We write a letter," I said. "We put it all down, we attach the relevant reports, we all sign it."

"That's a great idea, Tracy. What happens when we're all put on extended leave without pay while our 'allegations are investigated'?"

"So you'd rather wait? Just continue responding to calls and hoping that, when you call for backup, it's not him who shows?"

"We could transfer out of the North, move to another district."

"That's giving him what he wants," I said. "I won't do that."

"And it doesn't do anything for the next girl to come along," Jen added.

Sophie raised her hands, as if trying to ward both Jen and me off.

"All right," she said. "All right, you guys win. Write the letter, I'll put my signature next to both of yours."

———

I PUT THE letter in the following Monday, through channels, to the head of personnel, which meant that the letter had a lot of distance to cover before it would reach its destination. Putting it through channels meant that it had to start with my sergeant, then move up to the precinct commander, then over from the operations division to the services branch, finally to personnel. But putting it through channels meant that it would make the journey unmolested, that it would move along the chain of command without being rerouted, delayed, or denied.

Except that wasn't what happened.

Nine days after I'd submitted the letter, Jen, Sophie, and I all ended up rotating onto the third shift at the same time. We left briefing together, headed to the lot, and were finishing the checks on our vehicles when Morrison found us. It was almost eleven at night, the weather starting to turn crisp, and I saw him lit by the sodium lights of the lot, coming our way, and I figured he'd left something in his vehicle from his tour on second shift. When he corrected to head straight for me, I figured the car he'd used was the one I was checking.

"Hello, girls," he said.

"Something you need, Morrison?" I asked.

"Actually, yeah. I need you to stop pissing on my shoes, Hoffman." He pulled the letter from his back pocket, unfolded it, and held it up for all of us to see. "What the hell is this? Things you're saying about me. Why are you trying to make trouble for me like this?"

Off to my right, at her car, Sophie swore under her breath, turning away from Morrison. I couldn't tell if she was cursing me or him. To my immediate left, Jen had stopped her check, just staring at him.

Morrison looked at each of us in turn, still holding out the letter, anger flushing his cheeks and ears. He was a fair-skinned blond, and when he got mad, you could see it not only on his face but in his flesh.

"Where the hell did you get that?" I demanded.

"Never mind where the hell I got it. I got it, okay?" He lowered his hand, crumpling the letter in his fist and stepping forward, toward me. "You don't want to make accusations like this, Hoffman. None of you do. Saying that I don't give you ladies cover. You don't want to say things like that."

"You don't give us cover."

"I do, I always have. You get the cover you earn."

I tapped my badge with my index finger, hard and angry. "*This* means I get the cover whether you think I've earned it or not. If one of us needs backup, you give us backup, damn it, regardless of whether or not we pee standing up!"

He moved in closer, the flush in his face still riding high, and I was sure I could feel the heat coming off him. The muscles in my biceps were trembling from the sudden shift to fight-or-flight, and the tension in my voice was matched by the anger in his.

"A lot can happen on a call," Morrison said to me. "A lot can happen, things can get out of control real quick. You could find yourself on the ground before you know it, wondering where your cover's at. Any backup is better than no backup at all."

"You're threatening me?" I didn't know whether to be incredulous or outraged. "Honest to God, Morrison, are you threatening me in front of two witnesses?"

Morrison dropped the letter at my feet, not looking away from my eyes. "No, Officer Hoffman, I would never do that. I'm just telling you and your lady friends how it is. How you might want to remember to be careful. A lot can happen. A lot can happen."

Then he turned and walked off, leaving the three of us standing by our vehicles, none of us too eager to go on patrol.

———

I GAVE IT a lot of thought, and in the end, it came down to this: one of us would have to go.

It wasn't going to be me.

———

"JESUS CHRIST, TRACY, are you out of your mind?" Sophie asked. "You're talking about committing a crime, here. You're talking about committing a crime against a fellow officer."

It was four in the morning, the world dead quiet, with a light fog coming up from the river. We were in the lot outside the 7-Eleven on Greeley, on the edge of Sector 541, two days after Morrison had—as far as I was concerned—threatened all our lives. Jen and I had both called 10-81, then I'd used a landline to call Sophie in her car. She'd been patrolling 542, Grid 87655 on Swan Island, which was the largest patrol grid in the North and covered most of the industrial park and docklands along this part of the Willamette. It was a lonely grid to ride alone, especially late at night, especially when you weren't sure about your backup.

"He's no fellow officer of mine," I said. "He was supposed to be second shift until the next rotation. You know what he did after his little speech to us the night before last? He traded shifts with Jarrel. I've called for cover twice tonight, each time he's been the first one to respond."

Jen blew on the coffee in the cup in her hands. She'd gone with the jumbo size, and it made her look even smaller by comparison. "He responded to that alarm I had on Buffalo earlier. Never got out of his car. He's serious, he's willing to let one of us get hurt, or worse."

"It was a false alarm," said Sophie.

"Like he had a way of knowing that."

"So document it!" Sophie snapped. "Bring it to the commander!"

"And how's that going to help?" Jen shot back. "It was just him and me, Sophie! It's going to be my word against his, I've got no way of proving it. Even if he admitted to staying in his ride, it wouldn't amount to anything, he'd excuse his way out of it."

Sophie appealed to me. "He's going to screw up. Guy like him, he's going to make a mistake eventually, we'll catch him on it then."

"I'm not willing to wait," I said. "I won't speak for you guys, but for me, I can't let this continue. I go on patrol, I'm more nervous than I was on my first tour as a rookie. My stomach's killing me, I'm losing sleep, this is eating my life."

"You too?" Sophie looked surprised. "Seriously?"

"I can't keep anything down," I admitted.

"Wish that was my problem."

Jen snorted.

"God," Sophie said after almost half a minute of silence. "God, if it goes wrong, Tracy, we could all end up going down for it. I don't want to go to prison."

"He'd have to bring charges," I said. "He'll never do that. Not in a million years."

"You're sure?"

"I'm counting on it."

Jen blew on her coffee again. "That's not the part that worries me."

"No?"

She met my eyes. "He does carry a weapon, Tracy."

"So do we," I told her.

———

IT TOOK ANOTHER week before the stars aligned and everything was right. Sophie went off duty for three days, and Jen moved from third shift to second, but Morrison traded again, this time with Bowen, staying on third shift with me. It shouldn't have surprised me; he'd identified me as the ringleader, it was natural that I'd draw the generous portion of his ire. That week, it seemed like every time I called for cover, he was the first to respond to dispatch, and more often than not, he was the cover that dispatch sent to back me up.

The night I was assigned to Sector 521, Morrison pulled it as well, both of us in Grid 88090. I called Jen from the car on my mobile as soon as I went in service.

"Tonight," I told her. "Call it in by Germantown after three."

"I'll let Sophie know."

"You good for this?"

"Don't ask me that," Jen said, and hung up.

———

AT SEVENTEEN MINUTES past three in the morning, dispatch came over the radio with a report of a suspicious vehicle off the side of Germantown Road, asking if there was a unit nearby that could check it out. I'd been waiting on the call, and I jumped on it, told dispatch that I was in the area and on the way. Dispatch confirmed.

Germantown Road is a long and winding two-lane that climbs up from the west side of the river into the West Hills, through what remains of the forest that once dominated all of Portland. It was dark and it was quiet, and it was exactly the kind of place where drivers who had had too much to drink either wrapped their cars around trees or managed to find a spark of sense and pulled over to sleep it off. The call, in and of itself, wasn't anything out of the ordinary.

It took me a little more than four minutes to find where Jen had parked the pickup truck off the shoulder, and that entire time, I didn't see any other vehicles on the road. The truck was a blue-and-white Ford that belonged to Jen's brother-in-law, a plumber from Beaverton who'd married her youngest sister. As I came to a stop, Jen and Sophie climbed out of the cab. They were each wearing civvies, jeans and boots, Jen with a heavy black-and-red flannel and a watch cap, Sophie with a navy-blue sweatshirt, the hood up. Sophie had the camera, the little digital recorder she'd bought with the money we'd pooled together.

I switched the spotlight on, angling down toward the road, before getting out of the car. The bounce from the pavement threw illumination out to maybe twenty feet, enough that visibility wouldn't be a problem. Both women moved to join me in the puddle of light, Sophie handing over the camera. I switched it on, lined up a close-up of Jen.

"Go," I said.

"My name is Officer Jennifer Schaeffer," Jen said, and then gave her badge number.

I put the camera on Sophie.

"I'm Officer Sophie Gault," she said, and gave her badge number as well.

I turned the camera on me, lining up the shot as best I could.

"I'm Officer Tracy Hoffman," I said, and, like the rest, rattled off my badge number. Then I added, "It's approximately half past three in the morning, Thursday, September twenty-seventh. We're standing on Northwest Germantown Road, maybe a mile and a half east of the Last Chance Tavern."

I stopped recording and handed the camera back to Sophie, who took it without a word.

"I'm going to call it in," I said. "We're ready for this?"

Sophie and Jen both nodded.

I went to the car and killed the spot, watching as Sophie climbed back into the truck, this time getting behind the wheel. Jen had already disappeared into the darkness. I used the handset to call dispatch to tell them that I'd found the vehicle, then used the laptop in the car to log the stop and to run the pickup's plates. When the computer kicked back that the vehicle was clean, I called that in as well, and then added that I could see one occupant in the vehicle, male, apparently asleep. Then I requested a covering officer to join me before making contact.

Dispatch put out the request, and Morrison came back as if he'd been hanging on every word, saying that he could be there in three minutes. Dispatch relayed, and I confirmed.

Then I waited, feeling my stomach contracting and my hands

beginning to tremble, thinking that this was really the only way to make things right. I was committed now—we all were.

In the rearview, I caught the nimbus glow of headlights through the pines, and within fifteen seconds Morrison's car appeared, slowing as it came around the bend and he caught sight of my vehicle. I popped my door and got out, taking my stick and sliding it onto my belt, then pulling my flashlight. He parked behind me, and I watched him exit, waited until he'd approached before speaking.

"Single male occupant." My voice sounded strained, the way it had when we'd faced each other in the precinct lot, but this time I knew that it wasn't due to anger. "Think Caucasian, can't tell."

Morrison squinted past me at the pickup, raising his own flashlight and hitting the car with its beam. I watched as the pool of light drew itself over the license plate, then to the rear window of the cab, where Sophie's head, covered by the hood of her sweatshirt, seemed to loll against the driver's-side window. Morrison snapped the beam off, then grinned that smug grin of his.

"That little thing in there's got you scared, Hoffman?" he said. "I must goddamn terrify you. Tell you what, I'll handle the contact and you can take the credit for it. Keep you nice and safe."

"Just be ready in case I need you," I said.

Then, raising my own flashlight, I approached the pickup, snapping the beam on and shining it into the cab. I used the butt to tap the window, and Sophie showed me her hands in her lap without moving her head, so I could see the camera was on and recording. I tapped a second time, and Sophie moved her head slightly, as if waking up.

"Police officer," I said loudly. "Can I see some identification please?"

Then I stepped back and turned to face Morrison, putting

the beam from my flashlight directly into his eyes, effectively blinding him. The door, now on my left, opened, and Sophie slid quickly out, holding the camera with both hands, lining up Morrison in the shot.

Morrison had his free hand up, trying to shield his eyes. "The hell—"

"This is Officer Mark Morrison," I said for the benefit of the camera.

"Wait a—is that Gault?" Morrison demanded, still trying to free the light from his eyes. "Get your flash out of my eyes, damn it! Is it that little cocktease, is that Gault?"

"He's about to get the shit kicked out of him," I added, watching Jen as she came up behind him.

To his credit, Morrison shut up when he heard me say that. Then he started to turn away, and he dropped his hand from where it had been shielding his eyes. He was already half-blind from my flash, and there was no way he saw Jen until it was far too late for him to do anything about it.

"Try holding your breath," Jen said.

Then she hit him in the face with a shot of pepper spray.

Morrison gagged on a curse, staggered back, flailing in pain. I used my stick and took his right knee, and he dropped forward, managed to land on his hands, and I gave him another one in back to put him down, then dropped my own knees on him and put him in a choke hold. Jen had reached into my car by then, throwing the spot on again, suddenly making every detail in the scene brighter than day. She came back to us, began stripping the gear off Morrison's belt, going for his cuffs first. She did his wrists, then took his gun and his Taser and his stick, all of it, before running over to his car and dumping it inside.

Morrison shuddered and gagged, and when I released the hold, he collapsed heavily. A fountain of snot was running from his nose, his mouth open wide, dripping its own rush of fluid.

I got my feet under me and watched as Jen put a kick into his ribs, then I backed off to where Sophie was still standing. We traded: I got the camera, and she got my stick.

Sophie just looked at him for a couple of seconds at first. I could see the conflict in her face, see the shifting of her emotions from hesitation and even fear into anger. She was remembering what had happened to her, what could have happened to her. I could see it in her eyes.

"You bastard," Sophie said.

Then she brought the stick into his side. Not too hard, just enough to make sure he knew what was coming. Morrison choked, squirming, and she hit him on the opposite side, harder. He was still gagging, and he tried to lurch forward, but he couldn't get far without the help of his hands, and he gave it up when Sophie hit him a third time, harder, high in the back. Then she did it again, and again, and again, working along his side, until she'd reached the small of his back. Morrison was crying out, his inarticulate pleas filled with phlegm.

"You let him hurt me," Sophie said, and she rammed my stick viciously into his side, and Morrison stopped crying out, for a moment entirely unable to breathe. "You let him hurt me and you laughed while he did it, you son of a bitch."

Jen had the six-pack for me, and I gave her the camera and took it, then took my stick back from Sophie and replaced it on my belt. Morrison was struggling to regain his breath, trying to get his knees beneath him. I pulled the first bottle, felt it cool and heavy and smooth in my hand, a beer-filled rock that could crack a skull and end a life. Morrison managed to flip himself onto his side, and the spot from my car made the mess on his face shine like a glass mask, and through his tears he saw me, saw what I held, and he sputtered.

"Jesus Christ," he wheezed. "You can't do this, you can't—"

I threw the bottle, missing his head by six inches or so, and it burst on impact, glass shattering and beer spraying, and Morrison flinched. I took a second bottle, stepping closer.

"You can't—"

I threw again, this time harder, again missing him, this time just barely. More glass, more beer, and the scent of it mingled with the pines and the road and the autumn and the bile. Morrison choked back a strangled scream, and it wasn't enough, and I grabbed two more bottles and threw them at his head back-to-back, still missing, and this time he did scream, closing his eyes and trying to roll away from me. Sophie moved to cut him off, pushing him back with her boot.

"Now who's on the ground?" I told Morrison, and I threw my second-to-last bottle, letting it shatter beside him with all the others.

He screamed for me to stop, for Jen or Sophie to help him.

I picked up the last bottle, used the church key Jen had stuck in the pack to open it. Then I tilted it over his head and let gravity take half the contents, watching it run out and fall onto his face, washing away his tears and his snot as he spluttered and gagged some more.

Then I let gravity take the bottle itself, and it hit him just above the bridge of his nose, and what was left inside foamed out as it clattered onto the road.

"Bet you wish you had backup," I told him.

He blinked beer and tears out of his eyes, looking up at me, miserable, full of rage. Then Jen stepped closer, the camera still running, and he seemed to finally see it, and the rage abated in confusion.

"Yeah," I told him. "All of it recorded for posterity."

"You're all crazy," he croaked. "Fucking crazy."

"No, you've got it all wrong, Morrison," I said. "It's not for our posterity, it's for yours."

Jen handed the keys she'd taken off him to Sophie, who went

around behind and began unfastening his cuffs. Morrison tried tracking her, craning his head, then looked back to Jen, then finally to me. If he hadn't looked so pathetic then, I probably would have laughed.

"It's not for us," I told him. "It's for you."

He licked a thin line of mucus from his lips, blinking rapidly. Sophie rose, dropping the keys and the cuffs on the ground in front of him with a splash. He flinched again.

Jen lowered the camera, turning it off. She looked at me and I nodded, so she set it on the ground beside his cuffs and his keys.

"We're on it," I told Morrison. "Our names, our badges, all of it. Everything we just did, it's all there. Everything that just happened to you."

He forced himself upright, doubled over with a new fit of coughs, then swiped at his eyes and his mouth with a beer-soaked sleeve. The pepper spray still had to be working him something awful, but the beer had probably gone a long way to relieving the pain.

"Hand it over to Internal Affairs," I told him. "Give it to the commander. Take it downtown and hand-deliver it to the chief, send it through channels. Whatever you want, it's yours."

"You think I won't?" he asked softly, furious.

I looked to Sophie and Jen, then showed him my palms. "I don't know what you're going to do, Morrison. You could get yourself cleaned up and go back to District and spin some story about a drunk-and-disorderly call or some other bullshit to explain your sorry state. You might even get away with pretending this never happened. After all, we did a pretty good job of staying away from your face."

Morrison started hacking again, trying to clear his sinuses. I waited until he was finished to continue.

"Then again, you could drag your sorry ass back to District

right now," I told him. "You could raise holy hell, try to get the commander out of bed, hand him this camera here in person and tell him he's just got to watch what's on it. You could run it to your buddies downtown, you could give it to Internal, you could flip them to us and try to land our badges."

I paused, wanting him to hear the next part, to make sure he got it and got it clear. Sophie and Jen were each standing with me now, the three of us together, and I realized that my fear had gone. I realized that everything I was saying to him wasn't just the truth, it was what I believed. If I had to, I'd take the fall, and I knew Sophie and Jen felt the same way.

"I don't know what you're going to do, Morrison," I said finally. "But I do know this: you deliver this camera to *anyone* in the department come morning, and there will be *no one* who hasn't heard about it by lunchtime. And come roll call at third shift, they'll be making up details of their own, there'll be patrolmen in the Southwest talking about how you wet yourself, there'll be bicycle cops riding Central, swapping details about how you begged—*begged*—for someone to help you."

The radio on my belt crackled, dispatch asking my disposition. Looking Morrison dead in the eye, I radioed back that the situation had been resolved and that Officer Morrison and I were going 10-6. Dispatch came back with confirmation.

"Bring charges against us," I said. "Charge us all, you've got the evidence. We're agreed, we'll all plead guilty, if that's what it comes to. Each one of us is more than willing to stand up in open court and tell the world what we just did to you."

Morrison didn't move, and I thought that maybe he was staring at the camera, but maybe he wasn't looking at it at all. Maybe he wasn't hearing me anymore.

Sophie and Jen went back to the pickup, and I returned to my car, climbing in and killing the spot before restarting the engine. The light around Morrison vanished back into the night.

He was finally beginning to stir, but he was doing it slowly, and I watched him, because I sure as hell wasn't going to help. He made it into his vehicle and got it started, and I heard his 10-7 come over the radio, and I called mine in on top of it.

We headed in different directions, he toward the river, me up toward the top of the hills, the direction my fellow officers had gone, tiny Jen and gorgeous Sophie. We'd meet up after I got off shift, feel guilty and giddy as we waited to see if the phone would ring, if some officer we knew would be paying us a visit, asking us to clear up some confusion, to answer some questions.

Or maybe we'd find ourselves waiting for nothing, that Morrison hadn't dared to breathe a word. Maybe we'd find that we had gotten away with something we never should have done, something we never should have had to do.

Driving up that hill, I didn't fear the worst.

I knew I was covered.

RULE NUMBER ONE

BY BEV VINCENT

S he stands out like a cactus blossom in the desert, seated in the roll-call room beyond the eight men in sky-blue shirts and navy-blue pants huddled in the back row like juvenile delinquents in remedial math class. The minute Brett lays eyes on her, he knows she will be his for the evening.

Her attire is simple, understated: a white blouse and blue slacks with white pinstripes. Sensible, flat-soled shoes. Long black hair caresses the shoulders of her blouse, which is open demurely at the neck. In her right hand she grips a pen, which hovers over an open steno pad resting on the desk affixed to her chair. A burlap satchel sits at her feet. She doesn't look up when he enters.

The room is wide but shallow, containing three meandering rows of simple student desks, the sergeant's podium, and a TV suspended from the ceiling. Printouts listing suspect information decorate the podium. Behind it, next to the door, American and Texas flags flank an empty table. A poster features the sergeant from *Hill Street Blues* saying, LET'S BE CAREFUL OUT THERE.

It's nearly three o'clock on a Saturday afternoon, so the television is broadcasting a Texas A&M football game. The Astros play later on, which means Brett's radio will be filled with chatter every time someone scores.

Two bulletin boards sealed in glass cases cover the wall at the far end of the room. One features mug shots, wanted notices, and BOLO fliers. The other contains approved job postings for officers looking to supplement their income. Most are for night watchmen or nightclub-security positions. Brett has no interest in these—he already works the department maximum forty additional hours.

The comfortable weight of the gear on his utility belt—service revolver, radio, handcuffs, nightstick, and Taser—adds to his swagger. Two colleagues look up from their conversation when he takes the last empty seat in the back row. Phelps raises his eyebrows and tilts his head an inch toward the woman. Brett scrunches his mouth into an appraising pucker and nods. *Not bad* is the silent message they exchange. He doesn't waste any time checking her out, though. He'll have the next eight hours to do that. Guaranteed.

When the sergeant emerges from his office, he mutes the volume on the television but leaves the picture up. He reads a policy-change sheet and advises officers whose body armor is more than five years old that they have three more weeks to turn it in to be replaced. He has an orientation video available for anyone taking the sergeant's test. After reading the names of officers who need to sign subpoenas before they go on duty, he assigns cars by unit number.

"Hoskins," he says, "you have a ride-along."

Which comes as no surprise to Brett. Nine times out of ten, he gets the riders. The only question is why she's here. Most civilian passengers are either media or members of a mayoral task force. Her attire doesn't provide any clues, but he appreciates the way her blouse clings to her body. If he had to bet, he'd say media. It doesn't make much difference. Either way, he has to mind his p's and q's, keep the bawdy banter to a minimum, and not bust anyone's chops unless they deserve it. It also means, however, that he has an excuse to handpick the cushier calls.

The sergeant makes no introductions, merely points Brett in the woman's direction. She's already gathering her possessions and heading toward the podium. Her eyes are the color of roasted chestnuts. The long black hair framing her narrow face has been teased into gentle waves. He glances at her left hand—no ring. Her complexion is dark, making Brett wonder if she has Hispanic blood and whether that will be an issue during the shift. Many of the perpetrators he encounters over the next eight hours will be Hispanic.

"Follow me," he says. "It's a bit of a hike."

He leads her along the corridor, down a narrow staircase, outside the central station, across a gravel parking lot, into the garage, and up to the third level, where his ride, 1 Adam 25 E, is parked. The car is where he left it the day before, which probably means no one used it since then. The department is short staffed, so he's not surprised.

"Hoskins," he says by way of introduction when they reach the car.

Panting slightly from the stairs and the fast pace he set, she sticks out a hand. "Meredith Knight."

Her skin is smooth and soft, and he maintains his grip on her hand about two seconds too long. After he releases her, he pulls out a well-worn ignition key, opens the door, and clears the lock on her side. The car is seven years old and has more than a hundred thousand miles on it. He listens for the roof speaker to crackle when he starts the engine. "Some officers like to check all the lights, the siren and stuff. I know everything pretty much works. At least it doesn't change day to day, especially since the car's not driven around the clock. Means I don't have to change the seat, the mirrors, the radio station."

She starts taking notes immediately, which is a little strange. Reminds him of a high school keener, writing down everything the teacher says.

"How come I never get a ride-along?" Phelps says in a sing-song voice on his way to his car. Brett shrugs and grins.

The radio is set loud enough to hear the music without having it drown out the dispatcher or other radio chatter. He boots up the computer, which runs an obsolete operating system; loads the com software; and logs on with dispatch. The crowded quarters, the front seat jammed with computer equipment and other paraphernalia, makes it feel as if they're unusually close. Her perfume, mild and floral, reaches his nostrils. "Reporter?"

"Writer," she answers. "I'm doing research for a novel."

That's a new one. "Interesting." With two jobs and an ex-wife, Brett has no time for novels. Of the three, the ex-wife is the most demanding. Still, he relaxes a little knowing that his activities over the next eight hours likely won't end up in tomorrow's newspaper or in a report on the mayor's desk.

"They pretty much just give you paperwork to read over and then say come ride, right?" He knows the routine, but he's looking for a way to break the ice.

"If I get shot, beaten, or otherwise maimed, it's my own damned fault," she says. "At least that's what the forms I signed say."

"I'll do my best to keep that from happening. I've never lost a ride-along yet." He likes her spunkiness, so he answers in detail her questions about the minutia of his routine. He shows her how to use the outdated computer with attached microphone that is his lifeline to central dispatch. "If I'm getting my ass whooped, don't worry about calling 1 Adam 25 E. Just pick this mike up and say, 'Hoskins needs help.'" He points at a second microphone. "That one is for yelling at people on the PA. This is the one for saving my ass."

"Got it."

The computer pings every time a dispatch message comes through. If he ignores them long enough, a robotic female voice chides him. "Three new messages waiting." He picks some of the easier call slips to handle first to clear the backlog. Reports of suspicious people that rarely pan out or complaints about illegally parked vehicles that he will ticket and ultimately have towed if they stay there long enough.

Unsure of what she's looking for, he describes the neighborhoods on his beat and tells anecdotes about interesting calls he's taken in the past. Without mentioning his divorce or admitting that all he can currently afford is a dingy apartment in a rough neighborhood, he points out houses he's looked into buying, though they're all beyond his means. She compliments his ability to drive, operate the computer, and talk with her all at the same time. When she isn't writing in her steno pad, she's recording him on a digital voice recorder, a device smaller than a cell phone that beeps and chirps from time to time.

When he returns without getting a response at an apartment where a silent 911 was reported, he tells her, "The front door was locked. No noise coming from inside. Nothing more I can do—you just can't go around kicking people's doors in." He types "C UNF" into the computer and clicks "send." "That's 'clear/unfounded.' We get a lot of those around here. It's a Hispanic neighborhood, and part of Mexico has a 911 area code. Sometimes they forget to dial the '001' first, so they hang up." He waits to see how she will react, but she's too busy taking notes.

As work goes, it's drudgery, but Brett puts the best face on it. He feels compelled to both entertain and impress. He gets most of the ride-alongs because of his reputation for being easygoing, but he wants to be more than that for Meredith. *If I play my cards right, maybe I'll get to show her my billy club at the end of the shift,* he thinks with a barely suppressed grin.

She expresses interest in the mundane. The operation of the computer and what all the codes and responses mean. How he selects which call slip to answer. He allows a hint of pride to creep into his voice when telling her how he reads between the lines, discerning when a call should be assigned a higher priority than it seems to merit at first glance.

He elicits a laugh when he says, "Please don't steal the police car," before he goes to ticket a Hispanic teenager who ran a stop sign. The driver's-license number triggers a warrant flag, so he confiscates the ignition key and returns to the cruiser to await confirmation from TCIC/NCIC.

"Seven minutes is the timer on a stop," he says, typing a code into the computer. "I'm telling the dispatcher to restart the clock. Otherwise she'll start sending messages or calling me over the radio to make sure I'm okay." He twists in his seat to watch the occupants of the other car and make eye contact with Meredith at the same time. He has to be prepared in case the driver decides to run away. "Saturday usually starts out quiet like this and then picks up when the sun goes down. What's your book about?"

She shrugs. "I don't like discussing story ideas until they're finished."

"Have you published anything?"

"Some short stories. This is my first novel."

He wants to ask more, but he knows so little about writing and books in general that he's afraid to look stupid. Awkward silence fills the air between them, interrupted only by the garbled chatter on the radio, including frequent updates on the Astros game. Though it's early October, it's warm sitting in the car without the AC running.

When he notices her checking her watch after fifteen minutes, he decides to cut the driver loose with just the ticket rather than waiting for dispatch to respond. Priority-one queries, where the information determines whether or not someone will be arrested, are supposed to take less than ten minutes, but sometimes a request gets lost between the dispatcher and the person who keys it in. Thirty seconds after the other car drives off, the report comes back positive for two delinquent traffic tickets, so he flashes the lights, blasts the siren for a few seconds, and pulls the car over again, this time placing the driver under arrest. He turns the keys over to the passenger after ascertaining that he has no outstanding warrants.

Once he has the prisoner handcuffed and belted into the backseat, he says, "At least now you'll get to see the jail."

It takes nearly twenty minutes to drive to the Southeast Jail, where prisoners arrested on minor complaints are held. After they arrive, they have to wait another ten minutes for the garage door to open on the sally port, which is little more than a glorified parking garage with a few podiums. Here, the prisoner's handcuffs are removed, he is frisked again, and a jail employee asks in a bored tone if he has any medical conditions or any forms of mental illness and if he's ever attempted suicide. The guy is cooperative and untroubled by the process, which leads Brett to believe he's been through this before.

Brett ushers Meredith into the small office behind the podiums, where he hands over his paperwork. The other officers waiting in line look her over approvingly and give him subtle thumbs-up signs or winks.

By the time they leave the sally port, it's nearly six o'clock. Normally he'd have dinner with one of his buddies, but he called to cancel when Meredith was in the powder room at the jail. He doesn't want to share her with anyone.

"Hungry?" he asks. "There's a place up here I've been meaning to try out."

"Sure. My treat."

"You don't have to do that."

"It's the least I can do. You must be getting tired of all my questions."

"It's good to have the company, to be honest."

"On TV they always show the cops riding with partners."

"If we weren't so understaffed, maybe. You saw how many people were at roll call today? That was a big turnout for a Saturday. Usually we have two or three less than that. A couple of nights ago, there was a house fire, and another unit and I had to do traffic control. You should have seen the call slips piling up. I had nineteen when I got back to the car. Some of them had been holding for eight or nine hours from day shift."

He wheels into the restaurant parking lot and escorts her into the dim interior. It's a place where he knows he can get good food and quick service, two important factors to someone who could be called out at any moment. He likes the way she looks in the flicker of the candle on the table, and he takes the opportunity to discreetly appraise her while she studies the menu.

"This must be boring as hell for you," he says. "Nothing like what you see on TV."

"That's exactly what I'm looking for. Reality, not drama."

She focuses her attention on him, as if every word he says is gospel. Normally it's the uniform that makes him feel noticed. Today, it's being seen in the company of this beautiful woman. He wonders if it's too soon to ask her to join him at a nightclub after he gets off shift. He usually goes out on Saturdays because he has Sundays off. Maybe he should work that into the conversation first.

"You'll get a kick out of this," he says after they give their orders. "A woman was chasing a sexual-assault suspect the other day in her car. She calls 911 and tells the call taker where they're headed. Then she goes, 'I've got a pistol and I'm going to shoot him. . . . I'm getting ready to shoot him.' It goes out on the radio, and the responding officer calls back in this deadpan voice, 'Um, ask her to hold off on that.'" It's a funny story, much older than he lets on and always good for a laugh. A burst of adrenaline rushes through his veins when she reacts as if it's the funniest thing she's ever heard.

He tries to ask her questions, but she always turns the conversation back around to the job. Departmental hierarchy and the size of his beat, boring stuff like that, but if that's what turns her crank, he's only too happy to explain. He outlines the subtle but important difference between drawing his weapon—which he does occasionally—and actually pointing it at someone, which happens far less frequently. He admits that he has never fired his gun in the line of duty.

"I'm all for the Taser, as long as we can use it the way I feel it should be used. I shouldn't have to fight anybody anymore, because when you do, you sprain or strain something. People complain when some perp dies after being zapped because he refused to follow orders, but they don't want to pay officers injured on duty to sit at home because things got out of hand, you know?" It's one of his pet rants, and he stops himself before he really gets rolling. She has a few questions about the way the Taser works, which he answers simply and directly before changing the subject.

After dinner, he responds to a noise complaint—a band playing outside a restaurant—investigates a missing sewer grating, and calls a wrecker to tow an abandoned vehicle, identified by a chalk mark he made on the left rear tire during the previous shift. The work is so mundane, he's embarrassed. She's probably not going to think much of the reality of the job when all she sees him doing is writing tickets and getting cars impounded. If she expected *Cops*, she must be terribly disappointed.

He scours the screen for something a little more adventurous, a little sexier. Normally when he has a ride-along, he picks calls that are unlikely to turn ugly. Now he wants something that might give him a chance to impress her.

"What's that one?" She taps a coral-red fingernail on a new entry.

"Silent alarm on Westheimer."

"Like a break-in or something?"

He can tell she's intrigued by the way her breathing changes. Her right foot taps on the floor mat next to her burlap satchel.

Against his better judgment, he claims the call, knowing he could end up spending the rest of the night filling out paperwork instead of catching the perps in the act. He has a brief fantasy about Tasering a guy while Meredith watches in fawning adoration, after which she agrees to meet him at Numbers for a couple of drinks before sidling up next to him and suggesting in a steamy whisper that it's time to go somewhere else. Somewhere private.

"No lights or siren?" she asks. She sounds disappointed.

"Don't want to warn them we're coming," he says.

"Is another unit responding?"

"I'll call for backup if I need it. After I check out the situation."

"Do you get scared, answering calls like this?"

He considers lying but thinks the truth might impress her more. A chance to show his sensitive side. "I get scared every time I pull someone over for a traffic stop. You never know who's behind the wheel, what their day's been like. If they've just had a fight with their wife and are looking for someone to take it out on. Or if they've just robbed or killed someone and the only thing standing between them and freedom is me. I've got two rules for every shift."

He pauses, waiting for her to ask what they are. When she does, he continues. "First, to go home in the same condition I was in when I came to work."

"And the other?"

"Get a bite to eat sometime during the shift. That one doesn't always work out."

She laughs gently, tossing her long dark hair back. It's a good moment. He's about to broach the subject of nightclubs and drinks when he realizes they're a block from the scene. He keys in the code to let dispatch know he's on the scene and then focuses his attention on the surroundings. The address corresponds to a jewelry store squeezed between an antiques shop and a joint with a neon condom hanging out front.

The place is dark and looks empty. After wheeling around the corner to check the alley, he stops and uses the handle near his head to direct the spotlight at the back door. He's about to get out to make sure it's locked when a set of headlights materializes in his rearview mirror. His chest tightens when he considers the implications of a vehicle suddenly pinning him in.

Meredith bends over in her seat. Brett wonders if she saw something that alarmed her and is trying to get out of the way. Then he realizes that she's fumbling in her canvas satchel, though he can't imagine why.

He's about to reach for the dispatch mike when she straightens up and points a Taser exactly like his own at him. The red panic button on the corner of his keyboard is only inches from his hand. If he could hit it, an alert would go out to dispatch and all units in the vicinity, and his car's engine and computer would be disabled. The space between them is far less than the weapon's twenty-five-foot range. Its skin-piercing twin prongs would cover the distance faster than he could move an inch. The tension in her trigger finger is obvious—she won't hesitate to stun him. He shifts his gaze from her hand to her chestnut eyes, trying to comprehend what the hell is happening. How in a few seconds he went from thinking about asking her out on a date to staring down the business end of fifty thousand volts.

Two people arrive beside the car. They yank the door open, pull him out, and pin him to the ground in the filthy alley, next to a row of garbage cans and a stack of empty crates. He feels a tug at his belt. A moment later his own handcuffs ratchet around his wrists.

"Relax," Meredith says as she emerges from the cruiser. "Rule number one. Don't struggle, and you'll go home in the same condition as when you came to work."

A male voice speaks for the first time. "You all set?"

"Don't worry. I know all the codes to enter, and I've set up a few voice files on the digital recorder to answer routine pages from dispatch. I'll let you know if something comes up I can't handle."

The second male voice says, "Stay down if you know what's good for you. Don't try anything."

Brett is too frustrated and angry to answer. He shakes his head to acknowledge the order while trying to figure out how to extricate himself from this mess. He feels his service revolver, radio, baton, and Taser being stripped from his side. Without his weapons, all he has are some training and a badge, neither of which will stop a bullet or a paralyzing jolt of electricity. His body armor is in the trunk. He wonders if he'll get to turn it in at the depot for a new set like his sergeant ordered a few hours earlier.

Two sets of footsteps walk away from him. He turns his head far enough to see the dark figures disappear through the back door of the jewelry store. Another set of footsteps approaches from his left. He twists around to watch Meredith pull a crate from the stack and drop onto it. She has the Taser in a firm grip, though it isn't pointed in his direction at the moment.

"I don't understand," he says. "People know who you are. The community-relations officer who set up your ride ran a background check on you."

"He ran a background check on Meredith Knight. Getting into a police car for a ride-along isn't exactly like breaking into Fort Knox. Or," she says, with a nod toward the nearby building, "a jewelry store. We did the whole thing by e-mail, phone, and fax. He never met me. All I had to do was fill out some forms with fake information, fax them off to him, and that was it. No one even searched me at the police department."

"How could you know they wouldn't?"

"It's not my first ride-along. Just my first at your station. My first as Meredith Knight."

Brett closes his eyes. "Seems like a lot of effort for a burglary."

"Well worth it, though," she says. "The main problem was the alarm. We didn't know how to disable it, so the next-best thing was to distract whoever responded. If I couldn't persuade you to take the call, my associates would have ambushed whoever showed up—but that would limit their time inside. This way, we have a few extra minutes to get the safe open. Excuse me."

She steps past him and leans into the cruiser to enter something on the keyboard. He knows what she's typing. He explained it all to her in detail. Unless the dispatcher needs to get in touch with him about something unrelated or starts to wonder why it's taking so long to investigate, the next people likely to arrive on the scene will be the owners, to clear the alarm. They won't be of much help unless they notice something, and that's only if they're in town and get here before the thieves take off. For all he knows, they're at Minute Maid Park, watching the Astros game.

He still can't believe the lengths to which they've gone for a robbery. Later tonight, after they let him go, he'll sit down with the police artist and describe her so well that strangers will recognize her on the street. They'll have video of her too, from police headquarters and the jail. Her picture will be all over the six o'clock news tomorrow, regardless of how this turns out for him.

"You look lost in thought," she says, startling him. She's on the crate again, cradling the Taser in her lap.

His approach when interrogating people at a scene is to always let the suspects think they're winning. In this situation, at this moment, they are. All he wants to do is get through the night alive and with a minimum of humiliation. Losing his service revolver has been the biggest blow so far.

"I'm in a bad spot here."

"Not if you stay cool," she says. "Fifteen, twenty minutes, this will be all over. We'll be on our way, and you'll never see us again."

"This must be some haul."

"You have no idea. We've been planning it for two months."

He tries to decide how much to say. He doesn't want to give them any helpful information, but he also doesn't want the volatile situation to get any worse.

"If you're worried about the owners showing up," she says, "don't be. They're tied up at the moment."

Brett thinks she expects him to grin at the joke, but he doesn't. He curses himself for being so entranced by her that he overlooked the possibility that she might have some ulterior motive. Writing a novel. As if.

Her cell phone chirps. She flips it open and glances at the display. Brett deduces that she's speaking with her collaborators inside the building.

"Not long now," she says in a chatty tone after she disconnects, as if they're waiting for a pizza to arrive. "You probably don't want to go out with me after this, right?"

"Huh?"

"You've been working up the courage to ask me out all afternoon."

"You're nuts."

"A woman knows," she says. "Under different circumstances, I might have said yes."

"Fuck you," he says. He's in no mood for her banter anymore.

Still, no matter how angry he is with her for setting him up, he's more pissed off at himself for allowing it to happen.

"Yeah, and the horse I rode in on, I know. There, there." She checks her watch. "Oops, almost missed the deadline." She returns to the cruiser and resets the timer.

Brett releases a lungful of air and wiggles his hips to find a more comfortable position. Even without his weapons, his belt has enough pouches and compartments to make it awkward, especially lying on the ground in the paved alley.

"This is the point in the story where you're supposed to ask me to explain everything," she says once she's back on the crate again. "Where I reveal all our secrets before the cavalry arrives to save the day."

"I don't read much," he admits. "And you seem to have taken care of the cavalry."

"You're not happy with me."

He can't remember being madder in his life. Even his ex-wife never managed to get under his skin like this woman has in the past few hours. "No shit," he says.

"Your very own femme fatale."

"Don't flatter yourself."

"I can see the news tomorrow. Maybe they'll come up with a nickname for me, like the Ice Princess, in honor of all the diamonds we're stealing. That would be a good one. Feel free to use it."

"How many diamonds are we talking about? Out of curiosity."

"Let's just say I'll never have to work retail again. Are those dollar signs I see in your eyes? Looking for a cut?"

He turns his head away. More than anything, he hates the way she seems intent on taunting him. On humiliating him. It can't be personal, because she couldn't have known in advance that he'd be assigned to her for the afternoon. Unless it's because of the way he acted toward her during the shift . . .

"I went out of my way to be nice to you," he says. Even to his own ears, his voice sounds bitter and petulant.

"Yes, you did," she says. "You were very sweet."

Her phone rings again. She looks around the alley. After a car passes, she says, "All clear." A moment later, her accomplices emerge from the rear of the store. They stay in the shadows, so he never gets a good look at them other than to note that one is about five-six, a hundred fifty pounds, and the other is closer to six feet, two hundred pounds. Caucasian, he thinks, but can't be sure. He files these details away for later, but he knows he couldn't pick them out of a lineup or from mug shots.

The black pouch the taller man tosses to Meredith seems absurdly small. It has golden tie cords at the neck. From the way she presses her face against it, he figures it's made of velvet or satin. She tugs the neck open and sticks her hand inside, allowing the contents to filter through her fingers. Then she reseals the bag and tosses it back to the tall man.

After resetting the dispatch timer one last time, Meredith kneels on the ground beside Brett. "If we had a little longer, I'd show you," she says. "So you'd understand."

He doesn't want to look at her, but he knows this is probably the last time he'll see her, and he wants to remember her this way, framed in the amber light of a nearby streetlight, her features distorted by shadows.

"And you would," she continues. "One glance, and they'd steal your heart away."

He shakes his head, but he wonders if what she says is true. Look how easily she stole his heart.

She plucks the keys to his handcuffs from his front pants pocket. The brief contact is shockingly intimate and unexpectedly arousing. She grins. He knows that she sensed his reaction, but she says nothing.

"I'll leave these over here," she says, placing the keys on the ground in front of the trash bins. "Your gun and everything else are on the front seat. We have no need for them where we're going, and I know how much paperwork you'd have to fill out if you lost your gun." She winks at him. "You see, I've done my research. Maybe I will write a novel someday."

The two men take the front seat of their car. After Meredith opens the rear door, she watches him for a moment. He strains his neck to look up at her, to meet her gaze.

"Tonight you'll go home in the same condition as when you arrived at work. Maybe even a little better. It's up to you."

With that, she slides into the car and closes the door. A moment later, they're gone, blending into the Saturday night traffic on Westheimer.

Better? he wonders. *What did she mean by that?* He struggles to his feet, lurches toward the trash cans on numb legs, kneels, and picks up the handcuff key. Fumbling blindly behind his back, he finally manages to insert the key into the lock, and his hands are free. The next step is obvious but degrading. In succinct, professional language, he describes his location and the vehicle and its occupants to his dispatcher. He even has the license number to give them.

A few minutes later, the first cruiser arrives on the scene. The Investigative Division isn't far behind. They seal off the alley with crime-scene tape and make their way inside the jewelry store. Brett tells his story to one detective and again a few minutes later to another. His vehicle is part of the crime scene, so he can't touch it. He rocks his weight from foot to foot and pulls out his cell phone but can't think who to call. Which friend to share his humiliation with.

He puts the phone away and thrusts his hands into his pockets. Something sharp digs into the back of his right hand. It doesn't feel like his handcuff key. He gets up and strolls to the end of the alley, which is cordoned off with a yellow ribbon of crime-scene tape.

After ascertaining that no one is paying attention to him, he pulls the item from his pocket. It gleams in the yellow street-light, a little piece of carbon as cold as fire and as hard as the heart of the woman who placed it there.

WHAT A WONDERFUL WORLD

BY PAUL GUYOT

I n jazz I listen for her.
In rain.
Her laughter sends me to sleep at night and is the sound
that wakes me in the morning.

Her name is Kayla Lightfoot. I say *is* because even though
she's dead, her name hasn't changed.

———

THREE DAYS INTO a New Year, I was working the dark—the
shift from six p.m. to six a.m. The golfers, Trevino and Woods,
had caught a bunny in an apartment building at Broadway and
Dickson. Some hopper caught the hiv—the HIV virus—and
decided to hang himself instead of waiting for the disease to take
him. Don't hear much about the virus anymore, the celebrities
who schooled the country on it have long moved on to their next
cause, but it's still out there, killing people by the thousands,
mostly hoppers—heroin addicts—sharing needles, exchanging
sex for dope, etc.

A bunny was what we called a TGC, for *TV Guide* Cross-
word, and before that, a slam dunk. I can't remember how or

why we started calling them bunnies, but for the past year or two, any homicide that could be solved at the scene—a frozen homeless guy, a hopper hanging himself—was a bunny. Maybe the *TV Guide* Crosswords had gotten tougher.

So with the golfers out, I was next up. I say I instead of we because my partner at the time, Roland Park, was out with the flu. Every year, Roland gets a flu shot sometime in November, and within a month or so, he's in bed with the flu. I've never had a flu shot in my life and can count on one hand the times I've had the bug.

The call came in at just after one a.m. I was finishing up some pork fried rice from Mr. Lu's I'd found in the Homicide fridge—probably about the worst Chinese food in town, maybe even the Midwest. But it was the middle of the night, it was cold, and I was hungry.

Female DB. Delmar and Jefferson.

Usually it's an address. This simply said Delmar and Jefferson. A corner I knew well.

A couple of months before, just before Thanksgiving, I had been at an insurance place on Jefferson getting one of those umbrella policies for my home and car. Roland had dropped me off—I was going to walk to the office. I stepped outside the State Farm doors and found it had started to rain while I was signing papers and staring at fake wood paneling. I glanced around, hoping Roland had seen the rain and doubled back. Nope. It had been my idea to walk, and he was going to let me walk.

I pulled up the collar of my London Fog coat, started to cross Jefferson, heading for Clark, when something—to this day I don't know what—made me look north up Jefferson. There was a hot-dog cart on the corner of Jefferson and Delmar, the escaping steam mixed with the rain giving the image a surreal glow. And there, in the center of this gray, rainy, ethereal scene, was a girl.

Spinning.

Her arms were outstretched, her head was back, looking up into the rain, and she was spinning.

I'd been a cop for sixteen years, a Homicide detective for nine. I'd seen my share of craziness, and it would usually take a helluva lot more than spinning in the rain to blip my radar. But I suddenly found myself turning ninety degrees and walking up Jefferson through the rain.

As I neared the cart and the smell of bratwurst and onions, I realized that the girl—a rain-soaked blond bob, high cheeks, soft lips with a slight overbite—was not a customer but the proprietor of this cart.

She stopped spinning and said, "Hey, you," like we'd known each other for years. Looked to be in her early twenties but had the effervescent spirit of a toddler. I responded to her greeting with an eye blink, stunned silent by I don't know what. The friendliness so uncharacteristic of downtown? The brazen disregard for warmth or dryness?

She said, "Should've grabbed you an umbrella policy while you were in there, huh?" and then she laughed.

With her eyes.

A throaty chuckle followed a perfect smile, but it was her eyes that laughed. Blue eyes. Light blue. People call it ice blue, though I've never seen ice that color.

"Excuse me?" I managed, now wondering if she'd been in the insurance office and somehow my great detective skills had missed her.

She laughed and said, "You came out of the State Farm place down there, right? It looked like you did. I was making a joke. Insurance places sell umbrella policies, and you're out here without an umbrella. Hello? Is this thing on?" And there was the laugh again.

"Oh. Yeah. Right," I said. "Actually, I did get an umbrella policy, but they forgot to give me the umbrella." I was so witty.

"Bastards," she said, and her eyes laughed, lighting up the gray day.

"Dog lover?" she asked next.

She must have seen the confusion on my face because then she added, "I got dogs, brats, and Polish sausage. You look like a dog lover."

"Yeah. A dog would be great," I said, despite the fact that Roland Park and I had devoured a full breakfast not more than an hour before.

Her tongs grabbed a juicy link and flipped it end over end into a bun. She Grouchoed her eyebrows up and down, mocking her own talent with the tongs.

"You must be a professional" was the wittiest thing I could come up with.

"Not anymore," she said without missing a beat. "I went pro for a few years, but the hotels and groupies took their toll. I got back my amateur status last spring. Now I just do it for the love."

I took the hot dog and a coffee, paid her, and, as she handed over my change, managed, "So you like to spin in the rain."

"Don't you?" she asked, then proceeded to give me a three-hundred-sixty-degree turn. "Spinning is good for the soul. Especially when it rains. Come on, try it."

I watched her throw her head back and let the sky shower down on her flawless face, eyes wide open.

"Shouldn't you close your eyes when you do that?"

"I never close my eyes," she said. "I don't want to miss anything."

I realized—she wasn't crazy. She was happy.

"I think my spinning days are over."

"Why?" she asked, still turning circles.

"Too old."

"Oh, yeah. I'm too old too. I've been too old for years. Sucks, doesn't it?"

"How old are you?" I asked, sure I was about to be labeled a dirty old man.

"Nineteen. You?"

"More than nineteen."

"Ah, you're like my aunt. Major hang-up about her age."

"Forty-two," I confessed.

She stopped spinning and said, "Holy crap!" Then her eyes, her whole body, laughed. "Just kidding. Forty-two isn't old. No age is old unless you feel old."

"I feel pretty old sometimes."

"You should spin more."

My cell phone rang. It was Roland, asking me if I wanted him to come and get me. I said no, told him I was on my way in.

"Boss want you back at work?" she asked.

"No, my partner."

She looked me up and down, laughed, and said, "Must be a cop. If you were a lawyer, you'd have an umbrella."

I stuck out my hand and said, "Jim Dandridge. Detective."

"Kayla Lightfoot. Spinning dog flipper of Delmar and Jefferson."

My hand covered hers. I'm a little over six feet and a lot over two hundred pounds. She was maybe five-two or -three and barely over a hundred pounds, including the rain. I let go of her hand, and there was a moment—couldn't have been more than a second or two—where I just stared into those laughing eyes.

The rain fell harder, and she said, "Your dog's getting wet. And I don't mean that the way it sounds." She laughed, then turned to a pair of city workers who had walked up to her cart.

Between Thanksgiving and Christmas, I probably ate about six hot dogs a week. Kayla Lightfoot was always there, smiling, spinning, and laughing. She told me about her love of jazz— introduced to her by her aunt—and her favorites, Cannonball Adderley and Louis Armstrong. She asked my opinion *as a cop*

about her theory that if more people listened to the Cannonball Adderley Quintet and Louis Armstrong, there would be less
crime. I agreed.

"So, if you like Cannonball, you must like Miles and
Coltrane."

"Who?"

"You know Cannonball Adderley, but you don't know who
Miles Davis is?"

It was the only time I'd ever seen the light go out of her eyes.
But as quickly as it went out, the light reappeared, and she was
going on and on about Louis Armstrong and his amazing voice,
and how, if you really looked around, it *is* a wonderful world.

————

IT WAS RAINING as I drove up Clark to Jefferson. Typical St.
Louis January—twenty degrees and snow last week, forty-five
and rain this. I saw the familiar hot-dog cart as I climbed out of
my Impala. The rain was the same drizzling rain like the day I'd
met her, but there was no steam coming from the cart. I remembered her telling me that, even though most vendors shut down
after dark, she stays out until ten or later because "You never
know when someone's been working late, had no time to eat, and
just needs a dog."

Kayla Lightfoot's arms were outstretched like I'd seen so many
times. Her face was again looking straight up into the rain. But
she wasn't spinning.

And her eyes weren't laughing.

Her body was sprawled next to the cart, half in, half out of
the street. Her legs were up on the sidewalk, her torso hanging
across the curb, her head and shoulders on the asphalt of Delmar
Boulevard. I don't know how long I stared at her. Eventually, one
of the two patrol officers that were there put his hand on my arm
and asked if I was okay.

"Sure," I told him, not taking my eyes off Kayla's open, lifeless light-blue eyes. "Yeah, sure."

"We haven't checked for ID," he said. "Didn't want to touch the body, fuck up your crime scene."

"Her name's Kayla Lightfoot," I said. I knelt down and looked at what appeared to be a fairly deep stab wound, running about four or five inches up the right side of her abdomen. "Where's all the blood?"

I must have said it out loud because the patrolman offered, "Probably washed down the gutter there. You know, on account of the rain."

I sprang up. "I want a fucking crime-scene perimeter. From the insurance office down on Jefferson all the way to there. Now!"

The patrolmen shared a glance and moved off. I looked back down at Kayla. She was wearing those cargo-type pants she favored—the ones that sit so low on the hips, you think they can't possibly stay on. She had on a white turtleneck—same one she'd worn four days ago—but where was her jacket?

I looked around the cart. Nothing. She always had that thing on. Said it was from . . . where? Eddie Bauer? L.L.Bean? One of those types of places. It was lavender. Quilted. Hooded, with a strip of fake white fur around the edge. Said her aunt gave it to her. My detective mind kicked in. Was she killed for the jacket? A homeless person, maybe.

I looked up and down Jefferson, then Delmar. Visibility was lousy because of the rain. Was there a homeless person wearing Kayla's jacket right now? Sitting in some doorway, all warm and cozy, using the rain to wash off their knife blade?

I yelled at the patrolmen to call in more officers. I called the Homicide Squad and said I needed every available body. I wanted the area saturated with cops. Roust every homeless person they can find. Question anyone and everyone within a five-mile radius.

It would be days before I realized how unprofessional and just plain ridiculous I had appeared at the scene.

My lieutenant was a tall, wiry black man named Arthur Kincaid. He had twenty-four years in, the last three as one of the two lieutenants in Homicide. He was a good loot. Knew how to balance the cop work with the administrative and political bullshit that goes with wearing a bar on your collar. He had the respect of his men and the confidence of the brass. Lieutenant Kincaid showed up at the scene around four thirty.

He looked at the huge perimeter that I'd had patrol tape off. He took in the number of radio cars—five—parked in the area. He knew I had called Homicide and requested more men because he was the one who had told me no. He had sent Trevino and Woods to help me when they returned from their bunny—around three—and now he was here, wanting to know just what the hell all the fuss was about.

"She worked this hot-dog cart," I told Kincaid. "Somebody gutted her for no reason."

The lieutenant looked at me a moment before asking, "How do you know there wasn't a reason?"

I blinked. "Well, there's no sign of robbery. Her cart's still here, everything's in it, including her wallet, her DL, and sixteen dollars."

"Maybe the doer was expecting more of a take?"

"She had a jacket," I said, and watched Kincaid's dark eyes widen a touch. "I know her, Loot. Used to buy dogs from her on the way in to work."

"You live in Belleville," he said, probably thinking I must pass five or six similar carts that weren't out of the way like this one. I decided not to respond. He moved on to other matters, asking me about the need for all the manpower. I embarrassed myself by saying the first twenty-four hours after a murder was the best time to catch the doer.

"Yeah, I've heard that," he said. "Are you good for this, Dandridge? Is there anything about your relationship with the vic I should be aware of?"

"I didn't have a relationship, Lieutenant. I just bought hot dogs from her."

He gazed at me a few more seconds, then got into his Crown Vic and drove off. The golfers walked up. Jerry Trevino was a few inches shorter but must have had forty pounds on me. He spent every off-hour in the gym, trying to compensate for his lack of height. Albert Woods used to delight in people telling him he looked like Denzel Washington. But in the last few years, he had taken up golf, started wearing only clothing with a Nike Swoosh on it and talking about how he was distantly related to Tiger Woods. Few of us believed him.

"We did what canvas we could," Trevino said. "This hour, this weather, not much more than a couple of homeless."

"Couldn't you and Park have handled this one?" Woods asked.

"Park's got the flu," I said.

"Oh, yeah. January."

I thanked them for their help and let them get on home.

I looked down at Kayla's body again. I tried to hear her laugh, but all I could hear was the rain.

———

THE CRIME-SCENE TECHS had found nothing at the scene. They said there were so many prints on the hot-dog cart, it'd be impossible to get through them all. I had originally argued to lift any and all regardless of how many but came to my senses quickly. I spent hours at the corner of Delmar and Jefferson, asking every passerby if they knew the girl who worked the hot-dog cart there. I took down the name and address of anyone who said yes, mostly city workers and a few businessmen.

I ran every person who said they'd bought dogs from Kayla through the system. Nothing jumped out at me, but that didn't mean one of them hadn't killed her. I wanted to bring each one of them in, put them in the box, and make them talk. Lieutenant Kincaid nixed that idea—told me they weren't suspects simply because they admitted to buying a hot dog from the victim. I knew that. Kincaid suggested that if I really felt the need to speak with all of them, I should go to them, do some casual interviews.

Roland Park showed up around eight on the second night, carrying a box of Kleenex. Said he was feeling better. I brought him up to speed on the case. He blew his nose and said, "Booking some OT, sporto?" referring to the fact that I had been working right through the day shift.

"I didn't put in for it."

"Why the hell not?"

"I don't know," I said. "Just never occurred to me."

Roland squinted his Korean-American eyes at me and laughed, which turned into a cough. "So where are we?"

"Nowhere. I'm about to head over for the autopsy. Want to come?"

"Nah. My stomach ain't ready for a young girl's autopsy. Where are we on the Rickards thing?"

Rickards was the name of a shooting victim we had caught a couple of nights before. A young kid from England, he'd gotten into a beef with a bartender who refused to serve him and, in the ensuing brawl, wound up with a bullet in his head. Though there were more than a dozen witnesses, no one saw the shooter. It was one of three active cases when I caught Kayla's murder.

"Supposedly the bartender's sister is back in town," I said.

"You go to the cut, I'll work the sister," Roland said, then sneezed three times.

I nodded and left.

The medical examiner told me that Kayla Lightfoot was killed with a serrated blade, not unlike certain steak knives. Approximately four and a half inches long. She managed to find some microscopic filings from the blade that had lodged inside Kayla as the killer twisted and turned the knife.

The ME went on to say that the killer was most likely right-handed, had grabbed Kayla from behind, and had stuck her in her right side, between her kidney and oblique muscles.

The ME continued, but I didn't hear the rest. I was staring at Kayla—now laid out on a stainless-steel table, her eyes closed.

I was glad she was missing this.

I leaned down and kissed her forehead. "I'll find him," I whispered.

"What was that?" the ME asked.

"Nothing," I said, and walked out.

———

AFTER MY THIRD day with almost no sleep, after I had requested that Lieutenant Kincaid put me back on day shift, after Roland Park and I had a shouting match in the middle of the squad room over my wanting to go to every restaurant in St. Louis and check what type of steak knives they use, I was sitting in the lieutenant's office. He stared at me, palming his Ozzie Smith autographed baseball, the ink fading from the constant rubbing by his waxy brown fingers.

"You need to come correct, Dandridge."

"I don't know what you mean."

He set the baseball down and leaned forward. "Were you sleeping with this girl? This Lightfoot?"

"No, sir."

"Were you doing anything with her? Was she doing anything with you? To you? Hot dogs and blow jobs to start the day?"

"No, sir."

"Then what the hell is it? Your partner says you're ignoring your other cases, you two are fighting in the squad room, you're spending fifteen hours a day on this thing and *not* putting in for any OT. Something ain't right."

I looked out his window. Down on the street was a hot-dog vendor closing up for the night. "I met her back around Thanksgiving. Nothing between us. No sex, nothing. She was just . . ." I searched my mind for the right words. "She was just decent. Not a jaded bone in her body."

"And a tight little body she had," Kincaid said, letting me know he didn't believe there was nothing going on. "You need to put this case in the proper order and the proper perspective. Innocent girls get killed in this city every day. Sometimes we put them down, sometimes we don't.

"You got the shit luck that night and caught one that can't be put down." He picked up the baseball again. "Don't let it consume you. You've had a nice, solid clearance rate since I've been here. One of the better ones. But we all get these now and then. The ones we have to just chalk up to 'shit happens.'

"I've been there, I know how much it sucks when the golfers are catching bunny after bunny, and you and Park keep catching these twisters."

Kincaid went on to say, "If you need a break, a little time, let me know. But you're too good, Dandridge, for me to let you go back to the day shift. It'll all cycle around, but meantime you gotta work the dark like all of us."

"I just need the days—I have to run down all the restaurants, restaurant-supply stores. I'm trying to track down this aunt of Kayla's—"

"First of all, Park told me about this restaurant goose chase. That's bullshit, Detective. And second, who the hell is Kayla?"

"Kayla Lightfoot. The victim we're sitting here talking about."

He gave me another long look, then said, "Get back to work. And remember, you got people watching you now. Don't fuck up."

———

I FOUND KAYLA'S aunt living in a trailer park about twenty minutes north of the city. If it was the same Shawna Lightfoot, then she was about as different from Kayla as homicide is from shoplifting. A pop for prostitution, two for drunk driving, another for carrying a controlled substance.

Shawna Lightfoot was outside her trailer, stuffing a plastic trash bag into a metal can when I walked up. Despite the cold, she was in short shorts, sandals, and a severely faded long-sleeved T-shirt with the Harley-Davidson insignia on it. I showed her my shield, and she scoffed.

"That asshole Mooney give you a line of bullshit about me not checking in?" she said, then coughed. It was a nasty cough, a smoker's cough, not a sickness cough.

"Who's Mooney?" I asked.

"Yeah, right," she said. "My fucking PO. Guy's a stiff prick with the clap."

This was the aunt that taught Kayla about Cannonball Adderley and Louis Armstrong?

I told her I didn't know Mooney and wasn't there for any parole violations. I said I was there about Kayla. The second she heard the name, her whole demeanor changed.

"Oh, God. Come inside."

She led me into a double-wide that smelled of cheese, marijuana, and must. She grabbed an armful of laundry off a sofa that had lost its springs years ago. "Sit," she said.

I took a seat on one of two bar stools next to a Formica counter that held a saucepan with remnants of macaroni and cheese, a few cans of beer, and a photo of Kayla next to her hot-dog cart.

I picked up the photo without thinking. There was the face, the laughing eyes.

"She brought that to me this Christmas," Shawna said, balancing on the edge of the dilapidated sofa. "Last time I saw her. Please tell me she's not in trouble again."

I stared at the photo. "Trouble?" I said distantly.

"Come on, don't do the cop bullshit. Just tell me. Did she get fucked up again? Hurt herself? Crash a car? What?"

Finally, I managed to pull my eyes away from the picture and said, "Kayla was murdered five days ago."

Shawna Lightfoot sank into the sofa. She didn't cry or scream or say anything. She just sank. Physically. Emotionally.

"Do you know anyone who would want to do her harm?"

Shawna Lightfoot looked at me for what seemed like hours. Then she said, "You knew her, didn't you?"

"Yes."

"Do you know anyone who'd want to do her harm?"

"No."

Shawna nodded, then wrapped her spindly arms around herself. She began to rock slowly.

I don't know how long it was before I said, "Kayla told me you introduced her to jazz. Gave her that purple coat from L.L.Bean."

"Lands' End," she corrected. "Found it at TJ Maxx." A smile seemed to be fighting to make its way out of her mouth. "What else did she tell you?"

"She said you had a hang-up about your age."

She laughed, and with it came tears. Lots of tears.

"I tried so hard. So hard to keep her from being like me. The last thing in the world I wanted was for her to end up like me."

Over the next hour, Shawna Lightfoot told me about Kayla never knowing who her father was, about her mother—Shawna's older sister—being a meth dealer and user who got Kayla drunk at age nine, gave her her first joint at ten, and, during one three-day meth binge, told twelve-year-old Kayla that if she didn't get out of her house, she would kill her in her sleep.

Kayla ran off, was gone for months. Eventually, Shawna got a phone call—Kayla was in the hospital, having her stomach pumped of Jim Beam. Kayla had told the doctors that Shawna was her mother. That's when Shawna took her in. Even though Shawna was a hooker and a drunk, she knew that her sister was worse, and she knew there was something special about Kayla. Something worth saving.

She told me how she had no idea how to raise a kid, so she watched movies to learn. Said that it seemed like the people who were the happiest in movies were always listening to jazz. Shawna had never heard jazz in her life. But she went to the library and checked out two jazz records. The Cannonball Adderley Quintet and Louis Armstrong.

"It was alphabetical, you know? I just grabbed the first two in the bin."

That's how one knows about Adderley but not Davis.

She told me she brought them home and played them for Kayla over and over. Kayla loved them. Stopped listening to other music. Just fell in love with the jazz. Said Kayla memorized the lyrics to every Armstrong song and would even sing along to Adderley's instrumentals, making up her own lyrics.

"I still have them. I never took them back to the library. Sometimes I pull them out for kicks, you know? And I can still hear Kayla singing."

"So, Kayla sobered up?" I asked, still not comprehending how the girl I'd met could have had the life being described.

"Oh, yeah. She just needed love. She had so much love inside her, she just needed it pulled out. I guess the movies were right—jazz makes you happy."

"I think it was you, Shawna."

She started to cry again.

I got her a beer from the fridge. As I closed the door, I glanced into the sink. Saw a serrated steak knife. Shawna was lost on the sofa. I pocketed the blade, keeping as much of my prints off it as possible.

I handed Shawna the beer. She said she hardly drank anymore. She had made such a point not to have alcohol around while Kayla lived there.

"When did she move out?"

"After she graduated high school. First one in our fucked-up family to do that!"

She told me how she had made Kayla go to school. Made her study. Told her she could go to college if she could get a scholarship. But Kayla didn't want to go to college. When she graduated high school, she got a job. To pay back Shawna.

"Pay me back," Shawna said. "Little did she know, I owed her."

"I went to her address," I said. "The little place over off Kingshighway. Talked to some neighbors. No one seemed to really know her."

Shawna took a long pull from the bottle, wiped her eyes, and said, "Yeah, well, it ain't the greatest area. But she was so proud of having a place. So proud of herself. You're probably wondering how she could afford it, right? Outta high school, working a fucking hot-dog cart."

I nodded. "The guy, the landlord, was a former customer of mine. Know what I mean?"

"Yes."

"He gave her a great deal. He lives right above, gave her rent at half-price, long as every now and then, he gets a freebie from me, you know? Kayla never knew."

I nodded. "Did you and Kayla ever fight? Ever have problems?"

"No," she said, taking another pull. "We were best friends. I mean, in the beginning, she got pissed now and then. Called me a hypocrite, you know? 'Cuz I wouldn't let her do stuff I did. But once she got clean, we never had a problem. It was like having a daughter of my own. She was *my* daughter, more than she was my sister's."

I let her cry for a while. Thought about the blade in my pocket.

Shawna asked, "Do you know who did it?"

"Not yet."

"Do you know why?"

Why?

In my years as a detective, I'd come to learn that why was overrated. How plus why equals who is an old and outdated theory of police work. I learned long ago that why doesn't matter.

———

"Very likely" was the answer the ME gave me about the knife from Shawna's trailer. I literally ran up the steps of the station, took the stairs instead of waiting for the elevators, and burst into the Homicide squad room.

"I got her!" I yelled to Roland Park.

"Who?"

"Kayla Lightfoot's murderer."

My partner's face dropped. He shared a glance with the golfers. Kincaid stepped out of his office when he heard me yell. They all just stared at me.

I held up the baggy containing the knife. "The murder weapon," I proclaimed. "Her fucking aunt did it."

"Why?" asked Roland.

"Why? I have no idea why. Who cares? I've got her drunk, hooking ass." I bounced over to Kincaid. "Lieutenant, I want to bring the bitch in, put her in the box, and break her. She did it. She had the knife sitting right there in the sink!"

"The medical examiner called me, Detective," Kincaid said, his voice quiet and slow. "Said she told you it was a likely match based on type of blade, but the filings didn't necessarily match up."

" 'Very likely' is what she said. 'Very.' And the filings—there could be any number of reasons why they don't match."

"Like it ain't the right blade," Roland said.

"Detective Dandridge," Kincaid said. "Step into my office."

Kincaid picked up his baseball but didn't sit down. When I closed the door, he said, "Look in that mirror."

He had a small mirror on the back of his door. I looked.

"Yeah?"

"What do you see?"

"Lieutenant, we don't have time for this. We gotta grab up—"

"I see a burned-out cop. Look at your eyes. You haven't slept in how long? You haven't shaved since God knows when, which, by the way, is a departmental infraction."

"I'll sleep when I put this one down."

"You'll sleep today. I'm suspending you for a week."

"What? You can't. I've got the fucking murder weapon."

"I'll have Park and the golfers run it down. Question the aunt. If anything's there, we'll bring her in."

"No, they'll fuck it up. They don't care about her."

"About who?"

"Kayla!"

That was it. I put myself in the jackpot with that line. Maybe I could have talked my way out of the suspension before that.

————

I CALLED ROLAND Park's cell phone every day from my house. After three days, he returned my call.

"Got some interesting news for you, sporto," he said.

"You nailed her."

"No. The aunt's got a pretty solid alibi for the night of the murder. She was doing what she does best. But one of her johns, this guy who was renting the apartment to the vic, seems as though he had a little extracurricular whatnot going on with your honey. Me and Woods figure maybe he snatched one of Auntie's steak knives from her place at some point. Sound good?"

I hung up and left my house without locking the door. I don't know how fast I drove, but I was at Kayla's apartment in less than twenty minutes. I passed her door and took the stairs two at a time to the landlord's apartment.

He lives right above her.

I drew my gun and badge, and knocked. A small Hispanic man in his fifties opened the door, keeping the chain on.

"Yes?"

"Detective Dandridge, St. Louis PD. Are you the landlord of this building?"

"*Sí.* Yes. What's going on?"

"May I come in, sir?"

He closed the door and removed the chain. As he opened it again, I pushed inside, bringing my weapon up into his face.

"On the floor, now!"

"What is happening?" he said.

I spun him around, pushed him down, dropped a knee in his back, and began to cuff him.

"You're under arrest for suspicion of murder. What is your name?"

"What!"

"Name! *Nombre!* What is your name?"

"Edgar. Edgar Pablos. What is this? What did I do?"

I cuffed him and lifted him off the ground. Pushed him over and sat him down in a chair.

I found her jacket in his bathroom, along with some photos.

Shots of Kayla, obviously on the roof of the building, sunbathing. She wasn't nude, had a tiny bikini on, but there were close-ups of her breasts and crotch area, and there wasn't any doubt that she had no idea the photos were being snapped.

I had bloodied Edgar Pablos's face and was breaking his fingers when Roland Park and the golfers entered. As they yanked me off him, I heard someone screaming, "Why?" over and over.

It was me.

———

MY FIRING WAS official a month after the arrest of Edgar Pablos. The evidence, trace and circumstantial, was overwhelming. No doubt he killed Kayla. But my conduct, the subsequent lawsuit, and a good defense lawyer helped him go free.

There's another hot-dog vendor at Delmar and Jefferson these days. I don't go much anymore. Mostly I just stay at home, listening to Louis Armstrong sing about skies of blue and clouds of white. And what a wonderful world it is.

WINNING

BY ALAFAIR BURKE

Let me tell him for you, Jenny. You stay here and rest. I'll bring Greg in after—when he's thought it over a bit."

Jenny didn't have the energy to tell her partner, Officer Wayne Harvey, that there was nothing restful about lying in a hospital bed ten minutes after the completion of a rape kit. Thirty minutes after ingesting the morning-after pill and an HIV postexposure prophylaxis. Sixty minutes since the arrest. Three hours since the rape. That was her best guess—three hours, since it started, at least.

Talking to Greg would help her stop feeling this way that she didn't want to feel anymore. Weak. Embarrassed. Broken. She was ready to feel like herself again. Until the DA needed her testimony, she was finished with her duties as a crime victim. If she talked to Greg, she might feel more like Jenny. She would be the arresting police officer, delivering the news as gently as possible to the victim's family. She would also be his wife.

"No, Wayne. Go on home to Marcy. Just tell the nurse to get Greg for me."

Through the open slats of the drawn blinds in her room, she saw Greg talking to a young woman with bright-pink scrubs and a blond ponytail. She knew both this process and her husband well enough that she thought she could actually make out some of the words. *Your wife is ready for visitors now, Mr. Sutton.* Greg looking worried still. Asking her something. Something like *What happened? Was there an accident?* The nurse looking down at her hands, wishing there was a chart or a clipboard—some prop there to employ as a distraction. *Your wife needs you now. There's nothing more I can say.*

Greg opened the door and closed it gently behind him.

"You okay, baby? They won't tell me what's going on. Something happened on the sting?"

Jenny was one of two female patrol officers under the age of thirty-five working for the Missoula County Sheriff's Department. Tonight she was the one tapped to work as a prostitution decoy at the truck stops along I-90. She loved the job but not this assignment. Half-naked in the bitter wind, the cold, dry air freezing the insides of her nostrils while an unwashed trucker eyed her over so she could negotiate an agreement of sex for money. But once the nasty part was over, it was easy. It was supposed to be easy. *Drive around back, hon, and I'll meet you there.* Then the supporting officers would take him down. That's the way it was supposed to go.

She patted the edge of the sterile blanket covering the bed, and Greg sat next to her. She held his hand. "I'm okay. A hundred percent. You understand?"

Her husband nodded, and some of the tension fell from his face.

"A dark-green Bronco pulled in, not a truck-driving kind of truck, you know, but a regular Bronco, so he could maneuver better in the lot. Wayne was watching me just fine, but I wound up at the passenger side instead of the driver's. I made the deal."

"What's up, sweet thang?" Just looking for a date. *"How much will that run me?"* Twenty for a suck. Forty for straight sex. Fifty

gets you half-and-half. I'm worth every penny. "Well, all right, then. That last one should get us started." *Just pull around back and I'll meet you; sometimes the cops watch from the road.*

"So I told him to drive around back. It happened fast, but he pulled me into the car. He took me to a house out by Nine Mile Road, not far from the highway. He . . . he assaulted me, Greg, but I got away. I arrested him. Wayne came out and made sure the guy got processed just right. No technicalities for the courts."

"What do you mean, he assaulted you? You mean he—"

She looked him straight in the eye. Not one tear. Not even a quiver. "It was a sexual assault." *He raped me, Greg. And despite that look on your face, it was far worse than what you're imagining. So bad, I got to figure out a way for you never to know the details.*

Greg stood, leaving Jenny on her own in the bed. "I don't understand. How could they let this happen to you? How'd he get you out of that parking lot?"

"He sped right on out to the road. By the time Wayne got to his car, I guess a truck pulled in. The other guys were around back. It wasn't anyone's fault. It happened real fast, Greg." *No, it didn't.* "I'm all right."

"Where was your gun?"

"I can't carry when I'm a decoy." Underneath the tight outfits she wore undercover, the bulge of Jenny's Glock was as prominent as a road sign. "I guess we'll have to rethink the clothing in the future."

"You think that's funny?"

"I'll take humor anywhere I can find it right now."

"You couldn't fight him off? You're a cop. I've seen how strong you are."

"He was the one with the gun. I was lucky to get it away from him when I did, but the point was to come out alive." *I got my chance when he reached for the Vaseline on his dresser. He told me he needed it to get his fist where it would hurt me most. He kept his left hand on me while he reached with his gun hand. That's how he lost his balance.* "All I was focused on was getting out alive and getting back to you."

Greg's face was angry and injured at once. He worked his hands into claws while he paced the small room. "Baby, I'm sorry this happened to you. I can work more hours at the mill—"

"You work plenty." Jenny took her husband's hand and smiled up at him, hoping he'd see her face past the bruises that were starting to color. "How many times have you heard me say I'd keep working even if we hit the lotto?"

Greg helped Jenny change into the fresh clothes he'd been told to bring to the hospital. He even thought to take along his fleece-lined corduroy rancher's jacket for her, the one she loved to wear. When the nurse insisted she be wheeled to the exit, he did the honors. He even kept her mind busy in the truck on the way home to Lolo, making the antics down at the pulp mill sound like slapstick, the way he always did.

In their bed at home, though, with the lights off and with his back to her, he asked the question she knew he'd been thinking all along: "Why didn't you kill him, Jenny? When you got the gun from him, why didn't you do it?"

She gave him the answer she'd been working on since the hospital. "It wouldn't have been right. And I would've known it. And so I wouldn't have been the same person ever again. All the rest of it, I can get past."

Greg didn't speak to her again that night. If he ever turned to face her, Jenny didn't notice. Instead, she slept clenching Sushi, the stuffed purple goldfish that Greg won for her throwing rings at their first county fair together, the summer before they got married. *I told you I'd never let you down.* That's what he said when he won Sushi for her.

THE NEXT DAY, Greg called in sick so he could stay with Jenny. Everything might have been different if he'd gone to the mill. The phone rang around three in the afternoon. Jenny answered. It was Anne Lawson, one of the deputy county prosecutors. Jenny knew her pretty well from testifying in a few of her cases. She was tough but fair and always treated people with respect, even the defendants she imprisoned.

"You feeling a little better today, Jenny?"

"A hundred percent. Thanks." Greg walked past her and patted her arm. It was the first time she'd felt his skin against hers since he helped her from the truck last night.

"You did real good getting out of there alive. And it's a good case. We're gonna get him. No plea bargaining either. I'll carry the file myself through to trial."

"Thanks, Anne."

"Hey, you got a second?"

"Sure."

"We had the arraignment this morning in front of Judge Parker. And the bail hearing."

"Oh, yeah?" Greg was watching her now, concerned. She shouldn't have let the tone of her voice say so much.

"Yeah. He's got Rick Deaver representing him." Jenny knew him too. He was a decent public defender, a straight shooter as far as those guys went. "Anyway, we went for a no-bail hold. We thought we had a good shot."

"Did Judge Parker know it was me?" Jenny testified in his courtroom last year against a man who locked his wife in a closet for two days after she forgot to buy barbecue potato chips at the market. Parker said she did a good job getting the wife to cooperate with the Sheriff's Department. Jenny found out later that Parker told the prosecuting attorney the woman should have killed the SOB and called it a day.

"He said afterward to tell you he's sorry about what happened. But he also said there was more threat of witness intimidation with civilians. I pushed really hard, Jenny. I said your being a cop obviously didn't stop him from—"

"What'd it get set at?"

"Two hundred thousand."

"Does he own that place out near Nine Mile?"

"He inherited it from his aunt about eight years ago. It's not much to look at, but with all that land, and the way prices have gone up—"

"How long's something like that take? If he puts up the house?"

"He doesn't even have to use a bank. A bail bondsman will have him out in a few hours. I'm real sorry, Jenny."

"Not your fault. I appreciate the call."

The sound of glass shattering against the kitchen tile broke the silence that filled Jenny's head as she hung up the phone. She looked up to see Greg's juice glass scattered on the floor across the room, red V8 oozing into the grouted cracks.

"Am I supposed to clean that up?"

"Of course not." Greg began plucking at the shards of glass.

"Be careful with that." Jenny kneeled to help, but Greg pushed her hand away. "What exactly did I do wrong here? Why are you so angry at me?"

"I'm not angry at you," Greg insisted. "I'm angry at him. I'm angry at everything else. I'm angry because I'm a human being. What I can't figure out is you. How can you be so damn calm about all this?"

"You think I'm calm inside? You think my mind is peaceful today? You have no idea. It's because of what's inside me that I don't have the energy for outbursts. I don't have the luxury of a temper tantrum. What you're going through is natural, but it's not about me."

"Damn it, Jenny. Don't you see what's going on here? He's getting away with it. He did this to you, and nothing's happening. He's winning."

Jenny sat cross-legged on the floor beside her husband as he sopped up the remaining spill with a towel. "You and me, we've got different ideas about winning. You think the only way to walk out of a fight a winner is to beat the other man down. That's how men talk about fighting, right? Only a loser runs away. It's not like that for us. We win by getting away. We win by staying alive. This happened to me, Greg, and it's my right to say I won. I got away, and he didn't."

"I'm not stupid. I know why Anne called. He's getting bail."

"You know what? B . . . F . . . D. He buys himself a couple of months of freedom, but soon enough he'll be pulling a dime at Deer Lodge, and we're still us. In the meantime, you can bet that Wayne and the other boys will make sure that if he so much as jaywalks, his bail will get pulled."

She smiled at him, but Greg shook his head and walked to the sink. He wrung the towel beneath the faucet, watching a pink stream of water circle the drain. "It's not enough."

ONE WEEK LATER, Greg went back to the pulp mill. Jenny was still on leave and used the day to prepare Greg's favorite supper, grilled steak and fettuccine alfredo. Three hours after Greg's shift ended, the steaks were dry, black bricks in the oven, and the noodles were glued together in a clump. An hour after that, the phone rang. Jenny answered and heard her husband's heavy breaths in her ear.

"Greg? Greg, what happened?"

"Oh, Jesus. I . . . I don't know what to do. I . . . there's blood everywhere. It's all over my clothes. If I get in the truck—"

Jenny was already in the bedroom, opening the top drawer of her dresser. "My gun. My service weapon? The ballistics are on file. What did you do? What did you do?"

"I'm so sorry."

Jenny held the top of her head with her free hand, like that might literally help her collect her thoughts. "Are you cut? Did he touch you?"

"No. I didn't let him near me."

"So the blood's all his?"

"There's a lot of it. It sprayed or something."

"Have you stepped in it? Are there footprints?"

The pause felt like an eternity. "No. Some got on the tops of the boots, not the bottoms."

"All right. Keep it that way. Don't step in any blood. Your clothes. There's an attached garage there, Greg. And a tarp. I saw a blue tarp on the ground for painting." Jenny peered through the bedroom curtains. It was still snowing. That was good. "Stand on the tarp and strip off anything that's got blood. Put the gun in there too. Wrap it all up, and be careful. Wipe down anything you might have touched. Doorknobs, door frames, stairwells—"

"I wore gloves. I've still got gloves on."

"Okay. Good. How'd you get in the house?"

"I knocked. I told him I was an investigator with the PD's office, sent there by Rick Deaver. He opened the door for me."

"Good. Just make sure he didn't lock the door behind him." Jenny moved through the house, collecting the things she'd need. A spray bottle of bleach. A book of matches. "Leave it unlocked, you hear? And open the windows. Are you listening to me?"

"Why—"

"Just do it. Whatever room his body's in. Open all the windows so it gets good and cold. Do you know how many times you shot him?"

"Twice."

"You sure about that?"

"Yeah, I'm sure."

She took two cartridges from the top drawer. "What phone are you calling on?"

"Um . . . oh, my God."

"It's all right. We'll deal with it. Just don't get anything from his house or his body in your truck. Okay?" What else? One of the quick-burn logs near the fireplace. Lighter fluid too. She checked the mudroom. Greg's corduroy coat was missing from its hook. That was good. She began feeding the uneaten dinner to the garbage disposal. "It's isolated out there, so you've got enough time to be careful. Don't miss anything. Wrap the tarp up tight and put it in the back of the truck. And don't forget the gun. And drive perfect. Don't get yourself pulled over in your boxer shorts."

———

BY THE TIME Greg pulled onto their road, Jenny had everything ready. She pulled her shivering husband inside and washed his shaking hands under hot water in the kitchen sink. If they analyzed for gunshot residue, Greg would not be the one to test positive.

She checked him over for any blood he might have missed on his shorts and T-shirt, on his skin, in his hair. She poured him three fingers of Bushmills, made sure he downed it, then poured him another. She undressed him and tucked him into their bed, resting the whiskey bottle on the nightstand beside him. He'd wake from nightmares and reach for it. She stroked his cold, damp hair until his breathing was steady. She picked up Sushi from her side of the bed and tucked the little fish beneath one arm of her husband's resting body, kissed his cheek, and told him she was going to be gone for a little while to get rid of the tarp of clothing. To be safe, she grabbed his T-shirt, boxers, and socks, along with the kit she'd put together. She didn't wear a coat.

She used the quick-burn log to start a fire at a campsite along I-90 near the Clark Fork River. She burned his clothes—everything but the coat—using the lighter fluid to make sure the flames consumed it all. As a precaution, she poured half the bottle of bleach on the pile of charred wood and ashes. She turned the coat inside out, rolled it into a ball, and placed it gently on her passenger seat. She sprayed the empty tarp with bleach, then folded it and tucked it into her trunk. Finally, she held her familiar pistol and added two cartridges to fill the magazine. She fired two shots into a nearby tree and tucked the gun snugly into her waistband at the small of her back.

The drive to Nine Mile wasn't easy. The snow was sticking heavily, and she made a point of taking her Escort instead of the truck that Greg drove to work. The bad memories of the last time up this road didn't help. Neither did the current situation. By the time she neared the house she never wanted to see again, whatever tracks had been made by her husband's tires had been smoothed over by a perfect layer of white. She parked her car in the driveway, took a deep breath, ran through the plan one more time, and exhaled. She was ready. She retrieved the corduroy coat and blue tarp and walked through the unlocked front door.

The house was cold from the opened windows, like Jenny wanted it. The man's body was splayed on his living room floor. Two shots, just like Greg said. One near the bottom of his gut. One in the neck. The neck shot must have hit an artery. That's what caused the splatter. The gut shot probably took him down all mangled on his side like that. Jenny was grateful her husband wasn't a better shot. With a cool head and a well-formed intention to kill, Jenny could easily plug a man squarely in the middle of the brain and heart from this range. These wayward shots would allow a different narrative.

She tiptoed over the body to pull the windows shut, making certain not to traipse through any of the blood. Within a few minutes, she could feel the room temperature rising from the wood burning stove in the corner. Then she stepped near the body again, this time placing her boots firmly in the puddle that had formed beneath the man's torso. She took a quick look. The chill had kept the body fresh enough. Time of death wouldn't pose a problem. She walked to the phone and dialed a cell phone number she knew by heart.

"Wayne Harvey."

"Wayne, it's Jenny. I need your help."

"Anything. You know that."

Then she told Wayne the story. The man called the house during dinner. He said vile things about what he'd done to her. He said he'd tell everyone in prison. Montana is small. Her days in law enforcement would be over. Greg started drinking. She was at the Nine Mile house now and needed his help. She needed Anne Lawson from the County Attorney's Office to come out too.

Jenny hung up the phone and walked to the back of the house. It felt smaller now. Used. Threadbare. Diminished in ways that she could not quite explain to herself. She sat on the man's bed and looked into the mirror above the dresser. She remembered turning her head away from that mirror a week ago so she would not have to see her reflection. Now she did not have to look away. She touched a smear of lipstick on her mouth. It made her think of blood. For just a moment, only a moment, she felt her heart quicken with a strange sense of pleasure.

FATHER'S DAY

BY MICHAEL CONNELLY

T he victim's tiny body was left alone in the emergency
room enclosure. The doctors, after halting their resus-
citation efforts, had solemnly retreated and pulled the
plastic curtains closed around the bed. The entire construction,
management, and purpose of the hospital was to prevent death.
When the effort failed, nobody wanted to see it.

The curtains were opaque. Harry Bosch looked like a ghost as
he approached and then split them to enter. He stepped into the
enclosure and stood somber and alone with the dead. The boy's
body took up less than a quarter of the big metal bed. Bosch had
worked thousands of cases, but nothing ever touched him like
the sight of a young child's lifeless body. Fifteen months old.
Cases in which the child's age was still counted in months were
the most difficult of all. He knew that if he dwelled too long, he
would start to question everything—from the meaning of life to
his mission in it.

The boy looked like he was only asleep. Bosch made a quick
study, looking for any bruising or sign of mishap. The child was
naked and uncovered, his skin as pink as a newborn's. Bosch saw
no sign of trauma except for an old scrape on the boy's forehead.

He pulled on gloves and very carefully moved the body to check it from all angles. His heart sank as he did this, but he saw nothing that was suspicious. When he was finished, he covered the body with the sheet—he wasn't sure why—and slipped back through the plastic curtains shrouding the bed.

The boy's father was in a private waiting room down the hall. Bosch would eventually get to him, but the paramedics who had transported the boy had agreed to stick around to be interviewed. Bosch looked for them first and found both men—one old, one young; one to mentor, one to learn—sitting in the crowded ER waiting room. He invited them outside so they could speak privately.

The dry summer heat hit them as soon as the glass doors parted. Like walking out of a casino in Vegas. They walked to the side so they would not be bothered, but stayed in the shade of the portico. He identified himself and told them he would need the written reports on their rescue effort as soon as they were completed.

"For now, tell me about the call."

The senior man did the talking. His name was Ticotin.

"The kid was already in full arrest when we got there," he began. "We did what we could, but the best thing was just to ice him and transport him—try to get him in here and see what the pros could do."

"Did you take a body-temperature reading at the scene?" Bosch asked.

"First thing," Ticotin said. "It was one oh six eight. So you gotta figure the kid was up around one oh eight, one oh nine, before we got there. There was no way he was going to come back from that. Not a little baby like that."

Ticotin shook his head as though he were frustrated by having been sent to rescue someone who could not be rescued. Bosch nodded as he took out his notebook and wrote down the temperature reading.

"You know what time that was?" he asked.

"We arrived at twelve seventeen, so I would say we took the BT no more than three minutes later. First thing you do. That's the protocol."

Bosch nodded again and wrote the time—12:20 p.m.—next to the temperature reading. He looked up and tracked a car coming quickly into the ER lot. It parked, and his partner, Ignacio Ferras, got out. He had gone directly to the accident scene while Bosch had gone directly to the hospital. Bosch signaled him over. Ferras walked with anxious speed. Bosch knew he had something to report, but Bosch didn't want him to say it in front of the paramedics. He introduced him and then quickly got back to his questions.

"Where was the father when you got there?"

"They had the kid on the floor by the back door, where he had brought him in. The father was sort of collapsed on the floor next to him, screaming and crying like they do. Kicking the floor."

"Did he ever say anything?"

"Not right then."

"Then when?"

"When we made the decision to transport and work on the kid in the truck, he wanted to go. We told him he couldn't. We told him to get somebody from the office to drive him."

"What were his words?"

"He just said, 'I want to go with him. I want to be with my son,' stuff like that."

Ferras shook his head as if in pain.

"At any time did he talk about what had happened?" Bosch asked.

Ticotin checked his partner, who shook his head.

"No," Ticotin said. "He didn't."

"Then how were you informed of what had happened?"

"Well, initially, we heard it from dispatch. Then one of the office workers, a lady, she told us when we got there. She led us to the back and told us along the way."

Bosch thought he had all he was going to get, but then thought of something else.

"You didn't happen to take an exterior-air-temperature reading for that spot, did you?"

The two paramedics looked at each other and then at Bosch.

"Didn't think to," Ticotin said. "But it's gotta be at least ninety-five, with the Santa Anas kicking up like this. I don't remember a June this hot."

Bosch remembered a June he had spent in a jungle, but wasn't going to get into it. He thanked the paramedics and let them get back to duty. He put his notebook away and looked at his partner.

"Okay, tell me about the scene," he said.

"We've got to charge this guy, Harry," Ferras said urgently.

"Why? What did you find?"

"It's not what I found. It's because it was just a kid, Harry. What kind of father would let this happen? How could he forget?"

Ferras had become a father for the first time six months earlier. Bosch knew this. The experience had made him a professional dad, and every Monday he came in to the squad with a new batch of photos. To Bosch, the kid looked the same week to week, but not to Ferras. He was in love with being a father, with having a son.

"Ignacio, you've got to separate your own feelings about it from the facts and the evidence, okay? You know this. Calm down."

"I know, I know. It's just that, how could he forget, you know?"

"Yeah, I know, and we're going to keep that in mind. So tell me what you found out over there. Who'd you talk to?"

"The office manager."

"And what did he say?"

"It's a lady. She said that he came in through the back door shortly after ten. All the sales agents park in the back and use the back door—that's why nobody saw the kid. The father came in, talking on the cell phone. Then he got off and asked if he'd gotten a fax, but there was no fax. So he made another call, and she heard him ask where the fax was. Then he waited for the fax."

"How long did he wait?"

"She said not long, but the fax was an offer to buy. So he called the client, and that started a whole back-and-forth with calls and faxes, and he completely forgot about the kid. It was at least two hours, Harry. Two hours!"

Bosch could almost share his partner's anger, but he had been on the mission a couple of decades longer than Ferras and knew how to hold it in when he had to and when to let it go.

"Harry, something else too."

"What?"

"The baby had something wrong with him."

"The manager saw the kid?"

"No, I mean, always. Since birth. She said it was a big tragedy. The kid was handicapped. Blind, deaf, a bunch of things wrong. Fifteen months old, and he couldn't walk or talk and never could even crawl. He just cried a lot."

Bosch nodded as he tried to plug this information into everything else he knew and had accumulated. Just then, another car came speeding into the parking lot. It pulled into the ambulance chute in front of the ER doors. A woman leaped out and ran into the ER, leaving the car running and the door open.

"That's probably the mother," Bosch said. "We better get in there."

Bosch started trotting toward the ER doors, and Ferras followed. They went through the ER waiting room and down a hallway, where the father had been placed in a private room to wait.

As Bosch got close, he did not hear any screaming or crying or fists on flesh—things that wouldn't have surprised him. The door was open, and when he turned in, he saw the parents of the dead boy embracing each other, but not a tear lined any of their cheeks. Bosch's initial split-second reaction was that he was seeing relief in their young faces.

They separated when they saw Bosch enter, followed by Ferras.

"Mr. and Mrs. Helton?" he asked.

They nodded in unison. But the man corrected Bosch.

"I'm Stephen Helton, and this is my wife, Arlene Haddon."

"I'm Detective Bosch with the Los Angeles Police Department, and this is my partner, Detective Ferras. We are very sorry for the loss of your son. It is our job now to investigate William's death and to learn exactly what happened to him."

Helton nodded as his wife stepped close to him and put her face into his chest. Something silent was transmitted.

"Does this have to be done now?" Helton asked. "We've just lost our beautiful little—"

"Yes, sir, it has to be done now. This is a homicide investigation."

"It was an accident," Helton weakly protested. "It's all my fault, but it was an accident."

"It's still a homicide investigation. We would like to speak to you each privately, without the intrusions that will occur here. Do you mind coming down to the police station to be interviewed?"

"We'll leave him here?"

"The hospital is making arrangements for your son's body to be moved to the medical examiner's office."

"They're going to cut him open?" the mother asked in a near hysterical voice.

"They will examine his body and then determine if an autopsy is necessary," Bosch said. "It is required by law that any untimely death fall under the jurisdiction of the medical examiner."

He waited to see if there was further protest. When there wasn't, he stepped back and gestured for them to leave the room.

"We'll drive you down to Parker Center, and I promise to make this as painless as possible."

———

THEY PLACED THE grieving parents in separate interview rooms in the third-floor offices of Homicide Special. Because it was Sunday, the cafeteria was closed, and Bosch had to make do with the vending machines in the alcove by the elevators. He got a can of Coke and two packages of cheese crackers. He had not eaten breakfast before being called in on the case and was now famished.

He took his time while eating the crackers and talking things over with Ferras. He wanted both Helton and Haddon to believe that they were waiting while the other spouse was being interviewed. It was a trick of the trade, part of the strategy. Each would have to wonder what the other was saying.

"Okay," Bosch finally said. "I'm going to go in and take the husband. You can watch in the booth or you can take a run at the wife. Your choice."

It was a big moment. Bosch was more than twenty-five years ahead of Ferras on the job. He was the mentor, and Ferras was the student. So far in their fledgling partnership, Bosch had never let Ferras conduct a formal interview. He was allowing that now, and the look on Ferras's face showed that it was not lost on him.

"You're going to let me talk to her?"

"Sure, why not? You can handle it."

"All right if I get in the booth and watch you with him first? That way you can watch me."

"Whatever makes you comfortable."

"Thanks, Harry."

"Don't thank me, Ignacio. Thank yourself. You earned it."

Bosch dumped the empty cracker packages and the can in a trash bin near his desk.

"Do me a favor," he said. "Go on the Internet first and check the *LA Times* to see if they've had any stories lately about a case like this. You know, with a kid. I'd be curious, and if there are, we might be able to make a play with the story. Use it like a prop."

"I'm on it."

"I'll go set up the video in the booth."

Ten minutes later, Bosch entered Interview Room Three, where Stephen Helton was waiting for him. Helton looked like he was not quite thirty years old. He was lean and tan and looked like the perfect real estate salesman. He looked like he had never spent even five minutes in a police station before.

Immediately, he protested.

"What is taking so long? I've just lost my son, and you stick me in this room for an hour? Is that procedure?"

"It hasn't been that long, Stephen. But I am sorry you had to wait. We were talking to your wife, and that went longer than we thought it would."

"Why were you talking to her? Willy was with me the whole time."

"We talked to her for the same reason we're talking to you. I'm sorry for the delay."

Bosch pulled out the chair that was across the small table from Helton and sat down.

"First of all," he said, "thank you for coming in for the interview. You understand that you are not under arrest or anything like that. You are free to go if you wish. But by law we have to conduct an investigation of the death, and we appreciate your cooperation."

"I just want to get it over with so I can begin the process."

"What process is that?"

"I don't know. Whatever process you go through. Believe me, I'm new at this. You know, grief and guilt and mourning. Willy wasn't in our lives very long, but we loved him very much. This is just awful. I made a mistake, and I am going to pay for it for the rest of my life, Detective Bosch."

Bosch almost told him that his son paid for the mistake *with* the rest of his life but chose not to antagonize the man. Instead, he just nodded and noted that Helton had looked down at his lap when he had spoken most of his statement. Averting the eyes was a classic tell that indicated untruthfulness. Another tell was that Helton had his hands down in his lap and out of sight. The open and truthful person keeps his hands on the table and in sight.

"Why don't we start at the beginning?" Bosch said. "Tell me how the day started."

Helton nodded and began.

"Sunday's our busiest day. We're both in real estate. You may have seen the signs: Haddon and Helton. We're PPG's top-volume team. Today Arlene had an open house at noon and a couple of private showings before that. So Willy was going to be with me. We lost another nanny on Friday, and there was no one else to take him."

"How did you lose the nanny?"

"She quit. They all quit. Willy is a handful . . . because of his condition. I mean, why deal with a handicapped child if someone with a normal, healthy child will pay you the same thing? Subsequently, we go through a lot of nannies."

"So you were left to take care of the boy today while your wife had the property showings."

"It wasn't like I wasn't working, though. I was negotiating a sale that would have brought in a thirty-thousand-dollar commission. It was important."

"Is that why you went into the office?"

"Exactly. We got an offer sheet, and I was going to have to respond. So I got Willy ready and put him in the car and went in to work."

"What time was this?"

"About quarter to ten. I got the call from the other realtor at about nine thirty. The buyer was playing hardball. The response time was going to be set at an hour. So I had to get my seller on standby, pack up Willy, and get in there to pick up the fax."

"Do you have a fax at home?"

"Yes, but if the deal went down, we'd have to get together in the office. We have a signing room, and all the forms are right there. My file on the property was in my office too."

Bosch nodded. It sounded plausible, to a point.

"Okay, so you head off to the office . . ."

"Exactly. And two things happened . . ."

Helton brought his hands up into sight but only to hold them across his face to hide his eyes. A classic tell.

"What two things?"

"I got a call on my cell—from Arlene—and Willy fell asleep in his car seat. Do you understand?"

"Make me understand."

"I was distracted by the call, and I was no longer distracted by Willy. He had fallen asleep."

"Uh-huh."

"So I forgot he was there. Forgive me, God, but I forgot I had him with me!"

"I understand. What happened next?"

Helton dropped his hands out of sight again. He looked at Bosch briefly and then at the tabletop.

"I parked in my assigned space behind PPG, and I went in. I was still talking to Arlene. One of our buyers is trying to get out of a contract because he's found something he likes better. So we were talking about that, about how to finesse things with that, and I was on the phone when I went in."

"Okay, I see that. What happened when you went in?"

Helton didn't answer right away. He sat there looking at the table as if trying to remember so he could get the answer right.

"Stephen?" Bosch prompted. "What happened next?"

"I had told the buyer's agent to fax me the offer. But it wasn't there. So I got off the line from my wife and I called the agent. Then I waited around for the fax. Checked my slips and made a few callbacks while I was waiting."

"What are your slips?"

"Phone messages. People who see our signs on properties and call. I don't put my cell or home number on the signs."

"How many callbacks did you make?"

"I think just two. I got a message on one and spoke briefly to the other person. My fax came in, and that was what I was there for. I got off the line."

"Now, at this point it was what time?"

"I don't know, about ten after ten."

"Would you say that at this point you were still cognizant that your son was still in your car in the parking lot?"

Helton took time to think through an answer again but spoke before Bosch had to prompt him.

"No, because if I knew he was in the car, I would not have left him in the first place. I forgot about him while I was still in the car. You understand?"

Bosch leaned back in his seat. Whether he understood it or

not, Helton had just dodged one legal bullet. If he had acknowl-edged that he had knowingly left the boy in the car—even if he planned to be back in a few minutes—that would have greatly supported a charge of negligent homicide. But Helton had ma-neuvered the question correctly, almost as if he had expected it.

"Okay," Bosch said. "What happened next?"

Helton shook his head wistfully and looked at the sidewall as if gazing through a window toward the past he couldn't change.

"I, uh, got involved in the deal," he said. "The fax came in, I called my client, and I faxed back a counter. I also did a lot of talk-ing to the other agent. By phone. We were trying to get the deal done, and we had to hand-hold both our clients through this."

"For two hours."

"Yes, it took that long."

"And when was it that you remembered that you had left Wil-liam in the car out in the parking lot, where it was about ninety-five degrees?"

"I guess as soon—first of all, I didn't know what the tempera-ture was. I object to that. I left that car at about ten, and it was not ninety-five degrees. Not even close. I hadn't even used the air conditioner on the way over."

There was a complete lack of remorse or guilt in Helton's de-meanor. He wasn't even attempting to fake it anymore. Bosch had become convinced that this man had no love or affinity for his damaged and now lost child. William was simply a burden that had to be dealt with and therefore could easily be forgotten when things like business and selling houses and making money came up.

But where was the crime in all this? Bosch knew he could charge him with negligence, but the courts tend to view the loss of a child as enough punishment in these situations. Helton would go free with his wife as sympathetic figures, free to con-tinue their lives while baby William moldered in his grave.

The tells always add up. Bosch instinctively believed Helton was a liar. And he began to believe that William's death was no accident. Unlike his partner, who had let the passions of his own fatherhood lead him down the path, Bosch had come to this point after careful observation and analysis. It was now time to press on, to bait Helton and see if he would make a mistake.

"Is there anything else you want to add at this point to the story?" he asked.

Helton let out a deep breath and slowly shook his head.

"That's the whole sad story," he said. "I wish to God it never happened. But it did."

He looked directly at Bosch for the first time during the entire interview. Bosch held his gaze and then asked a question.

"Do you have a good marriage, Stephen?"

Helton looked away and stared at the invisible window again.

"What do you mean?"

"I mean, do you have a good marriage? You can say yes or no if you want."

"Yes, I have a good marriage," Helton responded emphatically. "I don't know what my wife told you, but I think it is very solid. What are you trying to say?"

"All I'm saying is that sometimes, when there is a child with challenges, it strains the marriage. My partner just had a baby. The kid's healthy, but money's tight and his wife isn't back at work yet. You know the deal. It's tough. I can only imagine what the strain of having a child with William's difficulties would be like."

"Yeah, well, we made it by all right."

"The nannies quitting all the time . . ."

"It wasn't that hard. As soon as one quits, we put an ad on craigslist for another."

Bosch nodded and scratched the back of his head. While doing this, he waved a finger in a circular motion toward the camera that was in the air vent up on the wall behind him. Helton could not see him do this.

"When did you two get married?" he asked.

"Two and a half years ago. We met on a contract. She had the buyer, and I had the seller. We worked well together. We started talking about joining forces, and then we realized we were in love."

"Then William came."

"Yes, that's right."

"That must've changed things."

"It did."

"So when Arlene was pregnant, couldn't the doctors tell that he had these problems?"

"They could have if they had seen him. But Arlene's a workaholic. She was busy all the time. She missed some appointments and the ultrasounds. When they discovered there was a problem, it was too late."

"Do you blame your wife for that?"

Helton looked aghast.

"No, of course not. Look, what does this have to do with what happened today? I mean, why are you asking me all this?"

Bosch leaned across the table.

"It may have a lot to do with it, Stephen. I am trying to determine what happened today and why. The 'why' is the tough part."

"It was an accident! I *forgot* he was in the car, okay? I will go to my grave knowing that *my* mistake killed my own son. Isn't that enough for you?"

Bosch leaned back and said nothing. He hoped Helton would say more.

"Do you have a son, Detective? Any children?"

"A daughter."

"Yeah, well then, happy Father's Day. I'm really glad for you. I hope you never have to go through what I'm going through right now. Believe me, it's not fun!"

Bosch had forgotten it was Father's Day. The realization knocked him off his rhythm, and his thoughts went to his daughter living eight thousand miles away. In her ten years, he had been with her on only one Father's Day. What did that say about him? Here he was, trying to get inside another father's actions and motivations, and he knew his own could not stand equal scrutiny.

The moment ended when there was a knock on the door and Ferras came in, carrying a file.

"Excuse me," he said. "I thought you might want to see this."

He handed the file to Bosch and left the room. Bosch turned the file on the table in front of them and opened it, so that Helton would not be able to see its contents. Inside was a computer printout and a handwritten note on a Post-it.

The note said: "No ad on craigslist."

The printout was of a story that ran in the *LA Times* ten months earlier. It was about the heatstroke death of a child who had been left in a car in Lancaster while his mother ran into a store to buy milk. She ran into the middle of a robbery. She was tied up along with the store clerk and placed in a back room. The robbers ransacked the store and escaped. It was an hour before the victims were discovered and freed, but by then the child in the car had already succumbed to heatstroke. Bosch scanned the story quickly, then dropped the file closed. He looked at Helton without speaking.

"What?" Helton asked.

"Just some additional information and lab reports," he lied. "Do you get the *LA Times*, by the way?"

"Yes, why?"

"Just curious, that's all. Now, how many nannies do you think you've employed in the fifteen months that William was alive?"

Helton shook his head.

"I don't know. At least ten. They don't stay long. They can't take it."

"And then you go to craigslist to place an ad?"

"Yes."

"And you just lost a nanny on Friday?"

"Yes, I told you."

"She just walked out on you?"

"No, she got another job and told us she was leaving. She made up a lie about it being closer to home and with gas prices and all that. But we knew why she was leaving. She could not handle Willy."

"She told you this Friday?"

"No, when she gave notice."

"When was that?"

"She gave two weeks' notice, so it was two weeks back from Friday."

"And do you have a new nanny lined up?"

"No, not yet. We were still looking."

"But you put the feelers out and ran the ad again, that sort of thing?"

"Right, but listen, what does this have to—"

"Let me ask the questions, Stephen. Your wife told us that she worried about leaving William with you, that you couldn't handle the strain of it."

Helton looked shocked. The statement came from left field, as Bosch had wanted it.

"What? Why would she say that?"

"I don't know. Is it true?"

"No, it's not true."

"She told us she was worried that this wasn't an accident."

"That's absolutely crazy and I doubt she said it. You are lying."

He turned in his seat, so that the front of his body faced the corner of the room and he would have to turn his face to look directly at Bosch. Another tell. Bosch knew he was zeroing in. He decided it was the right time to gamble.

"She mentioned a story you found in the *LA Times* that was about a kid left in a car up in Lancaster. The kid died of heatstroke. She was worried that it gave you the idea."

Helton swiveled in his seat and leaned forward to put his elbows on the table and run his hands through his hair.

"Oh, my God, I can't believe she . . ."

He didn't finish. Bosch knew his gamble had paid off. Helton's mind was racing along the edge. It was time to push him over.

"You didn't forget that William was in the car, did you, Stephen?"

Helton didn't answer. He buried his face in his hands again. Bosch leaned forward, so that he only had to whisper.

"You left him there and you knew what was going to happen. You planned it. That's why you didn't bother running ads for a new nanny. You knew you weren't going to need one."

Helton remained silent and unmoving. Bosch kept working him, changing tacks and offering sympathy now.

"It's understandable," he said. "I mean, what kind of life would that kid have, anyway? Some might even call this a mercy killing. The kid falls asleep and never wakes up. I've worked these kinds of cases before, Stephen. It's actually not a bad way to go. It sounds bad, but it isn't. You just get tired and you go to sleep."

Helton kept his face in his hands, but he shook his head. Bosch didn't know if he was denying it still or shaking off something else. He waited, and the delay paid off.

"It was her idea," Helton said in a quiet voice. "She's the one who couldn't take it anymore."

In that moment Bosch knew he had him, but he showed nothing. He kept working it.

"Wait a minute," Bosch said. "She said she had nothing to do with it, that this was your idea and your plan and that when she called you, it was to talk you out of it."

Helton dropped his hands with a slap on the table.

"That's a lie! It was her! She was embarrassed that we had a kid like that! She couldn't take him anywhere and we couldn't go anywhere! He was ruining our lives and she told me I had to do something about it! She told me how to do something about it! She said I would be saving two lives while sacrificing only one."

Bosch pulled back across the table. It was done. It was over.

"Okay, Stephen, I think I understand. And I want to hear all about it. But at this point I need to inform you of your rights. After that, if you want to talk, we'll talk, and I'll listen."

———

When Bosch came out of the interview room, Ignacio Ferras was there, waiting for him in the hallway. His partner raised his fist, and Bosch tapped his knuckles with his own fist.

"That was beautiful," Ferras said. "You walked him right down the road."

"Thanks," Bosch said. "Let's hope the DA is impressed too."

"I don't think we'll have to worry."

"Well, there will be no worries if you go into the other room and turn the wife now."

Ferras looked surprised.

"You still want me to take the wife?"

"She's yours. Let's walk them into the DA as bookends."

"I'll do my best."

"Good. Go check the equipment and make sure we're still recording in there. I've got to go make a quick call."

"You got it, Harry."

Bosch walked into the squad room and sat down at his desk. He checked his watch and knew it would be getting late in Hong Kong. He pulled out his cell phone anyway and sent a call across the Pacific.

His daughter answered with a cheerful hello. Bosch knew he wouldn't even have to say anything and he would feel fulfilled by just the sound of her voice saying the one word.

"Hey, baby, it's me," he said.

"Daddy!" she exclaimed. "Happy Father's Day!"

And Bosch realized in that moment that he was indeed a happy man.

ABOUT THE AUTHORS

James O. Born is the author of a series featuring Florida Department of Law Enforcement agent Bill Tasker. His newest novel, *Field of Fire*, follows the investigations of the ATF. His books capture the feeling and details of police work while following realistic procedure. He is a former U.S. drug agent and an agent with the Florida Department of Law Enforcement. He has been writing for eighteen years and is published by Putnam.

Jon L. Breen is the author of seven novels, most recently *Eye of God* (Perseverance Press), and three short-story collections, most recently *Kill the Umpire: The Calls of Ed Gorgon* (Crippen & Landru). He won Edgar Awards in the biographical/critical category for *What About Murder?* (1981) and *Novel Verdicts* (1984) and is a book-review columnist for *Ellery Queen's Mystery Magazine* and *Mystery Scene*. Retired as a librarian and professor of English at Rio Hondo College, he lives in Fountain Valley, California, with his wife and first line editor, Rita.

John Buentello is a writer who lives in San Antonio, Texas. He has published stories in a number of genres, including mystery, science fiction, fantasy, and horror. He and his brother Lawrence have published

ABOUT THE AUTHORS

the anthology *Binary Tales* and have recently completed the novel *Reproduction Rights*. John has been married to his wife, Ann, for sixteen years, which makes him the luckiest man on earth.

A former deputy district attorney, **Alafair Burke** graduated with distinction from Stanford Law School and is now a professor at Hofstra Law School, where she teaches criminal law and procedure. She is the author of four novels, *Dead Connection, Close Case, Missing Justice,* and *Judgment Calls.* Her fifth novel, *Angel's Tip,* featuring NYPD detective Ellie Hatcher, will be published by HarperCollins in 2008. She lives in New York City. Visit her at alafairburke.com.

Michael Connelly is the author of eighteen novels and one collection of nonfiction crime stories. Among his novels are *The Black Echo, The Last Coyote, The Poet, Blood Work,* and *The Lincoln Lawyer.* He is a past president of the Mystery Writers of America. He lives with his family in Florida.

About himself, **Jack Fredrickson** admits little other than that, after something of successful careers in productivity consulting and owning and managing an interior-design/commercial-furnishings firm, he abandoned productive employment to write in dark places. His first crime novel, *A Safe Place for Dying* (Publishers Weekly starred review), debuted in November 2006. He lives with his wife, Susan, west of Chicago. Check him out at jackfredrickson.com.

Leslie Glass is a playwright and the author of fourteen novels, including *Over His Dead Body, For Love and Money,* and nine bestselling novels of psychological suspense featuring NYPD detective April Woo. The founder of the Leslie Glass Foundation, Glass worked in advertising and publishing, was a script writer for a soap opera, and wrote the Intelligencer column for *New York Magazine* before turning to fiction full-time. She now writes a column for *Sarasota Magazine* and develops original screenplays with her daughter and partner, Lindsey Glass.

Paul Guyot is an award-winning television writer/producer whose credits include *Felicity, Snoops,* and the Emmy-winning drama *Judging Amy.* He is the creator and executive producer of the police drama *Crimes Against Persons* for A&E. His short stories can be found in numerous anthologies and online publications. He lives in St. Louis with his wife and family. More information can be culled from his Web site: paulguyot.net.

Diana Hansen-Young was born in Bellingham, Washington, in 1947, into a community of, as she called them, "depressed Mormon Swedish farmers." In 1966 she moved to Hawaii, ran for the State Constitutional Convention in 1968, and won a seat by ninety-three votes. She went on to run for the Hawaii State House of Representatives, a post which she won. After losing a congressional race, she started painting little scenes of Hawaii and selling them. For the next twenty-five years, she painted Hawaiian women, which grew into a business. But in 1996, after developing severe arthritis in her right arm and hand, she could no longer hold a paintbrush. During those twenty-five years, she had been writing plays, novels, and short stories, and tossing them in boxes. She dusted off manuscripts that she'd never submitted, closed the business, rented the farm, and moved with her two daughters to New York City. She received an MFA from NYU, where she met composer Brian Feinstein, her collaborator on her thesis musical, *Mimi Le Duck,* which premiered off-Broadway in 2006. A member of MWA, she now writes full-time in New York City.

John Harvey is the author of ten Charlie Resnick novels, the first of which, *Lonely Hearts,* was named by the *Times* (London) as one of the 100 Best Crime Novels of the Century. In 2007 he was awarded the British Crime Writers' Association Cartier Diamond Dagger for sustained excellence in crime writing. He lives in London.

Edward D. Hoch is a past president of the Mystery Writers of America and was a winner of its Edgar Award for best short story. He received the MWA's Grand Master Award in 2001. He has been a guest of honor at Bouchercon, twice winner of its Anthony Award, and recipient of its Lifetime Achievement Award. Author of some 950 published stories, he has appeared in every issue of *Ellery Queen's Mystery Magazine* for the past thirty-four years. Hoch and his wife, Patricia, reside in Rochester, New York.

Laurie R. King is the *New York Times* bestselling author of the Mary Russell novels, the Kate Martinelli series (including *To Play the Fool*, featuring Brother Erasmus), and five stand-alone novels, most recently *Touchstone.* She has won the Edgar, Creasey, Nero, Macavity, and Lambda awards; her nominations include the Edgar, the Agatha, the Orange, and the Barry. She is published in twenty countries.

Polly Nelson is new to mystery writing, having had her first story published in *Ellery Queen's Mystery Magazine*'s August 1995 issue, voted by *EQ* readers as among the year's ten best. The British Crime Writers' Association also selected a story for inclusion in the 2007 Fish anthology. Other stories have been published online at *East of the Web* and *Mystery Scene Magazine.* In a previous professional life, she directed children's theater and worked with individuals dealing with mental illness.

T. Jefferson Parker is the author of fourteen crime novels and a two-time winner of the Edgar Award for best mystery. He lives in Southern California with his wife and sons.

Peter Robinson was born in Yorkshire. After getting his BA Honours degree in English literature at the University of Leeds, he came to Canada and took his MA in English and creative writing at the University of Windsor, then a PhD in English at York University. He has taught at a number of Toronto colleges and served as writer in residence at the University of Windsor, 1992–1993. His first novel, *Gallows View,* introduced Detective Chief Inspector Alan Banks. It was short-listed for the John Creasey Award in the UK and the Crime Writers of Canada best first novel award. It was followed by fourteen more, the most recent being *Piece of My Heart*. The series has garnered many awards, including the Arthur Ellis Award, the Anthony Award, and the Barry Award, and has been nominated multiple times. He has also written the stand-alone novel *Caedmon's Song*. His books have been translated into fifteen languages. Robinson lives in the Beaches area of Toronto with his wife, Sheila Halladay, and he occasionally teaches crime writing at the University of Toronto's School of Continuing Studies.

Greg Rucka was born in San Francisco and raised on the Central Coast of California, in what is commonly referred to as "Steinbeck Country." He began his writing career in earnest at the age of ten by winning a countywide short-story contest and hasn't let up since. He graduated from Vassar College with an AB in English, and from the University of Southern California's master of professional writing program. He is the author of nearly a dozen novels, five featuring bodyguard Atticus Kodiak and two featuring Tara Chace, the protagonist of his *Queen & Country* series. Additionally, he has penned several short stories, countless comics, and the occasional nonfiction essay. In comics, he has had the opportunity to write stories featuring some of the world's best-known characters—Superman, Batman, and Wonder Woman—as well as penning several creator-owned properties himself, such as *Whiteout* and *Queen & Country*, both published by Oni Press. His work has been optioned several times over, and his services as a story doctor and creative consultant are in high demand in a variety of creative fields. Greg resides in Portland, Oregon, with his wife, author Jennifer Van Meter, and his two children. He thinks the biggest problem with the world is that people aren't paying enough attention.

Bev Vincent grew up in eastern Canada and lived in Switzerland before moving to Texas in the late 1980s. His American-born daughter recently moved to Canada to keep things in balance. He is the author of more than forty stories, including contributions to the Bram Stoker Award–winning anthology *From the Borderlands; Doctor Who: Destination Prague; All Hallows; The Best of Borderlands 1–5; Cemetery Dance;*

Corpse Blossoms; Shivers IV; and a mystery anthology featuring tales set in bathrooms called *Who Died in Here?* His first book, *The Road to the Dark Tower,* an authorized exploration of Stephen King's *Dark Tower* series, was nominated for a 2004 Bram Stoker Award. He coedited *The Illustrated Stephen King Trivia Book,* wrote reviews for *Accent Literary Review,* and is a contributing editor with *Cemetery Dance* magazine. He is a monthly contributor to *Storytellers Unplugged.* His Web site, with links to his message board and blogs, is bevvincent.com.

Persia Walker, a New York City native, is the author of *Darkness and the Devil Behind Me* and *Harlem Redux,* mysteries set against the glittering backdrop of 1920s New York. A former journalist, Persia has worked for the Associated Press and Radio Free Europe/Radio Liberty in Munich. She has degrees from Columbia University's Graduate School of Journalism and Swarthmore College.

In her four critically acclaimed Charlotte Justice novels, **Paula L. Woods** has focused on her protagonist, an LAPD Homicide detective. In "Divine Droplets," the focus shifts to Charlotte's nemesis, Detective Steve Firestone, and fast-forwards from the 1990s to present-day Los Angeles. "Since his debut in *Inner City Blues,* Firestone has been a deeply flawed but increasingly peripheral character in the series," she notes. "It was high time to tell his story and examine the errors he's made in his career." In addition to writing the series, Woods is also a book critic and pens reviews for the *Los Angeles Times.*

ABOUT THE MYSTERY WRITERS OF AMERICA

The Mystery Writers of America, the premier organization for established and aspiring mystery writers, is dedicated to promoting higher regard for crime writing, and recognition and respect for those who write within the genre.

COPYRIGHTS